Ruins of America

A Novel by

J. Schimschal

**The Ruins of America is the second novel in the Darken Realm
series of books and is the sequel to The Devil's Utopia**

Ruins Of America

Published by Fossil Ridge Books Inc.
P.O. Box 33218
Northglenn, CO. 80233

ISBN 0-9777327-1-1

Published in the United States of America

Acknowledgements
This book is dedicated to all of the people that enjoyed the first novel so much. I treasure your enjoyment. It is for you that I wrote this book.

About the Author

J. Schimschal is the author of the Darken Realm series of books. He lives in the western United States with his family. Additional information can be obtained by visiting www.darkenrealm.com.

Prologue

The refugee ships from the battered city-state of Rasheed managed to make it to the bustling port town of Eel Cove. As the last remnants of the Rasheed empire struggled to find their way in a darkening world, the fledgling mercenary team, Nova 7, determined to locate a nuclear weapon, headed out into the wasteland. Their goal was to locate a legendary arms dealer known as the Runner, reputed to make his home in the town of Shape Home, just south of the harbor town of Dune Station.

Leaving the safety of the refugee camp, the untested mercenary team worked its way across the Fire Ridge Desert, avoiding Reaper Kai tracker teams by using the expertise of the traitorous Mineera.

Knowing full well that an entire host of enemy scouts and assassins were close on their heels, Nova 7 procured a fishing boat, preferring to reach the harbor town of Dune Station by boat rather than on foot.

As the small boat carrying Nova 7 pressed onward through the sea toward Dune Station, dark storm clouds arose from the western wasteland, pushing out into the ocean with violent intent. As lightning flashed in the distance, the ocean, almost without warning, became turbulent. Within seconds, the tiny boat in the icy blackness of the night was pelted with heaving waves…

Chapter 1
Lost to the Sea

The rolling surf could not be contained. The darkness of the night was blinding, oppressive, and filled with confusion. With a crash and boom, the waves rolled in; their icy chill consumed all caught within the frigid water. Rolling and churning, the powerful ripples of the surf flung the hapless trio trying to stay afloat. In the darkness of the night, a thin outline of land was just ahead. This was the outline they had been pushing toward for many minutes, many minutes of panic as the salt water stung their eyes and clawed at their lungs. The coastline was nearby, serving as the salvation of the trio.

Banion struggled in the pounding surf. He fought to keep his head and Tani's above the crashing waves. Mineera was close to Tani, struggling on the other side of the young scholar, pulling him along, fighting to keep hold of the tribal in the chaos of the storm. With a heave, the ocean pushed, overturning the trio and landing them upside down in a wet mass. Gasping in the white sea-foam, the trio struggled with salt water stinging their eyes and nose. Finally, Banion felt solid land beneath him, just below the waves. His foot dug into the soggy sand and his mind was set at ease; the deranged gun fighter knew that the trio would make it ashore.

The waves surged and broke. Mineera also found a foothold. Urging Tani onward, she tried to stand in the fierce waves. Water, rushing back from the shoreline, sucked and tugged at the psychic maiden's feet. The pull was strong and the undertow flung her legs out from under her. Plunging head-first into the icy waves, Mineera held her breath and prepared to be drenched once more. Banion maintained a shaky foothold in the surf, still pulling on Tani, forcing his head above the water.

Fingernails hastily dug in the sand. Their fists closing around mounds of wet grit, the companions struggled for freedom from the waves, fighting to crawl ashore and escape the icy water.

Finally, with labored effort, the trio liberated themselves from certain death.

Tani rolled over and coughed uncontrollably. Water and mucous flowed from his open mouth as he fought to breathe air in hurried, quick gasps. With a cough, the young scholar felt his stomach constrict, causing him to retch on the sand. The fight to breathe was in earnest, and a mixture of bile from his stomach and salt water from his lungs was ejected onto the sand. Trembling violently, his nose stinging, Tani was happy to be alive.

A whisper erupted in the darkness. It was weak at first, and rose softly into a growing sensation. A spike of anger, like a pinprick, rose from the darkness, and Banion was its source. The pain rose in intensity and Banion was filled with a fury. Frustrated and filled with rage, Banion rose to his feet, his long coat hanging about his body in a wet mass. *Something* was missing, and Banion was none too happy about it.

"Jared!" Banion screamed as the pinprick of anger erupted into a burst of rage.

White, foaming waves responded with deafening crashes. Nothing else stirred in the surf. The winds were howling across the beach as black storm clouds blocked the stars of night.

"Jared!" Banion screamed as he stalked back and forth along the beach. "Damn it, kid! Where are you?" Like a caged animal he paced fiercely. With each pass, his pace became more frantic, more erratic. He wanted to pound at the imaginary bars, the bars that kept him away from his lost friend. Banion was lost in a prison of rage and anger. Jared was outside that cage, an intangible goal that he could not reach.

The fury of the storm responded. A chilling blast of wind hit the soaked Banion. Another series of waves assaulted the coastline. Lightning streaked across the sky and a boom of thunder rolled from the sinister clouds. In the flash of lightning, Banion looked out at the high waves and shook his head in anger. The light went out, the storm grumbled, but not another bolt of lightning broke the tortured clouds. The blackness of the night was haunting, keeping Banion from seeing much further than a few feet in front of him.

"Jared!" Banion yelled again and then fell silent. Despair was his companion and it was inside the cage. Jared, the intangible goal, was slipping away, somewhere outside the cage, somewhere in the blackness. Each moment, hope was fading further, further into the darkness of the swirling surf pounding the coastline without relent.

Mineera could feel Banion's anger rising at the very edge of his soul. It was a sickening wash of misery and hatred. She fought to remain in control. Her own feeling of loss was bad enough, but trying to contend with the full force of hatred in Banion was too much to bear. She shook her head back and forth, desperately forcing the invasive thoughts from her mind. Mineera had to remain in control. Finally, the psychic maiden pushed the hate-filled thoughts out of her mind and tried to calm herself. Breathing slowly, her focus began to change.

Mineera turned her thoughts toward young Tani. As her eyes fell upon the scholar, despair filled her. Young Tani clutched his laptop computer, hastily protected in a mass of plastic bags, hugging it tightly to his chest with a distant look. It was as if Tani was in a trance. His glasses had miraculously remained on his face during the swim ashore. His usually spiky hair was a wet mess, and he looked pitiful, crouched upon the sand with snot running from his nose. His lower lip was quivering and it looked as if he was about to collapse from defeat and exhaustion.

"Jared!" Banion screamed as anger took him once more. He stalked around in circles as his fury grew. Flailing his hands around, the deranged gun fighter was mumbling under his breath as he stalked about.

A white blast of water crashed against the shore. Sea foam sprayed and hissed as the bubbles broke and sizzled like hot oil in a frying pan. As the last sound of the foam left his ears, Tani sighed and became resolute in thought.

"He's gone." Tani spoke in a distant tone. "He never learned how to swim." His statement was so matter-of-fact that it brought the reality home to all three.

There was a silence between the trio. Like a pack of wet

dogs, the three faced each other in silent testament.

The reality was sinking in, but to deny death is the most wonderful of human yearnings. For what to be lost, that is not immortal. For when the silent heart fades and the distance of the darkness draws near, hope is rekindled. For an instant in death, all are immortal, and death is but an intangible thing, a thing that seems like a distant dream rolling from one's thoughts with a haunting whisper. In a blinding flash, the dream is gone and sorrow is a relentless companion, weighing down the spirit in pulses of sadness, guilt, and anger.

"He can't be gone!" Banion yelled and shook his fists at young Tani. Deny as he may, Banion could not avert the truth.

"He can't swim, Banion. He never could. We grew up in the desert. I barely made it and I can swim." Tani spoke while looking at Banion through his water spotted glasses.

"Some friend you are, bookworm!" Banion sneered at Tani. "Jared!" Banion screamed with a defiant look. The deranged rancher glared at Tani as he screamed.

"I can't feel his presence." Mineera said in a dull tone. The psychic maiden spoke while looking at the ground. She had a lost look in her eyes, partly from trying to feel the spark of life from Jared, partly from her own sense of loss.

"What the hell do you know?" Banion retorted. "You're the reason we are out here!" The caged animal struck back, hitting the bars, roaring inside. Mineera gazed at this beast and retreated a step back. His rage was a smoldering fire, about to erupt.

"What?" Mineera said in a shocked tone. Her thoughts had refocused and she was stunned awake from her daydream.

"You and your damn race!" Banion moved forward and stared at Mineera. The animal inside could not be contained. He was suffering and wanted repayment for his misery. Banion gave in to his dark heart. He shouted at her as anger took him. "If it weren't for you and the damn Reaper Kai, we wouldn't be out here! Jared would have never died!"

Like a hammer, the words hit her and did not slide off. The blunt words assaulted her hard and stuck. Tears welled up in

Mineera's eyes. Guilt filled her. No matter how many days she walked the earth, she could never wash away her past. Mineera could never escape her heritage. Slowly, the tears rolled down her face.

"Stop it!" Tani shouted back. The boy shot toward Banion and Mineera, stationing himself in between them, cheeks flushed in anger. "How dare you! Leave it be!"

"Why, kid? She is nothing more than a filthy dog, just like her race! A mongrel, a dirty mongrel that deserves to be put down! How dare I? I will tell you why! I am sick of the filth. Why are we made to suffer? Damn you, bookworm! Damn you, Mineera, and your kind!" His finger was pointed at Mineera as he finished his fit. Banion was out of control and nothing could return him to a state of sanity.

Mineera began to sob uncontrollably, partly from the loss of Jared, and partly from Banion's hate-filled words. Putting her hand in the air, she tried to put a symbolic stop to Banion's rhetoric.

Tani fell silent and averted his gaze from Banion. His mind began to return to his friend Jared. For as long as the scholar could remember, Jared had been there by his side. They were not just friends; they were more like brothers. They had shared a childhood, and it was as if Tani's twin had been ripped from his side. Tani shook his head back and forth, trying to escape the feeling. His mind didn't want to accept that Jared was dead. No matter how he fought, the weakness began to take him. Tani shivered in his wet clothes and his body began to wither in the cold night air. First he shook, and then the tears began to roll down his cheeks. They turned into a torrent; young Tani could not control himself and he began to sob. Like a defeated soldier, Tani collapsed upon the sand and wrung his hands together, wishing the pain would stop.

Banion looked at Tani and softness filled his eyes. He suddenly felt guilty. "I should have never taken you two runts along with me!" Banion said harshly.

Tani did not respond.

With that, Banion turned away from Tani and Mineera alike. He stormed off into the darkness. The night air was cool and inviting. The chill wind stung at his skin. He was half frozen, but the cold was strangely refreshing. It tensed his muscles, and was oddly familiar. Loss was a way of life for Banion. He was home again; a broken home, but home nevertheless. He walked along the beach and surveyed the violent surf, shaking his head in dismay.

"No matter what I do, they all die…" Banion whispered, lost in his thoughts. It was a profound statement, for his thoughts drifted to his mother, lost long ago; to his 'uncle', slain in Dune Station; to his dead wife, Lily. Finally, he thought of Jared. It was the first time Banion admitted to himself that he cared for the kid.

Banion leaned down and grabbed a wet fistful of sand. He crushed the sand in his fist and hurled it defiantly at the waves crashing against the shore. The sand hit the dark water and dissipated immediately.

"I am gonna miss you, Jared…" Banion whispered, and a single tear rolled down his cheek. It was only a single tear, but for Banion, it was all he had left to shed.

Chapter 2
The Return of Vertigo

The room had the stench of death. The rotting body of Father Vertigo was covered in a writhing mass of spiders and maggots. His sickly white flesh had been set upon by the insects, which were working feverishly to restore his battered body. Vertigo's body had been torn to shreds by the wicked aim and torrent of bullets unleashed by Banion O'Neil several months back, when the city of Rasheed fell to the Biogtech army. As the sickly swarm of maggots and spiders worked their dark magic, a host of unholy servants stood vigil around the Lord of Evil. Their twisted demonic faces glimmered in the shadows with dark intent.

Under their dark hoods, they peered out with black eyes and sinister red pupils. From time to time, a Goat Minion would bay and bleat in the dark tongue of its kind. The Goat Minions held a dark prayer around their fallen master, as they had done for nearly three months with little rest. Their red eyes did not veer from the corpse of Father Vertigo. Slowly, they chanted, their mouths uttering dark prayers in an unknown language, a language of dread.

The dark chamber was a mass of swarming spirits and specters. Blue, ghost-like entities, homeless demons, swirled endlessly around the corpse of Vertigo. In the dim light of the chamber, the blue forms would float about like vapor. Some would coalesce into forms with haunting faces, others would whisper in staggered phrases, mumbling a lost language. An icy wind swirled about the evil spirits, plunging the room into an unnatural chill. For the dark spirits were trying to return home, and their home was inside the twisted Lord Vertigo. Lord Vertigo himself was nothing more than a husk, a freakish home for lost souls and countless demons to invade. The dark lord was nothing more than the magistrate of all these dark souls. Or so it was until Vertigo fell in battle. When his body was torn asunder, the spark of Vertigo's own spirit was lost. Without his masterful will, the host of demonic spirits inhabiting his body could not be contained. And so they swirled about the room, wailing in agony, trying to return back to Vertigo's body.

The host of spiders worked feverishly and clattered across his body. As they worked, their black, engorged abdomens spun an endless coating of spider silk. The spiders worked intently, climbing to and fro across Vertigo's corpse. As the host of spiders moved, a thick coating of web covered the horrid wounds inflicted by dozens and dozens of bullets. The web became a thick matrix, a place for the maggots to work their own brand of demonic magic.

The swarm of maggots moved across onto the spider silk. The tiny worms soon became entangled in the silk and thrashed about. Slowly, they died, and a green filth encrusted the body of each maggot. This rotting green filth gradually restored the remains of Father Vertigo, creating a white putrid layer of skin atop the spider silk. And as each maggot died and added its essence into the body of Vertigo, a swarm of flies would replenish the maggot swarm immediately by laying a continual line of eggs upon his body.

The chanting continued as the spiders and maggots worked intently. Slowly, the wounds were disappearing, covered by the putrid white flesh which rendered the Lord of Evil's body intact, forming a new vessel for all the evil spirits hovering over his body to invade.

The Goat Minions bayed in the darkness. Sinister prayers were uttered in earnest. Although Vertigo's wounds were terrible, the dark magic was stronger. The wounds on his corpse finally closed, restored by the host of insects and dark prayers.

The white putrid flesh shuddered. Multiple convulsions rocked the corpse. Each tremor that rocked the body was evidence of a horrible fact: the body of Father Vertigo had been healed and made whole once more. The host of pale blue spirits roared in glee. One spirit after another dove into the corpse's mouth. With each spirit entering the husk of Vertigo, the body shuddered again and again. Finally, the last of the wraiths had made their way home. The corpse convulsed violently and then its eyes opened.

Black, sinister eyes surveyed the room. Vertigo sat up upon the unholy altar and looked toward his host of loyal Goat Minions, whispering in the dark. With shaky movements, the age-old dark priest tried to regain his composure. A seizure rocked him. With a gag, Vertigo retched a horrid mixture of black blood, spiders, and maggots upon the altar. He shivered as spasms coursed through his body.

The Lord of Darkness had returned. Father Vertigo, Lord of the Reaper Kai, was back from the dead, infested with a host of demons.

Several moments passed as Father Vertigo surveyed his followers. The spirit of Vertigo was focusing the thoughts and rage of all the other spirits trapped in his husk. If he did not take charge of all the demonic souls trapped in his body, he knew control of his own body would not be possible. Finally, the aged priest brought all of the demonic spirits into check, mastering them as he had done before his demise.

"Hail all ye fools," Vertigo said in a rasp. A look of hate was in his eyes. "Your failure could have cost us much!" he raged as he looked upon the Goat Minions. As he hissed at them, the Goat Minions bleated in submission and backed away from the naked Vertigo upon the defiled altar.

"Bring my council!" Vertigo hissed. A Goat Minion left the chamber as another moved forward to clothe the Lord of Darkness in a black robe, trimmed in royal blue.

Vertigo retched yet again and wiped the writhing maggots and spiders from his chin. He stood upright and looked around his coven of evil.

Three red robed forms entered the chamber.

Sister Nightshade was Vertigo's most trusted companion and aide. She was a hunched form with a twisted face. Disease and pestilence had ravaged her body. She was the master of the breeding pits, in charge of the monasteries of the devil, and a skilled military tactician. In addition, her skill and loyalty had earned her the right to control much of the Reaper Kai infrastructure; Nightshade was in charge of the biological weapons section of the Reaper Kai army.

With the support of a host of techno-biologists, the Reaper Kai arsenal for biological weapons was formidable. Several smaller towns had been eradicated and destroyed due to her plagues.

To look upon Nightshade was fodder for nightmares. Boils and lesions covered her body, and she kept her robes pulled close about her. Her pallid white flesh and disease-ridden body were a strange anomaly. For most, under the constant assault of pestilence, would have withered, but as for Nightshade, the pox upon her body fueled her with a supernatural power, infusing her with evil. If Vertigo were not in charge of the Reaper Kai, Sister Nightshade had both the leadership skills and the cunning to rule the Reaper Kai empire. Nightshade held the rank of Matron, essentially the queen of the Reaper Kai. Bowing in reverence to her dark companion, Nightshade paid him homage and then backed away, revealing another of Vertigo's trusted commanders.

Brother Feral was in charge of the great Biogtech armies. Tall and tan was Feral. Unnaturally strong muscles bulged upon his body. Praying to demons, Feral had mastered the ability to perfect his physical appearance. Vain he was, for his robes were opened so all could survey his perfect body. Neither scar nor mark marred his flesh. Feral's vice was perfection and vanity. He was a ruthless leader and master tactician on the battlefield, and had already led the armies of darkness to many victories. Though he was an excellent military leader, and a skilled scholar in technical issues, his leisure-time activities had gotten him in trouble on many occasions with Vertigo. Feral's lust for carnal pleasures had turned him into an insane killing machine on many occasions; often, he ended up killing the captives sent to his private chambers to pleasure him. Vertigo had grown tired of Feral's antics, and had threatened execution if he ever caught wind of such events. Feral took the threat seriously, and had carried out a campaign to keep his life a secret. The twisted lord of vanity bowed before the dark father, then took a step back, revealing the newest member of Vertigo's trusted inner circle.

The last member was Queen Toil, and she moved forward with a foul glimmer in her eye. Her new place in the Reaper Kai

Empire was apparent, for she wore the red robes of evil with a sinister pride. Marion Toil was the Great Betrayer, the Bitch Queen of Rasheed. Queen Toil had destroyed and usurped an entire empire for her own greed and ambition. Manipulation and underhanded plots were her specialty. Marion's new place in the empire was to bring about the ruin of the other great empires through deceit and mistrust. Her mercenary and assassin network was her pride and joy. She used hired guns and cutthroats to wear down the enemy by slaying their leadership or destroying key pieces of infrastructure. Though a fledgling leader, Marion had grown significantly in power over the years, first being taught by her mother, then communing with demons in secret directly after her mother's death. The Queen of Rasheed was a force to be reckoned with, boasting a unique set of psychic abilities not yet seen in the Reaper Kai empire. Her mastery of spiders and mental possession charms was formidable. Bowing, Sister Marion backed away from Father Vertigo.

"Ah, yes... my noble council," Vertigo hissed, looking at each in turn.

"Sister Marion Toil..." Vertigo's harsh black eyes fell upon the newest sister in the Reaper Kai order. "Your cunning betrayal of your people has given us dominion over the kingdom of Rasheed. You are much commended for your actions."

Marion responded to Vertigo's praises with a smile. But her smile quickly disappeared. Vertigo was displeased with her, and she could feel the hate rising in his heart.

"Your inept ability to deal with all the mercenary teams could have brought us to ruin, and could still bring us to ruin," Vertigo said in a heartless tone. "You failed to destroy Nova 7. And as a result, Banion O'Neil and a brat from the wastelands managed to bring the battle to me. Neither blade nor bullet had bit my flesh in more than a hundred years! Your incompetence almost cost me my life and station on this earth!" Vertigo yelled with a rasp in his voice. Black ooze poured out of his mouth.

"But..." Marion whined.

"Silence!" Vertigo yelled, and the Goat Minions secured the traitorous queen. "You will spend three days in torture for your failure! And after your arrogance and smug content are washed away, you will find this Nova 7 and slay all of them! Your quest for vengeance for your slain mother must end."

All was silent, and the Goat Minions pulled the horrified Marion away. She struggled but did not say a word. Marion knew better than to argue with the Lord of Darkness.

"Brother Feral, prepare the troops. Sack and destroy the surrounding towns and villages around Rasheed. This will allow us to maintain a tight hold over the region." Vertigo spoke softly to Feral. "Send word to the capital and prepare the troops to defend Detro Tech city. The foul Iron Kai are sure to assault it as soon as possible. I will not forget their attack against our troops with their gun ships as we moved on the city of Rasheed."

"Your will be done, master," Feral replied proudly. "Shall I make ready and defend the capital personally, my Lord?"

"No. You will stay here with me. Prepare the army here in Rasheed to push west toward the Steel Crag range. Our supplies of steel are running low. We were in need of fresh resources to construct more Biogtechs even before my absence," Vertigo ordered Brother Feral.

"If I am to stay here with you, who shall lead this army against the Steel Crag Guild?" Feral asked, his voice resentful. He couldn't believe another would lead the armies against the enemies of the empire.

"Nightshade will lead the army," Vertigo said forcefully, staring down Brother Feral. The intimidation worked, and Feral averted his eyes in an act of submission. "I grow tired of the populace of Rasheed," Vertigo sneered and turned his attention to his beloved Sister Nightshade, his most trusted emissary. "Kill half the survivors, send two thousand to the breeding pits, and splice the remaining to use as slaves." Vertigo smiled as he spoke to Sister Nightshade.

"Your will be done, master," Nightshade hissed, bowing before Vertigo.

"Nightshade..." Vertigo said, hatred flaring in his eyes. "Ready a plague... we should unleash it prior to the invasion of the

Steel Crag Mining Guild. With any luck, half the populace will be dead or too weak to fight during the invasion. Do this discretely. I will send Marion with you after she has been purified in the torture chambers. You can sneak into the city and taint the water supply. Marion is twisted and dedicated to our cause, but she is young. Teach her the way," Vertigo decreed, then fell silent.

"A plague we shall have, master," Nightshade replied.

A quite moment fell over the room. Vertigo was squinting, anger flaring in his black eyes.

"This boy..." Vertigo said in a dull tone. "This tribal brat who stabbed me. I want his home destroyed and his people slaughtered. Send out spies and find this tribal's home. After the fall of the Steel Crag Mining Guild, take one thousand Biogtech troops and..." Vertigo fell silent, and a smile graced his lips, "...kill every living person from his village. Make sure that this brat of a tribal pays for his arrogance."

"A thousand Biogtechs, my Lord? For a tribal village?" Nightshade quizzed in a confused tone.

"Yes." Vertigo spoke crisply and contemptuously. "I want his entire tribe to suffer horribly for what he has done. How dare a brat from the wastes attack me!"

"What of Banion O'Neil, my Lord? Banion was the one to slay you!" Nightshade hissed.

"I cannot destroy what I have burned already. Banion has no home..." Vertigo smiled. "I felt his mind... We have killed everything he has ever loved. He has nothing else to lose, this gunfighter from the wastes."

"True, but he is very dangerous, my Lord. Legends abound around this Banion! You know the stories! Dune Station fell because of him, master!" Nightshade spoke in an excited tone.

"I fear not a gunfighter, nor a tribal," Vertigo hissed. The Lord of Darkness then fell silent. His thoughts drifted toward the future, and a bizarre image entered his mind. A flash of precognition flooded him. In Vertigo's vision, the tribal was before him again, but this time his eyes were filled with madness and his mighty blue blade was bathed in blood. "Do my will!" Vertigo shouted.   Nightshade bowed and moved away from him.   As he looked at the Goat Minions, they sensed his fury and backed away, bleating in submission, leaving him alone in the room.

Collecting his thoughts, Vertigo let the hate of his existence fill him.   Thinking about the future, the Lord of Darkness plotted in his mind the demise of all that remained in the Darken Realm.

Chapter 3
And Then, There Were Three

The morning sun broke over the eastern sea, breaching the gray storm clouds that had turned the sea into a swirling maelstrom the night before. The first rays pressed outward from the clouds, shining upon the barren, desolate beach. Sea gulls huddled in masses along the edge of the sand dunes. Raising their heads, the gulls greeted the warmth of the morning sun. Green grasses swished back and forth in the moist breeze rolling off the gulf to the east. Waves crashed against the shore, and a trio of companions could be seen sitting quietly on the beach, still exhausted from the night; none of them had slept a wink, each lost in their thoughts.

The mood was somber. The sun had risen, and its warmth heated the trio of companions on the lonely beach. Like a collection of wet rats, Nova 7 gazed silently at the waves of the sea. The intense surf had diminished, but on the eastern horizon were a set of ominous dark clouds, the same clouds that had turned the sea into a writhing whirlwind of water; the same clouds that had spawned the deadly storm which had claimed the life of young Jared.

Not a single word passed between the trio. Each of them simply sat motionless, staring at the waves crashing against the shore. Each member was lost in dark thoughts; sadness mixed with guilt. Mineera was overwhelmed not only by her own thoughts, but by the thoughts of Banion and Tani as well.

Banion was filled with a haunting rage. Dark thoughts clouded his already fragile soul. Twisted fantasies floated through him. He trembled with a sense of loss overpowered by a blood lust. Banion wanted the enemy to be punished, and punished horribly. The deranged gunfighter focused his rage on the Reaper Kai. In his mind, the companions would not have been on the boat if it weren't for the insane quest initiated by King Toil to stop the threat of evil spreading from the northlands. The Reaper Kai were at fault for

Jared's death, plain and simple.

Tani, on the other hand, was filled with an intense sadness. Jared had been like a brother to the young scholar. Their families were close, and had spent countless holiday events together. Young Tani tried to keep from weeping, but no matter how hard he tried to hold back the tears, they trickled down his cheeks relentlessly. A knot had formed in the back of Tani's head and refused to leave. The painful pressure would not easily be forgotten.

Mineera was rocking back and forth, filled with Banion's rage and Tani's sadness. Her mind screamed, and she tried to force her companions' thoughts out of her own. Being able to discern others' thoughts was an advantage, but could also be overwhelming. Not being able to control her thoughts, Mineera cried silently, trying to return order to her consciousness while fighting back the rage building at the back of her mind as she focused on Banion.

White foam hissed as the waves receded back into the sea. The foam popped and bubbled. Soon enough, another wave crashed ashore and the process began anew. The daydream of the ocean waves was wearing off. Banion was becoming restless.

The deranged rancher had had enough of brooding, and hopped to his feet. He dared not look at Mineera or Tani, but spoke nonetheless. "We need to move. The enemy has spies everywhere, and I would hate to be caught out in the open like this. Especially defenseless." Banion's tone was low, almost a whisper.

Tani rose to his feet and turned away from the ocean. He looked down at the sand and stopped the tears. Gripping his hands together, he rubbed his stumpy fingers with his good hand. The young scholar shook his head and collected his thoughts. "My explosives are ruined, but my computer is fine and my dictionary can dry out." Tani displayed his laptop computer, wrapped tightly in plastic. His dictionary was a soggy mess, still soaked with salt water.

"No offense, bookworm, but I doubt we can beat off a mutant or gun down a Biogtech with your laptop or dictionary. We need some gear and we need it fast," Banion said in a grim tone, eagerly anticipating switching to a topic that did not involve Jared.

"I agree. We need to get moving." Tani spoke softly, not wanting to look at either of his companions.

"What about you?" the rancher asked in a blunt tone, looking at Mineera dressed in the blue robes she had acquired after the fall of Rasheed a few months back, in the refugee camp.

"I am ready." Mineera stood and managed to hold on to a good semblance of sanity. Both Tani's and Banion's thoughts had drifted, at least for the moment, away from the death of Jared. It was easier for her to collect her own thoughts. "I have no weapons other than my faith."

Banion looked at her with disgust, almost wanting to snort at her.

"Dune Station should be south of here. I recognize this beach. My 'uncle' and I came here often to fish when I was young. It's not far to Dune Station," Banion said, taking a step southward. He pointed at a large rock formation a few miles out in the gulf, half submerged by the ocean. "It's called Shark Rock. See how the rock formation looks like a shark's fin?"

Tani and Mineera nodded, staring out into the gulf.

"You're from here, then?" Tani quizzed Banion with a strange look in his eye. The young scholar was thinking back to the library in Rasheed. Suspicion filled his mind.

"Banion is from here," Mineera said in an ominous tone. The psychic maiden looked down at the sand as she walked. Banion shot her an uneasy glance. There was a hint of anger in his posture as he heard her speak.

Banion was dressed only in his long coat, shirt, pants, and combat boots. The sea had claimed his hat, weapons, and all other possessions. The deranged rancher's expression was cautionary as he walked. "We need to be careful. I know some good people in Dune Station who will help us, but we need to stay low. I don't want the whole damn town knowing that I've returned."

"I don't get it," Tani pressed again, trying to get Banion to expose his secret connection to the desert town.

Banion did not respond. Mineera simply looked at Tani uneasily. "Some secrets should stay hidden," she said in an ominous tone, staring at him with her intense blue eyes. Tani looked back tensely, letting the matter drop.

The trio continued on, with Banion O'Neil in the lead. The ocean breeze picked up and cooled the companions as they walked. The blue waves crashed against the shore as the sun rose higher in the sky. Soon, the trio could see the images of buildings coming into view just a few miles to the south.

A collection of wooden huts and houses filled their vision. Gray wooden frames, eroded by the salt air, were covered in a menagerie of mismatched wooden planks. Sand from the sea filled the streets.   Wooden boardwalks lined the avenues, and a ramshackle collection of town denizens could be seen milling about amongst the sand littered avenues.

Banion stopped at the edge of town and gave a loud sigh. Recollections filled his mind, and he looked white as a ghost. "So many memories…" Banion said in a dull tone.

"I bet," Mineera whispered. A chill rolled down her spine. A collection of memories filled the psychic maiden, fragments of sound and images, all from Banion's dark past, but none of them concrete enough to discern clearly.

"Stay close to me and keep quiet. Don't draw any attention to us. I don't want anyone to know I have returned." Banion spoke softly and moved onward slowly. "It's been a long time since I've been here, and I want to avoid word spreading that we were seen in Dune Station. The agents of the enemy would quickly be on our trail."

The trio pressed on and moved toward the harbor. A giant stone jetty pressed into the ocean. Large sailing ships and rusting steel freighters lined the stone jetty. Many of the ships were battered and damaged. Several were capsized in the harbor. The storm had not been friendly to the vessels in the harbor during the previous night, and had caused much damage to the waterfront. Such violent storms were rare in the gulf, and left many unprepared for their wrath.

Banion moved forward with his head down and pressed on into the middle of the waterfront. A strange collection of sailing folk were milling about the wharf district. Sailors smoked and drank while spinning tales about the sea and the world beyond. Small carts were arranged in a half circle, and the makeshift market was selling a collection of local wares and exotic treasures from distant ports. Banion smiled and kept walking, his mood getting better as he saw and remembered the kindred images of his childhood.

Homeless vagrants and derelicts from abroad were huddling near crates of garbage from nearby bars and shops, each hoping to collect small scraps of food that would make their lives a tad better.

Banion walked by without giving them a second look. He pushed on into a bar with a corroded sign that read 'The Ocean Rat'. The interior was dimly lit. Banion stood in the open doorway while the sun shone brightly behind him, obscuring his face from anyone within.

"We're closed," a man said in the darkness of the bar. "Come back after sundown."

"It's open for me," Banion said in an arrogant tone, still standing in the doorway.

"I guess you don't understand me, dipshit! Get the hell out of here, or I'll break your damn skull!" the man roared from the darkness.

Banion pushed into the dark bar with a nasty grin on his face. "Talon, you are the ugliest damn thing I have ever seen. I thought the years would have made you prettier, but I guess I was wrong."

"Banion?" The man moved from behind the bar, squinting in the darkness. A strange look of recognition was forming on his face. The tall black man moved forward and eyed Banion with suspicion. "Figures. The worst storm I have ever seen in my life has washed ashore the meanest damn thing in the entire Darken Realm, Banion O'Neil."

Banion smiled and slapped the barkeep, Talon, on the shoulder. Tani moved into the bar, with Mineera following close behind. She looked oddly at Talon, who stared back at her with a suspicious look.

"Who are these two dogs?" Talon spoke while squinting at Tani and Mineera.

"Close and lock the door," Banion said without answering Talon's question.

Talon stood still for a moment, eyeing the trio oddly. "Sure thing, Banion." He moved over to the tavern door and locked it shut.

"These are my two associates, Tani and Mineera," Banion said in a calm tone.

"Ok, well, good to meet ya. A friend of Banion is a friend of mine." Talon smiled and rubbed his bald head. "Come on over and let me give ya a drink."

The trio sat at a table and Talon brought out a bottle of whiskey. He poured four shot glasses and placed them down on the table.

Banion slammed his shot while Tani sipped the drink slowly, sniffing it as he drank. Mineera lifted the glass and swallowed the shot. Talon slammed his shot down in one gulp and smacked the glass down on the wooden table with a thud.

"What the hell happened to you, Banion?" Talon quizzed. "I heard stories... we all heard stories about you after that day..." Talon seemed to have a dreamy look on his face.

"I moved on," Banion said in a dull tone. "Worked for Rasheed and some mercenary guilds."

"Yeah, I heard you blew away Jimmie Skins, that gunfighter from Nar Whal," Talon replied.

Banion nodded, his face blank.

"What about Cline Redmond and his crew? You wiped them out too?" Talon quizzed.

"Yeah..." Banion sighed. "They fell in with slavers. I can't stand slavers."

"Guess so," Talon said in a submissive tone, eyeing Banion with an uneasy look. "So, what brings you here?"

"I need some gear." The deranged rancher got straight to the point.

Talon's expression was suspicious. "Gear? What for?" he asked, his voice helpful.

Mineera felt the skin at the back of her neck tingle.

Something wasn't right, but she couldn't tell what it was. She shook off the feeling and stared intently at Talon.

"I'm heading out into the western waste, going on an expedition," the gunfighter responded in a cryptic tone.

"Expedition? What are you looking for?" the bald, dark skinned man shot back.

Banion did not respond; he only stared intently at Talon. The barkeep avoided his gaze and broke eye contact.

"Fair enough, Banion..." Talon shook his head. "What do you need?"

"I need a submachine gun, several hundred rounds of ammunition, rations, canteens, explosives for the kid..." Banion said while nodding toward Tani. "And..." The gunfighter looked over at Mineera.

"A long knife or staff will suffice," the psychic maiden said, staring intently at Talon. Her blue eyes were unblinking as she considered him. Probing his mind, the traitor of the Reaper Kai was having a hard time reading Talon's intentions.

"I got just what you need." Talon rose and moved behind the bar. The strong, tall black man kneeled down and pulled open a trapdoor in the floor. He moved down a set of stairs into the cellar.

Nova 7 remained at the table, waiting for their host to bring out the gear. Talon descended into the dark armory, hidden beneath the bar.

"Talon was a gun runner, and a damn good one." Banion smiled as he poured himself another shot of whiskey. Eyeing Tani, he offered him another shot. Tani glanced back with an alarmed look; the tribal scholar had still not finished his first shot, continuing to take small sips.

After rummaging around in the hidden weapon cache, Talon emerged from the concealed basement and placed two backpacks on the table. One was filled with dynamite and the other with rations, canteens, and ammunition. The dark skinned man smiled at Mineera, jamming a hefty knife into the wooden table, making it stand on end. Mineera remained undaunted by the action, only eyeing Talon with a blank stare. Talon tossed Banion a submachine gun and then moved back behind the bar. Grabbing a black cowboy hat from a shelf under the bar, Talon returned to the table and handed it to Banion. "A drunk left it here a few weeks back. It smells bad, but it will keep the sun off your head."

Tani and Mineera surveyed the weapons and looked curiously at Banion.

After accepting all of the equipment and weapons, Banion looked at Talon and spoke. "I trust we are even now?"

"Not even close, Banion... you saved my life all those years back, you saved all of us. I still owe you... this town still owes you."

"Thanks for the drinks and the gear," Banion said in an appreciative tone while standing up, looking at the door.

"Can't you stick around a little while? I haven't seen you in years. Come on, kick back and have some drinks with me. You know, tell some stories."

"We don't have time for that. Next time I pass through, we can kick back. I just want to get the hell out of here as soon as possible." Banion walked over and stared at Talon intently. "No one needs to know we were here or that we are in Dune Station." A cold stare was on Banion's face as he spoke.

"Yeah, no problem."

With that, Banion turned around and walked out of the bar. Tani and Mineera followed. The trio disappeared into the streets of Dune Station, leaving Talon with an odd look on his face.

As the door to the bar closed, the odd look turned into a greedy, broad smile. Talon felt a rush hit his system. "No need to pay me back for my generosity, Banion," he chuckled. Moving over to the bar, he grabbed a radio transmitter, and spoke into it. "I got them," Talon declared triumphantly into the radio. "I got Nova 7."

"Excellent..." a sinister voice responded from the crackling radio.

Chapter 4
Prophecy of Doom

"Damn it, Mineera!" Jared screamed, his cheeks flushed red. There was a crazed look in his eyes.

Mineera stared at Jared dreamily. Her subconscious was screaming that something was wrong. "Jared?" Mineera asked in a confused tone. The hot-headed youth had Banion's revolver in one hand and the mighty Scar Blade in the other.

"Wake up!" Jared shouted angrily. "Snap out of it. We have a job to do."

Mineera looked around and found her surroundings unusual. Old, corroded rusty metal walls and steel girders rose around them. She spun around and caught sight of Tani sitting on the floor, leaning against the wall. There was a look of shock on Tani's face.

"He's gone!" Jared said in a matter-of-fact tone. "There isn't a damn thing we can do about it now. We need to get moving…"

The strange dream of Jared had ended. Something else moved into her mind, taunting her, baying at her. A powerful form moved into her dreams. A man, pristine in appearance, with shimmering blue skin and muscles bulging with an unnatural sheen filled her dreams. The form of the entity was perfect, except for his eyes. Instead of warm eyes, the perfect being had solid black eyes, devoid of all life and compassion.

"Morality is a fleeting thing, is it not?" the being taunted in the dream, as Mineera tried to rationalize the vision in the haze of her slumber.

"What do you want?" Mineera mumbled, responding to the specter filling her dreams.

"I want you back…" it hissed.

"That is something I cannot do. The suffering caused by our kind cannot be allowed to remain."

"Then stop him – stop Father Vertigo. Usurp him from his throne and lead the Reaper Kai the way you see fit." The man moved forward, toward her in the dream. A sickly haze clouded her mind. The spirit was powerful indeed.

"I only wish to end this war," she responded.

The being glared at her with its black orbs. *"You are powerful enough to overthrow Vertigo, but you must maintain control of our coven. Only through strength can one lead our race; only through a rigid hand can you dominate their minds and their will."*

The spirit was cunning, and Mineera was beginning to succumb to its words. She began to think about usurping Vertigo and leading the Reaper Kai as she saw fit. The glamour of power was alluring indeed. A burst of sickness washed over her, the same sickly feeling that had filled her before she betrayed the Reaper Kai. The sickly feeling was familiar, but perverse nonetheless. Overcoming the flood of evil coursing through her, Mineera fought back and drove the sinister thoughts from her mind, making a stand against the darkness.

"This is my final warning: submit to me and to your heritage, or I will make you submit."

"Do your worst, shade. I will not travel the path through the blighted lands again."

Twisted hate covered the face atop the perfectly formed body. *"In your most desperate hour, in your weakest slumber, I will find you. You are my child and you will follow me!"* the being hissed at her. The beastly vision of perfection began to falter; something else was approaching.

The vision began to change. Blackness filled her mind. The dark being bellowed as it was driven away, disappearing in a haze. The surreal dream was changing once more, and a point of light was the only thing that filled Mineera's slumber. The point of light exploded into a shimmering disk. Rotating, the disk pulsed with each turn, spinning faster and faster, until it exploded into a flash. A form moved in the bright light, and a being emerged from the disk and spoke.

"*Mineera...*" it whispered.

In a dream-like state, Mineera mumbled unintelligibly.

"*Mineera...*" The specter spoke more directly, with purpose.

The being flared and white light poured from it. "What do you want?" she whispered.

"*Do not despair, you must maintain your faith if the world is to survive this nightmare,*" the angel murmured in a calming, soothing tone.

"How can I not despair? Jared died so needlessly," Mineera replied in the dreamlike state.

"*It was the will of God.*"

"How can it be the will of God that Jared died? I don't understand. I do not believe you. How can the needless death of the innocent be divine will?"

"*You must believe and hold your faith. If you do not, all is lost...*"

Mineera thrashed about in her bed. She was talking in her sleep, and Tani eyed her suspiciously.

"Jared..." Mineera spoke dreamily. The psychic woman was having some sort of dream – a bad one, from Tani's perspective.

Over and over again, she called out. The hair on the back of the young scholar's neck was beginning to stand on edge. With each utterance of Jared's name, Tani became more uncomfortable. It was a pinprick striking at his mind. The scholar ran his stumpy fingers through his hair, clutching at it, pulling his short hair until it hurt. He was becoming enraged, and tried to force pain upon himself to make his anger stop.

Jared was my friend, Tani thought to himself.

"Jared..." Mineera said softly into the darkness of the room.

The pin kept striking at him. He quivered and anger took him. Tani fought his rage in vain. It exploded into a shout, a burst of anger.

"Shut up, you damn witch!" the young scholar shouted at Mineera. The psychic maiden awoke, sitting straight up in bed, looking bewildered.

"What?" she said in a startled tone, looking at Tani.

"I told you to shut your damn mouth," Tani shot back in an angry tone.

Banion simply looked at Tani with sympathy. The deranged gunfighter was unable to sleep himself, and had been lying on his bed staring at the ceiling before Tani shouted. He could relate to the youth, and wasn't in a mood to defend anyone, let alone Mineera. The deranged gunfighter watched through his dark brown eyes, a quiet spectator.

Mineera sat quietly, looking at Tani with a fresh feeling of guilt washing over her. In the darkness, their eyes met, and it was an uncomfortable meeting. Rage was flashing in the tribal's eyes, and Mineera knew that it was directed at her.

"I was talking in my sleep." The psychic maiden spoke confidently, but in an apologetic tone. "I was having a bad dream. I am sorry, Tani."

"He was my friend..." Tani said dully. There was a moment of silence, and then suddenly the fire flashed again, and Tani resumed his hostile tone. "Don't talk about him anymore. He was my friend, not yours." Tani fidgeted with his glasses as he fumed. His mind was racing, and he took a few seconds to collect his turbulent thoughts. Words began to flow from him. "I shouldn't be here right now, and there was no reason that Jared should have ever been on that damn boat."

Mineera was silent, allowing Tani to vent his simmering anger.

"I don't want any part of this war." Tani spoke passionately.

"At this point, you don't have a choice," Mineera countered with a blunt tone.

"I can walk out that door, right now. You watch me!" the scholar threatened, pointing his stumpy, gnarled hand at the door to their room, but remained sitting on the bed.

"Your leaving is not God's will." Mineera spoke softly,

staring out with a piercing gaze from the bright blue eyes set amidst the dark skin of her face.

"God? What God? Where is this God of yours? I have read about the ancient religions. Look what their God got them. The whole world is in ruins. It has taken centuries for mankind to crawl from the ashes, and it will take centuries more to reclaim this wasted land." Hostile words flowed from Tani and he didn't want to stop. He wanted more than anything to be out of control and make someone pay for what he was feeling.

"God will save us," Mineera pressed on, undaunted by the tribal's outburst.

"I say again, where is this God of yours? This land is full of suffering. If this God is here, in this place, then he is part of the suffering." The scholar stared at Mineera, hoping for a response.

"I am the only one that believes. If there were only one more person like me, this world would be a better place. I must trust in my faith." The answer was cryptic, but Mineera held her ground.

"The only thing we can trust in is our knowledge. Science – not *your* God – will put an end to this war."

"Science – not *my* God – is why the world is in ruins. Pride overrode wisdom and pride replaced the spirit. Why are we made to suffer? We make ourselves suffer."

"No, we don't make ourselves suffer. Your damn race, your damn people, that's what makes us suffer." Tani brought it home, and was all too happy to do so. He left Mineera in a shocked state of silence. Sure, the scholar knew it was a low blow, the same low blow he had defended her against just a few nights ago when Banion went into a rage. But this was different, Tani thought to himself; he was the victim. Tani was the one suffering, and he had to make someone feel just like him. It wasn't the right thing to do, but the young scholar didn't care. How can someone do the right thing when all they want to do is get even?

The deranged rancher smiled in the darkness. In a twisted way, he was proud of young Tani. The boy had come a long way. When Banion first met Tani, the young scholar was brilliant and timid. Now, the boy was showing some real backbone. Banion hated Mineera, and was all too happy to embrace the boy and initiate him into his own hate-filled world.

The rift had begun. Tani and Banion had the same thoughts. Mineera was now even more of an outcast.

Her intentions were genuine, but she could never escape her past. In a sense, she could not be in a worse place. She had betrayed her own people to save the innocent. Now, the very people she had fought to save were setting her adrift without a paddle. Mineera was caught in the center of two colliding worlds, two worlds that were now alien to her.

The room was silent, and the two combatants retreated into their own thoughts.

Tani lay back in his bed and stared at the ceiling. His mind was still fraught with fever and he was too pumped up to sleep.

Mineera sat on her bed and looked out the window. The harbor was silent. Wave after wave pressed against the stone jetty jutting deeply into the ocean. With each wave, her mind relaxed and a sense of peace came over her. She knew acceptance would be impossible. Mineera had no home. She shook her head sadly, and a gentle calm came over her. With a smile on her face, she watched the waves crash against the jetty. A thought came to her mind: *To be strong, you must first be weak. Submit to something greater than yourself. True strength lies in great abandon.*

In that moment, it didn't matter that the whole world was against her. She had a sense of duty and unwavering faith in something greater than herself. Sure, *everyone* was against her, but this only made the struggle all the more sweeter.

With these gentle thoughts, Mineera drifted into a deep slumber, one without interruption or visions.

Chapter 5
The Diplomat

The embers glowed and crackled as bright orange flames licked at the dry wood. With a pop, a bright ember flashed and whipped through the air, spiraling high into the dim light of the night sky and finally burning out. The bright orange flare of the ember was gone, disappearing into the darkness of the night.

The sight was ominous to a lone figure seated at the campfire. His eyes lazily watched more embers rise into the air and go out, extinguished by the chill of the dark night. With a sigh, the mighty Globulus averted his gaze and looked away, toward the encampment. Hundreds of campfires dotted the rock formation. In the dim light, at the edge of camp, guards wandered back and forth.

The last of our people... Globulus thought to himself. All of the survivors of the destroyed kingdom of Rasheed were camped along the rock face bordering the sea. It had taken weeks and weeks for all of the survivors to trickle in. Each day, Globulus hoped more would arrive, but alas, they did not. It had been days since any new survivors had staggered into camp. The mighty mutant hippo was beginning to believe that no more would come.

Globulus gave a large sigh. His thoughts drifted to Nova 7, and to hope. All of the other Nova teams had been slain in the battle of Rasheed. Nova 7 was the hope against the darkness. He smiled as he thought of each member of Nova 7. It was such an unlikely combination, but a strong one, nevertheless; they had survived against all odds and had emerged unscathed from the fall of Rasheed. And although the Reaper Kai were one step closer to victory, the Lord of Darkness had been slain in battle, which would slow down the leadership of the enemy.

It was strangely fortunate that the only team that survived was a team that required no compensation for its actions. Nova 7 was led by Banion, a crazed maniac who would carry on the mission without reward. Hate and vengeance fueled his fire, and he had more than enough gas left to finish the quest. Mineera, the homeless traitor, and the two tribals were along for the ride.

Breaking the silence and concentration of Globulus' thoughts, a soldier spoke to the mighty mutant who was lost in his daydream.

"Sir?" The soldier spoke softly, trying not to startle the mighty mutant hippo.

Globulus looked at the soldier standing before him. "You are my courier?" the hippo asked hesitantly.

The short soldier, young in years, stood with a sheepish look on his face. "Yes, sir," he replied softly.

Globulus snorted. The soldier looked green, real green.

"I was picked from all the others, sir." The soldier tried to sound confident.

"What is your name, soldier?" the mutant quizzed the recruit.

"Private Glenn, sir."

"Sit down, Private Glenn. Warm yourself by my fire."

"Thank you, sir," the soldier said while crouching down. He gave Globulus short glances, not wanting to maintain eye contact with the mighty mutant for too long.

"What makes you think you can make it all the way north without getting killed like the other couriers?" Globulus was blunt, his eyes locking with Private Glenn's.

There was an uneasy moment of silence while Globulus eyed the soldier suspiciously. Glenn was too frightened to speak, his heart stuck in his throat.

"I was first in my class for infiltration, sir." Glenn spoke softly while looking down at his feet.

"First in class, huh? Why haven't I heard of you before now?" the hippo pressed.

"Ah…" Glenn stammered.

"Out with it, Private!"

"No combat experience, sir. Not even the night Rasheed fell. I provided reloads to my unit the whole night. Never even fired my rifle." Glenn seemed embarrassed by his revelation.

Globulus let out a large sigh. "Not even a single shot fired that whole night?" The mutant hippo shook his head back and forth, as if trying to understand how such a thing could happen.

Glenn did not respond.

"Well, Private Glenn, it looks like you've been afforded the opportunity to serve your kingdom, what's left of it, anyway. What say you, Glenn?"

"I will serve, sir."

"Good." Globulus motioned young Glenn forward. "I charge you to take these papers into the northlands, beyond the Stone Wastes into the Iron Kai territory. These words you carry are my oath and are written in my hand as master of the remnants of the Rasheed Empire. They are words of urgency, and call for an alliance to be formed with the Iron Kai. They served in our evacuation, and we will pledge all of our remaining might to their great army. We have no home, but our purpose is clear. To surrender our fight against the Reaper Kai is unconscionable. Our world is gone, and to throw our lives needlessly against the Reaper Kai war machine would be futile. We will offer all of what remains to the Iron Kai." Globulus spoke softly, with a distant look in his eyes.

Glenn was stunned. It was official: Rasheed had been destroyed, and the remnants of a once great kingdom that had survived the cruel world for hundreds of years were shattered and broken. Now, their fate was to be assimilated into the army of another great empire struggling against the dread Reaper Kai.

"Your orders are to bring this transcript to Emperor Gunther himself. Pledge our allegiance, then return and muster our forces to aid the Iron Kai war effort," Globulus ordered.

"I am to muster the troops against the Reaper Kai? What of you?" Glenn quizzed in a concerned tone.

"Do not fear. I have left orders to my most trusted lieutenants; they will deal with military matters. You are simply a messenger. When you return, it is your direction that will mobilize all that remains of our army. And as for me? I might not return." Globulus's tone was ominous.

"Where are you going, sir?" Glenn's voice remained concerned.

"I am heading into the western wastes. The Steel Crag Mining Guild must be warned. All of our couriers sent west have not returned. I fear agents of the enemy have slain them. If all goes well, I can enlist the great mining guild to help in the struggle. Their might may well turn the tide of war against the Reaper Kai in our favor," the mighty hippo responded with a distant look in his eye.

"Why must you go, my lord? Why not another courier?"

"I will have the best chance of survival, and will be received favorably. The Steel Crags is where I was born; my tribe members are great warriors and friends of the Guild. I have the best chance to convince the Protectorate of the Guild to fight the Reaper Kai. And maybe..." His look grew distant and a sadness entered his eyes. His thoughts drifted to his long-ago home at the base of the mountains, amongst the reeds of the great marshes. Thoughts of his family, his real family, flowed through his mind with uneasy pulses of guilt and sadness. "Just maybe..." he whispered.

Glenn eyed him silently, watching the inner turmoil. When the mighty Globulus regained his composure, the young soldier spoke once more.

"The greatest warrior of Rasheed is now a diplomat. What happened to our world?" the soldier said, mystified.

"Our world is gone. All we can do is try to survive in this world." Globulus stared into the fire. Four glowing embers erupted and rose into the night. Instead of burning out, the embers returned to the fire and glowed intently. Globulus smiled to himself; four embers in a dark world. Hope returned, and Globulus thought once again of Nova 7, mired by the dark world but burning brightly against the night. Even if all the armies of the wasteland united, victory would still be scarce against the Reaper Kai. The world needed a miracle; the world needed nuclear retribution, provided from the unlikely band of heroes known as Nova 7.

"Well, Private Glenn. I think you need to get some rest. You will leave in the morning. It's a long haul into the northlands," Globulus ordered the young soldier.

"Are we gonna make it, sir?" Glenn quizzed with concern.

"I'm not sure, Private Glenn. I'm not sure."

Chapter 6
The Great Revolt

The citizens of Dune Station were mostly naked. Stark white bodies were pressed together in great cages. Most of the citizens had been rounded up and imprisoned in nothing but their bare skin. Whimpering filled the crowd as the masses pressed against each other. Fear was wild in the air. Like animals, they were crammed into pens, resembling a herd of cattle waiting to be slaughtered. Razor wire cages surrounded the citizens of Dune Station. Beyond the fences, Reaper Kai initiates and Biogtech soldiers walked the perimeter, ready to use any force necessary to keep the citizens of Dune Station imprisoned and at bay behind the fences.

"Stay close to me." Frank spoke in a hushed tone. The tall merchant eyed his bastard 'nephew' with a serious look. His 'nephew' knew that look all too well, and obeyed him without question, feeling frightened beyond belief. Old memories, memories of his mother, were slinking around at the back of the youth's mind, drawn forth by the sinister forms holding vigil around the pens.

The teenage boy was dressed only in his underwear and was wide eyed with fear. He gripped the wrist of his 'uncle' tightly, clawing his flesh. Feeling the youth's fingernails digging in, the adult took a moment to release his tight grip. Nodding in order to reassure young Banion, Frank was trying desperately to calm the youth.

Frank and young Banion pushed slowly through the crowd, through the masses of frightened victims, none of whom were prepared for what was about to occur. As they moved, the crowd bulged and heaved, shambling about in a frightened mass. Frank was staunch in his decision to reach the front of the holding pens, and this set young Banion on edge. His 'uncle' had a plan, and the youth was scared. Minutes passed, and finally, the two were standing near the front of the pen. A wooden platform rose just beyond the razor wire fences keeping the hopeless mass of Dune Station inhabitants caged like wild animals. The platform was brimming with the enemy. Reaper Kai initiates stood above the crowd upon the platform.

A host of robotic soldiers held guard around the pens. The imprisoned citizens of Dune Station eyed the automatons with great fear. Steel warriors, pasty white, giggling every now and again in a mechanical tone, their eyes flashing red, regarded their prized captives with sinister looks.

Banion, a mere fifteen years of age, stood with his gaze transfixed upon the robotic soldiers holding vigil over the scared and frantic captives. His mind began to wander, and visions of his past flashed into his mind. A tinge of burning flesh filled his nostrils. A horrid vision of burning bodies arose in his mind's eye. Banion began to tremble as thoughts of his past rolled through his fragile mind. The death of his mother so many years ago was washing over him in waves of terror. Even though Banion was only a few years old at the time, the death of his mother had been burned into his memory. The horrid events were beginning to paralyze the youth.

Frank saw his nephew wracked with fear. With a confident motion, he placed his hand on the shoulder of young Banion. Banion snapped out of his daydream and looked around him with startled glances. Frank nodded and gripped his nephew's shoulder tightly.

"We will be all right, Banion, don't you worry." Frank smiled, and Banion felt better. His 'uncle' had always known what to say. Frank could always console young Banion and make him feel better.

Banion gripped his 'uncle's' wrist tightly once more, trembling violently. Frank smiled and took a deep breath. With a confident gesture, Frank pulled Banion's hand from his wrist. He nodded at the youth and extended his other hand, allowing the youth to see what was clutched in it. Banion's eyes grew wide with fright. Clutched in Frank's hand was a silver, long barreled revolver, gleaming in the harsh desert sun.

"You are never helpless, Banion, you hear me, boy? You are

never helpless," Frank said, looking into his 'nephew's' eyes. Banion shook his head back and forth, unable to comprehend what was about to happen. The look on his 'uncle's' face was staunch, almost frightening to young Banion, who was looking up at the only family he had ever known. His jaw tense and tight, his hand flexed repeatedly around the grip of the revolver, Frank was ready for something desperate, something rash.

"Look at all the pretty tribal trash!" a woman dressed in crimson robes cried out while ascending to the platform near the edge of the cages. Her features were fine, pristine, as if she was born from royalty. Her bright blue eyes were deep and imposing. The priestess projected an air of confidence. It was easy to tell she often got her way. Two red robed initiates followed with grim looks on their faces. Serpent tattoos lined the fledgling Reaper Kai's arms, and they displayed them with pride.

"You should all be proud!" the woman shouted. "You will serve our empire well!"

"Reaper Kai scum!" a man yelled defiantly at the woman upon the raised stage.

Asagara Toil, the red robed woman upon the stage, was filled with rage. A grim look covered her face. "Bring him up here!" she screeched in anger.

The red-robed Reaper Kai initiates moved into the cage as a host of Biogtech soldiers trained their weapons on the helpless crowd. Forcing people out of the way, the young Reaper Kai grabbed the man from the crowd. He struggled and cursed his captors all the way to the stage.

"Let this man serve as an example to you all. Your only duty from this day forth is obedience to your new masters!" Asagara hissed and smiled. "Dune Station belongs to the Reaper Kai." The deranged Reaper Kai priestess motioned to her companions.

The Reaper Kai initiates pulled clubs from their robes. Without mercy, they pummeled and beat the man. Their intensity could not be swayed, and within a mere moment, the defiant man ceased to move, bloodied upon the stage, silent testament to failed defiance.

The crowd was shocked and horrified. An unnatural quiet came over the naked masses of humans crammed together in the cages. Not a single person stirred or made a sound. They breathed in shallow gasps, fighting the urge to close their eyes and wait for the darkness to take them.

Asagara gazed into the cages with a smile on her face. "I see you have already learned your place." A scowl covered the priestess's face as she looked out. "All of the women will now move to the gate. You will be used to aid our glorious race in breeding the next generation!"

A stunned silence followed. The women began to panic. Whimpering filled the crowd. Fear had taken over. Like wild animals before a butcher, hope had faded, and primitive terror replaced reason.

The women, too scared to disobey, moved slowly, pushing their way through the crowd. Mothers said hasty, tear-filled goodbyes to their families. Daughters whimpered in terror as they were stripped away by Reaper Kai initiates roving through the cages. Fathers stood stunned as their families were taken from them.

Frank had had enough of the terror. He held the revolver behind his back and prepared to make a stand. As the crowd of women pushed past him, he broke away from young Banion and allowed the mass of panicked captives to carry him toward the gate. In the chaos and pushing, the revolver slipped from Frank's hand. It hit the ground and disappeared in the flurry of fear. Young Banion saw the weapon fall to the ground, quickly lost in the shuffle. His 'uncle' was now defenseless and being swept away by the crowd.

Frank was trapped in the mass of frantic wives, mothers, and daughters, slowly pushed toward the gate by the herd. Banion was filled with fright as his 'uncle' slipped deeper and deeper into the crowd, further and further away. Shaking his head back and forth, a knot formed in his stomach.

"Uncle!" Banion yelled, but his voice was drowned out by the roar of the crowd. "Uncle!" he yelled again, but it was useless.

Blue eyes, callous and filled with hate, watched the crowd intently. Scowling, Asagara Toil caught sight of Frank, who was lost in the shuffle and being forced toward the gate. A grim smile covered her face. Shouting, she outstretched a single finger, pointing at Frank.

"I said women to the gate!" the priestess roared. Her white, slim finger, crooked in a gesture of command, pointed at Frank, stuck in the midst of the whimpering women. "I think we need another example! I will show you obedience!"

"Please, no!" young Banion whimpered, voice barely breaking the sound of confusion. He knew what was about to happen.

The red robed Reaper Kai pushed their way into the women. They moved in on Frank quickly. With a shove, they pushed him toward the gate.

Time seemed to stand still.

After sustaining a punch to the stomach, Frank fell before the red robed Asagara upon the wooden stage. Her wicked smile flashed in Banion's mind. Such cruelty and madness filled her. Banion was motionless, his heart pounding deeply in his chest. Her delicate features would forever sting his mind, after seeing her laugh, wicked blue eyes glowering at his 'uncle' as she prepared to do the unthinkable.

A club struck Frank on his back first. Pain filled his face as he doubled over. Again he was struck, this time breaking a rib. Frank fell limp upon the wooden stage, gasping, fighting to remain conscious through the pain. Blow after blow struck him. Like a rag doll, he was battered back and forth.

His fortitude was immense. Something inside kept him alive. Frantically, he scanned the crowd. As each blow fell, he winced in pain and then continued to survey the crowd. Finally, Frank found young Banion.

Their eyes met. Young Banion felt a shudder go through him. The hair stood on the back of his neck. Shaking his head back and forth, Banion screamed inside. Another club struck Frank. Tears rolled down the youth's face. Again, the club struck Frank. Even in all his pain, Frank smiled at young Banion. Even though he could not speak, Frank kept living long enough to say goodbye.

With a final smile and a look of compassion, Frank held his eyes
open and stared at Banion. With a whisper, he spoke: "I love you,
kid."

The fire went out of his eyes, and his body went limp.
Banion stood stunned in the crowd, unable to comprehend that his
only family was gone. A knot formed in his stomach. "Uncle..." he
whispered. "Don't leave me... please don't leave me." The loss he
was feeling could not be equaled. The sadness was a numbing ice
on his body. His blood seemed to freeze in his veins. A chill
captured his fragile mind. Time seemed to cease. "No..." Banion
whimpered.

Asagara Toil laughed at the sight of Frank's lifeless body
upon the stage. Each roll of laughter was a burst of fire. Each
horrid rise and fall of the twisted laughter threw new sparks at young
Banion. With the numbing, frigid sense of loss melting away with
each jeer and giggle, the youth was unthawing rapidly, and was on
the verge of exploding.

Unfrozen, the heartless laughter had awoken Banion's mind.
The sadness turned to a strange thought: the revolver, Frank's
revolver, was somewhere in the crowd. Sadness passed, and with
each roll of laughter that fell from Asagara's mouth, Banion felt a
strange twinge pull at his soul.

The twinge rose and it felt like fire. It pulsed through his
blood. Banion's face turned bright red and he shook with rage.
Nothing could stop him. Banion dove to the ground and fumbled
around on the earth. Finally, his hand found Frank's gun. The long-
barreled silver revolver quivered in his hands. How beautiful it felt,
cold steel clutched tightly in his burning hands, blood filled with
fire, sparks of madness setting the fuse for an all-out eruption of
insanity.

"You worthless bitch!" Banion screamed at Asagara.

The crowd was silent and turned to stare in horror at young
Banion.

"You will pay for your words, you insolent little bastard!"
Asagara yelled in rage. "How dare you defy me!"

Every revolution begins with a single act of defiance.

Banion was the fulcrum of change. The fuse was burning to its end and the world exploded.

The defiant youth raised the weapon and in a single instant, he was no longer a mere boy, but a deadly instrument plunging deeply into the heart of his enemy. Abandoning the helpless feeling, he trained the gun's sights upon Asagara. With an act of pure hate, young Banion pulled the trigger on the gun. The hammer fell and a blast erupted from the weapon. The bullet tore forth and struck Asagara Toil in the forehead. Her head whipped back and a spray of blood erupted. No smile graced Asagara's face as her lifeless body fell off the stage.

The huddled captives were shocked by what they saw. Sparks from Banion's action had set the fuses of many in the crowd. It was a chain reaction that could not be stopped. Hope had returned. The crowd was no longer a mass of helpless souls. Like a set of charges, pockets of anger flashed within them, waiting to explode.

"To hell with the Reaper Kai!" young Banion screamed as the gun erupted once more. "Fight! Fight for your freedom!"

A flash of anger exploded in the crowd. Like a pack of wild animals they roared. Without a sense of self-preservation, the horde rushed the fences. The onslaught was a terrifying sight; humans, dressed in nothing, charging like a feral herd, eyes flashing in fury. The robotic soldiers opened fire, shredding the hapless souls running forward. Bullets tore flesh and captives were ripped apart, but their fire, their spark of resentment, could not be contained.

Every time one of the captives fell, two more enraged townsfolk took his place. Using the fallen corpses of their brethren as shields against the gunfire, the crowd broke through the razor wire fence and engaged the enemy troops with their bare hands. Howling like wolves, they battered and pummeled the robotic soldiers, until their knuckles bled. Covered in sweat, blood, and motor oil, the mob growled as they dismembered their foes.

The Reaper Kai were strong but limited in number. Within a matter of minutes, the horde of naked captives had liberated themselves from the oppression of the sadistic Reaper Kai, and all thanks to the reckless courage of young Banion O' Neil...

"And that's how it happened. It was fifteen years ago." Banion spoke softly as he looked down into his ale. With tension in his face, he slammed back the beer stein and drained the rest of the ale into his throat.

Tani and Mineera stared silently at Banion with tears in their eyes.

"This place was my home so long ago..." Banion said quietly.

The young scholar rubbed the tears from his eyes and patted Banion on his shoulder. Mineera stretched her hand forward and caressed Banion's hand. For a moment, the deranged rancher let his companions console him. Suddenly, anger flashed in him, and he pulled away from both of them.

"Jared is the last person I will bury." Banion spoke softly. "If by my hand or by my will, the Reaper Kai will not survive. I know you both cared about him, I did, too. War has a cost, and we have all paid a horrible price. But enough with sorrow. Jared was an honored companion. Let us toast to him."

Banion grabbed a fresh stein of beer from the center of the table and raised it in the air. "To Jared of Scarskin. His courage and friendship will always be remembered."

Tani smiled and tears welled up again in his eyes. "To Jared."

Mineera smiled and crashed her beer stein into the others.

The steins clanked together and the three companions spent the rest of the evening talking about the lives they had all known so long ago.

Chapter 7
Beyond the Harbor

The scar was a mass of knotted flesh, stretching from the bottom of his right jaw, snaking upward along his face, ending at the tip of his ear. Pink, tough flesh was all that remained of the old wound, a wound Banion had received in a gun fight that was a little too close for comfort. It was just after the mighty revolt in Dune Station that Banion turned to the wastelands to comfort his rage. His first encounter was with a murderous cutthroat who came upon young Banion as he slumbered near the edge of the Steel Crag mountain range. The young Banion was stabbed in his sleep by the brigand. After missing his throat, the bandit quickly found what he was up against. The youth soundly gunned him down without a second thought. Frank's long silver revolver was still smoking as the bandit breathed his last breath, falling to the ground. Before his demise, the bandit managed to fire off a single shot, and the bullet rammed through Banion's cheek, leaving it a scarred mass, a testament to a violent life.

Banion, only a few weeks out from the revolt, surviving the lone bandit, was polarized by the events. Blood met more blood, and the only thing that could stay his sorrow was a never-ending romp through the backwater ruins of old, acting as a hired gun. The more he killed, the more he was intrigued by the feeling. After a while, he needed the rush of conflict and the pressure of danger to truly feel alive.

Banion fought like a wild animal when cornered. Ironically, the deranged gun fighter was always looking for the nearest corner. Most people go looking for trouble and get a sound lesson in discipline and humility. Banion, on the other hand, was so out of control and skilled at gun fighting, that he never got the sound thrashing he deserved. Instead, the scum of the wasteland were repeatedly gunned down by the rampaging youth. It didn't take long for the whisper of myth and legend to roll around the badlands; a new threat by the name Banion O'Neil was on the prowl. It was in this era that a wise king sought the aid of this crazed mercenary, the same mercenary who had gunned down his own wife. A strange relationship formed between the two, a lucrative one for King Toil, who hired Banion on many occasions to kill local warlords or religious zealots. The kingdom of Rasheed prospered under the watchful eye of King Toil and the directed purges of Banion O'Neil.

The gun fighter eventually found peace in the loving arms of Lily, sweet Lily. Coming to rest and giving up the bloodshed, the lost soul turned his focus from violence and simply lived his life, building a modest cattle ranch in the Frontier. It didn't take long for the hungry eyes of the enemy to bring a fight to his doorstep, ripping him from the world of peace once more.

Blinking repeatedly, Banion O'Neil pulled his long coat around him, shrugging off the images of his past. With a sigh of discontent, Banion whispered, *"Full circle... back where I started so long ago..."* His hand brushed across the whiskers on his face and found a barren patch of skin. The smooth skin of his scar and irregular ridges of flesh met his touch, and his mind flashed with anger. It was as if the scar on his face housed all the rage in his soul, a badge of torture to be shown to all the world.

Sighing again, he pushed fading memories out of mind and gazed around his home, the ocean town of Dune Station. With thoughts of bygone times still lingering, Banion decided to venture into his own past, moving about the town that was once his home. It was an uneasy homecoming for the gunfighter. A mixture of emotions filled him. Soaking in all of the haunted memories, Banion moved through the streets of his former home. His journey was short, and the weary gunfighter came to rest at the edge of the harbor. A distant expression was veiled behind Banion's dark eyes. With a look of hesitation, the gunfighter moved on.

Banion, being a local legend, was none too keen on being recognized. He knew that his reappearance in Dune Station some fifteen years after the bloody revolt would bring the town to his doorstep, something he was eager to avoid. With mercenaries and Reaper Kai operatives close behind, stealth was a primary concern. And in a small way, Banion did not want to look upon all those citizens who had shared that horrid day years earlier, during the great revolt.

Even though the enemy was close on their heels, Banion needed some time to himself, time to reflect on his past life, something he had not done since he left Dune Station. There were some memories he had to bury and some deeds he had to come to grips with. It was a way to clear his mind, bid goodbye to a long ago life, something he had avoided for half his years.

Banion looked longingly at the harbor and moved forward. He covered his face with his wide brimmed hat and avoided the citizens roaming about the waterfront.

A broad stone jetty pierced the ocean, extending several hundred yards into the harbor. Gray stone held fast against the waves crashing upon the solid rock. Giant chunks of granite were piled atop each other, creating a strong wall on the north edge of the harbor. Birds nested in the cracks between the rocks. Sea lions rested in the midday sun, holding their heads high with eyes closed, basking upon the jetty. Black shelled crabs and other sea creatures skittered across the stones, looking for food and shelter.

Banion smiled as he saw the jetty. It was a place where young Banion had spent many days as a child. With a heavy heart and a look of fascination, Banion walked out upon the jetty, sat upon the rocks, and let his mind wander. He closed his eyes and let his surroundings take over.

Salty, moist air rolled across his skin, as the smell of brine and fish wafted across the jetty. A cool breeze licked at Banion's face while the sun shone brightly upon him. Gulls cried out and dove into the rolling waves of the harbor. The caps of ocean waves were breaking upon the rocks with a white spray of foam.

Banion opened his eyes and smiled. A great sailing ship moved across the waves, cutting them with its bow. Waves broke upon the ship, and it bounced over each wave with a mighty heave.

The sails were not fully extended, but they bulged as the wind pushed against them. The sailing ship bounced repeatedly upon the water, pushing into the distance of the ocean beyond. Watching the scene with nostalgia washing over him, Banion felt at peace. With a dreamy look, he watched in silent fascination, feeling a sleepy wave wash over him as the ship pushed further and further away. Engrossed in the peace of the day, Banion was relaxed, and let the warmth of the day fill him.

Such a long time, Banion thought to himself with a smile.

When Banion was a boy, he had spent a lot of time down by the harbor of Dune Station. His uncle would often take him fishing on the old stone jetty. He remembered the long afternoons when Frank closed the shop and spent the day casting his baited fish hooks into the waves of the harbor. Banion loved those days. The memories washed over him, and the deranged rancher felt a smile cross his lips…

"Hey, boy!" Frank yelled with a frantic look on his face. "Hold on, boy, you got a big one!"

Young Banion held the fishing rod with all his might. Bending under the weight of some enormous fish, he struggled to maintain control over the fishing rod as it arced under the strain of the ocean denizen. Frank ran over and steadied young Banion. With a determined look, Banion pulled on the reel and began to pull the fish in. Slowly he cranked, while biting his lip and furrowing his brow. With his back tense and a frantic look in his eye, the boy fought to keep the fish in tow.

The mighty fish fought back. With determination of its own, the oceanic behemoth struggled against both Banion and Frank, who was steadying his nephew. The strain of the line could be heard as it groaned under the weight of the enormous fish. Banion placed his feet squarely upon the rocks and grunted with a look of determination on his face. The small boy tugged backwards, and the fishing rod bent even further under the additional strain.

"Hang on, kid!" Frank began to laugh. "You caught a

monster!" With a comical look in his eyes, Frank bent down and held Banion, keeping him from being pulled off the jetty into the waves.

"I got this one!" young Banion yelled in glee. His muscles were already sore, but the boy had a singular determination. With bursts of strength, Banion slowly reeled the fish toward the stone jetty. Finally, the fish emerged from the water. With a leap, it jumped into the air and thrashed about. Banion held his ground and pulled the mighty fish onto the stone jetty.

"Aha!" Frank slapped Banion on the back. "You got him, boy!"

Banion smiled in glee and stood up, proud of his fish, muscles tense and tired. He held the fishing rod in hand and smiled at his uncle. The fish gasped in the air, trying to find water to breathe. Its eyes looked around as its head flopped from side to side.

With a tremendous burst of strength, the enormous fish flipped up off the rocks and spun around in a wide arc. It hit the water with a loud snap. The fishing line broke, and the surprised boy lost his footing. Banion fell backwards and collapsed on the rocks of the stone jetty. With a grunt, the breath whooshed out of his lungs, leaving him gasping. He hit the rocks hard and whimpered, rubbing his backside with a look of embarrassment upon his face. Trying to maintain his dignity and not to cry, he fought hard to keep from feeling foolish.

"No!" Banion wailed as the enormous fish disappeared beneath the waves.

"Hot damn!" Frank roared. He began to chuckle as he looked upon the defeated Banion.

The boy held the broken line in his hand and shook his head in dismay.

Frank looked down at his orphaned nephew and patted him on the shoulder. With a smile, he pulled open his bait box and grabbed a piece of fish. He tossed Banion a new hook with a bright look on his face.

"Come on, kid, string up that new hook. Let's get that damn fish!" Frank said in a light tone.

The wet, dejected eyes of young Banion began to brighten. He looked at the waves and back at his uncle. With an open hand and a smile, Banion gestured for the new hook. The boy had been defeated, but his determination had been rekindled. He baited the hook and cast out his line once more. His imagination had been sparked, and the force of his will was set in motion. Victory was his only thought as images of the huge fish cooking on a grill flashed through young Banion's mind. He would get that damn fish!

Young Banion never caught that fish again. But Uncle Frank spent the rest of the day with him, laughing and telling stories. It was a day that Banion would always treasure, a day that seemed to live on forever in his heart.

Banion had a bright smile on his face as he remembered that day with his uncle. Abandoning his intensity, he let the warmth of the day enter his chilled soul. For a few hours, Banion sat upon the stone jetty and felt only warm thoughts.

The rest of his time was spent watching the white seagulls swirl around the harbor on the gentle winds. From time to time, a gull would swoop down and land gracefully upon the water, bobbing up and down like a cork on the rolling waves.

The gentle day moved on until finally, Banion rose to his feet and walked along the jetty, lost in pleasant thoughts of his childhood spent with Uncle Frank in the harbor town of Dune Station, so many years ago.

Chapter 8
Fallen Angel

The sun was shining bright. Mineera opened the door to the inn and stepped into the warmth. As the sun met her skin, she closed her eyes and let the new day fill her. A calm came over the psychic maiden. With placid breaths, Mineera inhaled and exhaled. Her mind was a clean slate. Giving in to the serenity of the day, the psychic maiden cleared her mind and allowed foreign thoughts drift in. Suddenly, a sickly feeling came over her. Something was wrong.

"Banion!" Mineera screamed a warning. It was too late; a bright sphere of energy hit Mineera in the chest. The blast threw the psychic maiden to the ground and left a hole burned in her robes where the blast of pure energy had hit. As the energy blast wreaked havoc on her nervous system, the helpless Mineera convulsed upon the ground. Finally, the convulsions stopped, leaving her incapacitated.

The warning was quick and the deranged gunfighter was instantly set on edge, set into action. With a fluid motion, Banion pulled a submachine gun free of his long coat, and took cover with a catlike dash. It took a brief second, and in the blink of an eye, the deranged rancher had disappeared from view.

Tani was caught unprepared and stood stunned, with a frantic look upon his face. Another blast of energy erupted from across the street. The bright white sphere of energy roared across the void with a sizzle, ionizing the air with a crackle as it hurled past Tani. The shot missed, but singed his hair as it whizzed past his head.

With panic filling him, the scholar from Scarskin dropped down below the entryway to the inn. As haste replaced the panic, Tani opened his pack and began to assemble a crude explosive device.

Banion looked out across the street from behind a water

trough and caught sight of two enemies. The dark skinned Talon crouched behind a muscle car with none other than a terrorist from the wastelands. Guillotine, the infamous opossum mutant mercenary, was exposing his toothy grin. Slowly, he licked his lips as he took aim with his pulse rifle. The mutant opossum was a deadly rival of Banion's, a scum born from the wasteland, the assassin who had attempted to slay Banion in Rasheed before its fall to the Reaper Kai.

"Oh, yes! Oh, yes indeed! Finally, I have found the foolish Nova 7!" With his narrow, sinister, beady black eyes scanning his surroundings, he spoke with a vicious tone. The mutant's gray and white fur was standing on end. The sinister opossum was excited by the thought of gunning down the most infamous mercenary in the Darken Realm.

"Talon, you worthless traitor. I trusted you!" Banion yelled. His friend from years back had sold him out. The bar owner had brought Guillotine right to their doorstep, hoping to claim a prize from the wicked mutant.

The sound of combat had brought many of the citizens of Dune Station to the scene. Curious onlookers crouched and watched the sinister encounter unfold. Peering out from behind buildings and water troughs, the citizens of Dune Station were drawn to the sound of battle with cautious, blank looks. None of the locals enjoyed conflict of any sort in their town since the revolt against the Reaper Kai so many years ago.

"Banion O'Neil!" Talon yelled back. "I would rather be on the winning side of this war! In the end, I will be a prince in the new world."

The crowd that had assembled was in awe. *"Banion O' Neil?"* The words rolled through the crowd. Many a citizen was filled with memories, memories of the great revolt that had occurred years ago. Even those who could not remember the revolt had heard the name Banion O'Neil. Their hero, their blessed hero, was under attack. It was something that most in the assembling crowd simply could not endure. Many members of the crowd felt a fury erupt in their hearts; they would not let the hero of Dune Station fall prey to a foul mercenary and a traitor of the town.

"Talon, I will bury you with the damn Reaper Kai!" Banion shouted and hopped to his feet. With a determined motion, Banion stood up and leveled his weapon at Talon. Pulling the trigger with the traitorous Talon in the crosshairs, Banion expected a swift death for his old friend. Instead, the weapon lay still; no bullets erupted from it. Talon had given Banion a faulty weapon. The betrayal was complete; Banion was now defenseless against Guillotine and Talon.

"Damn you!" Banion yelled as he hit the deck, fumbling with the faulty weapon. Talon laughed in glee as Guillotine aimed and blasted away at Banion with the strange electronic weapon. With eyes narrowed, Guillotine shook with a frenzy of excitement as he blasted away at Banion.

Several more spheres of light rocked across the street and slammed into the water trough behind which Banion had sought refuge. The blasts of energy reduced the trough to a smoldering ruin with only a few shots. The burnt wood lay smoking in silent testament to the battle.

Finally, Banion unjammed the faulty submachine gun. The trigger released and loosened as the deranged rancher fixed the weapon on the fly. With a satisfied look, he raised the weapon and trained the gun sights once again upon Talon.

The barrage of weapon fire ripped toward Talon and caught the inexperienced fledgling mercenary unprepared, hitting him in the shoulder. Several bullets bit flesh, and the force spun the bulky dark skinned man around in a wide arc. Spiraling backwards, Talon lost his balance and collapsed beside Guillotine.

The mutant was undaunted. Guillotine responded by firing another blast of energy at Banion. The sphere ripped forward, ionizing the air with a crackle. Banion was too quick, and was out of the way before the blast shredded a wooden support beam. Creaking under the duress, the post collapsed, and the wooden porch splintered and fell over with a crash.

The tribal from Scarskin had rebounded, finding his focus; the genius was ready with a surprise of his own. Hurling a lit dynamite stick, young Tani watched in anticipation as it landed at

Guillotine's feet. With a frantic look, the mutant flinched, preparing to meet an explosive death. Instead, the weapon failed to explode. Talon had given the tribal a fake explosive, another part of his twisted betrayal. Stunned, the youth was caught unprepared for the retaliation.

Guillotine's narrow, sickly eyes scanned the territory quickly and found the scholar perplexed by the dud explosive. Steadying himself, the mutant opossum clutched a gas grenade and pulled the pin. With a heave, Guillotine hurled the gas grenade at young Tani. Bouncing, the grenade hit the wooden boardwalk and ricocheted with a stream of green smoke emanating from it.

Just as the gas grenade landed at Tani's feet, Guillotine was pelted with gunfire. Banion's aim was true, and three rounds hit the opossum's chest. The bullets rammed into a thick steel breastplate covering the mutant's chest. With a spatter of sparks, the bullets bounced off the armor plating harmlessly, leaving Guillotine unscathed.

The mutant mercenary responded by returning fire. As bolts of hot white energy streaked across the urban battlefield, young Tani gasped and struggled to escape the gas cloud.

Gagging and staggering in the cloud of green gas, Tani fought to breathe. Dropping to his knees, the gas flooded his lungs. With tears streaming down his face, Tani began to cough uncontrollably. Each cough brought the scholar closer to succumbing to the gas. Quickly, the green cloud of filth overcame the scholar. With a coughing fit, Tani collapsed to the ground and lost consciousness.

Banion and Guillotine were locked in a chaotic gunfight. Streaks of energy and bullets alike were exchanged. The two combatants were both master marksmen and experts of evasion. Like a pair of cats, they stalked back and forth, weaving, attacking, and dodging.

Finally, Guillotine managed to gain the upper hand. With Banion caught reloading the poorly functioning weapon, another gas grenade was hurled, this time at the unprepared rancher. The grenade exploded only a few feet away from Banion, showering him in a cloud of thick, vile gas. Surprised by the attack, Banion gulped down several breaths of the toxic gas. His lungs stinging, Banion fought to remain standing, swaying back and forth as the vile fumes filled him with a dizzy flash of impending darkness. With tears rolling down his cheeks and the gas burning his lungs, Banion fell to the ground and the darkness took him.

Nova 7 had been defeated.

As Banion fell to the ground, the citizens amassing around the scene of combat were enraged. Their beloved hero had fallen. A tremor of rage rolled out. The bystanders ran from the scene, most of them yelling, trying to rally other citizens of Dune Station. The word spread like wildfire through the harbor town: Banion had fallen in battle.

With an arrogant leer, Guillotine laughed. "Oh yes! Nova 7 has fallen!" The mutant jumped up and down a few times in a twisted victory dance. His thin, white tail, covered in bristly fur, spun around him as he danced, flailing about like a tassel in a parade.

"Help me..." Talon moaned while clutching his wounded shoulder. "You have got to help me." Crimson blood seeped from the bullet holes in his shoulder. Sweat covered his brow, and he was almost in shock, pleading with Guillotine to help him.

"You've served your purpose. I need not share my reward with the likes of you!" Guillotine hissed, stepping over the fallen Talon. As he moved, he spat on the downed bar owner bleeding out in the street.

Without a second thought, Guillotine moved over to his black muscle car and popped open the trunk. Using both hands, the mutant pulled a silver disk from the trunk. With a sinister look flashing in his eyes, Guillotine brought the disk over to Mineera.

"Mistress Marion will pay much for the captured Nova 7, oh yes, oh yes indeed!" The mutant licked his lips, thinking of the money he would earn from their capture. After the fall of Rasheed, Marion had given secret orders to the opossum assassin to capture all of Nova 7. Marion had a sadistic side to her, and she wanted nothing more than the pleasure of torturing her new enemies.

Guillotine obliged the queen's orders and headed out into the wastelands with the intent of capturing Nova 7. His mission was now a complete success. All of Nova 7 was down.

The mutant grinned as he clutched the silver disk in both hands, eyeing Mineera. The twisted Guillotine stroked the device with his clawed hand until it fell upon a switch on the top surface. Flipping the switch on the device, Guillotine dropped the disk close to the fallen psychic maiden and then retreated quickly from the scene, hiding behind the edge of his black muscle car. He peered over the edge of the car like a frightened child, watching the strange events unfold.

A whirring noise erupted from the disk. A steel panel opened and slid forward. A series of popping sounds could be heard as a set of silver legs jerked from the open panel. Spreading outward, each leg was gripped with a mechanical spasm before it straightened, lifting the device off the ground. The disk now stood on six small legs. Another panel slid open and two copper tentacles emerged. Flailing about, the tentacles scanned the air for something alive, anything alive. Finally, the device turned around as the copper tentacles caught the scent of the fallen Mineera.

Suddenly, the silver disk skittered across the earth like a cockroach rushing for a crack in the wall. With quick and agile moves, the spider-like silver disk ran toward Mineera. Leaping, the disk hurled itself onto the helpless psychic maiden. The copper tentacles clutched and rolled Mineera over, exposing the back of her skull and spinal cord. The six silver legs positioned themselves upon her back. A cranking noise could be heard as each leg pierced her flesh, drilling into her back, drawing ever closer to her spinal cord. The copper tentacles moved toward the base of her skull. A thin needle emerged from the tip of each tentacle. With a rapid jab, the two needles pierced the back of Mineera's skull. The silver disk nuzzled deeper against her flesh. A flash of electricity flowed through the Splicer. Mineera convulsed as the electrical current wreaked havoc on her nervous system. With quick surges, the Splicer began to integrate itself into her system, taking control of her brain with a quick flurry of electrical impulses aimed at disrupting normal thought processes. Ceasing to convulse, her movements became calm; the Splicer had finished taking control of Mineera. The horrid process was complete, and the Splicer had integrated itself into Mineera, its new host.

Being spliced had stripped Mineera's identity, and she was now under the control of the Reaper Kai slave network. Electromechanical implants had complete dominion over her biological identity. No longer did Mineera have free will; she was nothing more than a slave of the enemy, an empty host, a vessel for the robotic device to reside within.

With a hurried rush, Guillotine ran over and dragged Mineera back to his black muscle car. With a grunt, the mutant tossed Mineera into the back seat.

Guillotine was about to splice Tani and Banion when a miracle happened. Word had spread quickly through the streets of Dune Station that Banion O'Neil was under attack; the beloved hero of Dune Station had fallen in battle. Fueled by memories of the past, a horde of locals had banded together in a huge mass to march against those who would do harm to their hero. Like a pack of animals they came, each brandishing crude weapons. They shouted and bellowed war cries as they moved toward the inn and the fallen Nova 7. The mob of inhabitants had drawn hundreds in the short span of a few minutes.

The enraged crowd came toward the scene with frightening speed. Guillotine was caught unprepared and the crowd was ready to tear apart anyone who stood between them and their hero.

Knowing that his prize was lost, the mutant abandoned the fallen Banion and Tani. Cursing at the crowd, hurling a gas grenade at the onslaught of citizens, Guillotine jumped into his black muscle car. He cranked the engine over and the car roared to life. As he punched the gas, the engine heaved and surged. The wheels spun in the sand as the back end of the car fishtailed. An inhabitant of Dune Station reached the car, pummeling it with a hammer. Others burst through the cloud of gas, hurling stones at the vile mercenary trying desperately to gain control of his vehicle. The tires gained traction and the muscle car whipped forward. Guillotine steered the car down the main street of Dune Station just in time to escape the enraged citizens charging forward to rescue the fallen Banion O'Neil.

The mutant drove like a maniac through the city; his cargo was a fallen member of Nova 7, the traitorous psychic maiden Mineera, now spliced and a hapless slave of the Reaper Kai empire. Where once there were three, another had fallen to the sadistic will of the enemy. Only two members remained, and hope was beginning to fade for the Darken Realm. The veil of darkness had fallen over the once proud band of heroes. Nova 7 was on the verge of ruin, and with it, the fate of all was in jeopardy.

Chapter 9
Voice From the Void

"You must not despair..." A weak voice resounded through Mineera's mind. It was distant, but was cutting through the haze, the only thing that was piercing the fog clinging to her enslaved mind.

Mineera was sitting on a bed in a dirty room. The sinister Guillotine was nowhere in sight, but it didn't matter. The Splicer had fully integrated itself into Mineera, robbing the psychic maiden of her consciousness and will. She was a prisoner but didn't require shackles. The electromechanical device attached to the psychic's spinal cord and brain stem was in charge, robbing her of any action. Her bright blue eyes stared ahead blankly while her mouth was slightly open. A thin trail of drool was dripping down from her open mouth. To the imaginative, Mineera looked like a drugged-up zombie that had lost its mind and was dozing the day away in some distant asylum.

The room was dark. The sun had set hours ago, and Mineera had been motionless the entire time. Unable to move a single muscle, Mineera fought an uneasy battle with herself. Try as she may, fighting with all her might, she could not even make herself blink. Though fully conscious, spliced slaves were unable to control even the most basic of motor functions. She could see, hear, think, and feel, but was unable to respond to any of her senses.

"You hear me, don't you? Through the haze and distance of the darkness..." The Voice was closer this time, a haunting wail in her conscious slumber.

Mineera's mind was still crisp, staring forward at the window sill that had been the only object in her sight for the last several hours. Unable even to twist her head or control her breathing, she listened intently as the strange voice in her mind returned once more.

"Do not let your faith waver. The enemy may steal your flesh, but your spirit is still strong. Do not lose hope," the Voice spoke once more in her mind.

"Can you hear me?" Mineera formed thoughts and forced them outward from her mind.

"I can hear you, Mineera."

A moment passed as the psychic maiden was formulating her thoughts. Was the voice she heard real? Was it just a delusion induced by her brain, lacking the stimulus of the rest of her body? Was her psyche already so starved that it was creating imaginary voices to keep her company in a time of need? All of these questions and many more flowed through her tattered mind.

Crash. An electrical impulse hit her mind like a dagger. The impulse disrupted her thoughts, forcing her to start over, to begin her thought processes once more. The Splicer attached to her skull was sending signals through her brain which were designed to disrupt thought patterns, thus further weakening the host, and making it nearly impossible to formulate concrete ideas, ideas that could ultimately lead to the host freeing itself from the iron grasp of the Splicer.

"Focus on my voice, do not let the Splicer drive me away."

Fighting back, Mineera forced her thoughts to repeat, over and over again, creating a never-ending series of similar thoughts. The Splicer sensed her defiance and fought back with equal force, jamming her mind with fragmented flashes of electrical pulses.

"Focus!" the Voice yelled in the background as more pulses warped her brain.

"I am here!" Mineera's mind screamed.

"Calm yourself and let go... allow my voice to flood you... let me in..." With a soothing series of commands, Mineera could feel a drowsiness flooding her mind. It was as if another presence was right on top of her own, masking the pulses from the Splicer. She retreated at first, the Splicer banging away at her brain, flooding it with a flurry of electrical blasts, trying to force her from thinking any cohesive thoughts. The pain of the noise in her brain was a deafening burden. Each time she let her defenses down, the foreign

presence of the Voice became stronger and the pain from the Splicer seemed to diminish.

"Be calm... I will help you stop the noise..." The soothing words in her mind rang out once more, this time much louder, much stronger.

The Splicer could sense her heightened brain activity and fought back with an intense blast of energy. Wracking her brain with high voltage shocks, the Splicer tried to override her conscious thought. The blasts were so intense that Mineera began to twitch. The more she fought the Splicer, the more it shocked her. As the pulses became deadly surges, Mineera began to convulse on the bed, drool streaming from her mouth as she shook.

"Don't fight me... I can make all the pain go away... let me in..." The Voice was urging Mineera to surrender what was left of her mind.

The pain was intense as her muscles convulsed under the force of the Splicer shocking her spinal cord and brain. The presence seemed somewhat perverse, but the thought of stopping the pain was becoming the focus of her conscious thought. Her fortitude was waning.

"I can make it all stop, have faith in me..."

Another series of shocks hit her. The pain was intense as the Splicer blasted away, trying to block her thoughts. On the verge of sheer agony, Mineera gave in to the haunting voice, letting her guard down. The foreign presence immediately rushed forward, charging onward, merging into her own fragile psyche. A sickening feeling washed over her as the spirit moved inside her own. The world seemed to grow dull. A deafening buzz filled her ears. Bright blotches of light filled her sight; orange blobs blocked out almost everything in her field of vision. Her skin crawled, as if a host of spiders were tickling her with hundreds of soft, furry legs.

The Splicer stopped its assault. The Voice had forced back the electrical will of the device, somehow forcing it to retreat. The foreign presence had defeated the Splicer for now, allowing the stinging pain to stop. Mineera felt at peace once more; the nausea from being shocked repeatedly had stopped.

"That's much better..."

"Thank you," Mineera responded, speaking with her mind.

"You are welcome... such pain cannot be allowed to last, especially for one of my servants..."

"I owe you much already. Your wisdom helped me save the man from my dreams. Due to your guidance, I was able to save Banion."

"Ah, yes... Banion... the man from your dreams..." The Voice was elated by the discovery. The foreign presence maintained a moment of silence as if pondering some great mystery. *"The enemy plots his demise as we convene here, in your mind..."*

"What? What do you mean? Is he in danger?" Mineera was confused by the revelation and none too happy about it. Banion was her chief concern, and the thought of him in danger once more was almost too much bear.

"The ones you betrayed... they have sent spies and assassins to slay Banion... they know of his importance and will stop at nothing until he is slain..."

"I must save him. I did it once, and I must do it again. I cannot let him come to harm," Mineera's mind screamed back at the Voice.

"Yes... you must be vigilant... you must not let anyone harm Banion..."

"I am useless. The Splicer is robbing me of independence. How can I be of any use in this condition?"

"Hold your faith, fallen angel of the Reaper Kai... only if you trust in me will Banion survive the agents of the enemy... you must have faith in me... I will deliver you..."

"Thank you. I have trusted you before. My faith in you will not waver."

And so she sat, as if in a trance, motionless, upon a dirty bed in an inn off the beaten path. The psychic was no longer alone. The presence, the Voice, was keeping her company, keeping her from the pain and torment of the Splicer which had burrowed its way into her mind and body.

Chapter 10
The Pact

The crowd of citizens held vigil around the Dune Station Inn. It had been a day since the vicious Guillotine and the traitorous Talon had ambushed Nova 7. An enormous crowd of townsfolk had amassed around the inn to give support to their hero, Banion O'Neil. Most of the people wanted simply to catch a glimpse of the legend, the man who had sparked the bloody revolt fifteen years prior, the same man who was known all across the southern wastes as a legendary hero and a brutal murderer. There were more tales told of Banion than of any other figure in all the lands. His mere presence was a thing of legend.

Banion sighed as he pulled back the curtain, looking out from the inn with a look of dismay. The event that he had been wishing to avoid had occurred. Banion had wanted to stay low and avoid any exposure. Instead, just the opposite had happened: the town had rallied behind their beloved hero and had saved both Tani and Banion from a horrid fate at the hands of Guillotine. With a reserved look, Banion turned away from the window and shifted his gaze to Tani.

Tani was lost in his thoughts, mulling over the information that they had both just received about the plot to capture Nova 7. The young scholar felt his stomach lurch as he pondered the information still being regurgitated over and over in his mind, locked behind his serious green eyes.

Talon had been interrogated by the town prefect before the gunshot wounds he had sustained took his life. The tale the traitor told was chilling. Marion Toil, The Great Betrayer, Bitch Queen of Rasheed, had put a bounty on the members of Nova 7. The maniacal Guillotine was sent to intercept and capture, not kill. Marion's plan was to toy with her prizes before killing them, especially Banion O'Neil, who had gunned down Asagara Toil fifteen years earlier.

The insane Queen of Rasheed who had betrayed an entire empire was now gripped by a blood vengeance and an ambition to torture all the members of Nova 7. These facts had put Tani on edge. The thought of the forces at work, tracking and plotting the demise of Nova 7, was almost too much to handle. Barely able to grasp the strange events, Tani felt as if he was somehow caught in someone else's nightmare, and as if his recent experiences were nothing more than someone's imaginary construct. But this sensation was to no avail: the stories were true, and Tani and his companions – or what was left of them, anyway – were now marked with a sizeable bounty on their heads.

The pieces of the puzzle began to fit. Tani sat on the bed, rubbing his hands together nervously. His intact hand rubbed the stumpy fingers on the mangled hand that had been injured in Tani's youth. The plot had come together, and was all too real. Hired mercenaries were stalking Banion and Tani. It was only a matter of time before others came calling, trying to claim Marion's sinister prize.

"What the hell are we doing out here, Banion?" Tani was lost in the surreal reality of what had just happened, and spoke slowly.

"Doing what's right," Banion responded in a flash of anger. "I don't like your tone."

"I don't really care if you like my tone or not. I shouldn't even be here. None of us should be here but you. I don't ever recall signing up for your quest of vengeance." The scholar's mind was frail, and he didn't give a damn about Banion. All he wanted was to make sure that the rancher knew what a mess he had made of the tribal's world.

"It's over, Banion." Tani was flushed and was about to start yelling. "I'm leaving. I am going to find my way home, leave this war, leave this chaos and death. I'm going home right now. I don't care if my village shuns me, I don't care anymore. I cannot live like this, constantly looking over my shoulder, watching my friends die around me. This is insane. We have lost, do you hear me? They have beaten us, the enemy is too strong, it's over." Trying to avoid the tears welling up in his eyes, Tani trembled violently, with his lower lip furled.

A silence fell over the room. Banion locked his gaze with Tani's, and neither of them conceded defeat. They simply stared at each other will hostile eyes, waiting for the other to make the next move. Finally, Banion spoke without removing his gaze from the scholar.

"What do you see when you close your eyes at night? What do you see when you awake with a startle? I have seen you many times in the night, calling out, thrashing about. Tell me, Tani, what are you seeing in your dreams, in your nightmares?" The direct question made the youth feel uncomfortable. Unable to maintain eye contact any longer, Tani conceded defeat and looked away.

Shaking his head back and forth, young Tani tried to hold back the tears already streaming down his face.

"What do you see, bookworm?" Banion pressed again.

Wiping the tears from his eyes, Tani felt a fresh wash of images roll through him. "The ship, Banion, it's always the ship..."

"When we escaped Rasheed?" Calmly, he pressed further.

"Yeah... the screams... the fire engulfing the city..." Tani began to stutter and his mind was distant. "It's their looks..."

"Looks?"

"Yeah... when we were safe aboard the ship and they were left behind. They were helpless, so helpless. I could see the fear in their eyes, and there wasn't a damn thing I could do about it. I was so powerless... Every night I see their faces, crying out with arms outstretched. Why did I survive? Why was I so special?"

"There's the door, bookworm," Banion said in a gruff tone, pointing at it. Tani looked shocked, not knowing what to think. "If you want to surrender, there's the door. Walk away."

Tani held fast. He stopped weeping and looked at Banion with an intensity that was close to rage. "What?"

"You heard me. If you want to go, I won't stop you."

Tani fell silent and almost walked out the door. Something stopped him. He didn't quite know what, but something inside him made him remain. He looked at Banion silently. Banion looked back and spoke once more.

"Your dreams are horrible; you can barely let yourself fall asleep at night. You have seen some terrible sights. Close your eyes and see those faces right now. Feel their pain, feel their terror. We cannot turn a blind eye. Do you hear me? We cannot turn a blind eye. To do so would allow the enemy a victory. I cannot allow it, you cannot allow it to happen. You said you felt so helpless on the ship that night, staring down at the ones that were left behind. You are never helpless, Tani, you hear me? You are never helpless."

Tani looked away and felt selfish. He finally understood. It wasn't about him anymore. It was about doing whatever was in his power to prevent another atrocity. Shaking his head, he looked at Banion and spoke. "I am never helpless," the scholar agreed with a solemn look.

Banion nodded back in acknowledgement.

"Mineera is gone. First Jared, now Mineera. What the hell are we going to do?" Tani asked in a quizzing tone. "We are falling apart. The enemy is too powerful, we don't stand a chance. There is no way we can succeed in this quest. Without Jared and Mineera, there is no hope."

"You are never helpless," Banion said once more, and Tani's despair began to dissipate.

"All right, Banion, I am not helpless, but I have no idea what to do," Tani replied earnestly.

There was a moment of silence between the two. The uneasy quiet spoke volumes. Banion was collecting his thoughts. The rancher moved over and flipped around a wooden chair so that its back was facing Tani. With a sigh, Banion sat on the chair, draping his arms across its back, supporting himself. He threw his hat on the floor and considered Tani with a serious look.

"I loved my wife very much, Tani. When I lost Lily, I lost the last, best part of myself. I struggled all of my life to put the horrid things I have done to rest. Just when I thought it was all over, my wife was taken from me. She didn't just die, Tani, she was taken from me. Taken by the same villains who just took Mineera, the same villains who forced us, not just me, all of us out here, into the wastelands, to creep through the ruins, trying to find a damn nuclear bomb." Banion's brow furrowed, and Tani looked at him uneasily as he spoke. The young scholar from Scarskin was frustrated, but managed to hold his composure long enough for Banion to finish his point. "We are out here to take this ride to the bitter end. While I can never forgive what happened to everyone I have ever loved, I cannot let Mineera face a fate of torture. After the fall of Rasheed, it was Mineera who kept us safe. Her extensive knowledge of the enemy allowed us to escape the Reaper Kai tracker teams time and time again. It was her wisdom that made us all invisible to enemy assassins. She saved our lives many times, and we didn't even give her credit. If it weren't for her, none of us would have survived long enough to be on that damn boat when it went down. I was harsh on her, Tani, too harsh. She never deserved my wrath or yours. I hate her race, but she is different. When I look at her, I see hope. I see someone who came back from the edge and is fighting for what's right. We can't let her die, kid. We can't abandon her." Banion was resolute, and Tani was elated.

"She has been captured by the enemy and Spliced. What does that mean? I heard the townsfolk talking outside the room about it." Tani was confused, and was hoping Banion would fill in the blanks. The tension between the two was lifting. Tani's tone lightened, and his psyche returned to its normal state. Banion also felt more at ease, sensing he had restored the scholar's confidence and had calmed his inner strife.

"The ancients were wise but reckless. Tani, you know better than me some of the wonders the ancients created. When the Reaper Kai disappeared after the civil war with the Iron Kai, it was said that they scavenged the wasteland for lost secrets. It's not much different from the reason your elders sent you and Jared out here into the badlands." Banion spoke softly and looked at Tani with a solemn expression.

"I take it the Reaper Kai emerged from the wasteland with something born of the ancients," Tani said in a matter-of-fact tone.

"You could say that. They found and restored great ancient foundries and brought back the mechanical terrors. First, the

Biogtech soldiers arrived. Their horror was but a taste of the fear that was about to be unleashed. The Splicers were the next wave of the Reaper Kai offensive. Splicers are robotic creations with only a single purpose: to enslave the innocent. I am not exactly sure how they work, but I have seen it several times. A normal person loses their soul, their very will to live. The Splicer attaches itself to its victim and becomes part of that person. Somehow, it takes over their mind and body, reducing them to mere slaves of the Reaper Kai. Mineera is now nothing more than a slave of the enemy."

As Banion finished explaining what had happened to Mineera, Tani was in a state of shock.

"I knew the ancients were powerful, but to interface electronics with organic life is way beyond even my comprehension," the scholar stuttered. His green eyes were looking at Banion, in the hope that the story was mere myth.

"The fate she has suffered is worse than death. Mineera is now a slave to the ones she fought so hard to escape. We cannot let her suffer. We have to save her." Banion was staunch in his decision.

Tani nodded in agreement.

"What do we do?"

"What do we do?" Banion repeated young Tani's words. "We make a pact never to rest until we save her. I hate to admit it, but I miss her. We need her, bookworm."

"Guillotine is gone. There is no way we can find him." Tani shook his head in disgust.

"You're right, kid, we can't find Guillotine, but I bet there would be enough volunteers in that crowd down there who would help us." Banion moved over to the window and stared out at the crowd of loyal townsfolk holding vigil around the inn. "Let's use my fame to our advantage. The citizens will track Guillotine down for us. We can send five people in every direction. That damn mutant has got to leave a trail. We will find him soon enough."

Tani shook his head in agreement. The plan was sound. Using the citizens to track Guillotine would work.

"Are you with me, Tani?" Banion spoke with a confident

look on his face. He held out his hand to Tani.

Tani looked at Banion with a wicked grin on his face. "I'm with you Banion." The tribal scholar gripped Banion's hand and shook it fiercely, sealing the pact. They would not rest until they had rescued Mineera from the maniacal Guillotine.

Chapter 11
Battle of Deception

The advance of the Iron Kai army was a full scale offensive. Nearly ten thousand infantry, an armored core division, and a host of small artillery units had pushed deep into Reaper Kai territory. The mighty army had met with little resistance. Biogtech scouts and small patrols had been the only defenses that the Iron Kai had met. The only skirmishes had been several incidents on the fringe of the main assault force. The objective was the siege and destruction of the Reaper Kai capital. It was the first time in more than two hundred years that the Iron Kai had mobilized a force of such magnitude. The directive and intention were clear; Emperor Gunther had initiated nothing short of a full-scale war.

A horrid smell filled the air. The rotting, death filled stench of Darkshade Moor was clinging to the mist riding the stagnant breeze through the twisted trees. Tall reeds and tangled roots hid the murky depths of the swamp. Swarms of bugs floated amongst the trees and vines. The air was hot and humid, draped over the marsh like a veil of heat.

The Iron Kai army was uneasy. It was less than twenty miles to the Reaper Kai capital, and they had encountered nothing but scouts. It was too easy. The dread Reaper Kai were a tough opponent, and getting so close to the capital without sizeable resistance was nothing short of unsettling.

The infantry formations were spread across a two-mile-wide front. Slowly they advanced, slogging through the mud and avoiding treacherous pools of murky water. The armored core, consisting of a division of tanks, had nearly ground to a halt several miles behind the infantry. Most of the tanks were creeping slowly onward through the thick mud. The assorted artillery teams were in the center of the mass of Iron Kai forces, still plodding through the slime but making quicker progress than the armored division.

"I don't like this," mumbled Field Marshal Mills, a veteran officer in the Iron Kai army. "This just isn't right. Our sworn enemy is letting us advance on their damn capital. It just isn't right."

"Maybe they underestimated us," a staff sergeant suggested in a soft tone, his eyes scanning the tree line. "Our advance may have caught them off guard. Their forces just sacked Rasheed. Maybe this is our lucky break. With their main force occupying Rasheed, maybe they are spread thin, and have pulled all their forces back to defend the capital. After all, it's a hell of a lot easier to defend a city than open territory."

A snap broke the air. A bullet hit the staff sergeant in the chest, spinning him around like a rag doll. A spray of blood erupted from the wound as he collapsed with a splash into the murky water. The attack was terrible, and the staff sergeant was the first to fall in the surprise assault.

"Ambush!" Mills yelled and took cover. Just as the field marshal hit the deck, a barrage of gunfire tore into the front ranks of the infantry. Automatic weapon fire shredded the hapless ranks of Iron Kai soldiers stuck at the front of the formation.

The attack was so quick and deadly that it left a dozen soldiers dead within a matter of seconds. The Iron Kai forces responded by taking up defensive positions behind the rotting trees and hollows. Using the natural vegetation and terrain for cover, the front line of the army dug in and prepared to fight off the attack. The Iron Kai leadership had been caught off guard. It took them about a minute of chaos to regain composure.

"Put some fire on those trees!" Field Marshal Mills yelled at a sergeant entrenched behind an adjacent stand of trees. The order was given, and several units responded by firing at the tree line. Several hidden attackers were hit by the gunfire. A pale soldier, devoid of hair and with a host of tubing jutting from his skull, uttered a shrill death cry and staggered through the murky swamp. He was caught by additional gunfire and crashed into the dark water.

The attacker was strange indeed, and caught the eye of many Iron Kai. The attacker who had just been slain was not a Reaper

Kai, but rather a Mord Tech. The pasty complexion and tubing sticking out of the soldier's skull had given him away.

Field Marshal Mills was stunned. The Iron Kai and Mord Tech had sealed a pact, forming an alliance to fight the Reaper Kai. It didn't make sense that Mord Tech forces had set an ambush in Reaper Kai territory. Something was amiss.

With a stunned look on his face, Field Marshal Mills gave an order over his radio. "Mord Tech forces have assaulted our front lines. I repeat, Mord Tech forces have assaulted our front lines. Open artillery barrage on coordinates 8.12.353."

"Please copy, Field Marshal, did you say Mord Tech forces?" a stunned voice responded from the radio.

"That is affirmative. We have engaged Mord Tech forces. Open artillery barrage on coordinates 8.12.353."

"Coordinates confirmed, sir. Artillery support acknowledged." The field marshal's headset crackled in response to the orders.

Within seconds, the boom of artillery resounded in the air. Shells arced across the battlefield and slammed into the hidden Mord Tech army stationed in the tree line. Loud explosions tore the swamp, spraying debris and filthy water. Bodies and blurry humanoid forms could be seen, hurled into the air by the explosions. The pounding from the artillery was horrendous. Casualties were mounting as the entrenched Mord Tech forces took the brunt of the attack. A continual bombardment of shells shattered the front line of the Mord Tech army. Scattering to minimize the effectiveness of the artillery, the Mord Tech forces spread out and continued the attack. Within a matter of seconds, more Mord Tech forms could be seen returning fire from the tree line.

Listening to the battle on his radio in the Iron Kai command room in the capital city of Stonen, Emperor Gunther, lord of the Iron Kai, sat in shock. He was barely able to comprehend what he was hearing. It didn't make any sense that the Mord Tech army would stage an ambush after a treaty had been formed between the Iron Kai and Mord Tech empires.

"What the hell is happening!?" Gunther boomed into the

radio. "Did you say Mord Tech forces are attacking your troops?"

Only static and short transmissions could be heard on the jammed radio waves. Heavy fighting had erupted in the Darkshade Moor. The entire front line of the Iron Kai army, over two miles in length, was taking enemy fire, and the Mord Tech forces had started to maneuver around, flanking the Iron Kai soldiers.

"Respond, damn it!" Gunther yelled into the radio as his war advisors looked on with stunned anxiety.

Gunther threw down the radio transmitter and rose to his feet. He walked across the throne room and stared out the enormous windows. Dark blue waves crashed upon the shoreline below the Iron Kai capital of Stonen. With a strange look on his face, the Emperor of the Iron Kai turned around and stared at his war advisors.

None of them had foreseen this. The Mord Tech diplomat who had been dispatched to form an alliance between the two mighty houses was convincing. Gunther eyed his advisors with a distant look as the sounds of combat crackled over the radio. It just didn't make sense. Gunther suddenly knew, deep in his heart, that all of this had to be some sort of cruel ruse or mistake.

With a resolute look in his eyes, Gunther moved back to the radio. Confidence was with him as he raised the microphone to his lips. "This is Emperor Gunther. I am giving a direct order to cease fire. I repeat, this is Emperor Gunther. All forces engaged in Darkshade Moor are ordered to cease fire."

There was an uneasy moment of silence on the radio.

"This is Field Marshal Mills. We are taking enemy fire, my lord! We cannot cease fire!" the Iron Kai leader in Darkshade Moor responded into the radio.

"Field Marshal Mills, that is an order! Cease fire!" Gunther yelled into the radio.

The battlefield was in chaos. It took nearly three minutes of fierce fighting and indecision for the cease-fire order to travel across the Iron Kai troops. The highly disciplined army followed orders. A lesser army, one without rigid training, would have never responded to the cease-fire order. The Iron Kai army was a monument to discipline. True to their commander's order, the Iron Kai army ceased fire and took up defensive positions, trying desperately to avoid the automatic weapon fire from the entrenched Mord Tech forces.

The Mord Tech troops continued to fire upon the Iron Kai troops. Holding defensive positions, the Iron Kai held their ground, stalwart and obeying their Emperor's order to keep from attacking. A minute of sustained fire continued. Finally, the gunfire trickled to an eerie silence. The two entrenched forces held a quiet stalemate, neither of them daring to move in the uneasy silence. The Mord Tech forces were mystified by the sudden lull in the combat.

"Field Marshal Mills," Gunther said in a confident tone. "Raise a flag of truce and do not fire until they accept a parley. If it takes until the end of eternity, do not fire on them. I cannot trust a lower ranking officer to do this. Mills, I want you to negotiate."

"But if you're wrong, the enemy will kill me, and our army will not have an experienced field commander." Mills spoke in a haggard tone.

"The reason that you lead my army is that you have the most stable personality. You are the best I have out there to negotiate a cease-fire. If you cannot put an end to this aggression with the Mord Techs, we will not survive the war with the Reaper Kai. You will parley with the enemy leadership, and you will put an end to this aggression. Those are my orders. Carry them out, Field Marshal." The Emperor was decisive in his verdict. His military advisors were crowded around the radio, wild eyed with fear. Each person in the throne room knew a war against the Reaper Kai was impossible without the aid of the Mord Techs.

"Yes, sir," Mills said with a confident tone into the radio as his heart leapt into his throat.

In the swamp, the bugs hummed and skittered. The smoking ruin of burning trees, shredded by artillery fire, still smoldered. The smell of death was in the air and the pungent odor of the swamp clung to the battlefield. All was silent, an eerie scene after more than fifteen minutes of open, heated battle.

The banner of truce was raised, a white flag stained with

blood and mud from the swamp. It was a symbol of hope set amidst the gore-stained moor. All who could see the banner could not take their eyes from it. It was a symbol of uncertainty, but a welcome sign, nonetheless.

With his heart pounding in his chest, Mills closed his eyes and stood straight up with his hands raised. He moved out from under cover with the banner of truce waving behind him. With slow, deliberate steps, Mills moved away from his hiding spot. He breathed hard while cringing at the same time. Mills kept envisioning a sharp, high caliber bullet ramming through his chest. With a shudder, he forced the thought from his mind.

Slowly he trudged, over the corpses of slain soldiers, through the bog filled with blood. Over remains of twisted, lifeless soldiers he moved, his eyes darting back and forth. Finally, his eyes came to rest on a figure.

With a bald head and pale skin came the soldier from the tree line. Tubing was fastened about his head and limbs. A strange blue liquid pulsed through the tubing as the Mord Tech commander moved forward. A tremble could be seen in his step as he crossed over his fallen kinsmen. His white eyes came to rest on Mills.

For a moment, the two stopped and regarded each other while standing in pools of blood, pools formed from an alliance gone wrong.

Taking uneasy steps forward, the two leaders moved. Finally, they halted just a few steps away from each other. They regarded one another in silence, each too hesitant to speak. Finally, Mills took the initiative.

"It has been a long time since our two great houses have shed such blood. I wonder what purpose this battle has served?" Mills spoke formally, trying to remain in control.

"This battle? It should have never happened. I wonder why your house, your empire, saw fit to return our diplomat in a mass of severed body parts?" the Mord Tech commander asked with a sneer.

Mills had a stunned look on his face. He had no idea what the Mord Tech commander was referring to, and stared at the other leader in silent shock. The Mord Tech commander picked up on

Mill's tense and baffled expression. Eyeing him carefully, the Mord Tech could tell that Mills had been surprised and astounded by his assertion.

"Your diplomat? Tell me of the foul deeds that befell him," Mills replied, trying to keep the quiver from his voice.

With a sneer, the commander spoke, still not confident that the Iron Kai had nothing to do with his countryman's demise. "Our diplomat was dispatched to your lands to secure a truce between our two great houses. He was returned to us with an act of war stuffed in the mouth of his severed head. The message was quite clear."

"Your diplomat was received with honor. His mission of peace was a success, or so we thought. We dispatched him back home, alive, with the intent of establishing peace between our two houses." Mills spoke with his radio transmitter open. Gunther listened on the other end while clutching his hands tightly.

"Alive, you say?" A silence fell over the Mord Tech commander. He eyed the line of Iron Kai troops who had initiated a cease-fire. If the Iron Kai truly wanted to wage war against the Mord Techs, the Iron Kai leadership would have never ordered a cease-fire. Something was wrong, horribly wrong. "We have shed much blood this day. I am not sure we can dismiss such carnage," the Mord Tech said softly.

"We cannot dismiss this day. For now I know the truth. It all makes sense. We have marched upon the Reaper Kai for many days. We have met no resistance. You know why? The only thing that makes sense is that the Reaper Kai orchestrated this whole mess. Our forces suffered no attack because they knew you were going to attack us. Why waste your forces on two armies, when you can destroy the weak army that survives? The Reaper Kai are cunning. It would be a shame if they destroyed us by using our two great armies against one another. I refuse to be a puppet. I am willing to end the hostilities with the Mord Techs, forget about the ambush, if you are willing to trust me, here today. I can offer you my word as a fellow soldier: the Iron Kai want a truce with the Mord Techs, not a war." Mills spoke methodically and logically, and his words rang true. Both of the commanders knew in their hearts that they had both been tricked by the Reaper Kai.

"The position of your army was given to us by Iron Kai traitors... supposed Iron Kai traitors..." The Mord Tech commander was speaking slowly and felt doubt rise in his mind. It was too perfect, and it smelled like deception. If the Iron Kai truly wanted to attack the Mord Tech empire, they would not have stopped the artillery barrage. The Iron Kai, with their armor and artillery support, had a clear advantage over the Mord Tech army, and would not have given up such an advantage if their true intent was all-out war. The Mord Tech commander was confident that the whole mess was a sinister Reaper Kai plot. Speaking slowly, the Mord Tech commander conceded his agreement to Mills' claim that the whole mess was a Reaper Kai ploy. "But on second thought, it doesn't make any sense. These traitors were probably born of this land, agents of the Reaper Kai, the true enemy. Our forces also only met scouts in these lands. For two armies to meet in the lands of the enemy without resistance is beyond reason. I think they have made fools of us. You are an honorable soldier. If we can dismiss this tragedy, we can fulfill our desire. Let us not forget the dead. Let our sorrow be our fuel not against each other, but rather, let our sorrow be the force that binds us together against the Reaper Kai. Our people are not puppets. Let us band together, here today, and kill the puppet-master, the cruel manipulator that orchestrated this ruse to bring our two great houses against each other." The Mord Tech commander spoke with a glimmer of hope in his eyes.

With a gesture of peace, Mills extended his hand. The Mord Tech commander grabbed it and sealed the deal. A new pact, one that could not be broken by simple treachery, had been formed. The Mord Techs and Iron Kai were now one force, a force dedicated to striking deep into the heart of Reaper Kai tyranny.

The Reaper Kai treachery had been narrowly averted. If not for the foresight of Gunther and the calm leadership of Field Marshal Mills, two great houses of the north would have annihilated each other under the watchful eyes of a master puppeteer, the dread Reaper Kai. With a renewed vigor, the two great armies marched toward the Reaper Kai capital with the intent of its utter destruction.

Chapter 12
Dark Tidings

The spiral staircase descended into the darkness. A humid stench of death rose from the pit. Cockroaches skittered along the floor, moving through the refuse. The staircase ended at a passageway dug into the earth. Cells lined the hallway, disappearing around a corner toward the end of the hall.

Laughing hysterically, one of the captives raved in his prison cell. Every now and again, the laughing would stop and the man in the cell begged for mercy, pleading to be released. No one responded, and the man would start giggling, eventually working himself back into a sinister laughter once more.

The dungeons of Rasheed had become a place of great suffering since the fall of the city to the demonic Reaper Kai. In all the years in which the mighty palace had stood, not a single person had been tortured. Since the infestation of evil, horrid deeds were being performed in the dungeons on a daily basis. Many of those being tortured were not strong enough to survive the agony they were forced to endure. The dead were already mounting in the cells, and it didn't bother the Reaper Kai priests one bit. Instead of removing the dead, the twisted jailors would simply add another victim to the cell.

Screams of agony pierced the darkness as The Lord of Evil, Father Vertigo himself, made his way down into the newly formed torture pits of the Rasheed palace. The stone staircase spiraled downwards into the darkness, and Vertigo, with a consortium of Goat Minions, descended into the dungeons. Baying in the darkness, the Goat Minions sniffed the air as they moved. The rancid smell of death increased as they pushed down into the depths of the palace. As the Dark Lord moved closer to Marion Toil's cell, wails of anguish echoed through the dark corridors.

Vertigo halted before a sealed prison cell. The Goat Minions bleated and bayed before the door, sniffing, probing the air for the life contained within the cell, hairy snouts held aloft. Vertigo unbolted the door to the cell and opened it with a creak.

Marion Toil, the Queen of Rasheed, lay on the floor in a pitiful huddled mass, her once beautiful blond hair matted and stained with her own blood. The traitor of Rasheed, the very woman who had sold out her own father and kingdom, was now a memory of her former grace and beauty. She squinted in the dim light; even the torches were a bright blast compared to the total darkness that engulfed many of her days while imprisoned within the cell. In a gesture of submission, she bowed her head before Father Vertigo.

"It's good to see that your stay in the torture pits has removed your arrogance and insolence," Vertigo declared in a harsh tone as Marion crawled toward the doorway. She was too weak to respond, and only glared at her twisted master. Exhausted, she winced in pain as the lacerations on her back, caused by continual whipping, throbbed terribly. The pain was so severe that she was almost on the verge of blacking out.

"I trust you will listen to my orders and execute them without hesitation from this point forward. My instructions were to eradicate Nova 7, and you decided, with your brazen bravado, that you would disobey my orders and capture them instead." The Lord of Darkness sneered and taunted the battered Queen of Rasheed. "Nova 7 escaped your foolish ambush in the Rasheed palace. As a result, they are searching for a nuclear weapon to use against our capital city. And now my sources have told me that your ineffective assassins have botched another strike against Banion O'Neil and his rabble of tribals. The wretched Mineera, that foul bitch and deserter of our cloth, has been captured..." Vertigo motioned to his Goat Minions. They charged into the cell, holding Marion roughly, pulling her head back so that she had no choice but to look upon the Lord of Darkness. "Why was Mineera captured? It leads me to wonder if you understand my intent!" Vertigo pointed at Queen Toil. The Goat Minions responded and struck Marion several times, beating her with their bare hands. "I want Nova 7 dead! Not captured! Dead, I say! Do you understand my orders?"

"Yes..." Marion Toil replied in a weak tone.

Vertigo motioned once more to the Goat Minions, and they
began to pummel her again. "I cannot hear you."

"Yes!" She moaned in pain.

"I am glad we have finally come to an understanding. I am
not accustomed to letting those who defy me live. It is fortunate for
you that your actions during the fall of Rasheed were so critical to
our goals. If it were not so, I would have executed you for your
impertinence." Vertigo's tone was suffused with hatred.

"I pledge my will to you, my lord. I regret my defiance,"
Marion said in a hushed voice, obedient to her master.

"I will let you out of this foul cell, but only to do my will!
You will send word to your mercenaries in the field who have
captured Mineera. I want her executed immediately!"

"Yes, master." Thrown to floor by the Goat Minions, the
Queen of Rasheed felt intense pain wracking her body. Marion
whimpered on the floor and crawled away from the open doorway.
Vertigo motioned to the Najaszim, the foul Goat Minions, to recover
the retreating traitor of Rasheed. They climbed into the cell and
grabbed the whimpering woman. With a mighty heave, they pulled
her to her feet and dragged her from the cell.

"Our ruse and deception with the Mord Tech diplomat has
failed. The dismembering of the Mord Tech diplomat was a sound
plan to drive a wedge between the Iron Kai and the Mord Techs.
Gunther and his commanders are wiser than I had originally
estimated. The Mord Tech and Iron Kai have reestablished relations
against my original intent. They are now a unified force marching
on the capital city as we speak. Our victory is still at hand, but our
momentum is slipping."

"What is your will, master?" Toil spoke in a weak,
submissive tone. The fight had gone out of her completely. She
dared not even think of defying Vertigo after spending time in the
torture pits.

"Nightshade is waiting for you. She is preparing a plague to
unleash against the Steel Crag Mining Guild. Your mission is to go
with Nightshade ahead of the main force. Contaminate their water
supply with this plague. If our plan is a success, the Steel Crag

Guild will be too weak to face us. The death and pestilence in the streets will usher in a swift victory for the Reaper Kai. After the fall of the Steel Crag Guild, return to Rasheed. I will have further use for your talents," Vertigo concluded ominously.

"As you will, master." Marion spoke while trying to avoid fainting. Her body and mind had been wasted to nothingness.

"Our resources are becoming scarce. The Biogtech production has been increasingly costly to our mines. Without the resources from the Steel Crag mines, I fear our military operations will grind to a halt. Without the demise of the Steel Crag, we will not be able to ensure our victory against the great houses in the north. Go now! Seek out Sister Nightshade, infiltrate the city of Rust Spire, and unleash this pestilence upon our enemies!"

The plan was sinister but commonplace for the Reaper Kai.

"Your will be done. I shall leave when the sun rises," Marion replied in a confident tone, still fighting the dizziness. The hate was rising in her soul. A focused bolt of anger and rage was directed at Vertigo. *How dare he make me suffer so!* her mind screamed.

Vertigo picked up on her rage and directed his black eyes to her own. "Your hate will make you pure." With that, Vertigo turned away from Marion and ascended the spiral staircase, leaving the torture pits.

Marion remained alone outside the cell in which she had spent several days and nights in torment. Rage and hate flowed through the Queen and revived her strength. The resentment she felt toward Vertigo fueled her recovery. Marion would go to Rust Spire and spread a virulent pathogen amongst the citizens. She would also tell her assassins in the field to locate and slaughter Nova 7. Marion, after all, was lucky to have escaped the wrath of Vertigo so lightly, a hazard she was not willing to risk again. No amount of torture or disgrace could normally change her actions, but she knew Vertigo meant what he said. Betraying him again would lead to a swift death, probably at the hands of the Goat Minions. The hate she felt for Banion could not be abated, but she dared not seek to capture him. Evil was a force which, once motivated, could not be halted, but it could be restrained by self preservation. She would attain vengeance upon Banion with his death and nothing more, a hollow sense of victory for the psychotic Queen.

Lost in thought, Queen Toil emerged from the darkness of her own dungeons and moved into the palace of Rasheed. Where once there was a mighty palace of beauty, only the stain of war could be seen.

As the new Queen moved through the halls, blast marks, stains of blood and other signs of conflict were displayed before her. The palace that had been the source of stability in the southern reaches of the Darken Realm was nothing more than a place of strife, a place where an ambitious young princess had betrayed many for her own twisted desires.

The very palace had been damaged spiritually as well as physically. The horrid deeds and terror of the fall of Rasheed had embedded themselves within the place. As she walked, Queen Toil could hear whispers in the darkness, screams in the shadows. The palace was forever tainted, a place haunted by so many souls that had fallen in grief and misery.

Queen Toil shuddered at all the energy that had been sealed in the palace. She moved hastily into a once splendid garden. The gardens had fallen to ruin. The plants had withered and died, the songbirds had moved on. The palace was lifeless and filled with dark memories.

Staring out into the city, Queen Toil gazed with sick fascination. The city had been burned almost completely to ruin. Charred timber and shells of finely crafted homes filled her view. The enslaved citizens walked in formation as Reaper Kai slave masters whipped them like animals.

Upon the balcony, Marion Toil stood amid the withered garden, looking into the battered city, while ghostly whispers wafted from the interior of the palace. The Queen of Rasheed was home, standing high above the city she had betrayed, with a sense of loneliness filling her. The cost of her soul was not just a stain on her existence but a jagged wound that had been torn in the heart of her subjects. Betrayal had a heavy cost, and never-ending loneliness was the price that Marion paid for her twisted ambition. She would be Queen forever, a matriarch over a set of ruins that had once teemed with life and happiness, secluded in her dark thoughts, sheltered by her own dark will.

Chapter 13
A Whisper of Myth

The lone figure emerged from the depths of the wasteland. Slowly, he plodded along in silence. The day burned brightly and bore down upon the wanderer. Weary with hunger and thirst, he held his hand above his brow to block the harsh sun. His eyes scanned the rolling dunes ahead. Sweat rolled down his face as he swayed back and forth. Dizziness was taking the young traveler. It had been several days of travel through the wasteland without food or water, and fatigue was taking its toll.

With a look of near despair, the wanderer gave a loud sigh and continued to move along the dry riverbed. It had been days of travel from the ocean. The youth had located the riverbed and decided to follow it inland. In a harsh desert world, life could exist only near a source of water, a source of freshwater. The youth had seen the dry riverbed and decided to follow it inland in the hopes of finding water and refuge. If there was a village out in the wastes, it would be near a water source, perhaps along the riverbed before it ran dry. As of yet, the theory wasn't paying off, and the riverbed was bone dry, lined with baked, cracked mud.

The sun was casting long shadows across the dunes of rolling sand. Stretching outward, a shadow had settled at the base of a tall dune, casting a swath of cool refuge against the harsh sun. The traveler moved slowly, unable to surrender just yet, enjoying the shade of the dune above him. He smiled and shook his head; it was only a few minutes of relief from the burning sun, but it was a miracle nonetheless.

Chasing the setting sun, the traveler trudged up the tan dune of shifting sand. The earth sheltered by the shadows had already begun to cool, offering the youth a chance to take off his boots and cool his feet. The leather of the boots grew more temperate in his hands as the heat of the day dissipated. Smiling, feeling the cold sand on his feet, the wanderer gave a loud sigh and pushed onward.

Ascending the mighty slope of sand, the youth looked off toward the ravine, the same riverbed he had followed deep into the wasteland in search of water. A jagged wound had been torn in the red sandstone. Like an enormous crack smashed into the rock, the sharp curves of the ravine drew forward toward a tall rock wall just west of his current location. As the youth moved, the height of the sand dune loomed above him, touching the brownish red rock formations which protruded majestically, towering several hundred feet in the air above the sea of sand. The rock formations ran in a northerly direction, separating the shifting desert sands from whatever lay within. Only a single opening could be seen in the giant rock wall: the sharply cut ravine gouged out of the tough stone. The top of the ravine was a jagged mass of razor-sharp rocks. The base was something different, its surface smoothed by countless flash floods and rushing water in ages past.

The traveler trudged up the dune, taking two steps forward for each step back, sand shifting endlessly under his weight. With a look of weariness, he reached the apex of the dune, and was finally able to rest atop the natural stone wall. Standing on the red rock wall, a smile graced the traveler's lips as he beheld the startling vision stretching out before him.

The youth surveyed the interior of the valley surrounded by the tall rock formations. The gorge was much larger than the lone wanderer could have ever imagined. As if a giant shovel had excavated the valley, the valley was enormous, at least several miles wide and a nearly a mile deep as it sloped away to the west. The tan and red sandstone rock walls protected the canyon from the desert beyond, hiding a series of rock spires smoothed by the blowing wind of countless centuries past. Hundreds of such spires were in the center of the valley, granting it a jagged appearance, as if needles of stone were springing outward from its floor. The jagged spires were a pale, whitish-tan hue, made of dense clay and earth, with red strands of color dispersed amongst their form. Clinging to the base of each spire were lush, brilliant green plants and vegetation. From each eruption of life, creeper vines sprung upward, clinging to the sides of each spire.   Wandering through the valley, a wide river ended in a small lake near the eastern edge of the canyon. The youth was elated by the find, and the small lake caught his attention immediately.   Pools of blue water glimmered in the distance, trapping the last rays of the setting sun and filling the traveler with hope. With lush vegetation and water at the bottom of the valley, a supply of food would not be hard to locate.

A shot of adrenaline hit the lone wanderer's system.   A paradise was just below, sheltered in the ancient canyon. His thirst and hunger overwhelmed his senses as a fresh burst of energy propelled him forward. With wild elation, he bounded down the sand dune along the rock wall, moving closer to the ravine and the entrance into the valley. Almost tumbling, the youth crashed down the sand with trembling anticipation. As he charged onward, the sun moved to the western horizon and began to sink past the edge of the world. The long shadows of fading light met each other and formed patches of cooling earth. No need to stay in the open wasteland; the lone traveler would spend the night in the shelter of the desert paradise, a welcome relief from his journey through the desert.

Hopping down from the shifting sand, the youth leapt into the dry river bed and followed the smooth, worn ravine into the valley.

The wanderer burst into the lush canyon and ran full gait along the bottom of the dry river bed. A cool pool of water rose to meet the newcomer; it was a small lake of standing water, filled with cattails and reeds. Laughing, the youth dove into the water and let the cold wash over him like an icy blast. Every inch of his body recoiled in the chill water as the frigid sensation washed over him. The sweat and stink were dissolving away from his body as his mind was set at ease. The threat of dying in the desert without provisions was now just a fading memory relegated to the youth's storehouse of undesired events. He splashed around the pool, and then came to rest by sitting in a shallow portion of the water.   Sighing in contentment, the youth grabbed several handfuls of water and drank them down, refreshing his body and soul.

Amongst the reeds and shallows, the youth caught sight of

another welcome benefit of the valley. A school of fish was slowly passing through the reeds and rocks. Their pink, scaly skin glimmered in the clear water. The traveler smiled and nodded his head in approval while his mouth began to water in anticipation. A fresh fish would make a welcome meal in the valley paradise.

The lone wanderer pulled a long branch from a spiny desert plant growing near the base of the mighty pool of water. Using the branch like a spear, it took the youth only a few moments to skewer a fish in the pool of water. The impaled fish wriggled and thrashed around on the branch, and the hungry wanderer smiled brightly while moving away from the water's edge. The fish twitched as he moved up the hillside amid the vegetation clinging to the edge of the pool.

A rock outcropping overlooked the pool of water. Collecting a pile of sticks and dry grass, the youth prepared to light a fire along the rock outcropping. He placed his weapons upon the rocks and pulled a lighter from his pocket, flipping the flint until a flame leapt into the dimming light. The dry tinder and wood erupted in orange flame as the fire consumed the fuel. Within minutes, the fire was large enough to begin cooking. The fish stopped flopping, and the wanderer propped the branch near the fire and began to cook the fish on the open flames. With a crackle, the fire popped as the youth stared at the fish, salivating wildly; his only focus was the meal at hand.

The sun was long gone from the world, casting darkness over the canyon. In the darkening sky was a set of purple clouds with a reddish tint. The sunset was brilliant, but began to dissipate as darkness slowly encroached upon the world. Bright, twinkling stars broke the night sky, and the lone youth looked into the heavens. Smoke and the smell of cooking fish wafted into his nostrils. He felt alive again, the thought of starvation and dehydration leaving his mind. The canyon was large enough to sustain the youth indefinitely. It was a true miracle that he had come upon the canyon.

With greedy, fervent hunger, he tore into the cooked fish. The youth chewed it up quickly, picking the bones from his teeth as he ate. Each savory morsel of meat tasted like a banquet. The lightly smoked fish was a real treat after several days without food. While the youth ate, his expression was distant, as if caught in some daydream.   With dull movements, the wanderer continued to consume the fish.   With only a pile of bones remaining, the youth smiled and pulled his knees against his chest. The onset of the cold night was abated by the glow and warmth of the campfire.

Feeling nourished and no longer thirsty, the youth drew closer to the fire and rolled onto his back. Letting his eyes shift onto the heavens, the young man looked at the night sky above. Stars and the white haze of shimmering constellations filled the dark sky. The youth's eyes shifted to the rim of the canyon.   A spark of light erupted from the ridgeline, a white spike of holy light rising higher and higher. The moon's edge pushed upwards, breaching the rim of the canyon, shining brightly in the dark. Staring in awe, with a tremor rolling through him, the youth looked on in anticipation as the moon rose. The event was not just another rising moon; it was a religious event. Each passing moment filled the youth with a jolt of adrenaline. Slowly, the radiant moon rose until the white glow of its perfect round form shone over the wasteland. Bathing the battered world in a sacred, holy white aura, the moon stood as a beacon in the darkness against the harsh backdrop of the shadowy night.

The youth looked at the rising moon with a sense of awe. Tears welled up in his eyes. Memories of the past filled his mind.

"Five moons…" The youth spoke dreamily in the darkness. He pulled his ponytail around and rested it under his head.

As he watched the full moon shining in the darkness, sadness filled him. The youth was alone. All of his friends were gone. A tragic night on the ocean had taken all of his companions…

With a thud, Jared rolled off the bunk and hit the floor of the ship hard. Something had hit the boat; or rather, the boat had hit something. Creaking had given way to a sharp snap. The hull of the boat had burst. Water rushed into the hold of the ship. Jared, wide eyed with fear, grabbed his gear and staggered to the top of the ship.

The damage to the boat was severe, and the vessel was in

real trouble. Shouting resounded on the deck. Waves crashed over the railings, obscuring the already dark night. A powerful storm had rolled in across the ocean, turning the sea into a swirling mass of chaos. In the madness of the night, the boat had struck submerged rocks near the coastline.

A powerful wave crashed over the sinking ship. Jared lost his footing and fell on the deck. The boat was sinking fast, and Jared clung desperately to the railing. Mustering his strength, the tribal rose and looked around for his companions, but they were nowhere to be seen.

"Tani!" Jared screamed in the howling wind. No one responded; his companions were fighting for their own lives, somewhere else on the ship. Recalling with fear that he was unable to swim, he knew that surviving the sinking of the boat would be almost impossible without help from his companions. Unwilling to lose his life in the disaster, Jared mustered a staunch expression. He had to find something to help him ride out the storm, and he had to do it quickly. Slipping again, Jared fell and cracked his chin on the tough wooden deck of the boat. Almost biting his tongue off as his chin hit the deck, he fought to remain conscious against the pain and to regain his footing. With a grunt, he rose again and staggered across the back of the boat. A large wooden deck plate leading to the cargo hold caught the tribal's eye. With a tug, the Scar Blade came free of its scabbard. With a mighty swing, the tribal brought the blue steel blade crashing into the hinges on the cargo door. The hinges shattered and the broad wooden deck plate came free.

Securing his weapons and gear, Jared climbed onto the deck plate just as the boat slipped below the chaotic fury of the ocean waves. The sound and spray of the waves was intense. The tribal gasped and coughed as wave after wave crashed over him. Clinging for life itself, Jared hugged the wooden plate and was battered time and time again by the waves of the sea. It seemed like an eternity, but finally, the wooden door deposited Jared on the shoreline.

Young Jared spent the night alone on the shore, and when the sun rose, he walked for miles and miles along the shore, desperately searching for Tani, Banion and Mineera. He found no trace of his companions; all he found was a dry riverbed leading west into the heart of the wasteland...

Jared stared up at the moon with a sense of loss. Memories of Scarskin, the journey to Pontiac City, the siege of Rasheed, the months of travel along the coastline, and finally the boat ride across the ocean were burned into his mind. It had been a long journey, and now the youth was staring at the rising of the fifth moon. Fifteen more moons would need to rise before he could return home to his village of Scarskin and take his place in society as an adult.

As Jared watched the full moon with a growing sense of awe, his worry and thoughts drifted to his lost companions. It had been many days since the ship wreck, without any trace of the rest of Nova 7. Jared was slowly coming to the realization that he might never find them or see them again. The stormy ocean was fierce enough to drown anyone, maybe even all of his companions. There was a good chance that some or all of his companions were dead, claimed by the brutal ocean storm.

Jared looked up at the night sky with a dull sense of loneliness. His hand moved to skim over his belongings. Banion's silver revolver met his hand. The youth grabbed the weapon and looked at it, his frustration mounting. Tears welled up in his eyes and he shook his head back and forth, fighting off the emotion.

"What am I doing out here?" Jared spoke softly. The fire crackled and was the only response to his lonely question to the night.

As fear stirred at the pit of his stomach, Jared looked into the night sky with a sensation of duty and terror. He held Banion's revolver in his hand and regarded it slowly. The memory of Rasheed being destroyed filled his mind as he stared at Banion's weapon. The gun was a symbol of death and a relic of Banion's wild fury and quest for vengeance. The weapon was now a silent symbol of a quest gone wrong, a symbol of a fading ideal that now seemed like a dream. Was the insane quest they were assigned by King Toil a reality? Was the horror seen in the fall of Rasheed a preview to even more horrid deeds unleashed by the enemy?

Young Jared clutched the weapon close and pressed the cold steel up against his face. The chilled weapon felt soothing to his skin. Memories welled up inside him as he thought about his journey thus far.

The sounds of the dying, the horrid flames leaping up to engulf the city, and the maniacal laughter of the Biogtech death squads laying waste to the citizens of Rasheed flashed in his mind. All of the visions came back in a fresh wash of emotion. With a grunt, Jared drove the visions from his mind. The boy sensed a thought forming at the back of his consciousness. The feeling flowed through him and struck the young warrior in his heart and soul. He knew that the enemy could not be allowed to last. Clutching Banion's weapon, his lonely frustration was beginning to mount into a seething rage.

"Everyone is gone..." Jared whispered with his gaze transfixed upon the fire. "What am I going to do?"

His thoughts kept lingering upon the razing of Rasheed. Try as he might, try as he may, he could not quiet the visions from that horrid night. His sense of loneliness sharpened into a frustrated sadness. "Why me? Why did this have to happen to me? I never wanted this."

Jared stood upright and stalked back and forth upon the rock outcropping, gripping his head in his hands, trying to remain in control. The face of Father Vertigo flashed in his mind, the twisted visage of evil itself. Jared fought back and thought of his home. The screams of the dying on the docks of Rasheed poured through his mind. The tribal youth struggled and forced an image of his family into his thoughts. The darkness pushed back, as a vision of the traitorous palace guards flooded his consciousness; their deceit and treachery could not be forgiven. The horrid events he had lived through could not be quieted by hiding in the shadows. The deeds must be erased by acts of daring and courage.

The battle Jared was waging against his own memories was failing. "I can't do this!" he shouted, frustrated.

Even though he felt helpless, he knew what must be done. In

order to stay the visions in his mind, to erase the nightmares, there was only one choice.

"I will finish this alone..." He shook his head slowly. Although frightened, Jared made a vow not to quit, not to surrender. He would take the insane quest all the way to the end, and he vowed to do it alone if necessary. It was the hardest decision Jared had ever had to make: continuing alone to fight a menace that could bring the world to ruin, a decision to stand against the darkness, no matter what the consequence. Clutching Banion's revolver, the emblem of the deranged rancher made him feel confident.

"Now is my time," Jared said in a resolute tone, staring at the moon, holding the cold steel revolver in his hand. The darkness responded; a blast of icy wind rolled through the canyon, an omen of the strife to come.

Chapter 14
The Legend of Navezgane, The Witch Hunter

Jared was spending a peaceful morning in the lush canyon. It was his first day in the secluded canyon paradise, and the youth from Scarskin was bright and cheerful, having already eaten another fish for breakfast. Young Jared had spent the morning thinking about his next course of action. With a confident demeanor, the tribal had resolved to search for the rest of Nova 7. Their destination before the boat sank had been the harbor town of Dune Station. It was Jared's goal to locate Dune Station and try to find his friends. If he could not locate them or a hint of their passing, Jared had resolved to finish the insane quest alone, locating a nuclear weapon somewhere in the ruins of the ancients.

With a dreamy look on his face, the tribal warrior continued on through the canyon, working his way between the clay spires jutting from the canyon floor.

His placid daydream was shattered as a loud, frantic scream rose suddenly in the distance. The hair on Jared's neck stood on end as his pulse raced and a tremor of fear ran through him.

Jared spun around and instinctively grabbed the hilt of the mighty Scar Blade. Another yell put the young warrior further on edge, his anxiety rising. Jared looked around the maze of rock spires through which he was traveling. The pleas for help ricocheted against the canyon walls, and Jared was frantic with anticipation; his ears scanned his surroundings, trying to discern the direction of the screams.

The canyon walls rose high above young Jared as he moved quickly in the general direction of the screams. Large boulders and pillars of rock blocked his progress. Like a rat in a maze, Jared pushed on. With a mighty tug, the Scar Blade cleared the scabbard, its light blue sheen glimmering in the sun. In and out of the shadows the young warrior pressed on, in the dim light of the rock formations rising high above. The sun barely reached the narrows in the canyon. The young warrior bounded forward in the cool shadows of the ancient clay monoliths, searching for the person crying out in terror.

"Gagghh!" A death cry was uttered just as Jared rounded an enormous tan boulder.

A chill shot down Jared's spine as he caught sight of the cause of this final cry. Like a coil of rope it was wound around a tree, gray in color, with yellow diamonds stretched about its enormous body in regular intervals. Its trunk was thick and split at the neck. Two serpentine heads rose from the junction. Yellow eyes, four in all, darted back and forth as two tongues extended, licking at the open air. The beast's tail was covered in thick rolls of hollow tissue. Shaking back and forth, the tail emitted a small tremor, a rattle that vibrated dully, clicking frantically as the gigantic two-headed serpent surveyed the area with hungry eyes. The mighty serpent lashed forward. Both mouths opened, exposing a series of fangs dripping with venom. The attack was swift and both sets of pale white, needle-like teeth hit their mark.

A dark skinned man dressed in leather clothes was struck in the chest and legs by the enormous fangs. Both heads bit into the hapless, defenseless man. Like hypodermic needles, the teeth sunk deep into the man's flesh. Poison, sickly burning poison, surged through the teeth, forcing its way into the victim's body. The amount of venom being infused into the man was so immense that it sprayed rapidly from the wounds; it was too much poison to be contained within his body. He gurgled, unable to speak, while twitching as the toxin took its toll. Within seconds, the man ceased to stir and fell limp. One of the heads recoiled from the dead man, and its forked tongue licked the air, searching for yet another victim, its white teeth stained in crimson blood. A second dark skinned man was down on the rocks, only a few feet away from the fifty-foot long serpent. He was crawling away from the monster with jagged, jerky movements. A trail of blood and poison dripped from his wounded chest as he crawled along the ground.

Jared stood motionless, witnessing the horrible scene. He

dared not stir and held the Scar Blade limply in his right hand. Still more than thirty yards away from the scene, he tried to regain his composure. He could not believe the sight he was witnessing.

The serpentine horror coiled itself more tightly around the tree. The enormous rattle at the end of its tail began to gyrate back and forth. The mighty Rattle Hydra licked the air once more. With a grotesque snap, one of the heads detached its lower jaw and began to engulf the motionless man, dead upon the ground. Slowly, the corpse slid into the enormous maw of the creature. The other head stared with fascination at the dark skinned man crawling away. The rattle boomed and clicked rapidly, gyrating with feverish intensity. The Rattle Hydra uncoiled itself from the tree and gave chase, wanting to envelop another victim with the saliva and venom dripping from its open mouth.

Jared looked at the beast and at the defenseless man about to be killed. A thought entered his mind as he looked at the engorged head swallowing the man. It was only half done with its meal, and that gave Jared an advantage. If he were to charge the beast, it could only fight back with a single head, not both. With a staunch look and his heart in his throat, Jared raised the mighty Scar Blade and charged the serpent terror.

Like a cat he charged, silent, bounding across the rocks. The mighty Rattle Hydra caught his scent a mere second before the assault. Jared attacked and drove the weapon at the head of the beast. It rocked backwards and dodged the attack. Anger flashed in its eyes as it reared back, its body forming a tight coil. The rattle gyrated intensely and the free head hissed in defiance.

Frustrated, the head consuming the man shook back and forth, trying to free its meal so it could defend itself. Its attempts were to no avail: the corpse clogged its mouth and would not come free. The free head darted forth, with fangs extended. Jared barely sidestepped the attack; it came so close that a spray of venom flew past the tribal's face.

The young warrior quickly jabbed at the beast. A gash opened on its neck, piercing the thick gray scales. With a hiss, it reared back and coiled more tightly. A fury was in its gaze. Yellow and sinister, its eyes fell upon the young boy wielding a blue blade smeared in red blood, the beast's blood. Rolling forward, the coiled beast struck out again. Jared was feeling a calm come over him. Instead of fear flowing through his veins, he sensed a resolute, cool calm flood him. The attack of the Rattle Hydra was quick, but not quick enough. Jared dodged again and swung quickly, not wanting to be too aggressive and leave himself open to a counterattack. Another wound opened upon the neck of the beast as the Scar Blade bit flesh once more.

The second injury drove the Rattle Hydra into a killing frenzy. It hissed and struck time and time again at young Jared. The tribal was now acting on instinct alone, allowing his combat prowess to take hold of his senses. For each hasty strike the beast made, Jared struck back and gashed the beast. Through a furious series of attacks and counterattacks by young Jared, the beast was left a bloody mess, with over a dozen open wounds bleeding profusely.

The other head was desperately trying to finish swallowing its breakfast to aid its twin in battle, but it was too late. The blood loss was already beginning to take its toll on the Rattle Hydra. Jared could sense the beast's weakness but stood staunch; he dared not hazard giving in to a hasty attack. With an exhibition of patience, Jared continued to slowly injure the beast until the wounds were too much.

The snake began to swagger back and forth, weak from battle and blood loss. Sensing victory, the tribal warrior eyed the beast intently; he knew it was time to end the creature's life. Jared inhaled and stepped forward, preparing to strike. With a mighty cry he exhaled and swung the blade directly at the base of the free head. The snake was weary from battle and never even tried to avoid the attack. The blue blade struck the neck and ground through completely, severing the head. With a spray of blood, the stump rocked back and forth as the lifeless head crashed to the ground.

Jared inhaled again and raised the gore stained blade above his head. He directed another attack directly in between the necks of the serpent, where the beast was at its thickest. The blade crashed down and tore deeply into its body. The sharp weapon found its mark and cut into the chest of the beast, splitting the heart of the monster in two. With a grunt, Jared placed his foot against the beast and pulled the Scar Blade from its twitching serpentine body.

The Rattle Hydra crashed to the ground and ceased to stir. Jared, a youth from the wasteland, had slain the terrible monster.

The tribal sighed and felt the adrenaline subside. He stared in shock at the corpse of the creature before him. It was a mighty kill indeed. Jared shook his head in amazement, then suddenly realized that he was not alone. Whirling around, the tribal of Scarskin caught sight of a host of dark skinned male warriors wielding spears. All had witnessed the end of the battle.

With a wide eyed look of fear, a dark skinned man dressed in leather clothes stepped forward and pointed at Jared. He yelled in a foreign tongue, "Navezgane!"

Many members of the war party moved back in terror as they stared at Jared. It was as if the natives were looking at a ghost, a haunting specter that had crept from the spirit world. Many pointed and uttered phrases in their native tongue in excited bursts.

Without warning, a sudden dizziness took Jared. He staggered back and forth and felt a sharp pain in his arm. With hazy vision, Jared surveyed his arm and found a deep gash and sickly yellow venom surrounding the wound. During the battle, he had been so focused that he failed to notice that the mighty Rattle Hydra had stung his arm, and that deadly venom from the beast was now coursing through his body. His vision began to blur. The Scar Blade fell from his hand as his arm began to spasm under the influence of the poison.

As the venom flowed through his mind and body, the host of dark skinned warriors drew near, holding out their hands as if preparing to touch a thing born of the spirit world. Each native reached forward, trying to touch young Jared. With many hands upon him, the youth from Scarskin staggered back and forth. The weaker he became from the poison, the more they held him. The last thing Jared heard before he lost consciousness was the word of the strange warriors, stinging in his mind with a sinister whisper: "Navezgane... Navezgane..."

Chapter 15
The Mission

The poison had taken its toll. For three days, young Jared had been caught in a horrid daze of confusion and misery. A high temperature had spiked and turned into a raging fever as the venom coursed through his veins. Tortured by the fever, Jared was caught in a whirlwind of chaos. Slipping in and out of a haunted sleep, the tribal fought a war with his dreams. Day after day passed without the fever breaking. Visions of crusades long past and wars not yet waged were the focus of his fever-induced madness. Rolling back and forth with sweat streaming down his face, Jared mumbled and spoke of lost history hidden beneath the shifting sands of the world.

From time to time, the tribal would awake and sit upright in the straw bed. He would find himself surrounded by strange people, mumbling in an unknown tongue and stretching their hands outward, trying to touch him with frightened gestures...

The fever had broken. It was dark when young Jared awoke from the horror of the last three days. His eyes opened slowly. A dull orange glow filled his vision. His sight was blurry, and he blinked several times and rubbed his eyes, trying to clear the haze from his vision. He exhaled slowly and fought to rise. As he did, a sharp pain filled his temples. Fighting back the feeling of nausea, the tribal sat at the edge of the straw bed. His focus came to rest on the orange glow. A candle, a solitary candle, illuminated the darkness.

His focus broke from the flame to examine his surroundings. He rose and took a shaky step forward. Dizziness took him and he staggered toward the wall. His hand came to rest on a dark stained, brownish-red, finely crafted wooden panel lining the wall, which was worn with age but smooth to the touch. The youth was in a small square room with an ornately carved door sealing him within. Devoid of windows, the tiny room felt confining.

The youth pressed forward in his exploration. He halted before the closed door, and stretched out his hand, grasping the cold metal rung hanging down. Fidgeting with the handle, Jared pushed the door open and moved into an enormous room beyond. With a feeling of awe, Jared entered the expansive room.

As he emerged from the small room, the walls towered above the tribal, several stories high. Darkly stained wooden beams soared upward, meeting in vaulted arches suspended high above the young tribal. Dark wood paneling surrounded the perimeter of the room. Carved into the wood were intricate patterns with a ridge of raised wood surrounding a diamond pattern of raised circles. Interlaced with the fine woodwork was dull gray stonework. Raw stones were painstakingly assembled, with mortar sealing the cracks between the grey stone. Jared's eye followed the edge of the wall as it rose upward. Brightly colored stained glass caught his eye. The sun was pushing through the glass, creating a spectrum of warm colors. Red, orange, and purple light streamed through the stained glass windows surrounding the topmost portion of the church. The warm colors against the backdrop of the dark wood and earthy stonework gave the mighty room a unique, warm appearance. It was a place of peace, a refuge from the desert wastelands and harsh world beyond.

The quiet of the sanctuary was a stunned silence. Young Jared could hear his own heart beating in the calm serenity. It was almost too quiet for the tribal, making him feel a little anxious. The smell of age wafted through his nostrils. The scent of old wood and the gritty smell of earth filled his nose. A waft of old books, with their smell of worn paper, rolled through the enormous room and mingled with the odor of burning candles. The mighty sanctuary was filled with a unique aroma.

Jared took another shaky step forward. Row after row of wooden benches stretched before him. Walking among the rows, the tribal had a dull sense that he was not alone. Still dizzy from the ordeal with the Rattle Hydra, Jared dismissed the feeling, walking along the empty rows of benches. At the other end of the expansive room, past the wooden benches, was a raised dais with an altar upon it.

Jared stumbled down the aisle between the benches. As he moved, he became even more aware of someone's eyes upon him. Giving in to his curiosity, Jared turned around slowly to find a person cloaked in the shadows, near a wooden column, watching him very carefully. The tribal was instantly set on edge. His hand moved instinctively to his belt. This movement was in vain; the mighty Scar Blade was not at his side.

Jared held his ground and stared nervously at the form. Slowly it moved, with staggered and jagged movements. The aged form hunched forward. As the stranger moved, light and shadow interrupted Jared's vision. Watching the strange figure move toward him was almost like watching a mirage. Finally, the stranger had crossed the distance to the youth.

A dark skinned man stood before Jared. Deep lines of age cut the man's face. Gray hair was braided about his shoulders. Each of the man's eyes was a different color. One eye was hazel, while the other was a sickly white, affected by a cataract, dimming his vision and making it hard to maintain eye contact with the aged shaman. The elderly man considered Jared with an unwavering gaze. Jared looked back at him, frowning as he surveyed the drooping cheeks that gave him the appearance of a wizened holy man. Animal bones, feathers, and other earthen artifacts hung around his shoulders in an assortment of crude necklaces. The stench of roots and herbs wafted from him, and a nostalgic feeling filled Jared as the medicinal smell filled his nostrils. The scent reminded the tribal of his friend Tani and his room back in Scarskin, filled with odd smelling chemicals.

"Navezgane..." the old shaman muttered.

Jared stood dumbfounded, and it took him a moment to speak. "What...?" Jared quizzed in a confused tone.

"You speak a lost tongue, my boy." The shaman spoke in a dull tone, staring uneasily at Jared. "Your speech is that of the ancients."

Jared remained silently bewildered, not knowing what to make of the strange man or his surroundings.

"Your wounds are healed, boy. We spent much time with

you, breaking the fever, holding prayer over you. The dark spirits were about you, and it took some time to drive them back." The shaman spoke softly, with a look of dispassion, his white clouded eye quivering as he spoke.

"Evil spirits?" Jared quizzed.

"In the heat of your fever, you spoke of horrid things, wars long past, hidden in the passage of time. The visions you were wracked with brought you back to us. The Great Spirit broke the demons from you and brought you back to life. It is powerful magic."

"I don't understand," Jared said, dumfounded, while rubbing a bandage on his right arm. He pressed his hand against the bandage and the wound stung underneath.

"We have a legend here in this place." The shaman spoke in a whisper, moving away toward the west wall of the ancient church.

"My ancestors lived far beyond the seclusion of this canyon before the fall of the ancients. The land was all people's until the ancients subjugated the land with the tools of pestilence and war. My people persisted. Reservations were formed, and my people were forced to live in the wastelands of the earth. Slowly dying on these reservations, our way of life began to wane and pass out of knowledge. As our way of life was about to disappear forever, an event occurred that brought the world of the ancients to ruin."

"The apocalypse..." Jared whispered as he moved to follow the old man through the dark church.

"The world came to a ruinous end. The civilized world was over. The sky rained poison upon the land. Sickly clouds of dust rained down, and our people began to die of strange diseases. Their eyes bled, their hair fell out, their souls withered and wasted away. Both men and beasts fell sick. The crops withered and died. The springs of water ceased to flow. A great many of our people fell to the shadow. Our tribe was on the verge of extinction." The shaman moved closer to the young boy and stared at him, his gaze unwavering. "The shaman of our tribe fell ill, and hope seemed lost. Our wise leader had succumbed to the poison falling from the heavens and passed into death. Without our leader, despair was the only focus of our people." The shaman then fell silent and considered the youth with a serious look. Jared stared back and a chill ran down his spine. The shaman was a menacing presence, wisdom etched into his face. "After the rites of death were performed upon our shaman, a stranger gripped by darkness, driven by madness, appeared at the edge of our reservation."

Jared gazed at the wise shaman, motionless. The youth of Scarskin breathed softly, his head still throbbing in pain, trying to discover why the strange story was being retold for his benefit.

"The stranger was a priest of old world religion, staggering from the desert on the verge of death. He was weak from his journey through the desert and fell into unconsciousness. Three days passed, and his fever was filled with dark tidings. It was whispered that evil spirits had inhabited his body during this time, trying to poison his soul. The priest awoke much as you did, boy, ripped from nightmares and forced back to the world of the living by powerful magic." The shaman considered young Jared with a distant look, clearly on edge, for whatever reason. The aged man motioned Jared to follow and they pressed further into the church.

"The priest related a strange tale to my people on the reservation. He claimed that spirits had come to him in a vision and had shown him the way through the desert and had ordered him to bring my people from suffering. Our tribe was broken by the ruin of the world and the passing of their kindred by the plague raining from the sky. Without leadership, the tribe was desperate for guidance. The priest, with hope in his eyes, convinced my people to leave their home and press on into the harsh desert on a pilgrimage into the wasted earth. The priest claimed that spirits would guide them to a place of refuge far from the death of the contaminated land and sky. The tribe followed, and the priest led my people to this valley, this paradise, hidden in the canyon."

Jared was awestruck by the story, but still felt confused. "Why are you telling me all of this? I don't understand."

"The priest saved our people from certain death, but he fell into madness after coming to this place. He abandoned reason and built this very church, stone by stone, timber by timber, upon our mesa, refusing all help from our tribesmen. Throughout the time he toiled, he was wracked by horrid visions of the future. It took his lifetime to build this church stone by stone. When the church was finished, the priest became reclusive and refused to leave the safety of this place. The remainder of his life was spent scrawling drawings upon the walls of this church. All that remains of his legacy are these pictures…" The shaman ceased to speak. A look of indecision clouded his visage. There was a moment of silence in the dimly lit church. "These drawings were from his visions of the future…" The shaman regarded Jared with a look of sympathy and then led him to the front of the church.

Bathed in the brightly colored light shining in through the stained glass windows was a series of crudely drawn pictures scrawled upon the walls.

Jared gasped as he viewed the pictures upon the wall. The largest of the pictures filled him with fright. Drawn upon the wall was the image of a young man wielding a blue blade in one hand and a severed snake's head in the other. Surrounding the man were a host of beast men, their heads twisted in the shape of goats.

"How is this possible?" Jared asked with horrified fascination. "What is this?"

"This is what the priest envisioned. This is what drove him into the wastelands. It is said that he was haunted by these visions and that he sought out my people to deliver them from sorrow."

Jared was appalled by the scrawling upon the wall. The tribal was unsure how a man living hundreds of years ago could have glimpsed the insanity that Jared had seen. The vision of the man holding a blue blade surrounded by a host of goat men was almost too much to bear.

Jared felt the hair rise on the back of his neck.

"Our people believe this church holds powerful magic. Legends were formed from these pictures scrawled upon the wall. It is part of our heritage. We believe that some day, a savior will appear from the wasteland and will deliver our world from evil." The shaman stared intently at Jared, and the young tribal shook his head in fear. "The visions, I believe, were of you." The shaman spoke in a resolute tone, considering young Jared with a piercing gaze, his white clouded eye trembling.

"What? That's impossible," Jared countered, fear rising in his soul.

"Is it?" the shaman quizzed. "Behold." The shaman moved to another set of drawings upon the wall.

Jared followed hesitantly. The tribal youth gasped as he viewed the scrawling. Another crude drawing depicted a young man holding a blue blade in one hand and a silver revolver in his other hand.

"This is the legend of Navezgane, the demon hunter." The shaman shot Jared another piercing gaze.

"I don't want any part of this." Jared stumbled backward, not wanting to believe the strange tale.

"It is unavoidable. These drawings contain chronicles of things you have already done and things you will do. You cannot change that."

"I don't want this," Jared countered again, his mind spinning.

"I cannot tell you where the road you are on will lead you. These pictures are a fragmented record of the priest's maddened visions. But the one thing I do know is this: I do not doubt that you are the one in these pictures."

Jared was dizzy and shook his head back and forth, not wanting to believe. With a sick frustration filling him, he scrambled along the wall, looking at the drawings. At staggered intervals, a full moon was etched in the wall. A picture of a mesa hauntingly reminiscent of Scarskin could be found in many of the pictorials. The final and most horrifying was a portrait of a sickly pale man with a forked beard.

"Vertigo…" Jared whispered.

The blood drained from his face and he turned ashen white. Attempting to put as much distance as possible between himself and the drawings, the youth was frantic to escape. With eyes rolling about, he found the exit to the mighty church, staggering toward the enormous doors of the church and flinging them open. As the doors opened, sunlight flooded the space of the church. Jared squinted in the light and stumbled outward from the sanctuary. A crowd of villagers was stationed outside the mighty doors. They all gasped and pointed.

"Navezgane," the crowd whispered.

Hearing the sinister name, Jared was horrified. He found himself fleeing from the people whispering and pointing outside the church.

"This cannot be happening…" Jared whispered in horror, trying to awaken from a dream that was his reality.

He stumbled back into the church and slammed the doors shut, pushing his back up against the doors and sliding down.

Holding his head in both hands, Jared fought the strange feeling inside him. He closed his eyes and then opened them. It was no dream. Jared stared about the church in disbelief; the church was a monument to *him*.

Chapter 16
The Village of Song River

Lost in deep thought, young Jared was sitting at the edge of the Indian village near the side of the cliff face. He stared down into the lush canyon far below the precipice upon which he perched. Two hawks circled endlessly around a crisp blue pool of water, trying to catch sight of field mice or fish for a morning snack. The hawks let out a piercing wail as they rode the thermal winds over the canyon. Spiny plants such as yucca and cactus lined the periphery of the canyon, while more leafy plants clung to the riverbank in the center of the canyon valley. The green vegetation climbed the white clay spires lining the floor of the canyon. A herd of antelopes, at least three dozen, grazed on the grasses near the stream meandering through the valley. The healthy herd contained several young antelopes which were walking on shaky, thin legs, following their mothers very closely.

Jared had been silent for some time. The unusual events which had transpired in the ancient church were still clinging to his fragile mind. Unable to comprehend the strangeness, young Jared was forced into an uneasy silence. Feeling someone's eyes upon him, Jared tensed abruptly. He sighed and looked behind him, scanning the area. Three dark skinned children were hiding at the edge of a nearby building, whispering and pointing at Jared. He shot them a dirty look and they yipped and ran away toward the center of the village.

The village of Song River was built on top of a mesa in the center of the lush valley. All in all, it was very similar to the village of Scarskin. Adobe and mud houses clung to the edges of the jagged rock walls that fell away more than a thousand feet to the bottom of the canyon. Crops, mostly corn, were on the northern rim of the mesa. The center of the mesa was dominated by an ominous site: an enormous church made of stone, wood, and stained glass rising high into the sky, casting long shadows upon the rest of the buildings in the village. The mighty church looked out of place and was an imposing sight to behold. The architecture and construction of the building simply didn't seem to fit among the crude adobe houses.

The church caught the young warrior's eye as he gazed toward the town. He looked up at the edifice with hesitation. It was as if the monstrous building was a silent enemy, an object toying with the young tribal, urging him to come inside and view all the wonderful pictures scrawled upon the wall by a madman who had died nearly eight hundred years ago.

"Come inside, my boy! Come inside and take a look!" the church seemed to call out, and Jared shuddered as he tried to put his imagination to rest.

No matter how many times the tribal tried to force the images from his mind, they kept slinking back softly, sneaking up on Jared. Next thing he knew, the images Jared had seen upon the wall of the church were flashing through his mind like a demented primitive picture book.

"Argh!" Jared said out loud, rising to his feet, forcing the images from his mind.

"Navezgane is displeased?" the shaman inquired. He had crept up softly behind the tribal and caught him unaware.

"Don't call me that," Jared whined with a frustrated look on his face.

The shaman fell silent and looked gruffly at Jared.

The tribal from Scarskin sighed out loud, then apologized for his outburst.

"Follow me, boy, we have much to talk of," the shaman ordered, and Jared followed him silently.

The youth from Scarskin moved away from the edge of the cliff and followed the wise shaman into the heart of the village. As they passed, the locals gasped and whispered, pointing at Jared. The tribal turned bright red and tried not to get annoyed. He shook his head in frustration and moved on in silence. The shaman led the youth to a circular hut made of rows and rows of wooden timbers with dried mud jammed in between the cracks. Using timbers of wood in one's home was a sign of status. Since trees were rare in the valley, only the most important members of the tribe had such wooden huts. The church, in contrast, had intricate woodwork. The size of the structure and the amount of wood used in its construction were another aspect that made the building so ominous. It was a monument that would always inspire awe and legend in the village.

The shaman moved into his wooden lodge and Jared obediently followed. Urging him to make himself comfortable, the shaman sat down upon the floor of the hut, which was lined with soft animal hides and furs. Jared sat as well, eyeing the shaman suspiciously.

Taking flint and a wedge of metal, the old man struck the two objects together and let the sparks light the dry kindling in the fire pit at the center of the hut. The flames rose softly, and the shaman fanned the orange flare, watching the fire grow in size. Finally, it sprung to life and illuminated the hut.

As the light erupted, Jared looked around in confusion. Animal hides covered the walls. Skulls of desert creatures adorned the entryway. Dry plants hung above the fire, giving off a pungent odor. It was almost as if Jared had stepped into Tani's room, back home in Scarskin.

"Our tribe owes you a debt of thanks," the shaman said, nodding his head.

Jared looked on dully, wishing he could escape the strange village, preferring the company of loneliness to his eccentric host.

"Your bravery was appreciated, young Jared of Scarskin. Even though you could not save our tribesmen from the Rattle Hydra, your courage was respected nonetheless. We have waited long for you to come to our village. Generation after generation has known your story. You are a myth and a legend to our people. I am glad you came to us in my lifetime, so I could help you on your journey." The shaman produced a pipe from the animal hides lining the floor. He packed the pipe with some of the foul smelling herbs from the ceiling and pulled a burning branch from the fire. Lighting the pipe, the shaman took several puffs, then handed it to Jared.

With hesitation, he sniffed the burning herbs and almost

gagged. The shaman gave him a stern look, so Jared put the pipe in his mouth and took a puff. The smoke was strong and stung the tribal's lungs. Coughing and gagging, Jared fought to breathe in fresh air. With a wave of dizziness, he rubbed his eyes as the powerful tobacco coursed through his veins. His vision blurry, he looked to the shaman with a dazed expression.

"This plant is powerful medicine for my people. Those who smoke often are brought visions by strong spirits. I am glad we could share such medicine."

Jared giggled and looked up at one of the animal heads above the entrance. The coyote head seemed to grin at Jared. The tribal laughed and pointed. The shaman smiled and took another mighty puff from the pipe. Jared took another puff as well. The anxiety was dissipating the more Jared smoked. The young tribal just didn't care anymore.

"There is another medicine I wish to share with you, Navezgane."

The shaman moved to the back of the hut and recovered a finely crafted wooden box. He touched it with a sense of hesitation, rubbing the cover of the box with his rough, aged hand. Finally a sparkle lit his eyes and he nodded and whispered to himself. The shaman crept back and placed the wooden box before Jared.

"Our ancestors communed with nature and maintained peace with spirits of the world. A powerful medicine man, Spotted Coyote, an ancestor of mine, took a great pilgrimage into the wilds of the earth. It was said that this medicine man traveled a great many days, refusing both food and water on his journey. To become one with the spirits, he walked the line between life and death, starvation driving him into a focused state. The spirits of the world brought Spotted Coyote many visions, and it was whispered that many spirits entered his body and taught him the mysteries of the great void." The shaman looked at the wooden box with a solemn face. After a moment of silence, he collected his thoughts and continued the tale.

"During the spirit journey, Spotted Coyote was commanded to seek out a ruined tree in the forest, one that had been burned by lightning. From that very tree, the spirits commanded him to craft a totem, a mighty totem of a great bird, a raven born from the sky. Spotted Coyote did as the spirits commanded. He crafted the totem from the tree scarred by lightning, spending a great many days in the wild. After the raven totem was complete, Spotted Coyote communed with the spirits once more.

"The spirits then commanded Spotted Coyote to travel back home and to pray, chanting all the way. The medicine man did as the spirits bid him to do; he chanted and prayed all the way home. Without food and water for many days, Spotted Coyote entered the village and collapsed. His body had failed. The tribe ran to his aid, but it was too late. Spotted Coyote would never awake, consumed by spirits of the great void, infused with knowledge and power from the spirit world. As the tribe held vigil around the fallen shaman, a fierce storm appeared from the empty sky above the village. The tribe saw this event as a powerful omen and fled, leaving Spotted Coyote upon the earth. A mighty flash drove down from the heavens and the thunder clapped in the sky. A bolt of lightning struck Spotted Coyote, and his body turned to ash. The storm clouds vanished and the tribe returned to view their beloved shaman. The only thing that remained was the totem of the bird, smoking amongst his ashes, its eyes burning brightly, licked once more by lightning."

Jared was lost in the thick fog of the pipe smoke, but he had an uneasy, solemn look upon his face. He eyed the wooden box in front of him with an anxious gaze.

"The totem of my ancestor is yours, Navezgane. It is powerful medicine and will keep you safe from evil spirits. I do not doubt that you are the one upon the walls of the church. You are our hero, our chosen. This is the most powerful gift we could bestow." The shaman eyed Jared sternly and motioned the youth to take the box and accept the gift inside.

Even under the influence of the strong tobacco, Jared knew to be respectful and nodded in reverence to the shaman. With a shaky hand, Jared reached forward and touched the wooden box. It hummed at his touch, small tremors shaking it from within. Jared recoiled, frightened by the response to his touch. The shaman nodded in support and he reached forward once again, this time placing both hands upon the box. Jittering, the vessel housing the magic totem rocked about once again. With the hair rising on his neck, Jared opened the box. Two red, piercing eyes glowed in the darkness of the vessel. Like fire trapped within the totem, the eyes burned with fierce intensity. Jared's eyes opened wide; he could not avoid the gaze of the raven totem. Finally, the wooden bird ceased to stir, and the flames were extinguished in its eyes.

Jared clutched the wooden totem. It was small, about the size of his hand, and had a strange chill about it, almost a faint, icy presence. Its wings were extended and its head looked straight ahead. The wood was worn, gray in color, and there were places on its body that were burned to a blackened cinder.

Jared looked uneasily at the totem in his hands. The shaman reached out with a piece of twine, offering it to young Jared. The youth accepted the twine and wrapped it around the totem's neck, fashioning a crude necklace out of the powerful relic. Jared eyed the shaman, who nodded in approval. With hesitation, Jared placed the totem around his neck. The wooden bird rested at the center of his chest, the icy chill pervading its wooden body. At that moment, Jared felt something tug at his soul. It was as if a powerful presence was now with the tribal, an ancient presence protecting him. Even in his stupor, Jared could tell that the spiritual power emanating from the totem was formidable.

The shaman nodded in approval and placed his hands on Jared's shoulders, looking into his eyes, speaking softly. "Now you are ready for your journey."

Chapter 17
Of Myth and Legend

The horse neighed and shook its head. Jared wiped the sweat from his brow and looked onward. After a ride from the primitive village of Song River which had lasted more than three days, the youth from Scarskin could finally see the outskirts of a small farming town just ahead. The youth shifted uneasily in his saddle as he reined his horse, which had been a gift from the tribe, to a halt. He surveyed the village with hesitation; each town had to be considered carefully. Each town had its own set of hidden dangers. With agents of the enemy abounding, Jared had to be vigilant. It was the first time he would be back in *civilization* since the fall of Rasheed.

Images of his journey since the ill-fated boat ride which had separated young Jared from his companions were beginning to creep into his mind while he hesitated at the edge of town. The indecision and doubt whether his companions had survived the ship wreck, the encounter with the Rattle Hydra, the horrid dreams from being poisoned, the strange church dedicated to the tribal from Scarskin, and finally, the animal totem given to him by the shaman were all events that put Jared on edge. Throughout all of the fantastic events, Jared was the center, the focal point, and this fact was changing him. The events were altering the youth's psyche, polarizing the highly skilled warrior, transforming Jared into something different, something deadly.

Moving his hand to his neck, Jared rubbed the strange wooden bird totem. Over the last few days, the tribal had developed an uneasy twitch. The totem felt odd, resting silently in the center of his chest. He wasn't sure if it was just his imagination, but the object felt strangely cold, almost as if it were radiating a chill. The tribal dismissed the idea as nothing more than fanciful nonsense. How could an ancient wooden relic exude a chill? But still... it just didn't seem right...

Snapping out of the daydream and sighing, Jared gave a light kick and his horse started forward, pushing toward the ramshackle farming town. The landscape had become more temperate, and the desert had given way to sparse patches of earth which could support vegetation. Crude crops were grown around the perimeter of the town. The fields were irregular in shape, since the blasted landscape could barely support the crops withering in the blazing sun. The wheat crop was dried and burnt in several places, creating an impression of disease. In any event, the crude wheat fields were the only real staple of the wasteland town, the only real profession of its inhabitants. Avoiding passing through one of the fragile fields, Jared steered his mount around and soon reached the edge of civilization.

Shacks and crude houses made from a collection of wood and rusted scrap metal were the prominent features of the ramshackle town. Mismatched wooden planks were either nailed together with rusted nails, or bound together with twine and other crude fastenings. None of the windows had glass; instead, dirty rags and worn blankets covered the openings. Refuse and decay were all about. Many of the homes had been abandoned and turned into repositories of garbage. Old world devices such as battered bathtubs, tarnished toilets, ruined refrigerators, and withered washing machines were piled about in the abandoned properties, giving the town the appearance of a landfill.

To say the town was poor greatly understated the poverty of the environment. A child, covered in dirt from head to toe, was chasing an equally filthy, three legged mutt with one eye down the main street of the town. The child stopped and eyed Jared with a look of suspicion. Once he had an eyeful, the lad resorted to chasing the dirty dog through the streets once again.

Jared stared on in shock. The youth had never seen such poverty and detritus. Leading his horse through the ruins masquerading as civilization, Jared surveyed the town, attempting to locate either an inn or tavern. The youth needed some information about the surrounding wasteland if he was going to make his way to

Dune Station in search of his lost companions.

A two story building stood in the center of town, with a crude wooden sign tacked up over its doorway. The tribal smiled as he read the word 'saloon' painted on the sign in dull washed yellow. Tethering his horse, young Jared dismounted and stared at the entrance with an uneasy measure of anxiety. *"Here we go,"* he whispered as he pushed his way inside.

The interior was dimly lit, and a host of desert scum huddled around the poorly crafted tables inside the ramshackle bar. Several bar patrons were seated around wooden crates acting as crude tables. Everyone in the bar jumped when the tribal walked in the door. It was as if the crowd was awaiting a visit from some sinister monster. A sigh of relief rolled through the bar as the half-drunk patrons eyed Jared. The anxiety of the bar patrons was clearly high, and the youth was suspicious of their response. He eyed them uneasily, as if to discern the cause of their distress, to no avail; the hopeless patrons failed to divulge any knowledge in their silent stupor.

Many members of the drunken mass eyed the tribal's weapons, each noticing that the youth was armed with a revolver and a sword. One man snorted, but the rest didn't even flinch; they looked away and went back to their business of drinking away the afternoon. Even though Jared was young, it wasn't every day a drifter walked into the bar armed with a sword, let alone a gun. Weapons in this part of the wasteland were crude. Only people of consequence had such fine armament. In many areas of the wasteland, guns were a wicked status symbol; only the dangerous and combat savvy carried such gear. Such individuals were granted respect and a wide girth.

Jared moved over to the bar and sat down on a crude stool. One of the legs on the bar stool was shaky, causing the tribal to steady himself or else fall over outright. Gaining his balance, Jared gripped the counter. The barkeep moved forward and eyed him oddly.

"You sure gave us a startle, boy. Where did you come from?" the barkeep quizzed the youth, his voice soft.

Wondering why everyone in the bar was on edge and

attempting to act confident, Jared slowed his speech, trying to sound imposing. "I pushed out from the northeast. I've been riding for three days. What is this place, this town?"

"You're in Baker's Grove. What brings you in? We don't get many visitors out here these days, with the rumor of war and all."

A moment of silence stretched out. Jared was trying to formulate his thoughts. He knew locating his lost friends would be his first plan of action. "I am on my way to Dune Station."

"Dune Station, huh? Why does a drifter need to head into Dune Station? You looking for work?"

"No, just my friends," Jared said in a quiet tone, his look distant. "I need some directions, if you don't mind. I've never been to Dune Station."

The barkeep eyed the tribal's weapons with an uneasy look. Finally, he spoke in an equally uneasy tone.

"Head east, and four days ride will bring you to Shape Home. Once you're on the coast, it's a week's ride north to Dune Station." The barkeep spoke softly while looking back and forth, evading eye contact with the tribal from Scarskin. He was still on edge, looking nervously at the door to the bar, speaking in a near-whisper.

"Four days east to Shape Home, then seven north to Dune Station?"

"Yeah, kid."

The tribal fell silent and felt a spark of hope. He knew Dune Station was the destination of Nova 7 before that fateful night on the ship, and that their ultimate destination was Shape Home. If the others had survived, his best chance of finding them would be in Dune Station or Shape Home. If his quest to find his friends failed, the youth was prepared to head out and search for a nuclear weapon by himself, undoubtedly a daunting task.

"Thanks," Jared replied.

"No problem, kid. You want a drink?" As the barkeep spoke, his eyes widened; someone had pushed into the bar and the owner was none too happy.

At that moment, something strange happened. The totem around Jared's neck began to vibrate violently. A frigid blast of cold air erupted from it, startling Jared. The confused tribal grabbed the totem and stared at it in surprise. The eyes of the wicked relic were glowing red and a chill was emanating from the raven totem.

Jared spun around and his heart leapt into his throat. The person who had pushed into the bar was clad in red. The robes fell about the initiate, branding him an agent of the enemy, a foul Reaper Kai. The patrons were terrified as well, and stared on with fright. It was now apparent why all the patrons were so uneasy when Jared entered the tavern; a sinister agent of the Reaper Kai was in town.

With a jolt, Jared jumped off the bar stool and his hand fell instantly to the hilt of the mighty Scar Blade, knowing that the enemy had been tracking Nova 7 since the fall of Rasheed. The initiate was startled by Jared's response and took a step back. It wasn't often that anyone, let alone a mere boy, went for his weapon in the presence of a Reaper Kai. A twisted look covered the initiate's face, and he shot the tribal a hate-filled glare.

"Where did you come from?" the initiate hissed. "You little brat! What do you think you're doing?"

Jared stood his ground, with the totem around his neck vibrating violently. Each passing moment, the Scar Blade slid further from its scabbard, exposing the light blue metallic sheen of the ancient weapon. Jared locked his eyes on that of the initiate. He knew his chance of surviving an attack from the Reaper Kai would be slim. Jared had encountered such foes with little success. A Reaper Kai often had the ability to kill several opponents simultaneously with ease. Jared knew that escape was impossible and that there would be no support from the locals to aid him in this struggle. There was no Banion to mercilessly gun down the enemy; there was no Tani to hurl explosives; there was no Mineera to shield him from harm.

Jared had to act and he had to act fast if he was going to survive. The fragile thread of weakness broke in the boy. Instead of the blood thickening inside of him, as it had done in previous battles, a smoldering fire began to stir within his heart. Normally, combat filled Jared with fright, but this time, something was different; the panic was gone, the uncertainty had diminished. Jared had to depend on himself, and this forced maturity was refreshing to his soul.

With a resolute look, the blade cleared the scabbard and Jared charged the Reaper Kai. Stunned, the initiate retreated back a step before dropping into a meditation. A calm came over the initiate. Channeling evil energy, the startled Reaper Kai extended his hand forward, fingers outstretched, and a bright orange lance of fire shot forth from it. The blast of fire roared ahead, right at Jared. Bracing for the impact of flame, Jared gritted his teeth.

Expecting a fiery death, the tribal halted his charge and prepared to be turned to a fiery cinder. That is when it happened, the event that would forever change the fate of the tribal youth. As the fire raced forth, the totem around Jared's neck sprung to life. A white swirl of energy spun out from the totem, creating a vortex of supernatural energy around Jared. The fire slammed into the vortex and dissipated immediately. The strange relic had absorbed the psychic attack, leaving Jared unscathed. As the vortex of white energy vanished, Jared exhaled with relief, his breath freezing in the chilled air spreading in front of his mouth like a fog. The eyes of the totem burned brightly, hungering for more spiritual energy, vibrating even more violently while spewing forth a frigid blast of chilling air.

Jared and the Reaper Kai alike were stunned. All in the bar were stunned. Jared had repelled the psychic attack of the Reaper Kai without a hint of damage.

"How can this be?" the Reaper Kai hissed. Never in his life had a mortal man, especially a puny boy, survived a psychic attack, let alone unwounded. Fumbling quickly, the initiate pulled a crude wooden club from his robe and prepared to engage Jared.

The youth from Scarskin looked at the totem around his neck, its eyes glowing bright red. Next, he looked at the Scar Blade. Finally, his eyes fell upon the Reaper Kai. A feeling of confidence surged through him. Charging, the youth uttered a loud, aggressive war cry and set out to slay the initiate.

The Reaper Kai was ill prepared for what he was about to face. Without the use of his psychic powers, he was nothing more than a fool with a club and no skill in using it.

Jared closed the distance quickly, and the Reaper Kai swung the club in a desperate attempt to parry the tribal's vicious attack. The club blocked the assault, but the Scar Blade sheared through the crude weapon and kept going like a bear smashing through a wooden door. The blade roared forward and struck the Reaper Kai in the throat. With a spray of blood, the initiate staggered backwards, trembling violently with a wicked wound on his neck. With a look of fright, he clutched at the bloody wound, knowing death was near at hand. Cowering, the initiate tried to retreat. Jared took the advantage and, recoiling from his swing, brought the blade in for another strike. The weapon struck true and impaled the Reaper Kai, piercing his heart. Suffering from two mortal wounds, the initiate crashed to the floor and died.

The patrons of the saloon were stunned, and with good reason. A drifter, a mere boy from the wastelands, had slain a wicked Reaper Kai, the same Reaper Kai who had been tormenting the town since his arrival, five days prior.

"Who the hell are you?" the barkeep stuttered, staring in awe at the corpse of the Reaper Kai initiate, dead upon the floor.

Jared did not respond; he spun around and checked the bar for more enemies. None could be seen, so the tribal turned to confront the barkeep.

"How did you do that? How... how did you stop his fire?" a bar patron asked in confusion.

"Are there more of them?" Jared inquired in a commanding tone. The barkeep did not respond, still amazed by the sight he had just witnessed. "Snap out of it! Are there more of them in town?"

"No..." the barkeep stuttered. "He came into town five days ago, claiming to be a missionary of the Reaper Kai. On the first night, he killed the local sheriff. Since then, two more townsfolk have disappeared. We were so scared, we didn't dare oppose him. He told us not to tell anyone that he came into town. He said he would kill us if we did."

"I suspect more of them will be on the way soon. Rasheed fell about three months ago, and it looks like the enemy has set its sights on the rest of the wasteland. Enemy agents have already wandered into your town," Jared said, shaking his head in disgust. "It is in your best interest and the interest of all in this town to leave as soon as possible."

"Who the hell are you, kid?" the barkeep asked again.

Jared fell silent, holding the totem in his hand. The chill from the relic had dissipated and its glowing red eyes had fallen silent. The violent vibration had ceased. Looking on with amazement and intrigue, the tribal remembered the pictures scrawled upon the wall of the church in Song River. It was somehow beginning to make sense, all of the uncertainty and mystery. Shaking his head in disbelief, he looked at the barkeep and whispered, "Apparently, my name is Navezgane."

Chapter 18
The Search for Nova 7

Over and over, the event played out in his mind. With a sick fascination, young Jared mentally recreated the battle, time and time again...

The Reaper Kai fell backwards, gasping in pain, clutching his bleeding throat with a look of shock and fear. As if in slow motion, Jared's hand reeled back and a foul thought entered his mind: *kill him, kill him quick!* Submitting to the strange urge, he attacked, letting his training take over. The blade crashed forward, piercing his opponent's chest, killing the Reaper Kai with blinding speed.

And then it was over. The man's life had ended and his dead body rested on the floor in a pool of blood.

Jared was worried about the vision replaying itself over and over again, not because of the violence, but mainly due to the lack of emotion that he felt about it. Just before the battle reached its bloody climax, the tribal had been nervous, as if hungering for something more, something substantial. But alas, Jared felt *nothing,* and that's what put him on edge. The youth had taken a life and he felt *nothing*; no guilt, no sadness, no regret, no anger... *nothing.*

What should I be feeling? he pondered. *Why am I so damn numb?*

Unable to supply an answer to the newest mystery facing him, Jared shrugged off the strange feeling and directed his attention to the journey at hand.

The day of travel had left the youth exhausted. Pushing eastward into the heart of the wasteland from Baker's Grove, Jared had put two days travel between himself and the town which was under the watchful eye of the Reaper Kai. With a dead missionary, it wouldn't take long for other Reaper Kai to hear the tale and inquire about the one who had killed the initiate. Jared already knew he was in a dangerous position, being tracked by mercenaries. Now his deeds would bring about the vengeful wrath of the enemy, a circumstance the youth would rather avoid.

The desert outpost of Black Rock lingered in the distance. It was only an hour before sunset by the time Jared rode toward the gates of the fort. The fort of Black Rock was a haven, a station of refuge against the burning sun along the road between Baker's Grove and Shape Home. Jared had discovered the existence of the outpost earlier in the day, when he encountered a merchant caravan pressing westward toward Baker's Grove. The caravan master was more than happy to share some information about the road ahead with the lonely tribal. Since then, the post had become his objective for the day, a safe haven, if only for a single night.

The fort of Black Rock rested upon a hill overlooking the trade route running through the parched valley. A dry riverbed, long since forgotten by the waters of the world, had turned into a road for merchants passing through the region. Black Rock fort rested above this path, giving refuge to anyone who needed it.

The fort itself was constructed of thick, earthen clay walls, standing two stories high, surrounding the outpost on all sides. Wooden support beams were embedded within the clay walls, giving them an unnatural strength against the harsh sun and any possible aggressive attack from brigands and raiders. A catwalk encircled the top of the wall. Battlements surrounded the fort on all sides, allowing defenders cover against gunfire in times of conflict. On this particular day, as Jared rode toward the outpost resting off the main road, about a mile up a meandering path, the battlements were lifeless; not a single person could be seen atop them.

Jared led his horse through the gates of the outpost into the empty courtyard beyond. The heat of the day was still high, and the inhabitants of the outpost were eluding the heat in the shelter of their homes. Shrugging with indifference, Jared reined his horse toward the middle of the courtyard while surveying his surroundings.

The base of each wall contained a series of shops and living quarters. Near the north wall, in one of the corners of the fort, a small tavern had been built. The tribal eyed the tavern and sighed. Leaping off his horse, Jared tethered the beast to a railing. He conducted a quick check of his gear, making sure that his weapons were accessible, still remembering the encounter which ensued last time he frequented a tavern.

After the harsh heat of the day and the long journey, Jared was on the verge of collapse, wanting nothing more than to spend the remainder of the day in solitude to once again ponder his own psyche.

With a staunch look and his heart once again leaping into his throat, the anxious young warrior pressed into the tavern. Only a few patrons could be found inside.

A short man with fiery orange hair and a sunburned nose sat at one of the tables, exhibiting a frustrated expression. The other man sharing his table was a tall, lanky individual who was balding, and who looked equally irritated. The two talked quietly amongst themselves and eyed Jared with suspicion as he entered. Their eyes scanned him, checking his weapons as he walked, sizing him up. Jared sensed their watchful gazes and shot them an uneasy glance. The two men looked away quickly and continued their conversation in hushed tones.

"What can I get for you, stranger?" a female barkeep asked in a commanding tone as the tribal moved toward the bar. She was large and haggard. Appearing to be in her late forties, she jostled about in her dirty skirt and revealing blouse, cut a little too low for a woman with so much mileage. Her face was a mass of angry wrinkles. It was apparent to the tribal that the woman spent way too much time scowling.

"Give me a shot of something, anything," Jared mouthed with an exhausted look on his face. He was wiped out, and was too timid to ask for a cold glass of water.

The barkeep handed the tribal a dirty glass filled with a strong smelling, brownish liquor. Jared smelled it and hesitated. The youth didn't drink often, especially alone. "One silver piece, stranger," the barkeep said, noting Jared's hesitation.

Jared produced a single coin from his pocket, placing it on the worn bar. The barkeep scooped it up quickly and went about her business, 'cleaning the bar'.

Jared cradled the dirty shot glass in his hand, smelling it carefully. A small sip revealed a taste similar to tar mixed with rubbing alcohol. *"Wonderful..."* Jared said under his breath, watching the barkeep carefully, drastically regretting his choice to have a shot. When she turned around, the tribal emptied his shot glass out on the floor then put the empty glass back on the bar.

The two men saw his displeasure with the alcohol and considered him with amused looks. The tall, lanky man chuckled as he saw the foul liquor dumped on the floor of the bar.

"The first shot is rough, but the next one isn't so bad," the man with orange hair snorted at Jared.

The tribal turned around, feeling his cheeks spring to life, blood filling them and turning his face bright red.

"Yeah, if you don't mind the taste of radiator fluid." The other man snorted as well, holding an empty shot glass. The two were mildly drunk. Jared, somewhat timid, didn't say a word, returning their gaze with flushed cheeks.

"That's a fancy gun you got there, kid, especially for a tribal," the red haired man commented in a quizzing tone.

"I'm holding it for a friend," Jared answered, trying to avoid looking foolish again.

"Yeah, I bet he's the kind of friend you wouldn't want to mess with," the other man said, turning around in his chair to face the youth as he spoke.

"No, definitely not, people have a habit of turning up dead around him," Jared agreed earnestly, thinking of the hot tempered Banion.

Both men chuckled, and Jared began feeling more at ease. Neither of the two men seemed too dangerous.

"You been out in the wastelands a while then, tribal?"

"Yeah... a little while." The young warrior was purposely trying to remain vague.

"Heard any rumors, kid?" the orange haired man blurted out

with an uneasy look in his eye.

Jared chose to maintain his silence. He did not want to divulge any of his dealings in Baker's Grove, and keeping his mouth shut in this situation seemed like the best course of action. Stuttering, it took him a moment to respond. "N...No..."

"Yeah, of course not. You're only armed to the teeth, but you haven't heard a damn thing?" the balding man who was the taller of the two responded with a tone of sarcasm.

"Well, we have heard some damn vicious rumors, kid," the orange haired man added.

"Oh, yeah, like what?" Jared's interest was piqued as he spoke.

"Looks like bounty hunters and hired guns are swarming the area. A hefty bounty has been placed on Banion O'Neil and his entire crew. Looks like the Reaper Kai are calling in all the scum of the wasteland to track them."

"Banion O'Neil, eh?" Jared mused aloud, his heart skipping a beat. "I thought he was just a myth. I didn't even think he was real."

"Myth? You're joking, right? Banion is real enough. We just passed through Shape Home, and word on the street is that a mutant mercenary captured one of Banion's crew. More and more Reaper Kai have been seen in the area. Rumor has it Reaper Kai have even been seen as far out as Baker's Grove." The orange haired man was speaking quickly, looking around as if terrified to even be talking about such things.

"One of Banion's crew was captured?" Jared quizzed, his interest turning to dread.

"Yeah, we heard the mutant is hanging around in Turner's Corner, probably waiting to collect on the bounty. I suggest you steer clear of that place until things start calming down. With Reaper Kai and bounty hunters swarming, no one is safe."

"You're damn right no one is safe. Rumor has it people have started disappearing out here. A few here and there, usually the local prefect or sheriff. Ill deeds are abounding, tribal. You best keep that gun of yours loaded. Ever since the fall of Rasheed, strange things are going on in this region."

Jared proceeded with caution. Acting naïve, the tribal spoke once more. "Turner's Corner… where's that?"

"What? Why the hell do you want to know that?" The orange haired man was stunned; after everything he and his friend had described, the youth still wanted to know the location of the town.

Jared fell silent and pondered a suitable answer. "Sounds like a dangerous place. I want to make sure I stay clear of it."

Both the men nodded and bought the lie.

"About an hour's ride north of Shape Home, on the road to Dune Station. Turner's Corner is a rough place. It's a mercenary hangout. Biker thugs, gun runners, you name it."

"I will make sure to keep away," the tribal said in a resolute tone as hope filled him. The rumor was just a bit of lore, but was well worth investigating all the same. Jared had a new focus: locate Turner's Corner and investigate the rumor fed to him by the unsavory bar patrons. "Thanks for the information." The tribal rose and headed for the door.

The two patrons shot each other quick glances of concern as the youth left. His departure had been a hasty move that made them both feel that the tribal was anxious to act on the information.

Jared bolted out of the bar and made for his horse. The tribal was exhausted beyond belief, but a spark of intrigue had flared in him in reaction to the rumors told in the bar. Launching himself onto his horse, Jared kicked the beast hard; the horse responded by neighing and bucking its head. The tribal was not amused, and gave the beast another healthy kick. The horse bolted forward and charged out of the gate into the open desert. As it charged forth, Jared felt the blood pounding in his veins. The youth was resolute in thought: he must reach Turner's Corner and investigate the rumor regarding Nova 7.

Chapter 19
Hero

Young Jared crept forward, concealing himself along the side of the building. Moving stealthily and cautiously, the tribal tried to catch sight of his objective. He had heard a rumor while passing through the small desert outpost of Black Rock and the town Shape Home. Word in the wasteland was that a mercenary had captured a Reaper Kai traitor, a former diplomat. This fact had piqued Jared's interest, causing him to set out immediately. Two days travel had brought the tribal youth to the crossroads of the southern reaches of the Darken Realm, a mercenary hangout known as Turner's Corner.

Slinking against the wall, Jared rested his hand lightly on the mighty Scar Blade. His other hand rested on Banion's silver revolver. With a quick glance, Jared peeked around the corner of the building. A black muscle car was parked just a few feet away. A sinister looking mercenary, a mutant opossum, was grinning and bouncing about. He was obviously elated by something and wasn't paying very keen attention to his surroundings.

Jared held his breath when he caught sight of a familiar witch, a lost soul who had betrayed her own people to save the lives of the innocent. Mineera was standing behind the car with a blank expression on her face. A metallic disk was stuck to her back, and copper tendrils ran from the disk into the base of her skull. Her hands and feet were shackled. The psychic maiden made no movement; she stood in the burning sun without even blinking. It looked as if she was in a daze.

"What the hell?" Jared whispered as he surveyed his old companion. It was apparent to the tribal that Mineera was somehow restrained, unable to move or act on her own. The stories of Splicers rolled through the tribal's mind. Banion had spoken of such topics, though Jared had never seen such a thing. His eyes fell upon the strange silver disk attached to her spine and skull. With brow furrowed, Jared tried desperately to comprehend what was wrong with Mineera.

Shaking off the confusion, the tribal considered the situation, figuring out a plan of action. The sinister mutant mercenary, Guillotine, was by himself, still hopping around with a twisted grin on his face. Jared knew that if he closed fast on the mutant, he could take him down with little problem. But if the mutant drew a gun, Jared would be on the losing end of the exchange. The tribal warrior was legendary in close combat, but was pitiful with ranged weapons.

Just as the fervid mind of the tribal was working out a plan of action, a chilling blast of air erupted from the raven totem around the youth's neck. The blast of cold instantly began to freeze the air. Even in the burning heat of the day, Jared's icy breath could be seen like a trail of mist leaving his mouth every time he exhaled. The totem began to jiggle violently, its movement eventually turning into a rhythmic gyration as it oscillated furiously. The cold black eyes of the totem sprung to life, burning bright red.

"*Uh oh...*" Jared whispered, clutching the totem in fear.

Another chill blast of air rolled from the totem. Jared exhaled, panic rising in his mind, his breath freezing in the chill air. Vibrating slowly, the totem rocked back and forth. "*Great...*" Jared whispered. The last time the relic awoke from its slumber had marked the entrance of a Reaper Kai initiate. Jared knew something wicked was drawing near, very near.

A low rumble erupted at the edge of Jared's hearing. The noise increased in fury and in strength, turning into a loud jumble of clattering metal, whining engines, and cries of terror.

A convoy of trucks, covered in red dust and battered by the wasteland, lumbered slowly toward the mercenary station at Turner's Corner. Old world cattle trucks lurched into view, bouncing from pothole to pothole, metal screeching and clanging as they moved.

As the trucks came into view, Jared gasped in terror; the cargo they transported was sickening. The trailers of each truck were a horrid sight. People, hundreds and hundreds of people, were packed into the cattle cars like animals. Arms desperately emerged from the openings, brushing the free air, and cries of sadness echoed from within.   Most of the people were dressed in their undergarments alone, while some had no clothes at all. The sight was so sickening to the tribal that he gasped repeatedly and shook his head in despair, trying to drive the horrid image from his soul. Those enslaved within the trucks were a humiliating testament to the cruelty of the wicked.

The convoy of three trucks ground to a halt. The diesel engines sputtered and belched a cloud of thick black grime. Rattling back and forth, the trucks sounded ominous, like ancient rusted furnaces about to explode. The paint had long since fallen away from the trucks, and the bare metal was corroded, giving the lumbering monstrosities the look of a moving scrap yard.

The totem, the ancient bird relic, vibrated violently. Burning brightly, the red eyes hungered softly. Jared grabbed the relic tightly, feeling the freezing cold rolling from it.

Emerging from the cab of the lead truck, a ghastly priest garbed in red jumped down and approached the mutant opossum who was still giggling like a maniac. Bald, with horrible scars on his face, the Reaper Kai priest was an intimidating presence. His cold, piercing eyes projected a commanding, dominant persona. The priest had definitely seen war, and looked as if he could handle himself even in the most dire situations.

"I see you kept only part of your word. Queen Toil ordered the capture of all of Nova 7. I have not spoken to the Queen in months, but I'm certain she will be most displeased. Where is the remainder of our prize?" the priest hissed with a look of disgust.

"I only managed to capture the traitor. But I shall find them all soon," Guillotine hissed back with a wicked grin on his face. His furry white and gray snout sniffed the air, catching the scent of the priest before him.

Jared maintained his position.   He knew that attacking Guillotine and a Reaper Kai priest would be certain death, not to mention the added hazard of any other enemies concealed within the filthy slave trucks. The tribal's time to strike would have to wait.

"Here is your money, mercenary." Handing over a packet of

bills, the Reaper Kai priest glared at the mutant. "One more thing, Guillotine."

"Yes..." Guillotine replied softly, licking his yellow teeth with his gnarled tongue.

"No one, and I mean no one, is to know of our dealings, even other Reaper Kai. There are many in our coven who would be greatly displeased if they knew of our transaction. It is in your best interest to keep this quiet."

"*Our* secret is safe indeed."

"It had better be, for your sake," the Reaper Kai hissed while pushing the shackled Mineera toward the cab of the truck. "Get in, you traitorous bitch!" the Reaper Kai ordered, and Mineera responded to the command, climbing into the cab of the truck. "I need to get these fresh slaves back to Rasheed quickly before they spoil. Update me of your progress after you capture the other three members of Nova 7."

"I will..." the mutant answered, lost in his own thoughts as he thumbed through the wad of money he had just received.

With a whine, the starter growled to life. Finally, the engine rolled over and an eruption of foul fumes burst forth from the exhaust stacks on the truck. The truck rattled as it lurched forward at a snail's pace, heading northeast along the ancient road. Moving slowly, the convoy faded into the distance with its cargo of slaves wailing in anguish.

As the convoy drove off, Jared knew that Mineera was receding further and further away. If the tribal lost the convoy, the chances of recovering the psychic maiden would be slim. Eyeing Guillotine's car, the tribal had concocted a plan: take out the mercenary, steal his car, then chase down the convoy. After that, he didn't really know what he would do. The plan to stop the monstrous trucks and kill the Reaper Kai holding Mineera captive would have to be put on hold.

Guillotine was envisioning more and more money when the attack came. Jared emerged from behind the building, charging with the Scar Blade glimmering in the mid-day sun. Bounding forward like a tiger, silent and deadly, Jared prepared to kill the mercenary.

Something felt wrong. The sound of displaced air and a flurry of motion at the edge of his vision were enough to startle the opossum mercenary. Guillotine whirled around just in time to see the tribal charging with his blue blade shining in the sun. Swinging with a precise slash aimed at killing with a single blow, Jared attacked the mutant mercenary. With an agile move, Guillotine managed to sidestep the wicked attack from the youth.

The mutant opossum stumbled backwards and went for a knife at his waist; all of his guns were in his black muscle car. Brandishing the blade and hissing like a cat, he bolted forward, swinging his knife like a madman. "I was wondering where you'd snuck off to, little boy! I didn't see you in Dune Station!"

Jared held his ground. The mutant was nothing new to Jared, and Guillotine severely underestimated the tribal's skills in close combat. Concentrating on the battle, the tribal let his training overcome his senses. With calm moves, Jared batted away the slashes made by Guillotine. The flurry of hasty attacks was averted with ease. Overextending himself, the mutant left himself open. Counterattacking with a slash, Jared brought the blade across the mutant's forearm, tearing a gash in the muscle.

Guillotine gasped but was undaunted. Leaping forward while kicking his clawed foot, Guillotine made contact with the tribal. Jared was caught in the chest and collapsed backwards. Gaining a few seconds of time, the mutant mercenary ran to his car and fumbled for a weapon. Jared leapt to his feet and charged again.

With a mighty yell, Jared brought the Scar Blade around, swinging with all his might, an attack that would easily cleave a man in two. The sword charged forward and Guillotine jumped back, the blade barely missing his belly. The blade rammed forward and crashed into the side of the car. The Scar Blade bit metal and sheared into the frame of the car.

With a tug, Jared felt the ancient weapon holding fast, stuck in the frame of the car. Knowing Guillotine had probably recovered a weapon, Jared abandoned the Scar Blade and sought to engage the mutant with his bare hands.

The mutant had recovered his pulse rifle, but Jared was too

quick. With a hefty grunt, he brought his elbow into the opossum's jaw. The blow was terrible, and Jared broke several of the mutant's teeth. Dizzy from the attack, Guillotine stumbled backwards. The tribal continued the assault and wrested the rifle from the mutant's hands by spinning the weapon around until Guillotine lost his hold.

The mutant, still dazed and with blood dripping from his mouth, fumbled to defend himself from the agile tribal. Jared never wavered; he took the advantage and used it to end the conflict.

Still holding the mutant's gun and taking shaky aim, Jared started firing the weapon at the stunned mercenary. The first shot whizzed past Guillotine's head, the bright sphere of electrical energy ionizing the air with a sizzle. The second blast hit true as the tribal brought the weapon under control. With an explosion of sparks, the sphere of energy hit the mutant's steel breast plate. The bright flash of electricity shocked the mutant as the energy surged through his body. Crashing to the ground, Guillotine began to shudder and convulse. The attack had fried the mutant's nerve endings, shutting down his body within a split second. Smoking upon the ground with the smell of burnt fur in the air, Guillotine did not stir or shudder; the sinister mercenary had been gunned down by the wild fury of the tribal.

Jared, seeing his enemy down, moved to recover the Scar Blade. When he tugged at it, the blade held fast, stuck in the steel frame of the car. Although he yanked with all his might, the weapon was embedded deeply within the metal and would not come free. With panic filling him, Jared cursed in anger. "Damn it!" Time was running out. The convoy was already moving out of view. His mind spinning frantically, the tribal jumped into the car. Fumbling wildly with the pedals and gear shift, he fought to animate the black muscle car, to no avail; Jared could not figure out how to operate the vehicle. Cursing again, he jumped out of the car and tried to recover his sword once more. It still held fast in the frame, and the youth grabbed his head with both hands, trying to figure out what to do. The convoy was moving further and further away each moment, Mineera's freedom slipping away with each passing second.

With a look of despair, Jared paused, staring at his ancient sword stuck in the frame of the car, a sword that had been kept safe since the beginning of his tribe, hundreds and hundreds of years ago. The Scar Blade was no ordinary sword; it was an heirloom of legend, a mighty symbol of Jared's tribe. Looking at the convoy escaping down the road, Jared made a difficult decision. Shaking his head, he abandoned the mighty Scar Blade and grabbed Guillotine's pulse rifle, favoring a chance to save Mineera over the possibility of recovering the fabled weapon of the Scarskin tribe.

The youth ran behind the tavern, mounted his horse and charged after the convoy lurching slowly down the ancient road. With heart pounding, Jared had decided to do the impossible: hurl himself into the fray, risking his life to save a long-lost companion.

Chapter 20
Roads Converge

"Move it, bookworm!" Banion said in a harsh tone while thundering down the side of the hill. A trail of dust clouded around the gun fighter's boots as he ran. The winded Tani followed close behind, with both hands clutching the straps of his backpack. Beads of sweat were rolling down his face and he puffed heavily, trying desperately to keep up with the deranged rancher.

Banion and Tani were rapidly nearing the mercenary hangout known as Turner's Corner. A trader from Dune Station claimed he had ran across the vile mercenary Guillotine and the newly enslaved Mineera at Turner's Corner. The tidbit of information was too tempting to ignore, so the scholar of Scarskin and the deranged gunfighter had set out to see if the rumor was true.

Both Tani and Banion caught sight of Guillotine's black muscle car parked near the entrance to the bar at Turner's Corner. They knew the mutant mercenary was near and that this might be their best opportunity to rescue their captured companion. If they hurried, there might still be time to save Mineera.

"Watch your flanks when we move in. Keep your eyes open and do not falter. Commit to your actions and never look back. If you can do that, we will both survive this," Banion said in a confident tone. Tani nodded while breathing hard.

Banion had slowed his pace, holding his weapon against his shoulder; the submachine gun fit perfectly against his body, and its crosshairs moved across his field of vision with sweeping motions. Stalking forward like a cat, Banion moved in quickly on Guillotine's black muscle car. Tani, with a look of worry, fidgeted with the pin on a hand grenade.

Banion motioned to Tani, and the deranged rancher advanced on the car. Rounding the front, he aimed the submachine crosshairs directly at the interior. Slowly he crept forward, with trigger finger twitching in anticipation. Finally, Banion closed in and was confronted with an odd and unexpected sight. Guillotine was lying on his back and did not stir. The mutant opossum had been taken down. A black blast mark was on the mutant's thick steel breast plate, and Guillotine was unconscious from the wounds he had suffered. Confused, Banion whirled around and surveyed the outskirts of Turner's Corner. He looked around and finally caught sight of a convoy of trucks disappearing into a cloud of dust about a mile down the road. *Someone* on horseback was giving chase and was slowly gaining on the trucks.

A motley trio of thieves, trash of the wasteland, exited the mercenary bar and looked at the stunned Banion, holding his submachine gun at the ready, and at the shaky Tani holding a live hand grenade. The leader of the thieves was taken aback by the scene. All three thugs were set on edge by the sight of the heavily armed duo.

Banion was in panic mode. He shouted at the thugs, "What happened here?"

"You missed quite a show. Some punk kid just wiped Guillotine's ass," the brigand leader said with a sinister tone.

Banion was none too happy with the situation, and reacted by returning his focus to trying to locate Mineera. He moved forward with his submachine gun at the ready. "Did you see a woman with Guillotine?"

"Huh?" one of the weasely brigands grunted.

Banion raised the weapon and trained it on the trio, crosshairs pausing on each one of them. "I said, did you see a woman?"

"Whoa, pal! Take it easy! Yeah, we saw a woman. That slave convoy came through and picked her up. Nasty company at that. Reaper Kai priests were all riding as passengers in the trucks."

"That convoy?" Banion threw his thumb up and pointed behind him.

"Yeah, yeah, man, just take it easy," the brigand said, holding his hands up in submission, not wanting to get shot by the hot tempered Banion. "The convoy just left a few minutes ago."

"You got a set of wheels?" the deranged rancher asked, a look of dispassion on his face.

"Uh, yeah…" the brigand answered, shaking his head in disgust. He knew exactly what was about to happen. "It's right there, the bike." With another look of disgust, the brigand pulled a set of keys from his pocket and tossed them to Banion without another word. He knew better than to mess with a deranged gunman holding a fully automatic weapon. All three thugs saw the look on the gun fighter's face and knew that he meant business.

"I'll be back, bookworm," Banion said as he rushed over to the motorbike. Hopping on, the deranged mercenary inserted the keys in the bike's ignition, cranked and revved the engine. The tires screeched and the bike reared up. Throwing his weight forward, Banion brought the front wheel of the bike back on the ground and the tires dug into the pavement. Burning rubber, the bike tore forward with rapid speed. Punching the gas, Banion hit the road, preparing to engage the convoy.

As Banion disappeared down the ancient highway, Tani gave a sigh and looked around with a look of disgust of his own. It was almost comical that Tani was alone, staring through the trail of dirt and dust left by Banion as he rushed off down the road, jumping once more into the fray.

"Your friend is a real asshole!" the brigand said, eyeing the hand grenade in the tribal's hand.

"Yeah, Banion's not real friendly," Tani agreed, conceding to the derelict brigand. "You're lucky he didn't kill you."

"Banion?" The brigand spoke with a look of fear.

"Yeah, Banion," Tani nodded.

The trio of brigands turned tail, hopped on their remaining two motor bikes and sped away in the opposite direction to the one in which Banion had disappeared. Tani smiled, almost feeling proud.

Standing in a cloud of dust once more, the scholar of Scarskin looked around with a look of bafflement. It took the tribal a moment to formulate a plan of action while the dust settled. Finally, a bright sparkle illuminated his eye. A smile of mischief and a jolt of adrenaline hit his system. The spark of insanity was growing. His mind filled with a crazy thought, Tani pushed his wire-rim glasses up his nose and stared at Guillotine's black muscle car. A smile graced his lips and he moved over to the fallen Guillotine. The tribal began to rummage through the mercenary's belongings until he found what he was looking for: the keys to the car.

"You won't be needing these," Tani concluded, grabbing the keys, speaking to the fallen mercenary who was still unconscious upon the burning asphalt.

Nearly shivering with anticipation, the youth ran over to the black muscle car with the intent of hijacking the vehicle and chasing after Banion and the convoy.

The tribal stopped dead in his tracks as he approached the car, keys almost falling from his stumpy fingers. An odd feeling coursed through him. Jammed into the frame of the car was an ancient steel blade, glimmering blue in the sunlight. The tribal recognized it immediately and a jolt of adrenaline hit his system. Shaking with excitement, the scholar took several steps forward, his gaze transfixed on the weapon. With his heart pounding and mind racing, the tribal *knew* the glimmering weapon stuck in the frame of the car was no ordinary weapon. Tani knew it was the Scar Blade, the ancient heirloom given by his tribe to his friend, Jared.

"What the hell!" Tani yelled, looking at the blade in astonishment. Suddenly, the vision of the stranger on horseback chasing the convoy was beginning to make sense. "Jared... it can't be... Jared...it must be!" The tribal blinked several times, thinking the Scar Blade was a mirage. But it was a reality; the weapon was evidence that his friend was alive. Almost breaking down in tears, Tani fought to control himself. Wrestling with the emotion, he set off to recover the weapon from the frame of the car.

With a mighty grip, the tribal genius tugged on the weapon and found that it held fast. Analyzing the situation, Tani used intellect to achieve his goal. Utilizing his knowledge of pivots and fulcrums, Tani applied leverage on the blade while wiggling it back and forth. The screeching and grinding of metal could be heard as the ancient weapon began to come loose from the frame of the car. With a grunt, Tani pulled the weapon free and held it in his hand triumphantly. Smiling, he tossed the weapon into the black muscle car and jumped into the driver's seat.

Thrilled by the discovery of the Scar Blade, credible evidence that Jared had survived the ship wreck, the scholar smiled and looked at the controls of the muscle car, recognition flooding his eyes. Tani had never driven a car, but he had read a great many books on how to control various ancient vehicles. Drawing upon his phenomenal photographic memory, he set out to commandeer the vehicle.

"Let's see, the right pedal is used to accelerate the vehicle... the left pedal slows the vehicle..." Tani mumbled while fidgeting with the windshield wiper controls. "No, that's not right..." With a snap of his fingers, Tani fumbled with the right side of the steering wheel column. His stumpy fingers brushed across the ignition and he pressed the keys into the opening. With a flick of his wrist, the engine rolled over and hummed. Without thinking, Tani placed the car in Drive. The scholar was satisfied, turned around to see what was happening *behind* the car, and pushed down the accelerator. The car jumped *forward*, smashing into the brick wall of the bar, while the impact hurtled the scholar forward in his seat.

"Damn it!" Tani mouthed as the bartender and several others came out to see what the hell was happening. Seeing the patrons emerge, Tani found Reverse, shifted the car, then punched the gas again. Its wheels grinding and kicking up a cloud of dust, the black muscle car whipped around backwards.

Fumbling wildly for the gear shift, the tribal put the car in Drive and punched the gas again. The black muscle car roared forward, and Tani swung the wheel, trying to turn it. The back end of the car fishtailed, whipping around with dirt flying everywhere. The young genius fought to control the car, and finally succeeded just in time to see the cursing barkeep charging toward the side of the car. His hand outstretched and his face red with anger, the barkeep intended to put a hasty end to the young scholar's joyride.

His heart pounding and his eyes wide with excitement, Tani

managed to bring the car around. With calm movements, the genius regained control of himself and the vehicle. Smiling broadly, Tani let the exhilaration of his first car ride fill him. He had once again done the impossible: hijacked a vehicle and escaped with it just in time to avoid the enraged barkeep. Learning the flow of the controls, Tani smiled as sweat rolled down his brow. He quickly picked up the basics and controlled the car with relative ease. Sighing with relief, the young scholar looked in the rearview mirror with a smile. The barkeep held his middle finger high while cursing.

Thundering down the road, Tani learned how to steer the car with a broad grin on his face. "Go any direction but east... ha! Look at me now, Mogi, look at me now!"

His heart was still pounding, and Tani glanced over at the Scar Blade in the passenger seat. Though the tribal was not spiritual by nature, the glimmering blue weapon was an omen, an omen of victory. Jared *must* have survived the ship wreck.

Feeling the thunder of the powerful engine, Tani grinned and placed his stumpy fingers on the Scar Blade.

"Hold on, you guys... I'm on my way!" Hitting the accelerator, Tani blazed after Banion, the mysterious person on horseback, and the truck convoy carrying the captured Mineera.

Chapter 21
Thunderblood Road

As the engine hummed, Banion O'Neil fought a desperate battle. The ancient highway was marked and marred by enormous fractures and potholes. Pushing nearly fifty miles an hour on the motor bike, the crazed mercenary was throwing all caution to the wind. With focus, Banion dodged potholes and launched the bike over shelves of cracked concrete. In reality it would have almost been easier to grind across the naked desert than to travel down the highway of the ancients.

Banion had a single focused thought: take out the convoy and save Mineera from the dread Reaper Kai priests holding her hostage.

As he bumped along the highway, the convoy came into view on the battered road ahead. A strange person was chasing the convoy on horseback, but that individual was fighting a losing battle. The horse was running out of steam and the convoy was beginning to pull ahead.

Back and forth, he rocked on the bike, swerving wildly along the road which the locals called Thunderblood Road. The mysterious rider was coming into view.

Like a pinprick in his mind, Banion's consciousness screamed, and a strange sense of the familiar filled him. Straining his eyes, the deranged rancher blinked several times, his brain trying to rationalize what he was seeing. Shaking in disbelief, Banion viewed the rider on horseback.

"Can't be..." he muttered while jumping the bike over a rough patch of road.

Watching the strange rider, whose hair was bouncing up and down in a ponytail tied back and who was dressed in primitive clothing, Banion was almost convinced he was seeing one of the tribals, a tribal thought to have been lost to sea in a violent storm. Flipping his wrist, he pulled down the throttle on the motorcycle and charged up behind the horse. The rider heard the bike and spun around in the saddle, training a hi-tech rifle on the deranged gun fighter. Jared, tribal from Scarskin, was stunned as his eyes met the cold, heartless eyes of Banion O'Neil.

A wild, manic look covered Banion's face. He blinked several more times before the reality set in. Jared had survived the storm and was charging to save Mineera from the slave convoy. A jolt of adrenaline hit the gunfighter's blood, screaming with a mixture of joy and a wild battle cry. "Jared! You sorry son of a bitch! Damn, am I glad to see you!"

Jared smiled back and a huge weight was lifted off his shoulders. Finding Mineera was a shot in the dark, but seeing Banion was a powerful catalyst, polarizing the youth to a heightened state. Adrenaline hit Jared's blood, burning like fire. The thought of rescuing Mineera was no longer just a possibility; the youth felt that nothing could stop them from achieving their goal.

Banion nodded at Jared and yelled, "Let's take 'em out, kid!" The tribal warrior nodded in response, grinning broadly.

The black muscle car driven by the whimsical scholar roared into view, with Tani's head poking out the window. Tani waved excitedly, catching a glimpse of the long lost warrior from Scarskin. Jared smiled back as he saw his best friend, his brother from Scarskin. The trio had been reunited, and nothing but death itself could stop them from thundering down the road toward the convoy. The trio felt a powerful sense of rage settle over them. Feeling the call of battle, they prepared to assault the convoy.

Jared's horse was on the verge of exhaustion, so he reined it toward the black muscle car which Tani was driving. As Jared eyed the car with quick glances, Tani got the idea and slowed the mighty vehicle so that it kept pace with Jared's charging horse. With a leap, Jared launched off the horse onto the hood of the car. Landing squarely on the front of the car, the tribal warrior clung precariously as the vehicle roared down the battered road. Guillotine's strange electrical gun fell from Jared's belt, hitting the road in a shower of parts and debris. Jared grumbled as he saw the high tech weapon shatter. Ignoring the loss, the tribal set out to climb into the black muscle car through the open passenger window, a task which he quickly and deftly accomplished.

Tani grabbed Jared's shirt in his fist and tugged on it, roughing him up a bit. "It's so good to see you – I thought you'd drowned!"

"I thought you'd *all* drowned," Jared responded and then shifted his focus to the convoy. "Mineera is in that convoy, lead truck."

"Yeah, that's what Banion and I were hoping." Tani jammed on the gas, charging toward the last truck in the convoy. "I brought you something," the scholar said, pulling the Scar Blade from the back seat of the car. "Don't lose it again," he chuckled.

Jared slapped his friend on the shoulder and his heart lifted. The thought of never seeing his friends again was already becoming a distant, bleak memory.

Allowing Tani to catch up alongside him, the deranged gun fighter shouted, "Good idea, bookworm!" motioning to Guillotine's muscle car. "Let's focus on the last truck in the convoy! Support me as best you can! Jared, where is Mineera?" The deranged rancher had to return his focus to the road, almost losing control and bouncing through a deep pothole.

"Lead truck," Jared shouted back with a grim look on his face.

Gritting his teeth, Banion punched the gas and screamed toward the back end of the last truck in the convoy. The imprisoned humans, crammed together, reached out from the back of the truck, waving in terror, pleading for help. Acknowledging their panic, Banion drove closer to the back of truck. With a bold move, he grabbed onto the back end of the vehicle, letting the motorbike fall away and crash into the battered highway. Pulling with all his might, the crazed rancher moved himself up the side of the cattle car, using the openings as hand- and footholds. Finally, he reached the top of the truck, while the caged humans kept wailing for help. Banion moved on, forcing their pleas from his mind; he wouldn't allow their distress to cloud his judgment or concentration.

It didn't take long for Banion to cross the top of the cattle car. Jumping down, the gun fighter landed behind the cab. The passengers inside the cab were stunned and unable to react in time. Banion was merciless, opening fire at point blank range with his submachine gun, spraying both the driver and passenger with a hail of lead. The attack was so fierce that both were dead within seconds. The truck was out of control, but it didn't matter. Banion opened the vehicle's door, swung around and pulled the dead driver out of the cab. The body hit the highway with a crunch, and the satisfied gun fighter was left to enjoy his commandeered truck.

The other two trucks in the convoy knew something was up. The Reaper Kai priest in the lead truck had psychic powers keen enough to tell that the last truck had been hijacked. He motioned to the other truck and the fight was on.

With a sneer, Banion hit the gas. The truck lurched forward and he steered it toward the next truck in the convoy, intent on thoroughly smashing and battering it.

Tani and Jared rolled onward, trying to get in position to aid Banion. Their black muscle car thundered down the road, bouncing from pothole to pothole.

Banion managed to reach the next truck in the convoy. Using his own hijacked truck like a steel behemoth, a deadly battering ram, he smashed into the second truck. The imprisoned slaves screamed as the sound of crushing metal resounded throughout the wasteland. The second truck took some damage; the back axel had bent under Banion's attack, and the vehicle slowed considerably.

The tribals roared up on the right side of the crippled truck.

"Take the wheel!" Tani said in a frantic tone.

"What?" Jared was horrified; he had no idea how to steer the vehicle. As he fumbled with the wheel, the black muscle car spun out of control. Jared was trying with all his might to control the car. Swerving back and forth, the muscle car squealed as its tires clung to the torn concrete road. It took a few moments for Jared, with the aid of Tani, to get the vehicle under control.

"You got it now?" the scholar asked, looking at Jared. His friend nodded that he was fine.

Tani grabbed his backpack and rummaged through it. The tribal scholar located a pair of hand grenades and smiled. "Keep it steady…"

Banion was on the left side of the truck, ramming into it without mercy, battering it beyond recognition. With each hit, the enemy truck slowed a bit. The driver behind the wheel was panicked, and frozen with fear. The passenger priest was yelling orders at the initiate, but it was in vain; the young Reaper Kai was too scared to function.

With an accurate toss, the tribal hurled a pair of live grenades into the cab of the truck through the open window on the passenger side. The Reaper Kai were caught unprepared – neither saw the grenades land inside the cab. A few seconds passed and the deadly explosives detonated, shredding both the Reaper Kai to a bloody pulp. Banion nodded his head in appreciation after seeing the second truck taken out by the wily scholar, brought to a halt by Tani's demolition skills. The truck was out of control but was losing speed quickly.

A lance of fire rushed forward and exploded. The front end of Banion's truck was struck with a fiery projectile. The head priest, now standing atop the last remaining enemy truck in the convoy, had channeled his potent psychic powers and directed a powerful blast of hellfire at Banion's truck. The smoke stung Banion's eyes as he flinched back from the fire rolling across the windshield. Just after the first blast cleared, another lance of fire rolled from the Reaper Kai's outstretched hands. Ducking down, Banion concealed himself – and none to soon. The blast of fire hit the front of his truck, shattering the windshield and spraying Banion with melted shards of liquefied glass and metal.

"Damn it!" Banion cursed, trying to regain his composure.

The priest would not yield. Another burst of fire rocked the truck, hitting the grill, racing around the sides. The blast was so strong that the heat melted the right tire of the truck. Popping under pressure, the tire blew and the truck lurched violently to the right. The assault was brutal, leaving Banion's truck a smoking ruin. The tire shredded off completely and the rim hit the ancient highway with a shower of sparks. Unable to continue with a blown front tire, Banion cursed and watched the lead truck escape the battle.

Tani and Jared watched Banion's truck come to a halt, and they knew he was done. Looking at each other with hesitation, the tribals knew that it was up to them. If the last truck in the convoy escaped, Mineera was doomed.

"I've got an idea," Jared said in a confident tone, holding the strange bird totem, which was still emitting chilled air.

"Really?" Tani quizzed. "What?"

"Get me to the back of that truck. I will do the rest."

"What are you talking about? You saw that priest. What are you gonna do about him?"

"I am going to kill him." There was a wicked look in Jared's eye. The tone of his voice was ominous, and it set Tani on edge. Something had changed in his friend, and the scholar found this change unsettling. Tani looked uneasily at Jared. There was a flash of madness on the young warrior's face.

Tani did not respond; he felt reluctant to be part of Jared's mysterious plan. "That is a Reaper Kai priest, Jared. You saw what he did to Banion's truck. He is going to do the same to you."

"Trust me, Tani, get me to the back of that truck and I will do the rest," Jared repeated, while the ancient relic around his neck vibrated violently. There was a darkness in Jared's eyes as he spoke. A chill rolled down Tani's spine. The look in Jared's eyes was all too familiar; it was as if Tani was looking at Banion, not at his childhood friend.

"All right..." The scholar was worried but went along with his friend.

Pushing down the accelerator, Tani steered the car down the ruined highway, getting ever closer to the last enemy truck in the convoy, the truck that held the imprisoned Mineera.

The priest tracked the approach of the black muscle car with derision. Channeling more fiery energy, the Reaper Kai flexed his hands forward and a lance of fire shot forth. Tani was prepared for the attack, after witnessing the demise of Banion's truck. Swerving to the right, the muscle car screeched and the lance of fire flew past, striking the road behind with a deafening boom.

Tani was undaunted; he punched the gas and the car roared forward. Jared grabbed the Scar Blade and sheathed it on his back. With a resolute look, the tribal warrior climbed onto the hood of the car. The priest smiled and forced a spike of fire from his hands. Tani responded quickly, veering the car to the left, and watching Jared cling precariously to the hood. Clenching his teeth, Tani was elated that Jared hadn't fallen off the hood of the charging car.

Closing the distance quickly, the young scholar brought the muscle car alongside the final truck in the convoy. With a deft move, the young warrior clutched one of the slats on the side of the cattle car and let his feet fall away. Clinging to the side of the truck, Jared pulled himself up the side while the slaves held within the cattle car cried out in terror. "Save us!" they wailed in anguish, holding out their hands, touching him as he climbed the side of the truck. His muscles tense, Jared pulled himself onto the top of the truck.

Jared stood upright on top of the moving truck. His gaze fell upon that of the Reaper Kai, who was stunned by the young man's daring. Without wavering, the youth pulled the Scar Blade free of its scabbard. A chill wind poured from the bird amulet around his neck, as its hungry red eyes flashed. The Reaper Kai priest was smiling in response to Jared's bravado.

"Astounding, I admit, but rather rash and foolish!" the priest scorned the youth. With a flick of his hand, a lance of fire sped forth toward Jared. With a sense of calm, Jared held his ground and let the burst of fire strike his body.

Banion and Tani both clenched their teeth as they saw the fire strike their friend. There was no way that the tribal could survive such an attack, which could burn steel and melt glass.

The totem hungered for evil energy. Its eyes burned brightly. As the hellfire struck Jared's body, the ancient relic responded by absorbing the energy. With a swirl of rising chilled air, a vortex enveloped the tribal, shielding him from the sinister psychic attack. Jared, tribal of Scarskin, had survived the assault unscathed.

"What the hell?" Banion mumbled, unable to comprehend

what he had just seen. The tribal scholar almost ran into the side of the truck, equally stunned by what he had just witnessed.

As the smoke cleared and the frigid wind subsided, Jared opened his eyes and trained them upon the Reaper Kai priest. A wicked look was in the tribal's eyes. With blade in hand, the young warrior advanced without fear.

"What are you?" the Reaper Kai hissed in panic.

The tribal did not respond; instead he closed on his enemy quickly as the wind rushed by him.

The priest pulled a curved dagger from his belt as the wind whipped through his crimson robes. He considered the youth with respect and prepared to battle him hand to hand.

The totem vibrated fiercely as Jared moved in for the kill. The priest made the first move. With a precise strike, the Reaper Kai slashed at Jared's throat. With expert skill, the tribal warrior moved back, avoiding the attack. The priest was filled with a bloodlust, erupting into a battle rage, and did not stop the assault. With another hurried set of attacks, the Reaper Kai whirled about like a crazed wolverine, slashing at Jared without relent. Parrying and dodging, Jared evaded every one of the attacks.

Overstepping his bounds with the wild flurry of the battle, the priest left himself open to a counterattack. Jared took the advantage and screamed forward with a dizzying series of slashes. The Scar Blade slammed into the priest's stomach, piercing it violently. With a sickly spray of blood streaming off his body in the fierce wind of the moving vehicle, the priest retreated while Jared struck again and again. More wounds opened, and the Reaper Kai's life began fading rapidly. Choking on his own blood, the priest made a feeble attempt to communicate.

"I know not... I know not who you are..." the Reaper Kai gasped. "You will not... you will not survive our race...or the coming war..."

Jared had enough of the threats. As the totem around his neck burned brightly, the tribal warrior leveled his mighty, gore-drenched blue blade with a grim look on his face. Inhaling and drawing the blade back, Jared prepared to end the priest's life. With a swift, powerful stroke, he exhaled and swung full force, nearly cleaving the Reaper Kai priest in two. The mortally wounded priest gasped and fell off the side of the truck, hitting the concrete road, body rolling across the highway like a rag doll.

Tani and Banion both saw the blow. Something inside of each of their minds screamed. Jared was no longer a boy from the wasteland; he was something more menacing, something much more sinister.

Collecting his thoughts, Jared pulled out Banion's silver revolver. Leaping down into the back of the cab, Jared pointed the weapon at the driver's head. "Stop the truck," Jared commanded. The Reaper Kai initiate nodded in compliance, looking in the rear view mirror; he knew better than to argue with anyone who had bested a priest, a seasoned veteran of the Reaper Kai.

The truck ground to a halt in the desert. A cloud of dust settled over the battlefield. The Reaper Kai initiate left the truck with his hands up the air, responding to Jared's aggression with an act of submission. Jared moved forward with the gore stained Scar Blade in one hand and Banion's mighty silver revolver in the other.

"Tell Lord Vertigo about this day. Tell him Nova 7 send their regards." Jared was angry as he spoke, and the initiate nodded in acknowledgement. "Get out of here." With that, the Reaper Kai ran for his life, into the heart of the wasteland, never looking back.

The relic around the tribal's neck ceased to vibrate. Jared shook his head slowly as the haunting rage was leaving him. Regaining control of himself, Jared climbed into the cab of the truck. Mineera was staring ahead with a blank look, the Splicer still robbing her of conscious thought. Nodding and letting out a sigh of relief, Jared smiled. He had succeeded in his goal, rescuing Mineera from the dread Reaper Kai, an amazing act of courage and heroism. At that moment, the tribal warrior from Scarskin was no longer a scared boy; he was, instead, a force to be reckoned with, a legendary presence that would forever shape the battered world.

Chapter 22
Reunion

"I don't think so, Banion. This is *my* car," Tani protested as he looked at Banion holding his hand outstretched, waiting for the keys to Guillotine's black muscle car.

"Your car? Come on, Tani, give me the damn keys." The deranged gunfighter spoke in a nasty tone.

"I stole it, I am driving it," the scholar said triumphantly, cherishing the keys in his stumpy hand.

"You just remember that when Guillotine comes looking for it."

It was nearing sunset. Nova 7, the reunited mercenary team, had pulled off the road to take a brief break before heading on into Shape Home. It had been only a few hours since the legendary mercenary team had wiped out a Reaper Kai slave convoy, liberated hundreds of slaves, and rescued the psychic traitor, Mineera. Already, the hundreds of freed slaves were retelling the story of heroism and daring deeds committed by Nova 7 in the mercenary hangout of Turner's Corner. Nova 7, wanting to put as much distance between them and their deeds, hit the road in Guillotine's car, attempting to elude the horde of freed slaves that viewed them all as heroes.

As Banion and Tani argued about the muscle car, Jared was distant, lost in silence, not wanting to put words to the acts he had just committed. Breathing softly, his right hand rested on the hilt of the Scar Blade, while his left hand brushed against the sinister raven totem hanging around his neck. With soft strokes, Jared fondled the perverse totem, staring ahead with a blank expression.

"Let's get moving," Banion ordered, shaking his head in defeat at the tribal scholar; the crazed mercenary would let him drive the car, for now.

Jared stayed put, still lost in a daze.

"Jared?" Tani said in a concerned tone.

The tribal warrior did not respond.

"Hey, Jared!" Banion shouted while walking up on the tribal.

Finally, he spun around with a bewildered look on his face. "Sorry…" Walking slowly toward the car, Jared elected to divert his gaze, avoiding the looks from his companions.

Banion shot Tani an uneasy glance. The young warrior had been gone for quite a while and had only returned a few hours ago. A lot could happen out in the wastelands, far from reason, far from law and order. Jared was hiding something – Banion could tell. Sizing him up, Banion watched him carefully. The tribal's usually clumsy moves had been replaced by confident motions. He had grown considerably during his absence from the rest of Nova 7. There was something unsettling about the youth. Banion still had flashes of the recent violence rushing through his mind. He could still see the heartless look on Jared's face as he butchered the Reaper Kai on the back of the semi truck. The actions of the tribal warrior were bold, rash, and somewhat uncontrolled. The youth was in a dark place, hiding from *something*.

The trio climbed into the black muscle car. Mineera was sitting quietly in the back seat, not even blinking. The Splicer was still stuck to the back of her neck and spine, robbing her of conscious freedom. The trio piled in and the tribal scholar hastily put the keys in the ignition. With a flick of his wrist, the engine thundered to life, and Tani put his lead foot down on the accelerator. The wheels dug into the dirt, eliciting a screech from the tires. The car lurched forward with a jerk, launching back onto the battered roadway.

"Next time, I'm driving," Banion said with a look of disgust.

Tani smiled, with his cheeks flushed bright red.

Nova 7 bounced down the road, toward the coastal town of Shape Home. The conversation ended, as no one seemed too eager to talk about the events of the day. With flashes of memory, the chase down the road came back in waves of sound and images. Banion sat quietly as if still trying to size up the situation, still suspicious of Jared's actions and his uncanny ability to survive an attack from a veteran Reaper Kai priest. It just didn't make any sense. Banion had seen a lot of things in his travels, but never had he seen anyone withstand an attack from a Reaper Kai priest. It was more than luck; it had to be.

The deranged rancher was riding in the front passenger seat of the car. He turned around and stared at Jared for a moment as if soaking in information. The tribal avoided his gaze, remaining silent and electing to look out the window instead.

"What happened out there?" he asked the tribal warrior directly. Tani looked in the rearview mirror, trying to see his friend's reaction; the young scholar was also interested in the strange events of the day.

Jared tried to act as if he hadn't heard the question, but then changed his mind and shot back, "Out where?"

"What happened after that night, the night on the boat?"

Jared fell silent. A fresh wave of memories washed over him. He felt too uncomfortable with what had happened to him in the village of Song River to even respond. The strangeness of the church, and the monument to *him,* were too much for Jared to handle, let alone telling anyone about it. "I was lost for a while. I had a hard time getting my bearings and finding a town. There was a dry river bed where I washed up on shore. I followed it inland several days and came to a valley. After that, I ended up in Baker's Grove, and tried to make my way to Dune Station, looking for you."

"Baker's Grove?" Banion repeated in a quizzing tone.

"Yeah, that's right, Baker's Grove," the youth responded, shifting his eyes away from Banion's. The crazed mercenary picked up on his discomfort and pressed on.

"Those slaves we liberated from that convoy, many of them were from Baker's Grove. I talked to one of them for a little while. Told me an odd story. Seems that a drifter came into town and killed a Reaper Kai in the local bar. The freed slave said that drifter was you."

An icy silence washed over the car. Tani was shocked. Banion had kept much of that information to himself.

"Maybe he was wrong," Jared countered.

"Was he?" Banion pressed.

The tribal did not respond.

"Tell us what happened out there." His voice was soothing as he spoke. Banion was trying to get the tribal to open up and let his guard down.

Jared sighed and almost burst in tears. The weight of his journey was overwhelming, and he wanted nothing more than to tell someone, anyone, but it was still too near, too raw. Jared would need some time to digest the journey before he could open up.

Banion saw the distress on his face and backed off. "I thought I would never see you again, kid. I thought you were dead." After a brief pause, Banion smiled and spoke once more. "It's good to have you back. If it weren't for you, we would have never rescued Mineera. That truck would have escaped and we would still be chasing it. I am proud of you, Jared." Banion stretched out his hand and slapped Jared on the shoulder.

Turning back around, Banion abandoned the interrogation of Jared. "Damn it, Tani, can you speed up a bit? I want to reach Shape Home before sunset. Let's get a room at an inn, and then you need to use that oversized brain of yours to figure out how to get that damn Splicer off Mineera."

"Sure thing, Banion," Tani said, still darting quick glances at Jared through the rearview mirror. It had only been a few hours since their reunion, but the interval seemed to be an unexpectedly strained one. Jared's familiar carefree and prideful exuberance seemed to be gone. Instead, a deadly, staunch warrior had taken over. Something had happened to Jared during the mysterious period of his absence, something that had drastically changed his best friend. With concern for both Mineera and Jared, Tani steered the black muscle car down the lonely road toward the coastal town of Shape Home.

Chapter 23
The Consortium of Arms

The sun had set nearly an hour ago. The wasteland was washed in an eerie darkness. The waves of the nearby ocean crashed against the shore with a spray that glittered in the icy blackness of the night. Banion O'Neil crouched below a low dune just on the outskirts of Shape Home. The seasoned mercenary was watching a fortified building just to the west of him. Nothing stirred within the fortified compound, and Banion watched on with bemused trepidation. He was a survivor, a patient hunter who was carefully surveying his target.

Banion had been drawn to the sinister compound by his extensive knowledge of the southern reaches of the Darken Realm. The Consortium of Arms was the best mercenary outfitter in the Darken Realm. While other arms dealers sold and traded stolen weapons from the great northern houses, the Consortium of Arms had an extensive collection of pricy old world weapons, weapons created by the ancients themselves. The weapons were taken from old world military installations scattered about the southern and western reaches of the Darken Realm. The Consortium of Arms was an elite market for mercenaries or wealthy nobles seeking exotic, high-end items. Banion knew that if anyone in the entire Darken Realm knew the location of a nuclear weapon, it would be the Consortium of Arms.

A nuclear weapon was the holy grail of artifacts in the Darken Realm. Any army with such power would be unstoppable. The mighty houses of the north had scavenged and raided many ancient military installations and had never recovered such a fearsome armament. It was whispered that none remained. Banion knew otherwise. With the majority of the western Darken Realm ravaged by nuclear fire during the Armageddon ages and ages ago, much of the land still remained toxic and unexplored. If a nuclear weapon could still be found, it would be found in the western reaches.

The Runner, the most infamous and deadly of arms dealers in all the wastes, was in charge of the Consortium, and he was the object of Banion's search. He knew that there was a good chance this Runner had an idea where to dredge up a nuclear weapon from the wastelands.

The compound was silent. The night had bathed the sinister outpost in a haunting blackness. Nothing had stirred since Banion had arrived. The Consortium was only open at night, and the front gates were still shut tight. A lone building, nearly thirty feet high and armored in thick steel plates, sat in the middle of a fortified area surrounded by high, razor wire fences. The sharp, menacing fences were designed to cut and capture anything brushing across them. Beyond the fences, surrounding the lone building of steel, was a flat expanse of sand where nothing grew. At uneven intervals, small bulges protruded slightly; they were subtle to most, but not to Banion. The battle-hardened veteran had developed the keen senses necessary to spot them and decipher their meaning. The bulges in the sand were most likely land mines, anti-personnel explosives designed to detonate if disturbed. Beyond the mine field, at each corner of the building, were concrete bunkers with ports cut to allow gunfire to spew forth if the building ever came under attack. Banion smiled and sighed in the darkness. It would be a sad thing to see anyone ever assault the fortified compound. The defenses were formidable, and were putting the deranged rancher on edge.

Banion was about to give up, thinking he should try again tomorrow, when a click echoed in the darkness. The locking mechanism popped open on the front gate. A buzzing sound erupted as the mechanical gate slid open. Banion eyed the compound with tension and suspicion. Clutching his newly returned revolver, he stood up and moved slowly toward the front gate of the compound. He could see no one inside the compound, but a shadow moved inside one of the concrete bunkers. Someone was inside, probably training a machine gun on Banion as he edged forward.

Breathing heavily, Banion let his senses take over. A

rustling sound erupted from another one of the bunkers. The inhabitants of the Consortium were aware of his presence and were watching him carefully. With a confident motion, Banion approached the front gate of the compound. A flagstone path led from the gate to a doorway set in the steel plating of the lonely building at the center of the compound. Banion moved inside, beyond the gate. Knowing better than to step off the path, the crazed mercenary began the long walk to the steel building ahead.

Halfway to the door, Banion caught sight of a crater near the north fence. Bone fragments and fur were spread around the crater. His suspicion had been confirmed: the area just inside the fence was an active mine field. The remains must have been from an unfortunate animal which found its way into the compound, detonating one of the explosives.

The long walk came to an end. Banion stood before an iron door with no handles. With a groan, a heavy draw bolt slid back on the other side of the door. With a creak of corroded metal grinding, the door opened inward. Banion drew in a fortifying breath and entered the Consortium of Arms.

The interior of the square building was lit only by a single source of light, a lantern sitting on a wooden desk opposite the entry, which bathed the interior with dim shadow. Banion took a step forward, and the door behind him creaked shut. Turning around, the deranged rancher could hear something shuffling across the floor near the door, but he could not see a thing in the darkness.

Seated behind the wooden desk was a small form, cloaked in brown robes, face and body hidden completely from view by the cloth. Even in the dim light, the wall behind the small cloaked figure revealed itself to be covered with hundreds of weapons. Guns, hand weapons, explosives, and other rare military equipment were all on display, an irresistible source of attraction to any seasoned mercenary or man of war.

Banion moved forward, toward the cloaked figure seated at the desk ahead. As he walked, a sickly smell greeted his nose. It smelled like wet animal inside the Consortium. A sense of foreboding washed over him. Shuddering, the deranged rancher could tell that many eyes were upon him, gazing at him from the darkness of the strange building. If anything went wrong, Banion knew that an ambush would come from the shadows around him. As he reached the middle of the room, several fibers of hair rained down from above. As Banion made his way through the dim light, this falling fur put him on edge. Looking upwards, he could see shadows moving, hunched over, up on the rafters. The faint light was too scarce to make out anything definite. Whatever it was crawling around in the shadows, it wasn't human, based on the sickly smell and the tufts of fur falling from above.

Banion came to rest in front of the wooden desk, feeling his skin crawl in the bizarre environment, still sensing many eyes upon him. The figure seated at the desk appeared to be the size of a child. The head of the figure was elongated, and the stench of wet animal increased significantly. The arms of the figure were garbed in the same brown cloak which shrouded its body, and the hands were covered in brown leather gloves. Whatever the creature was, it wanted to keep its identity a secret.

"It's a bold move for someone like yourself to come to a place like this with a bounty on your head." A raspy voice rose from the robed figure. More movement could be heard above, in the rafters. Banion could have sworn he heard a squeak rise out from the darkness. He immediately dismissed the notion as nonsense. "Your name is Banion O'Neil, if I am not mistaken."

"You are not mistaken," Banion said in a confident tone.

"We watched you for quite some time, outside the Consortium. What brings a mercenary of legend into our wondrous market?"

"I am looking for the Runner."

There was a hesitant moment of silence. The form shifted uneasily in its chair. Its robes ruffled and unfurled, revealing a hunched back beneath them. Banion looked on at the creature before him; he knew without a doubt that it wasn't human.

"The Runner? Now that is a tall order, Banion O'Neil." The thing spoke with a rasp. "Why would we be interested in such a meeting?"

"I have money, a considerable amount," the deranged mercenary responded.

"From the plundered treasuries of Rasheed, no doubt? What makes you think we need your money at a time like this, a time when war is all around, a time when all races fight to survive the coming darkness?" The creature shifted again, and another waft of stench rose from it. Banion breathed through his mouth to avoid getting sick.

"I seek to fight the darkness that is engulfing this land."

"I know you seek to put an end to the Reaper Kai, but we struggle against another type of darkness in *our* land. Money is a useless tool for our fading people. What we need is a way to survive the hordes that would seek to destroy us. You want to meet the Runner? Then you must do *our* will. If you seek an audience with the Runner, you must be *our* champion. You are a legend of this land. Help us, and we can help you."

"How can I strike a bargain when your asking price is such a cryptic mission?" Banion inquired with a grumble.

"You must seek out my people and our tribe. Beyond the shifting sands and dunes to the west, in the Concrete Barrens, is where you must go. The road is long, but you will be well rewarded."

"Rewarded? You have no idea why I am here, what I seek. How can you give me what I want?" Banion scoffed at the sinister creature at the table.

"You are seeking a nuclear weapon, are you not?" the creature shot back with a slow, measured tone. Its words caught Banion off guard. How could the strange creature know his quest?

"You are correct about what I seek. Are you willing to swear an oath that if I lend aid to your people, you will give me the location of a nuclear weapon?" Banion moved forward, eyeing the strange creature.

"Yes…" it responded immediately with a rasp. "This is my pledge to you…" The creature extended its gloved hand. Banion clasped the hand and shook it, sealing the deal. A disturbing fear rolled into Banion's mind. The deranged rancher has just sealed a pact with some sort of creature, and he had no idea what it would cost him or the rest of Nova 7. With his obsessive need for vengeance, Banion would have sold his very soul to see the Reaper Kai destroyed. The deal he had just made would be costly, but it didn't matter. As long as he had a chance to do the impossible, that was all that Banion needed.

"The Concrete Barrens is a long haul. It will take a long time to reach the ruins," Banion said in a dull tone.

"Of course," the creature rasped. "It would be a shame if *our* new hero was unable to reach the Concrete Barrens alive. I suggest you re-outfit yourself and your team with some of our gear before you go."

Banion moved to pull money from his pocket, but the creature waved its hand in disagreement. "How can we charge *our* new champion? Take whatever you like, free of charge..." Banion shuddered at this generosity. It felt as if he had just sealed a deal with the devil himself.

As Banion moved forward, he surveyed the ancient weaponry with a glimmer in his eye. Fueled by greed and a sense of abandon, the reckless mercenary further entangled himself and the rest of Nova 7 in the twisted will of the sinister creature. It was a means to an end, he told himself; yet Banion knew he had crossed the line, pulling the rest of Nova 7 into a mysterious pact with a deadly tribe hailing from the ruins of an ancient city.

Chapter 24
Anatomy and Technology

"It's not coming loose. I can't get to the bolt, Tani, it's against her back. In order to get to the bolt, the Splicer has to be off her, but we can't get the Splicer off unless we release that bolt," Jared said in an exasperated tone, holding the rusted wrench.

Tani gave a loud sigh while looking at the Splicer still attached to Mineera's back. "I don't know how to get it off of her. It was designed not to be messed with once it's attached."

"There's got to be *something* you can do."

"If I could get to the electronics, maybe I could do *something*. Let's try cutting into the case with that hacksaw," Tani said, grabbing another crude tool.

"What about cutting the legs off with the saw?" Jared suggested enthusiastically.

"The legs are stuck in her spine. If we make a mistake, we could paralyze her."

"Um... then let's cut into the case."

"That's what I just said, Jared."

"Fine, give me the saw, then." Jared grabbed the saw and looked dumfounded. "Where should I cut?"

"I don't know!" Tani whined again. "It's not like I ever learned about extracting mechanical implants from a living person! Cut just below the tentacles."

Jared grabbed the hacksaw and began to saw into the casing. The metallic cover was slick and the saw slipped several times, making broad scratches in the soft metal. Finally, the blade bit in, and the tribal warrior made slow cuts into the casing. Working feverishly, the tribal managed to cut a crude opening in the convex cover of the Splicer. With a triumphant tug, the cut plating came free, exposing the Splicer's innards. Wires, electrical boards, and a host of motors were revealed.

Jared's eyes opened wide as he surveyed the interior of the Splicer. "I think it's your turn," he said as he backed away, allowing the scholar to survey the technology contained within.

"This a little better," Tani said, shaking his head with a mingling of dismay and fascination. A calm came over him as his eyes darted back and forth, figuring out the internal workings of the metallic creature. "These motors at the base of each leg are all tied into this main control board here." As Tani pointed these features out with his stumpy fingers, Jared simply looked on in stunned silence. "I don't see any external power cable, so if we disable this control board, we should be able to retract the legs from her spine."

"Can we just cut the power to the whole thing?" Jared quizzed, trying desperately to understand.

"We could, but if the Splicer is integrated into her brain, we might cause lasting damage. I am not sure what would happen if we turned off the electrical impulses to the Splicer while it was still integrated within her brain."

Jared nodded in meek agreement.

The mind of the genius was set aflame. He had read dozens of books about electronics and had even created crude control boards of his own back home in his makeshift laboratory. Surveying the mechanical creature, the scholar found it strangely simplistic. All of the motors and controls were ultimately wired into a main control board, a control board with a remote access port...

"Whoa!" Tani said as he caught sight of the access cable port. "I can hook my damn computer up to this access port." With a wild, fervent look, the scholar jumped to his feet and recovered his laptop computer. With trembling hands, he opened the laptop and attached the remote cable directly into the main board on the Splicer. Jared simply furrowed his brow, trying to look as if he knew what was going on. In reality, young Jared had no idea what his friend was doing.

"The Splicer is autonomous. That means all of the information it requires to operate is inside it. All we have to do is access the functions." Tani was smiling as he began to bang away at the keyboard on his computer. Using a program to access command functions, Tani started to probe the device with the aid of the software. Jared sighed as the tribal scholar dug into the device. He slunk against the wall and watched his friend hack into the programming of the Splicer. Feeling increasingly drowsy, Jared finally fell into a light slumber as Tani banged away at his computer.

It took several hours of varied strategies before the scholar hacked into the internal programming of the device.

The door to the inn room opened. Banion strode into the room with an odd expression on his face, seeming deeply concerned about something. Jared examined him with a quizzing look while yawning; the tribal warrior had just awoken once more from his intermittent nap. Banion avoided his gaze as he moved into the room.

"You have been gone a long time. Did you get any food?" Jared asked. The intent of Banion's absence was to 'get food', or so the tribal thought. In reality, Banion had been consorting with deadly arms dealers. The deranged rancher placed a large burlap rucksack filled with weapons on the floor of the room. Jared raised an eyebrow as he saw the bag and its contents.

"I lied. I was getting some information and new weapons," Banion said while looking at young Tani plugging away at his keyboard. "Any luck yet?"

"Yeah, I think so. Tani hacked into some sort of command library in the Splicer. He's trying to figure out how to tell the Splicer to release. He's been at it for a while."

Banion came over and eyed the project. As he saw the innards of the Splicer and Tani at his computer, he shrugged and started rummaging through the rucksack filled with weapons.

The time passed with dull intensity. Jared and Banion both were beginning to think that the tribal scholar would never figure out how to remove the Splicer. Just as hope seemed to fade, a look of recognition flashed through Tani's green eyes. "I think... yeah. I found a command chain that resets the state of the Splicer. I'm not sure what it means, but if we can reset the Splicer, it might detach from her."

"Try it out, then," Banion said, with a yawn. The deranged

gunfighter rubbed his eyes while shrugging off the drowsy feeling overtaking him.

Tani hit the Enter key with a loud bang. The command shot into the Splicer. With a whir, the implement came alive. A grinding sound issued from it. All of the legs retracted from Mineera's spine, and the tentacles released the back of her skull. The disk stood on the floor, and then the legs disappeared into a panel within the Splicer. The two copper colored tentacles shot back into the disk. The Splicer had detached itself from the psychic maiden, and all in the room who had witnessed the event were stunned. Though free of the Splicer, Mineera was still silent, eyes rolled in the back of her head. The recent liberation from the Splicer would require some time to take hold; the psychic maiden was still unconscious.

"You have got to be kidding me... how the hell did you do that?" Banion asked, shocked, looking at the tribal genius as he grinned, holding his laptop with pride.

Jared started laughing; that was Tani, brilliant and dedicated.

A loud whir rolled through the room. A panel opened on the Splicer. The legs shot out from the opening and the disk stood up once more. Another panel slid open. The two copper tentacles erupted and began to probe the air for life. The tentacles pointed toward Banion and maintained their position.

The trio was stunned and eyed the Splicer with curious looks.

Leaping forward, the Splicer launched itself toward the deranged gun fighter with frightening speed.

"Damn it!" Banion yelled as the Splicer began to grapple with him. The tentacles wrapped around his arms, trying to force them out of the way. After being reset, the Splicer was now looking for a new host.

Jared jumped to his feet and bolted toward his bed. Moving swiftly and deftly, the tribal warrior grabbed the mighty Scar Blade and pulled it free from its ancient scabbard. With a battle cry, Jared charged forward and with a precise strike, chopping through one of the copper tentacles. Coming under attack, the Splicer abandoned the crazed mercenary and focused its fury on young Jared.

Leaping forward with its needle-like feet extended, the

Splicer looked like an enraged swarm of wasps lunging forward, stingers at the ready. The youth sidestepped the creature and it embedded itself within the wall; each spiked foot pierced the wooden planks like a sharp nail.

Banion pulled a massive assault rifle free of the bag of newly acquired weaponry. Slamming a fresh magazine into the mighty weapon, he set out to destroy the Splicer. Taking shaky aim, Banion opened fire, sending a hot hail of bullets into the Splicer and the surrounding wall. The bullets rammed into the Splicer, fracturing its body in many places. Other bullets pierced the wall and slammed through the room next door. As the Splicer shuddered and exploded into a shower of sparks and twisted metal, screams of panic rose out in the neighboring room. Whoever was in the room had narrowly escaped the hail of gunfire, and was none too happy. The screaming patron was then seen running out the front of the inn with backpack in hand, desperate to escape the chaos. The inn owner had also fled the building and was looking up toward the second floor of the inn with a tremor of fright, but was not courageous enough to check out all the commotion in person.

With the barrel of his weapon still smoking, Banion kicked the remains of the Splicer and sighed. "Next time, bookworm, let me know it's going to attack us!"

"Sorry..." Tani said with a sheepish look on his face.

"And one more thing, bookworm... great job," Banion said in a sincere tone. The tribal genius had done the impossible once again: figuring out how to save the enslaved Mineera from the Splicer. Nova 7 was back. With Jared returning from the dead and the enslaved Mineera now free of the Splicer, the mercenary team was back on the road to victory.

Chapter 25
The Lost Tribe of Ceibla Moralis

The tower rose high above the city. The Lord of Evil was standing on its topmost deck with his arms folded against his back. His black eyes surveyed the ruins of Rasheed far below the tower of the palace. Father Vertigo was lost in his thoughts. Something was irritating the ancient priest of the Reaper Kai, something tugging at the edge of his mind.

"My Lord?" a young initiate addressed him in a trembling voice. It was the first time that he had been given an audience with a high priest, let alone Father Vertigo. It was an uncommon event for such a lowly Reaper Kai to be given an audience with the Lord of Evil.

Father Vertigo turned around slowly, still holding his arms folded behind his back. His pasty white skin was gruesome to the sight, but his eyes were the focal point of all who came into contact with the evil priest. Black globes, rotten orbs, rested in his sunken eye sockets. He looked like a rotting corpse.

"What is your name, initiate?" Vertigo asked, staring at the youth.

"Initiate… Fallow." Still nervous, the initiate was stuttering. Vertigo was not amused.

"I have heard rumor that several of our priests have been murdered by dissidents. I find this news most troubling."

"Yes, my Lord." The initiate spoke while bowing his head in reverence.

"The thing that I find curious is the murder of *two* of these priests. The ones slain by a boy…"

"Yes, my Lord. I saw this boy, a youth dressed in primitive hides and cloth. Brother Malice engaged him, but he did not survive."

"Brother Malice fell in combat to this boy?" Vertigo was

stunned. The exploits of Brother Malice were well known in the upper ranks of the Reaper Kai. He had an extensive and glorious reputation in the empire. The wicked Brother Malice had fought in the front lines against the northern tribes when the Reaper Kai emerged from their silence. He had slain dozens and dozens of soldiers over the years, and was an accomplished psychic warrior. Malice would have gone far in the Reaper Kai empire if it were not for his demise at the hands of the tribal warrior.

"Yes, my Lord, Brother Malice was slain in combat against this youth." Still uneasy with Father Vertigo, the initiate chose his words very carefully, not wanting to enrage him further.

"Tell me more about this *boy*," Vertigo hissed, hate rising in his soul.

"The boy wielded an ancient weapon, a blue steel sword, and when Malice assaulted the youth with his powers, the boy was immune. He escaped a direct psychic assault unscathed, totally unwounded. I have never seen such a thing, my Lord."

Vertigo's face twisted into a sneer. "Blue steel sword... that brat from Scarskin bested Brother Malice... he survived unscathed... impossible!" the dark lord roared in displeasure.

"You know of this boy, my Lord?" the initiate asked in a meek tone.

"Indeed I do!" Booming in anger, Vertigo began to lose control of himself. A wail pierced the room. A haunting scream arose as he twitched while the demons inside him roared in anger. Fighting back the torrent of emotion barely contained within his frail husk, Vertigo sought to calm himself and bring the raging demons within him to rest.

Regaining his composure, the dark father began to concentrate once more on the issue of the tribal. "Brother Malice fell in combat, and if my sources are correct, the missionary we sent to Baker's Grove met a similar fate. I could classify one such murder as blind luck, but two priests falling to this boy from the wastelands is more than luck. It is not possible for someone to survive our dark powers, unless..."

"Unless what, my Lord?"

"In your teachings, have you knowledge of the Lost Tribe of Ceibla Moralis?"

"No... my Lord," the initiate admitted in a baffled tone.

"I suspect their memory is only a myth to most of our race. I fear it is no longer a legend."

"I don't understand..." the initiate admitted, taking a step back from Father Vertigo.

"After our kind was driven from the Iron Kai empire during the witch hunts and civil war, we retreated into the darkness of the northern territories. Our fragile race desperately clung to this world for survival and was splintered into many houses, each led by a powerful priest. Most of these priests were too arrogant or corrupt to lead effectively. The power struggle that ensued was bloody. The remnants of our race fought against one another, vying for control over all. It was in this time that a priest named Ceibla Moralis emerged, a gifted psychic, touched by visions from the spirit world. As corruption rocked our people, this traitorous priest began to commune with the enemy. It was said that he abandoned our ways and took favor with angels of old. His teachings spread and a faction of our kind turned away from our heritage and began to embrace the putrid will of these angels. The angels began to hone Ceibla Moralis, who had been gradually twisted by their teachings, into an instrument of their design. By embracing the light, this risen father began to convert many others. In a short course of time, the ranks of Ceibla Moralis began to swell." Vertigo continued the lesson in Reaper Kai history while the initiate merely gazed at him nervously.

"Our kind could not stand for such sacrilege, so the other houses made a brief truce to destroy Ceibla Moralis and his traitorous faction. In an epic battle, the proud troops of our race banded together and slaughtered Ceibla Moralis and his followers... or so we thought. Lost in our legends are tales of several survivors from Ceibla's order. In our legends, the remnants of this tribe struck deep into the barren wasteland, avoiding our wrath, growing strong in the silence, hoping that one day, they could rise up against us. I had considered most of this to be nonsense. There has not been any

credible evidence that any of Ceibla's followers have survived...
until now."

The initiate was engrossed in the tale and was astounded that
the leader of their order had seen fit to recount the story. The lowly
initiate remained silent and attentive the entire time.

"In your training, who are the only ones who can withstand a
psychic attack?" Vertigo quizzed the youth.

"Another psychic," the initiate responded. "A psychic
cannot harm another psychic with their powers."

"Indeed. Only other psychics can withstand an attack from a
Reaper Kai."

Vertigo fell silent and stared at the lowly member of their
order as if anticipating an intelligent response.

"I... don't understand," the initiate replied softly, trying to
avoid Vertigo's wrath.

"Of course you don't! I only gave you all the knowledge you
require! The Lost Tribe of Ceibla Moralis is not a legend. It must
be a reality. This Scarskin... this village must be where those
dissidents hid all of these years. It is the *only* explanation. The
reason Jared of Scarskin is immune to our powers is because his
ancestors are our ancestors." Vertigo was elated by his conclusion,
not knowing of the strange raven totem that Jared had in his
possession. "The bloodlines must still be strong enough for that brat
to be immune to psychic attack. We must double our efforts to
locate this Scarskin. We must destroy it utterly and slaughter all that
remain."

The initiate was stunned and unable to react. He simply
stood before Father Vertigo, dumbfounded.

"When this Jared attacked, what did you do to stop him?"
Vertigo became irate, staring at the youth with a sinister gaze.

"I... I..." the initiate stuttered and stammered, taking several
hasty steps back from the age old Lord of Evil.

"...did nothing!" Screaming, the lifeless husk stepped closer
to the initiate. A host of bleating rose from the darkness. Najaszim,
Goat Minions, closed in from the shadows. Their eyes were flashing
with rage as the will of Vertigo forced them from the darkness of the

room. Vertigo's power was so great that he could command the Goat Minions by thought alone. Dozens moved in quickly, surrounding the frightened initiate, baying and bleating in a sinister tongue. Horns rose out of their skulls, tufts of fur jutted from their chins, and their sickly yellow teeth could be seen in the dim light of the tower.

"Weakness is a curse of the pitiful. Fleeing from an enemy of the empire is punishable with death!" As Vertigo projected his thoughts outward, the Goat Minions heard his orders and seized the initiate.

"Please, no…" the initiate began to plead.

"Only through fear do we grow strong. Only through punishment do we purify our souls!" A Goat Minion struck the initiate in the jaw with his furry hand. The pain was intense and the young man grew dizzy from the blow. "Do I sense weakness in you, or strength?"

The initiate was nearing the end of his life. He knew that if he did not think carefully and give a suitable response, the Goat Minions would kill him immediately.

"I will not whimper, my Lord. Through pain, I will grow strong." The lowly initiate looked up at Father Vertigo in respect.

"Indeed, through pain, you will grow strong. I sentence you to three days of torture for your weakness. When your soul has been purified, I trust you will never waver, never flee from an enemy!" Vertigo addressed the young priestling in a heartless, imperious tone.

"I will not flee an enemy ever again, my Lord. My will is bound to you and to this order. I thank you for your kindness, and will accept purification through pain willingly."

"Perhaps you have some use after all. When you are done with your repentance in the torture pits, I have a job for you to perform." Vertigo moved forward and clutched the initiate's chin, forcing him to look into the dark lord's lifeless, black eyes. "You are my new courier, initiate. Go forth into the wasteland. Seek out Sister Nightshade in the Steel Crag mountains. Your mission is to tell her of this news. Tell her that the destruction of Scarskin is her primary goal after the fall of the Steel Crag Mining Guild. This goal must be absolute. Tell Nightshade to bring the Abomination. With his power, the Lost Tribe of Ceibla Moralis will not survive!"

"Yes, my Lord," the initiate replied in reverence.

"One more thing, initiate!" Vertigo hissed. "You are to tell no one but Nightshade about this conversation. Do not use a radio to relay any of this information. If I discover otherwise, your life will be forfeit."

"Yes, my Lord." With that, the Goat Minions dragged the initiate away to the torture chambers beneath the palace of Rasheed.

Chapter 26
The Oracle of Saints

A series of black storm clouds were moving in from the western mountains, gradually engulfing the snow capped peaks. Wisps of cloud were breaking away, flowing downward in sheets just across the ridgeline. Bright bolts of lightning crackled, arcing from one cloud to the next, filling the sky with a low rumble. A soft, moist air preceded the storm, spreading a fresh smell of renewal all around.

A figure stood in the center of the fields, looking out upon his crop of wheat. Long golden stalks were about knee high, each stalk flourishing with a clutch of grain. The darkness of the coming storm washed over the land, blocking out the warm rays of the sun, creating a chill in the air. The light and warm hues of the golden wheat faded and turned almost ashen gray in color.

"Samuel?" a woman in a bright blue dress called out in a concerned tone. Long flowing brown hair rolled about her shoulders. Soft, warm, loving eyes stared uneasily at her mate. "Samuel?" She moved forward and gripped her husband's hands with a concerned look on her face. "Come back to me..."

The man blinked several times as if lost in a daze. Finally, he came back to reality and smiled at his wife. He had light colored hair, cut short about his ears. Bright blue eyes, shining even in the dimming light of the coming storm, considered his wife with compassion. A deep wisdom was reflected in his demeanor. He wore a heavy mantle about his shoulders, one that he could not easily forget. Smiling, he responded to his wife's caress and turned to commune with her.

"Where are you?" As she clutched his hands with an even tighter grip, he responded by rubbing the back of her hands with his thumbs. He looked back with a sheepish look on his face, not wanting to confront his concerns.

"It's nothing," he responded in a dull tone. "I am just tired and worried about the harvest. With so many bad years of drought, this will be the first year in seven that we will have a decent crop."

"The crop?" she echoed, knowing that he was hiding something. "Come on, what's going on?" she pressed again, her smile dropping, fading from her face. He avoided her gaze and looked away, toward the coming storm washing over the mountains. The clouds had dropped down, showering the grasslands in a warm, refreshing rain. Turning away from the mountains, his blue eyes fell upon his wife and conceded defeat; Samuel could no longer contain his grief.

"I've been seeing things again." He sighed and felt ashamed. Samuel never liked admitting that he was tormented by what he saw. Visions of horrid events would come to him in dreams, dreams that were not easily evaded.

"What was it this time? Did you dream about that *woman* again?" his wife quizzed, still holding his hands in her own, consoling him with her compassion.

"Yeah, and battles, horrible battles. Battles with red robed priests. I think our time of peace is coming to an end. Our ancestors are apparently on the rampage again. I fear this time we will be forced to face them." The man's eyes were lined with worry. He spoke softly while rubbing his temples with his worn hands. "It was not our fate to escape our heritage. No matter how many generations separate us from them, our dark forefathers will never give up their insane quest to master all others. This woman is somehow involved in all of this mess."

"Tell me about her, this woman in your dreams," Samuel's wife quizzed, trying to figure out what was happening. The two had a truce between them. She believed that he was having visions, but Samuel insisted strictly that this information stay between them. It was unconscionable for an outsider to learn about his dreams and visions. Many in their town would consider such visions a link to their dark past, a past where legions of demons were the focus of worship. Such abandonment of the old ways was a binding and committed lifestyle, a way to separate themselves from the darkness their tribe had escaped.

"She has strange eyes in my dreams. They are bright blue, and her skin is dark. Black, long hair streams down her dark blue robes. She is troubled but holds a distinct power. The spirits of good have found favor with her. She is some sort of leader, *our* leader." Samuel was having a difficult time relating the strange visions to his wife. "Half the time, I don't even believe she's real."

"What do you mean, *our* leader?" His wife was picking up on his distress as he spoke.

"I am not sure. I have a strong feeling that there are others *like* me. I see others in my dreams that are drawn to this woman." Samuel spoke softly. "She is some sort of beacon, a focal point for something... Somehow, this woman will bring *us* all together."

"You're talking about *us* again. You don't even know if this woman exists, let alone others like you. Could this just be a dream? Does it really have to mean anything?" The strange tale Samuel was telling was a little too much even for his own wife. Sometimes, she felt that his mind was fragile, and that his dreams were simply constructs of an overactive imagination.

"At this point, I don't think they are just dreams. There is some sort of significance to them. I think something is about to happen, a profound event that will forever change this world. I fear my peaceful time here is over. Soon we will be called to this woman, drawn to her from across great distances. I think a great battle is about to erupt, and somehow, I will be a part of it."

"Just make sure you don't get caught up in something you don't understand," his wife said in a severe tone. She was growing increasingly irritated by all the talk about visions, battles, and the ancestors of their people. In her heart, she only cared about their peace and happiness. The world down the road didn't matter to her; it was simply a distant land, a place where forgotten dreams fell away.

"I don't know what to say. I trust your heart and I do not think you would be led astray. I only worry about your safety and our home. I am selfish, I guess." Tears began to well up in her eyes. "I just want you here with me, that's all. All this talk is scaring me.

When I go to sleep every night, I imagine that all the stories we were told as kids were just fairy tales. I want to escape from those stories and imagine we live in a world without our ancestors and their ruinous pride and ambition. No matter how much I wish, and no matter how I imagine all the darkness away, we can never escape our heritage. The ill deeds of our ancestors must be put to rest. I don't doubt your visions. I only wish we lived in a time without the need for such omens. "

"I know..." Samuel looked away into the distance. The storm had engulfed the fields. A light splash of rain was falling, offering much needed relief from the dry climate. The thunder boomed in the heavens. Bright flashes lit the sky. The sound of falling rain increased its intensity.

Samuel and his wife hugged each other. The falling rain grew harder, but the couple stayed put, lost in thought, lost in each other. It felt reckless to stand in the falling rain, a way to defy heaven itself as the wild flames of war engulfed the tender fading memory of a civilized, fragile peace.

Chapter 27
Return from the Darkness

"Those who would bring the world to ruin are at your doorstep..." A loud boom rocked Mineera's slumber. The Voice erupted in her fragile mind, pulling her toward consciousness. *"Be careful... the agents of the enemy are close at hand..."*

The Voice began to move into the background of her thoughts. Sensations began to flood her senses. Nerves twitched and sound filtered into her dormant state. A flash of fire came next into her consciousness, dull throbbing flashes of pain which could be felt at the base of her neck and lower back. The hurt and suffering of her body, her physical form, were rushing into her focus. With a jolt of panic, Mineera opened her eyes and sat straight up in the bed. As her blue eyes opened, a foggy mirage of light and color swirled about in her field of vision. The rush of color and sound almost overwhelmed her. Fighting back a feeling of nausea, she blinked slowly several times, trying to focus her sight. Finally, the swirling mass of colors came together and a frightening image appeared.

The youth's face was fine featured, almost childlike in appearance, and exposed by the long hair tied back behind his head. His skin was tan and his dark eyes looked at Mineera with reservation, with a mixture of shock and compassion. Mineera gasped at the tribal warrior, and held up her hands in a feeble attempt to defend herself from the person standing in front of her.

Jared eyed the stunned Mineera with a look of concern.

"Who are you?" Mineera gasped, staring at Jared. Her consciousness had returned. Probing forward with her psychic powers, she found herself unable to reach Jared. It was as if her psychic powers had crashed into a wall, and nothing could be sensed behind that impenetrable barrier. There was nothing but emptiness. It was the only time in her entire life that her powers could not reach inside someone's soul and take a look around. The lack of feeling, the lack of emotion, was almost like having her powers stripped away. Whenever she looked upon someone, bits of their life would flood her. Whether it was a flash of emotion or a vague memory of the past, the psychic maiden could always discern information from anyone she surveyed with her extraordinary powers. But when she probed Jared, there was only an empty void, an unsettling chasm of nothingness. Her mind was frantically trying to comprehend what was happening. For a brief second, Mineera actually believed that she was dreaming and that the lack of emotion was a phenomenon akin to dreaming that her legs would not move or that she could not talk. It was such an unnatural feeling for the psychic maiden, that it brought panic inside her mind and soul.

"Get away from me!" Mineera flung herself backwards in the bed, putting as much distance between her and the phantasmal Jared. "You are dead!" she gasped.

"Calm down. You have had quite an ordeal." Tani rushed over to help comfort the dazed psychic maiden. She looked abruptly upon Tani and felt his essence fill her senses. It felt just like Tani, and she was comforted. She could sense the tribal scholar, just not the *thing* in front of her that *looked* like Jared.

"Be still. You have been asleep for a long time. I know you must be confused." Banion reached forward and touched Mineera on the hand. As he did, a flash of madness filled her senses, and tender emotions and chaotic anger coursed through her; it was definitely Banion. "Guillotine gunned you down in Dune Station and used one of those Splicers on you. Do you remember anything?"

Mineera was calming down after feeling Banion's touch, but she was still uneasy with the void of emotion emanating from Jared lingering near her bed. Ignoring the tribal warrior for the time being, she focused on trying to remember her ordeal.

Vague images were filling her mind. There was a weak memory of walking out of the inn and seeing a blinding sphere of light hit her. Another series of memories revolved around a being, a supernatural presence aiding her under the influence of the Splicer. Another series of memories coursed through her; she was unable to lift a finger, blink her eyes, or scream out in terror. The ordeal with the Splicer was a nightmare in which her soul and free will were stripped away.

"I can remember feeling helpless..." she whispered as tears filled her eyes. "How long was I gone?"

"It took us a while to track you down and save you. Five days to find you, and several more days to get that damn Splicer off without killing you. I had a hard time getting it to release. I finally had to hack into it with a remote cable and my laptop. You have been unconscious for almost a day since we pulled the Splicer off you," Tani responded with a serious look on his face. The young scholar had his arms folded across his chest as he spoke.

"Thanks for coming after me..." The weak psychic was speaking in a low tone. "I don't deserve anyone's kindness, let alone you risking your lives for me."

"Thank Jared most of all. If it weren't for the kid, I suspect you would be dead or in the clutches of the Reaper Kai," Banion answered, nodding toward Jared, who had fallen silent since Mineera's initial outburst. Turning back to Jared, Mineera tried to probe his thoughts. Nothing, she could feel nothing. Worried, in a sad state of confusion and exhaustion, the psychic maiden blurted out, "I think I just need some sleep." What she was really thinking was: *That's not him. Jared is dead.*

"You sure? It's been days since you have been awake. Are you sure you don't want some company?" Tani responded, not wanting to abandon her just yet, feeling that keeping her awake and lucid for at least a few hours would be good for her in the long run. The tribal warrior looked at her without adding a thing.

"Just get him away from me!" Mineera shouted, flinging her hands around in a rage, pointing in Jared's general direction.

Tani shot Banion a look of concern.

"Just calm down. You're still shaky from the Splicer. We need to get you some food and drink. You're not yourself." Banion reached forward and placed his hand on her shoulder.

Staring back at Jared, she shook her head back and forth. "I don't trust him. That's not Jared. Just leave me alone!"

Sighing with a startled look, Banion motioned for the two tribals to follow him out of the room. The trio moved into the hallway of the inn and let Mineera get some rest.

"Don't sweat it, kid." Banion slapped Jared on the shoulder. "She has been through quite an ordeal."

"Yeah, I know," Jared conceded. "We are damn lucky we even found her."

"We are damn lucky we found *you,* Jared. You're the one that saved the day," Tani responded, eyeing his friend with a serious look on his face.

"Let's get some air." The tribals agreed, and followed Banion out into the street.

The small town of Shape Home was right on the coast, and was essentially a fishing village, with a population of merchants and career fishermen. The town was nothing more than several hundred people living in wooden huts just beyond the shoreline, on the hill overlooking the beach. An ancient brick lighthouse stood at the north end of the village and was the home of the local mayor and his family. An old wooden dock, consisting of layer after layer of worn, water-rotted boards, extended several hundred yards into the ocean. Fishing freighters and sailing ships were tethered to the dock.

Earlier that day, a thick fog had rolled in off the ocean, plunging Shape Home into a grungy darkness. A chill clung to the fog, and the tribals shuddered in the cold. Banion pulled his long coat around him as they moved away from the inn.

Walking forward, Banion led the tribals to the dock and looked around in the fog with suspicion.

"Keep your voices low," Banion ordered, and the tribals nodded in agreement. "While you two were tending to Mineera last night, I took the opportunity to meet a contact here in Shape Home. They are gun runners who distribute to the southern Darken Realm. I quizzed them about some more exotic weaponry. We have a weak lead on a nuclear warhead, but it is a lead, nonetheless."

Tani and Jared were both uncomfortable with talking about a nuclear weapon, especially out in the open.

A form emerged from the fog, a fisherman moving forward

slowly with a net in his hands. A pipe was sticking out of his mouth and he puffed on the tobacco. The trio fell silent and considered him with suspicion. He moved beyond them and disappeared into the darkness of the fog.

Seeing that the fisherman was gone, seemingly swallowed by the mist, Banion spoke once more in a hushed tone.

"The gun runner's supplier hails from the west, far west. Beyond the wasteland is a battered, ruined, ancient city. The supplier makes his home somewhere in the ruins. Based on the technology they have, it is a strong bet they know the location of a nuclear weapon or a good place to start looking. This isn't a sure thing, but we can use this arms dealer as a source of information. If anyone knows about a nuke, it will be this gun runner."

A fog horn roared in the white darkness. It bellowed and was followed by the ringing of a bell. A fishing freighter lumbered into view. Fishermen jumped off the ship and landed on the wooden dock. Securing the boat, the crew tethered the mighty ship. Within seconds, they were unloading their catch of fresh fish and crabs.

Banion moved off the dock, away from the fishing crew. Jared and Tani followed while looking around in suspicion; having their conversation overheard was not an option.

"Where is this city?" Jared asked in a quite tone.

"Far to the west of here, about three to four months travel if we are lucky."

"Three or four months?" Tani gasped in amazement.

"The road to the battered city is not pleasant. The arms dealer has given me several maps of the way to the city and several maps of the city itself. The hell-blasted area is known as the Concrete Barrens to the peoples of the southern Darken Realm. In ancient times, the city had millions of people living inside its giant spires of glass and concrete. Now, nothing remains but the twisted, burned out husks of the once mighty buildings. Tribes of mutants and humans still fight over the region in war-bands, roaming from building to building, looking for the wealth of the ancients while trying to survive the harsh environment."

The tale had piqued the interest of both the tribals, and they were too enthralled to interrupt.

"During the Armageddon, the city was hit with nuclear weapons, reducing its center to a radioactive pile of ash. Since then, the earth itself has ravaged what remains of the once mighty city. Earthquakes and volcanic eruptions have destroyed almost everything else. All that remains are the splintered buildings and the tribes of mutants that haunt the ruins."

"And the most powerful gun runner in the southern Darken Realm lives there?" Tani questioned in a strongly skeptical tone.

"That's what the rumor is, bookworm," Banion responded.

"We can't cross a city that has been hit by a nuclear weapon. The earth must still be contaminated," the tribal warrior asserted, trying to support the scholar of Scarskin.

"You're right. We are not passing through the city, we will travel under the city," Banion shot back with a wicked look in his eyes.

"Under the city?" Tani protested again.

"A series of passages, some made by the ancients, some made by earthquakes, and other tunnels made by mutants, will be our road. The underbelly of the ruined city is riddled with passages and catacombs."

The tribals both shook their heads warily.

"This doesn't sound like a good idea to me. Sounds really risky for such a vague lead," Jared said in an arrogant tone. His eyes met Banion's. The defiant youth had an edge about him now. No longer was the tribal warrior a punk kid from the wasteland; instead, there was something unsettling about his demeanor.

Banion shot Jared a withering look. "We are heading to the Concrete Barrens," he said harshly to the defiant tribal from Scarskin. Jared held his gaze for a brief moment then looked away, conceding defeat to the wily gunfighter. Backing down, Jared took a step back. Tani sensed the tension and broke it by speaking to Banion.

"When do we head out?" he asked.

"Soon, in a few days, when Mineera is back to her old creepy self," the deranged gun fighter responded. "I don't want to move out with her yet until she can move about on her own. I want to give her a few days to recover from everything she's been through."

"It's not wise to linger here any longer than we need to. Mercenaries found us once, they can find us again," the young genius concluded knowingly. Hanging around a town with bounty hunters and mercenaries on your trail was risky.

"So what's the plan?" Jared asked, trying to be respectful of Banion.

"There are several small towns in between here and the ruins. Our goal is a wasteland town called Green Isles, the last civilized location on the road to the Concrete Barrens. From there, it's a five day journey along a trail leading to a mountain pass. On the other side of the mountain pass is the Concrete Barrens."

"Green Isles, then?" Jared nodded.

"Green Isles, kid. Come on, let's head to that tavern on the docks and get some dinner for ourselves and some food for Mineera."

The tribals agreed, and a plan of action had been made. Nova 7 would push into the western reaches of the Darken Realm with the intent of reaching a dangerous, hell- blasted city known as the Concrete Barrens. Unbeknownst to the tribals, Banion had made a sinister pact with the mysterious gun runners hailing from the ruined city. Still feeling indecision about the future mission, the trio pushed into the fog, disappearing like wraiths in the mist.

Chapter 28
The Front Lines

An explosion rocked the landscape. Enemy artillery fire was pounding the front lines of the Unified Army. The Mord Tech and Iron Kai forces were entrenched within the suburbs of the once great city. The ruins were excellent cover for the Unified Forces, but better cover for the enemy troops who had been fortifying their position for weeks and weeks as the Unified troops slogged through the treacherous Darkshade Moor.

"I need aerial support at my coordinates 162.36.05. I repeat, aerial support at 162.36.05. Targets are artillery batteries!" Lieutenant Jackson Heismann screamed into his headset. As he yelled, additional Reaper Kai bombardments screamed in, turning the ground into an exploding mass of debris and shrapnel.

Green helicopter gunships roared into the urban battlefield. Flying fast and low, they came into view, three in a series. Maneuvering through the ruined office buildings of old and battered skyscrapers was a daunting task, especially when the buildings were filled with enemy troops. As they roared into view, the gunships came under heavy attack. Biogtech troops reinforcing the perimeter opened fire, and a barrage of rounds pelted the assault aircraft. With thuds from small arms fire, heavy machine gun fire, and small bore anti-personnel cannon rounds, the helicopters' armor plating was taking a real beating. Several rounds managed to pierce the armor, and bullets were zinging through the interior of the gunships. Soldiers manning the heavy caliper machine guns cringed, each hoping the bullets ramming through the helicopters would miss their mark. This pass, none of the soldiers fell; the interiors of the gunships were still stained with the blood of fallen soldiers from the last pass through the ruins of the city.

The gunship formation reached the coordinates, and the helicopters strafed the enemy artillery batteries. Humming with an intense fury, the machine guns opened fire, and a stream of hot lead and bright tracer rounds tore forward. Hundreds of bullets streaked forth, slamming into a concrete barricade surrounding several artillery cannons. The Reaper Kai priest controlling the artillery battery dove for cover. The machine gun fire pelted the artillery crew, a squad of mindless Biogtechs. Gunship after gunship strafed the battery until all three helicopters emerged from the death zone. Their assault was well placed, and the artillery battery was shot to ruin. Not a single Biogtech death machine survived. The priest was also slain in the hail of hot lead.

"Artillery neutralized, Lieutenant," the lead gunship sent a radio transmission to Lieutenant Heismann.

Cheering, the troops in the surrounding squads under the control of the Iron Kai field leader rallied and prepared to push forward into the city, taking enemy ground.

"This is Heismann. I need artillery support on the two large buildings near location 162.36.05. I repeat, artillery support on the two ruined buildings at location 162.36.05," the lieutenant said with urgency into his radio headset.

"Artillery support confirmed. Commencing ordnance barrage of sector 162.36.05," the radio crackled back in response.

Booms filled the air. Whistling, the artillery rounds came crashing into the sides of the ruined buildings. Loud explosions echoed as explosives slammed into the buildings. Fragments of concrete, melted steel, and the shredded remains of mangled Biogtech soldiers pelted the ground around the ruined buildings. As the artillery shredded the enemy troops holding the buildings, the lieutenant ordered a full charge. Three squads of Iron Kai troops, clad in green military garb, charged the ruins.

Uttering war cries and accompanied by the explosions of artillery slamming into the enemy positions, the three squads advanced quickly. Running full speed, the soldiers hurled themselves over concrete debris and razor wire barricades. With several well placed bursts of assault rifle fire, the advancing squads of Iron Kai troops shot down several Biogtech death machines holding the courtyard in between the two towering buildings. With a final quick push, the Unified Troops now held the courtyard.

"Courtyard secure.   Send reinforcements to take the buildings," Heismann ordered hastily into his radio headset.

"Acknowledged, Lieutenant, we have three more squads on the ready and moving on your position," the radio responded.

All hell broke loose.

"Bombardiers!" a soldier yelled. "Take them down!"

Spliced slaves, human slaves acting against their own volition, under the will of the Reaper Kai, were charging the courtyard, strapped with explosives. The suicide bombers were a twisted tool of the Reaper Kai and in their condition, were mindless drones with a single purpose: inflict as much damage as possible.

Gunfire hummed as dozens of Spliced suicide bombers poured into the courtyard. The crack-shot Iron Kai troops dropped five or six immediately, but they kept coming, crawling over the rubble and running straight toward the Iron Kai soldiers with blank, lifeless expressions on their faces, covered in deadly explosives.

There were too many of them. Although most were dropped by gunfire, several managed to race through the lines. As they reached the perimeter of the Iron Kai troops, they exploded in a shower of destructive energy. Screams of anguish pierced the air as the bombers detonated themselves in the middle of the squads. Several soldiers were killed outright and others were left severely wounded. The three squads were panicked, as more suicide bombers charged forward and the stalwart soldiers mowed them down as fast as they could; each soldier knew that one stray shot could mean the difference between life and death. The three squads, left in ruin, braced themselves for another onslaught.

Biogtech soldiers, fresh from the factory, had closed in on the courtyard. Laughing in glee, they advanced while firing upon the Iron Kai troops. Pinned and having sustained heavy losses from the bombardiers, the Iron Kai were demoralized and scattered around the courtyard. Hope was a fading glory for these troops.

"I need support now!" Heismann screamed into his radio with fear in his voice. The lieutenant was brandishing his pistol, firing on incoming enemy forces.

A hand grenade exploded in the midst of the laughing, advancing robotic soldiers. The blast killed two of the robots and threw several others to the ground.

"Victory!" a Mord Tech soldier yelled. Blue liquid was flowing through the tubing on the soldier's neck, filling his body with a burst of medicine and chemicals designed to enhance combat prowess and survival in hazardous environments. Several Mord Tech squads closed in on the courtyard. They were firing at the enemy troops while charging. As the Mord Tech troops breached the courtyard, additional Iron Kai troops flooded in from the west, putting the advantage back in the hands of the Unified Forces.

With efficient speed, the Mord Tech forces had closed on the Biogtech troops. Pulling out an assortment of hand weapons, the drugged-up super-soldiers let the chemicals fill their minds and bodies with a staggeringly aggressive battle fury. Engaging the Biogtechs hand to hand, the Mord Tech troops attacked without mercy.

The Biogtech troops were too slow to be a real threat to the superhuman strength of a chemically pumped Mord Tech. Within a matter of seconds, the Mord Techs had torn the Biogtech soldiers apart. Covered in motor oil, blood, and hydraulic fluid, the battle-crazed Mord Techs sounded a cry of victory. The troops wounded in the attack had blue goop bleeding from their wounds. Within seconds, moderate wounds had closed completely; the strange chemical cocktail contained a powerful coagulant as well as combat enhancing drugs.

The Iron Kai troops eagerly thanked their brethren from the north; the alliance was becoming more and more of a necessity, rather than a luxury. The Iron Kai squads under the leadership of Heismann had pushed the front line of the Unified Forces ahead another hundred yards, a hundred yards closer to the heart of the Reaper Kai capital. With other bold moves, and strong tactical advances on enemy positions, it would only take a few more months to push another eighteen miles into enemy territory, eighteen miles closer to the Biogtech factories – the same factories that were producing more than a hundred Biogtech troops a day.

The battle lines were slowly moving forward, but this progress wasn't rapid enough. With the enemy producing so many soldiers, it was a tortuous battle to gain any ground. Without significant advances and hindrance of the Biogtech production, the Unified Forces knew that they were fighting a losing battle.

As the Unified Forces cheered their victory, the ground shook and the sounds of distant booms rolled in. Taking cover, the troops prepared for another artillery barrage. As the enemy shells roared toward the Unified Soldiers, the battle for the Reaper Kai capital ground onward.

Emperor Gunther moved away from the radio. He had been monitoring the battle transmissions the entire afternoon. With a somber look, he grabbed a stein of beer and took a great drink from it. A dribble of beer ran down his chin, and he wiped it away with a sigh.

With a somber look, he moved over to the great window that looked down from the mighty fortress of Stonen upon the enormous lake below, a lake so large that only on rare occasions could one see all the way across. As the waves of the lake surged and heaved onto the crude rock shoreline, Gunther felt a rush of confidence fill him. He could not despair in such times; to do so would be certain death. Even in times of great strife, a leader must never waver, never show fear or indecision. Gunther knew that to empower his troops, he must be resolute, strong, and never concede defeat.

"Emperor?" A war advisor had entered the mighty Truce Hall and was seeking an audience with Gunther.

"Yes, Captain?" Gunther turned around and faced the war advisor with an air of confidence.

"I have news on many matters, several of which you might find quite interesting."

"Out with it, then. Enough of these formalities," the red bearded Emperor boomed.

"A mercenary team just wiped out a Reaper Kai slave convoy outside Turner's Corner, a weigh station and crossroads in the southern reaches of the Darken Realm."

"And what is so *interesting* about that?" Gunther asked, hoping his direct attitude would spur his advisor to get to the point.

"The witnesses claim it was Nova 7, my lord. It appears they are still alive."

A smile graced Gunther's lips. "That is good news indeed. It has been a great many months since the fall of Rasheed, and we have heard nothing about Nova 7. I am glad one of the mercenary teams survived that horrid night in Rasheed."

"I knew you would be pleased, my lord. And that's not all. It is also rumored that Nova 7 killed a missionary in Baker's Grove. A drifter came into town and killed the Reaper Kai missionary. The rumor is, it was Jared, a member of Nova 7. The southern reaches of the Darken Realm are polarizing, my lord. The tales and legends of Nova 7 are driving a defiant wedge into the populace. The southern lands are under attack and are being pillaged by the Reaper Kai. The fear generated by the invasion is turning to rage as the tales of Nova 7 spread. Recruits, my lord, thousands upon thousands of recruits, are migrating from the southern reaches with the intent of joining our army! They want to fight the Reaper Kai!"

Gunther was stunned and elated by the news. "Continue, Captain."

"Just today, we received over three thousand new recruits, and our scouts manning the roads into the southlands are reporting thousands more are on the way. The peoples of this land are taking sides, and they are rallying to our banner."

"Interesting. The goal of Nova 7 is to bring about the nuclear ruin of the enemy. Now they are a defiant force, blazing a trail through the enemy, creating legend and daring deeds. The scared and fragile provinces are accepting these legends with open arms. Nova 7 has given these people hope, a focal point for change. No longer do these people feel helpless, but rather empowered by Nova 7. I would have never imagined such fortune."

"Yes, my lord, our fortune has truly changed, but we still need to be careful. We have received word that the army that destroyed Rasheed is now marching across the southern wastes, carving a bloody path toward the Steel Crag Mining Guild. We have received emissaries just now from that great mining guild calling for aid," the advisor informed the mighty Emperor.

"We do not have the resources to fight a battle on multiple fronts. The siege of Detro Tech City has drained our resources. We are barely keeping the enemy in check and are slowly progressing into the city. Each step forward, our troops are met by staunch and ever-stronger defenses. We will ally ourselves with the Steel Crag Guild, but we mustn't draw our resources away from the front lines of the enemy." Gunther fell silent while a plan of action filled him. "These volunteers, all these men from the south – I have an idea what to do with them."

"Yes, my lord?"

"Send all of them to the front lines of Detro Tech City. Draw three thousand veteran troops from the Reaper Kai territory and send them to aid the Steel Crag Guild. With our added might and use of experienced troops, we should be able to hold the southern wasteland. These new troops, these recruits from the south, should be kept in reserve long enough for them to be trained."

The decision was sound, and the captain nodded in agreement. "I will send word that we are supplying aid to our new allies in the south."

"Since the Reaper Kai troops are already en route to the Steel Crag, will our troops reach the southlands in time?"

"I am not sure, my lord. The distance is far, and with the current advance of the enemy, the Steel Crag territory will almost be surely under siege by the time aid arrives."

"Understood. Tell the Steel Crag Guild to bolster their defenses and to prepare for a siege. We will march our troops quickly to aid them. I only hope that by the time we reach the south, our new allies are still left standing. If the Steel Crag Mining Guild falls, the Reaper Kai will have enough steel and petroleum to increase their production of Biogtechs. If our victory is to be assured, the Steel Crag Guild must survive the Reaper Kai assault." Gunther spoke as he strategized.

"I agree, the Steel Crag Guild will be ill prepared for the

army that marches against them. What they need is a miracle," the captain concluded.

Gunther concurred. A miracle, a wild act of fate, was needed to ensure that the Steel Crag Mining Guild survived the dread armies of Biogtechs marching in on their territory.

Chapter 29
Carla Reins

The patrol ahead of the main Reaper Kai army was closing in on Globulus quickly. He had concealed himself behind a clutch of boulders, high upon a slope. The scouting patrol, comprised of eight Biogtech soldiers and a Reaper Kai initiate, was on the mutant hippo's trail. He had managed to avoid the main force and several other scouting groups, but this time, his luck was running out. The mutant hippo would have to face an entire squad of enemy troops by himself.

The psychic felt a twinge at the edge of his senses. He could feel that someone was concealed, hiding up in the boulder fields. With a grim smile, the initiate ordered the Biogtech scouts to advance up the hillside. The feeling became stronger, and the initiate focused his powers, giving orders to his troops, and trying to flush out the hidden mutant. Globulus and the Reaper Kai scouting band had been playing a game of cat and mouse for the past several days. Though Globulus was faster, he had made several critical navigation errors, and had been forced to backtrack to find his way. Another such mistake had brought the scouting party directly into contact with the mighty mutant. The initiate was powerful enough to know that the hidden prey wanted nothing more than to elude the scouting party, and that made him all the more hungry for the kill. Like a lion chasing a gazelle, the Reaper Kai smelled the scent of fear and was closing fast.

Cackling, the mindless robotic soldiers began to slowly stagger up the steep hill. The landscape was broken with rocks that had fallen away from the mighty mountain range known as the Steel Crags. The boulder field was incredibly steep, extending all the way to the base of the giant stone peaks which made up the eastern fringe of the mighty mountain range. Large fragments of rock dotted the steep hill, giving exceptional cover but little way to escape.

Globulus had retreated into a cove of stone. Behind him was a sheer rock face ascending more than one thousand feet straight up. The only way out was straight through the enemy squad now ascending the steep terrain. Cursing, the hippo prepared to engage the enemy troops closing on his position.

Seeing the troops move in, Globulus took the initiative. With a grunt, the mutant hippo's arms strained and his muscles rippled. With a burst of strength, he pulled a large rock off the steep hillside. Clutching the boulder, he took a brief moment to target the lump of stone at his enemies. Globulus hurled the rock down the hillside with a determined look, aiming for the enemy soldiers. The mindless robots were caught unprepared. One Biogtech looked on as the boulder came tumbling down the mountainside. Cackling as doom rolled near, the Biogtech never even made an attempt to flee the crushing power of the rock thundering downward. With a crack, the boulder slammed into the robotic soldier, crushing it immediately. Like an orange being crushed by a hammer, fluids burst from its robotic body, as the stone hammered forward without hope of stopping. The initiate had to retreat from the deadly projectile bounding down the hillside, rushing quickly to the right as it thundered past.

"Kill him!" the Reaper Kai yelled, pointing his finger up at Globulus, who was now exposed on the hillside. The robe on the initiate's arm fell away, revealing the diabolic snake tattoo which branded the man as a servant of evil.

Responding to the orders, the Biogtechs clumsily raised their weapons and opened fire. As bullets whistled past and ricocheted off the rocks, Globulus moved for cover. Concealing himself behind an outcropping, the mutant hippo pulled a brace of shotguns, small enough to enable him to hold one in each hand. With a look of dispassion, Globulus crouched behind the rocks and fired the shotguns like a pair of pistols at the advancing soldiers. The blasts were hasty and too far out of range to be effective. The robots responded by returning fire. As seven automatic weapons fired on his position, Globulus hit the deck. He could shrug off a few bullets, but being hit by bursts from seven automatic weapons was a certain death. The mutant hippo was beginning to feel that his options were running out. He was outnumbered, and his guns didn't have the range to pose a real threat to the enemy. If he didn't do something quickly, Globulus knew his death would be close at hand.

A precise blast ricocheted through the air, and the sound of thunder erupted, echoing off the rocks of the boulder field. The Reaper Kai priest was ill prepared for the attack. A high caliper sniper round hit his throat, whipping him backward like a rag doll. The priest was unable to withstand the attack and crashed backwards, splitting his head open on the rocks. The trauma from the fall was terrible, but paled in comparison to the hole that had been blasted through his throat. The priest fell silent, staining the rocks with his blood. Globulus was stunned. The assault had come from higher up in the boulder fields, from a concealed attacker. There was *someone* hidden in the boulder field, lending aid to the hippo pinned by gunfire.

The Biogtech soldiers were undaunted by the death of their leader. Without new orders, they continued to move up the hillside with the intent of killing the mutant hippo.

Another clap of thunder resounded through the boulder field. A Biogtech soldier was struck by a high caliber bullet, which sheared its head clean off. Globulus stared in awe, rolling onto his back, looking upwards into the boulder field. The mutant could see nothing. Whoever was lending him aid remained well hidden and extremely deadly.

As he scanned the hillside, a shot rang out again. Another Biogtech soldier was felled by the precise shooting. The battle had turned around quickly. The Reaper Kai initiate and three of eight Biogtech soldiers had been slain already. Seeing an advantage, Globulus felt a crazed notion fill his mind. Rising from cover, the mighty hippo launched himself downward, descending the slope, uttering a fierce war cry. With a shotgun in each hand, he opened fire, blasting into the troops as he charged. Two more Biogtechs were slain in the attack, and the others were ill-prepared to engage the mighty one ton hippo at close range.

Like a crazed juggernaut, Globulus blasted into the

Biogtechs, scattering the remaining ones as if they were mere toys. Using his shotguns like clubs, he pounded away at the cackling robotic soldiers. Whirling around, he battered and smashed his way through them. He swung wildly, scattering motor oil and fragments of plastic with each blow. Several quick attacks smashed into the Biogtechs, causing frightening damage. Killing two in a fury, the hippo launched himself toward the last Biogtech with the intent of slaying it. As he charged with a yell, the Biogtech leveled its weapon at the oncoming hippo, attempting to drill the charging mutant with a burst from its automatic weapon. Instantly assessing the situation, Globulus knew that his chance of survival was slim.

Prepared to be shredded by hot lead, Globulus charged onward, screaming valiantly while knowing full well that the bullets were about to bite his flesh.

Another loud snap rolled through the boulder field. The Biogtech suffered a severe wound, sustaining a deadly shot. The gun arm of the robot had been sheared off at the shoulder by the concealed sniper, and a splatter of motor oil erupted from the wound. The submachine gun fell harmlessly to the ground, still clutched in the severed robotic arm. The Biogtech rocked back and forth, confused by the sniper shot that had ripped off its right arm. Within seconds, Globulus had closed in on the last Biogtech and was beating the robot to death, hammering it without mercy; it only took half a dozen hits from the mighty Globulus to slay the Biogtech.

The battle had ended. The Biogtech scouting party had been destroyed. Globulus looked up into the rocks and saw nothing. The hidden attacker was remaining concealed. Knowing that the sniper could kill Globulus at any moment, he shouted upwards into the boulder field, hoping that the sniper did not harbor any ill will against his kind.

"I owe you a debt of gratitude!" Globulus yelled out. "Come out where I can see you! I mean you no harm!" The mutant hippo holstered his weapons and held out his empty hands.

A moment of silence gripped the boulder field. A wind rose, whistling through the barren rocks and lonely shrubs dotting the hillside. A line of dust spiraled around the silent battlefield as

Globulus scanned the rocks high above. Finally, a form emerged up on the rocks, several hundred yards away. From his distant viewpoint, the hippo could barely see what it was. It rose from the ground like a sentient pile of earth, dressed in a brown burlap sack with shrubs and other camouflage pasted to its outer surface. The suit was perfect for the environment, offering the deadly sniper a high level of concealment. The form was small but walked upright like a human. Walking delicately downward, the sniper passed amongst the boulders like a shadow. The mighty mutant had to keep from blinking, for if he did, the sniper would disappear into the background.

It took a mere moment for the sniper to come before the mutant hippo. Standing only twenty feet away, with weapon ready, the dangerous soldier considered Globulus silently. Observing the deadly assassin with a look of fascination, the mutant hippo was stunned to see the face of a woman peeking out from underneath the sniper suit.

"You must tread softly, master hippo, in the Steel Crags. The enemy is in full advance and their scouting parties are littering this passage into the mountains." The small female sniper spoke with a confident tone. She was short in stature, just over five and a half feet tall, and had short brown hair that fell just past her ears. With hazel eyes looking out from a face covered in brown and gray camouflage face paint, she was an ominous sight in the barren foothills leading deep into the mountains.

"I am pleased you came to my aid. There are not many willing to risk life and limb to rescue a stranger from the Reaper Kai." The hippo nodded in respect. "What brings a lone person into this forsaken landscape?"

"I have my reasons. I am but one woman, but I can wage a lonely war on those who travel under the flag of pestilence and death. I have no love for the Reaper Kai. I would gladly give my life to purge their foul presence from this earth." As the sniper spoke, an innocent, almost child like grace illuminated her eyes. "Any enemy of the Reaper Kai is a friend of mine."

Globulus smiled at the young sniper and shook his head in

amazement. "Well spoken, lass. I am Globulus, former warmaster of the late King Toil, monarch of Rasheed."

"Rasheed? I have heard that the city was set ablaze by the armies of darkness."

"It was. We were betrayed from within. The city fell in one night of chaos and carnage."

The female sniper stared at Globulus with a look of sympathy.

"When I saw you, I thought you were a local. A tribe of your people is not far from this passage into the mountains," the young woman said, scanning the territory around her from time to time, constantly on the lookout for enemies.

"I know..." The hippo had a distant look in his eyes as he spoke. "I left the Steel Crags a long time ago..." His distant look turned to a misty eyed expression of heartbreak. In the hot, dry air, the mighty hippo appeared to be fighting back a fresh wash of emotion. Something raw and unsettled was just beneath the surface. "This is the first time I have returned in a great many years."

"Carla Reins," she declared matter-of-factly. The hippo blinked several times before the statement sunk in.

"Carla Reins?" The young woman nodded in affirmation "Good to meet you. I think it's best to move on."

"I agree. The enemy has many patrols ahead of their main army. It is unwise to linger here. Where are you headed, Globulus, master of the fallen Rasheed?"

"To Rust Spire. I need to get to the capital of the Steel Crag Mining Guild," the hippo responded as the two moved away from remnants of the battle. Normally, the mutant would be suspicious of outsiders, but in this case, he was a little more receptive to the stranger. It was rare that someone would oppose the Reaper Kai and risk their life to save a stranger. The selfless act of heroism exhibited by the young woman was more than enough to make Globulus feel at ease.

"Rust Spire? I can take you as far as Black Rock Canyon. From there, you can catch a train to the Gold Road, and after that, it is a half day's journey to Rust Spire," Carla said while scanning her surroundings like an eagle looking for a fish in a lake.

"I don't need an escort," Globulus boomed back.

"Neither do I. But it's wiser to travel together than alone," she shot back, staring at him with a smile on her face. "With the recent increase in enemy troops in this region, I can do little more by myself. I will slowly retreat and do what I can to hinder the advance of the Reaper Kai. I will help you find your way."

"You don't even know me," the hippo countered.

"I know of your exploits. I travel in dangerous circles. Your deeds of daring are known throughout the southern wasteland. Many have heard about King Toil's warmaster. I trust you well enough. If I didn't, you would be dead in those rocks back there. I didn't have to intervene, but I did. Let's just trust each other."

"Fine. I will travel with you. And what about you? Is it your custom to roam around the outlands, killing at will?" Globulus quizzed the young woman. "Whom do you serve?"

The silence stretched on. Carla failed to respond to the hippo's question. There was a distant look in her eyes, hidden beneath all of the camouflage and war paint. With a tense tone, she responded after several moments of silence. "I serve no one."

The duo continued onward, deeper into the mountains, which greeted them with a wondrous vision.

The slope rose higher and higher. Small grasses began to dot the hillside and wild flowers clung to the base of the boulders lining the mountain pass. The rock walls of the Steel Crag mountains rose thousands of feet into the air. Jagged, grey granite outcroppings jutted outwards, like a fanning of knives, cutting the air with their sharp spines. The mountains were imposing and awe inspiring. Snow-dotted peaks sloped downward, forming broad snow fields in the saddles between the ridges. Cold air whipped the snow-capped peaks as plumes of blowing snow rolled off the heights of the mountains. The blowing snow rose hundreds of feet into the air, creating clouds of billowing haze, swirling around the peaks of the mountains like a hurricane of mist. A cool, frigid wash of air rolled downwards from the chilled peaks, flooding the valley with an icy air. The sight of the majestic range looming closer made the duo feel small and insignificant as they made their way through the mighty shadows looming outward from the Steel Crag Mountains.

As Globulus caught sight of the peaks rising thousands of feet above them, memories began to course through his mind. "It's been a long time..." he whispered, looking at the awe inspiring peaks surrounding the two as they pressed deeper into the heart of the mountain range.

"Long time?" Carla echoed. "How long has it been?"

"Too long. I was born here... ages ago. I was taken into King Toil's house at a very young age. I was trained to protect the royal family." Globulus spoke with a misty eye. The betrayal of young Marian Toil still stung like a hot knife in his mind. Forcing the thoughts from his mind, the hippo eyed his companion.

"Welcome home, master hippo." Carla smiled at Globulus as she spoke. The mutant saw her smile and chuckled. He already had a liking for the young woman. She was confident, a menace on the field of battle, and had a warm, caring heart.

"I was born here, too." Holding her fifty caliber sniper rifle, she trudged onward, while Globulus thought, on many occasions, that the young woman was about to fall over from the weight of the weapon. "Come on, if we pick up the pace, I know a great campsite near the Mirror Pools."

Globulus nodded, and the two pressed deeper into the Steel Crag range, drawing ever closer to Rust Spire and the inevitable siege by the dread Reaper Kai.

Chapter 30
Black Rock Canyon

The duo had pressed deep into the Steel Crag mountain range. It had been a few hours travel from their campsite at the Mirror Pools, a series of small ponds fed by glacier flows, which, true to their name, glistened like mirrors. The day wore on at a comfortable pace, with the two new companions pressing ever closer to the Gold Road, the giant tunnel cut underneath the mountains, which was used by the Steel Crag Guild as its primary source of gold and iron ore. At present, Globulus and Carla were still far from the Gold Road and were pushing slowly through Black Rock canyon.

Tall, jagged, grey rock walls rose high above them, marking the boundary of Black Rock canyon. Spires of rock towered high into the air, piercing the cold wind. The canyon walls were narrow, and the chill crisp air was blowing in from the western, snowcapped peaks, which were surrounded by a congregation of white, puffy clouds. The sun had passed its zenith, heading always west, casting long shadows into the canyon. Patches of sunlight and shadow intermixed and mingled, creating a patchy effect of light and dark. Where the light fell away from the walls of the canyon, the rocks in the shadow looked as if they were cut from black stone – hence the name of the canyon.

An eagle cried as it rode the thermals. Its brown head scanned the canyon below, moving back and forth rhythmically as it attempted to spot the slightest movement of a rabbit or vermin, hoping it would soon find a midday snack. Crying softly, the eagle voiced its displeasure with the two travelers stomping around the bottom of the canyon. The duo continued undaunted, ignoring the cries of the mighty eagle, and instead, watching a creek fed by the snowfields head away to the east.

The stream meandered through the canyon. Smooth, worn boulders, eroded by thousands upon thousands of years of rushing water, lined the streambed. Shrubs and plants hugged the rocky, broken earth near the water. Clinging greedily to the moisture, the plants grew out of any crevice in the rocks that could support life. Bubbling over the rocks, the stream pushed onward toward the base of the mountains where the mighty deserts began.

Carla Reins and Globulus were walking along the bottom of the canyon, following a set of train tracks that pushed deeper into the mountain range. The Steel Crag Mining Guild had used the railway for centuries to move ore and other precious wares to the eastern fringe of civilization, most often trading with the kingdom of Rasheed.

Globulus found the company of the female sniper to be comforting. He enjoyed talking with her as they journeyed.

"So, why are you out here, anyway?" Carla asked, still clad in the burlap sack sniper suit, her face covered in camouflage face paint.

Globulus was silent. He did not want to reveal the purpose of his travels to a stranger, no matter how well he liked her.

"Oh, come on, if I wanted to kill you, it would have been easy. I would have shot you in the head from three hundred yards. You would have never seen me," the sniper said in a heartless tone.

Globulus was astounded by her bravado. "Is that so?" He shook his head. "You are a bold little brat, aren't you?"

"Yeah, I guess so," Carla agreed with a grin on her face. "So, come on, why are you all the way out here?"

"You're not going to stop asking until I tell you?" the mutant quizzed.

"Nope."

"Fine," Globulus grumbled. "You must promise not to tell a soul."

"Don't be so serious. What am I going to do? Walk up to the next Reaper Kai scouting party and tell them I ran into a mutant hippo from Rasheed?" As she slammed him repeatedly, the hippo was almost on the edge of barking at her. If he could blush and be flustered, the mutant hippo would have been. "I wouldn't be so obnoxious if I thought you were *weird*."

"That's a real comfort."

"So, why are you out here?"

"You may be a brat, and you may be dangerous with your little rifle, but if you don't knock it off, I am not above crushing you with my bare hands." He glared at the tiny companion walking by his side. She got the idea and stopped her attack. Considering her with a serious look, he asked, "Are you finished now?"

"Yeah... for now..." she said with a grin.

"After Rasheed fell, our people were scattered. Knowing that the enemy would not yield, I gave orders for our people to join the Iron Kai army in fighting the enemy. My goal is to travel to Rust Spire and seek an audience with the Protectorate, the wise leader of the guild. Hopefully, I can convince the Steel Crag Guild to join in the struggles against the dread Reaper Kai."

"Well, that is a noble goal. I suspect with the Reaper Kai armies already marching on Rust Spire, the Steel Crag Guild will be more than happy to ally themselves with the other great empires of the land."

"I hope so. If the Reaper Kai gain control of this region, the mineral and oil supplies would give the enemy a sizeable advantage in this war." He talked softly, feeling comforted by Carla's company. He had only known her a few days but trusted her nonetheless. "So, what brings a brat like you out here?"

"Me? This is my home," she responded.

"This canyon?" the mutant shot back, trying to purposefully fluster his companion the way she had done to him.

"No, no. The Steel Crags are my home."

"So you just wander around in your rags, with dirty leaves stuck all over you, killing things?" Globulus was the one being a brat now, and had turned the tables on the petite woman walking beside him.

"Not *exactly,*" she whined.

"So where is your village?"

"It's gone." Carla sighed.

"Gone?" the mutant quizzed.

"Yeah." She sighed again. "I grew up with my grandfather.

My parents died when I was very young. My mom and dad owned a general store and were getting supplies from Rust Spire. When they were making the journey through Ice Ridge Pass, an avalanche hit and killed both of them. They knew better than to travel so late in the season, and that poor decision was a costly one. I was three when it happened, and have only vague memories of them. My grandfather raised me and we lived a quiet life." Carla fell silent as if trying to collect her thoughts. A few moments passed and she continued once again in retelling the tale of her life.

"I lived with my grandfather until just a few years ago. Our home was a small town named Dawn Ridge, in the foothills of the Steel Crags. It was autumn, and the fields of wheat had just been cut. A few of the farmers came down with some sort of illness. We thought it was just a cold, at first. Later, it became evident that the disease was no common ailment. The sickness began to spread, first amongst the farmer families, and then throughout the town as a whole. Those afflicted spent the last days of their lives coughing to death, spewing up bloody phlegm. Most of the sick lasted only a few weeks." Carla was distant as she recounted the tale. It was clear to Globulus that the story was having a profound effect on his companion. "I never want to see a world filled with sickness ever again..." she whispered.

"My grandfather was the closest thing to a doctor in Dawn Ridge, and he tried to treat the people. He sent me to Rust Spire for medicine. By the time I got back, the town was abandoned. All those still left in their homes had passed into death, leaving the town deserted. I ran home and found that my grandfather had also succumbed to the plague..." Her voice began to quiver. "I still remember the look on his face when I found him. He had died with his eyes open. When I came into the room, he seemed to be staring at me, through those glassy eyes of his..."

"I am sorry for your loss," Globulus responded in an earnest, heartfelt tone. Carla nodded back, trying to smile.

"I took a torch and burned the entire town to the ground. Hopefully, the next poor souls who passed through would be safe from the plague. And that's how I ended up here."

Globulus was suddenly frustrated. The story was intriguing, but didn't make much sense. "So you put on a sniper suit and started roaming around the Steel Crags?"

"No, no!" She shook her head. "I wandered off and headed east, spending time in the wasteland, traveling from town to town. I hooked up with some gun runners and we took up some business in the southern reaches. The gun runners taught me how to shoot and survive out in the wilds. One night, our camp was ambushed by highwaymen. We were overwhelmed, and everyone was killed – everyone except me. When the attack started, I ran off into the hills and hid until the battle was over. I waited until morning and then went back to camp. The highwaymen were gone, and had taken damn near everything, except some rifles. In the darkness, they had missed a crate of weapons. I took this gun and headed off. Since then, I have been making a living, hunting big game in the wasteland. You would be surprised how much money you can make off a giant Gila Monster skin." Carla spoke quickly and frantically, so quickly that it was almost hard for Globulus to keep up.

"That's a tall tale, young Carla."

"Yeah, I have been out here ever since, stalking around and hunting, honing my skills." Carla sighed as if something was bothering her.

Globulus picked up on her distress and prodded her further. "Are you troubled?"

"I am good at what I do. Damn good. But where I have great skill, I have little courage."

"I don't understand," the mighty mutant questioned.

"Three days ago, some travelers were passing through the boulder field where I found you. They were ambushed by a Biogtech patrol. None of them survived. I was scared and didn't help them. All I did was watch them get gunned down through the scope of my rifle." She shook her head in despair. Globulus remained silent, eyeing her with concern.

"I felt so ashamed, but didn't know what to do. When I kill something, it's usually some sort of beast that can't fight back. The scouting party, on the other hand, would kill me without a second thought. It took me the rest of the day to gather up the courage to do something about what I saw. I crept down the boulder field that same night. The priest was edgy; he could tell something was out in the darkness. He stalked around, staring out into the night, probing the darkness with his psychic powers. I concentrated so that the only thought in my mind would be that of a rock. I imagined that my body was a stone, a boulder. I concentrated without any other thought in my mind. Over and over I said to myself: '*I am a stone. I am a rock upon the hill.*' It threw off the Reaper Kai's senses, so I crept closer and closer. It took hours to get near enough for a solid shot. All the while, he was staring up the boulder field, suspicious. I let my breath grow even and I concentrated. I emptied my mind, and finally, the priest was unable to sense me. That's when I hit him, shot him dead at almost three hundred yards. With the priest dead, the Biogtechs were an easy kill. I wiped them out in a matter of minutes.   Since then, I've stationed myself up in the rocks, waiting for more scouting parties to come through. I know I can't win a war, but I didn't want any more innocent travelers to die needlessly." The young woman sighed and looked at Globulus with a serious look.

"I am glad you came to my aid," Globulus said in earnest. A silence passed between the two.   Globulus broke it with a spontaneous suggestion. "Why don't you come with me? Come with me to Rust Spire. With your skills, you would be a real asset in the coming war."

"I don't know…" Carla said in a dull tone. "I am not sure I have the stomach for it."

"Come on, you said it yourself. You have no home, no real purpose. Come with me. Help me gain the support of the Steel Crag Mining Guild."

She wavered, her eyes growing distant once more. "I get so damn lonely out here," she confessed, a sly smile beginning to sneak onto her face. "It would be good to have some company. I will go with you on one condition."

"What is it?" Globulus asked solemnly.

"You have to take a bath every once in a while. You stink

like a musty river!"

Growling, Globulus reached out to grab Carla, but she was too quick. "Remember, I can crush you like a grape, you damn brat."

Carla laughed, and the mutant hippo shook his head. Grimacing, Globulus finally conceded a smile.

"So what's your plan when you speak to the Protectorate?" Carla changed the subject.

"I haven't figured that out yet."

"Well, don't you think you should figure it out? Maybe before you're standing before him dumbfounded?" she started to ride him once again.

The mutant hippo's irritation level was beginning to increase drastically. The obnoxious Carla Reins was almost too much to handle. As he shook his head in disbelief at her tone, a whistle bellowed in the distance, and the clatter of machinery grew audible. Pushing along the train tracks was a coal fired locomotive. Pressing on from the east, it moved toward the companions.

As it neared, the whistle blew once again. The train slowed as the engine belched black smoke. The conductor was eyeing the two travelers upon the tracks and had slowed the engine considerably. Finally, the train ground to a halt.

"Ah, sweet Carla!" the conductor yelled, smiling at the young woman through his soot covered glasses. Carla waved back and smiled. "It has been months since I have seen you out here. You and your oversized friend there need a ride? It's a hell of a long walk, wherever you are headed. It's at least a day on foot to civilization."

"Thanks for stopping. A ride would be nice," Carla responded in a bright, cheery tone.

"Where you be headed, lass?" the conductor boomed back, his face covered in black filth from the coal fired engine.

"Rust Spire," Globulus answered.

"Fine, fine… I can take you as far as the Gold Road," the conductor agreed.

"You have my thanks," Globulus replied.

"Climb up onto one of the ore cars, and hurry, I have a deadline to make!" the conductor yelled at the companions.

Carla and Globulus did as the conductor asked, climbing aboard one of the ore cars. Just as soon as they had found a place to sit, the grinding of the locomotive sounded once more. With great strain, it moved forward slowly, so slowly that Globulus thought about getting off and pushing the damn train. In a matter of minutes, the train was chugging down the canyon, pushing closer and closer to the Gold Road.

"You ever been on a train before?" Carla quizzed Globulus.

His irritation was already beginning to mount. The mutant hippo knew that he was only a few moments away from another ridiculous, never-ending conversation with Carla. "No, I have never been on a train."

"That's really interesting. How is it that someone like yourself, someone from the Steel Crags, has never been on a train? How on earth did you ever get around these parts? I think a train ride is nice. Now we don't have to walk all that way." The young woman was already beginning to gab incessantly, and the mutant hippo was beginning to drift away. He let his thoughts wander and became drowsy. Slipping into a light slumber, Globulus napped in the noonday sun, resting in the ore car of the train. All the while, Carla continued to jabber away, even through the hippo was engulfed in the comfort of a nice, soothing slumber.

Chapter 31
The Legend of the Beastling, Globulus

The shadows flashed across his face. Globulus blinked several times and opened his eyes. The sunlight streamed into his consciousness. The train was still moving, pushing in a westerly direction through the canyon. The mighty hippo had fallen asleep inside one of the ore cars. Coal smoke wafted through his nostrils as sounds began to flood his ears. The pumping of the coal train's engine pounded into the dim haze of Globulus' mind. With a sigh, the mutant sat up and looked around.

"You're finally awake," Carla said in a chipper tone. Scrunching up his nose, the reality of his travels caught up with Globulus. The chattering nightmare was a reality, and its name was Carla Reins.

"Please spare me," he grumbled. "I am not in the mood for any more of your stories."

"Fine," Carla said, acting hurt. Actually, she didn't care, but was trying to drive the hippo over the edge once more. "I'll leave you alone, but you have to tell me a story instead."

"What a bargain..." Globulus boomed, shooting her a dirty look.

"Come on, you know *all* about me. Tell me a story about you."

"You promise that we can just sit here quietly the rest of the day if you get your story?"

"I do," she said with an impish smile.

With a loud sigh, Globulus grew calm and his gaze withdrew, becoming distant. Memories of his past rolled into his mind as he began to recount a tale, a story about his youth before he came to the city of Rasheed.

"I once lived in another place, before my time in Rasheed. Beyond the mountains, south of the Steel Crags, is a marshland fed by the spring run-off from the adjacent glaciers. My home was in that place, lost amongst the reeds and waterways. It was a wonderful home. My people were strong and filled with life… until…" A flash of tortured memories was flowing to the surface as young Carla watched in fascination. It was the most emotion she had seen in the mighty mutant thus far.

"The snows ceased to fall for an entire season. The Steel Crags were gripped by a drought. The once cool waters that cascaded off the mountains and fed our marshland, our home, ceased to flow. The heat of the desert was insatiable. Slowly, the burning heat pushed into our home. The once lush marsh was turned into a mud pit. Our crops failed, and my people were on the verge of ruin. Starvation gripped our tribe. Hundreds of my once proud brethren fell prey to hunger and passed into death. With a famine gripping our tribe, hope had failed." Globulus looked disheartened, and Carla was enthralled by the tale.

"Far away, beyond the harsh burning desert, a young king heard the plight of our people. That monarch was none other than King Toil of Rasheed. He was a young ruler, new to his throne, but his compassion was unmatched. With a gentle heart, King Toil sent shipments of food and provisions to stay the horrible famine in my village. The supplies were eagerly welcomed, but came too late for some…" Almost in a whisper he spoke, emotion choking his speech with sorrow. "My mother was so kind. In the hard times, she refused to eat, preferring to give her ration of food to me and my siblings. By the time food arrived from Rasheed, it was too late for my mother. She had slipped into unconsciousness and never woke again. The ultimate sacrifice had been made so that her children could survive." A tear rolled down the hippo's cheek. "I was very young at the time…"

Carla had tears in her own eyes and reached out to comfort Globulus. With a grumble, he pulled away from her. The mighty hippo did not take sympathy very well.

"The shipments of food from King Toil stayed the famine. Our fragile people subsisted until the rains, the blessed rains, finally arrived. For nearly two weeks, a series of violent storms rolled over the Steel Crags, flooding the mountain streams. The water rushed from the mountains, filling the marshlands once more. The battered plants, dried out nearly to death, sprung to life once more, and the brown, sun-blasted marsh was rekindled. The lush green splash of life erupted once more. My people were saved and the drought was transformed into a painful memory for my tribe."

The mighty mutant let out another sigh. It had been a long time since the hippo had talked about such things. Feeling comfortable around young Carla had allowed him to open up about his past.

"The drought had ended, but had cost our tribe much. Hundreds of my people had starved to death. Burying their strife, my people rejoiced and embraced King Toil as their savior. Vowing to aid the King and offering a life-long debt to Toil, my people offered their very lives to serve the compassionate king of Rasheed. Toil, in his wisdom refused such a debt of service. Instead, he asked for only one thing..." Globulus shook his head in despair. "King Toil asked for the largest male child of the tribe as payment for his kind deeds. The chief of the tribe selected me to be given to King Toil. I was very young, only eight years of age."

"Amazing. So that is how you came to serve the kingdom of Rasheed."

Globulus nodded. "King Toil welcomed me into his family with open arms. Over the years, I was trained in combat and came to serve the king as his warmaster and bodyguard. His kindness and leadership made me feel like part of his family. King Toil was more than just my king; he was my father."

"I was sorry to hear about the fall of Rasheed," Carla said in earnest. As she spoke a flash of anger rolled through him.

"That traitorous witch of a daughter, Marion, was responsible for his death. King Toil died at the hands of a hired assassin, and Rasheed fell to into the clutches of the Reaper Kai."

"Is this your first time back to the Steel Crags?" Carla asked the mighty mutant.

The hippo warrior answered with a look of reservation. "Yes. I have dreaded this trip back home my entire life."

"Why?" Carla asked, prodding yet again.

"My tribe cast me out as a youth. It's not an easy prospect to return home after such a thing. I have lacked the courage to face my past. I have been hoping to avoid it all my years."

"Your tribe made a hard choice, but they didn't cast you out. Everything that you have learned and everything that you have seen has made you stronger. It was a hard choice to cast out one of their own, but they did it to honor King Toil. You said it yourself: Toil was a compassionate king. It was an honor that you were sent to Rasheed, not a curse."

"Whether it be a curse or an honor, it's a long road home, one that I am too weak to walk," Globulus admitted in a somber tone.

"Some day, you will walk that road," she responded in an empowering tone.

The mighty hippo smiled warmly at Carla. The young woman smiled back at her companion, still basking in the warmth of the sun. The train whistled as the black coal smoke belched from the stack. The screeching of metal sounded and the locomotive came grinding to halt along the tracks.

"Gold Road!" the conductor boomed.

"Guess that's our stop," Globulus said as he jumped down from the ore car. Following the mutant hippo, Carla jumped down as well. The duo had reached the Gold Road, a series of tunnels and mineshafts that led through the heart of the mountains to the city of Rust Spire, a city which had drawn the focus of the enemy, and was currently the target of a full scale invasion.

Chapter 32
Seeds of Ruin

Holding her breath, Sister Nightshade fell into a light meditation. Her eyes rolled back into her head, exposing ghastly, gelatinous white eyeballs, wreathed in a crimson mass of pulsing blood vessels. As she quivered, her eyes vibrated violently within the sockets. The sinister Reaper Kai priestess began to shiver and shake. Her skin and body convulsed wildly and energy seeped from her twisted mind. A wave of deception flowed from her. Marion stared at her with an intent look of surprise. Right before the queen's eyes, Nightshade began to transform.

Where there were once pustules and pox upon her face, the blemishes of pestilence had now receded, leaving smooth, healthy skin. The cracks on her lips which dripped a constant flow of blood closed, and her lips became full of life. No longer did mucous drip from her eyes; instead, a youthful vigor flowed into her. The plague had gone out of her. Sister Nightshade, once twisted by the diseases she had so lovingly cultivated, was no longer marked by such evidence of her evil deeds. Her appearance was that of a vivacious, young, and beautiful woman.

Queen Marion reeled back as the transformation took hold.

"You have grown young!" Marion gasped as she placed her hand on her chest. The thought of eternal life had sparked a greedy interest in the traitorous Toil.

"I have not grown young. My powers are not what you think. You see me as young and beautiful; that is the extent of my power. My actual body is still withered, but my powers make you *think* I have grown young. It is nothing more than tricking your mind into seeing what I want you to see," Nightshade hissed softly, her face still radiating beauty. Marion Toil gasped. Such power to disguise one's self was a potent ability. "We can now attempt to pass into the city."

Marion stood dumbfounded before Sister Nightshade.

Where there was once a haggard, misshapen witch, there was now a vision of loveliness.

"Get rid of your robes. We will change into the clothes of commoners to pass into the city. I do not want anyone to suspect us of any mischief," Nightshade ordered, already removing her crimson gown of evil.

With that, the two women disrobed, hiding the crimson garb near the side of road, behind a line of bushes. Dressing hastily, they donned long skirts and flowery blouses with long sleeves. After the change of clothes, the two sinister Reaper Kai looked like ordinary peasants.

"Do not roll up your sleeves for any reason. If anyone suspects our heritage and sees your tattoos, we will not likely escape the city alive." When Nightshade spoke, the hiss in her voice was gone. A crisp, bouncy tone had replaced her habitual rasping speech.

"Amazing..." Marion whispered, hearing her voice change as well. The powers of Nightshade were formidable indeed. "Why can't I see through your illusion? I should be immune to the powers of *our* kind. Your psychic abilities should not affect me."

"How arrogant you are, child!" The hiss had returned once more and there was a flash of anger in Nightshade's eyes. "Father Vertigo is the patron and I the matron of our race. The darkness grants expanded capabilities based upon our servitude. A balance must exist so we can cleanse our people of lesser subjects. Without absolute power at the head of our order, chaos would reign. The lesser priests would squabble and bicker over pointless exploits, while the real goal of our masters would go unnoticed. Father Vertigo and I are that balance. Our powers are absolute, and the lesser subjects still tremble under our fist. Those that do not conform are cleansed by death. There is only one will, *our* will." Nightshade fixed her eyes upon Toil, her hatred building. Her presence was intimidating, and Marion backed down immediately, remembering all too well how quickly the order was issued for her torture in the dungeons of Rasheed. Young Toil would be respectful, for now.

"Let's be on our way. We need to pass into Rust Spire before nightfall. The gates are closed after sunset, and I do not want to spend another night out here in the frigid air of the Steel Crags." With that, Nightshade moved forward, a vision of loveliness, with the equally gorgeous Queen Marion close behind.

Passing out of the hills, the two women found themselves upon an ancient concrete road pressing westward down a shallow ravine. The sun was edging toward the western horizon. Shadows of the coming night were drawing into the ravine. Casting long patches of darkness, the shadows increased in size, engulfing the two women upon the road. Pressing on quicker, with a sense of urgency, the two travelers fought and raced the setting sun.

At last, the ravine twisted hard into a hairpin curve, which nearly wrapped around itself inside the narrow gorge. With quick movements, Nightshade and Marion reached the bottom of the ancient road and stared in awe at the sight before them.

A bridge, an ancient monstrosity from before the apocalypse, stretched out before them. Steel girders, corroded but still strong, rose upward into the air, more than a thousand feet above the base of the bridge. Cables arched downwards from the girders, bolted into the base of the bridge. The concrete structure sprawled over a large expanse, a void several thousand feet above the floor of the desert. The bridge was situated at the western edge of the Steel Crag range and crossed over a chasm, an enormous canyon below. The other end of the bridge was a chain of jagged mountain peaks which were smaller than the Steel Crag mountain range, running about ten miles in length and known as the Giant's Spine. Situated upon these jagged peaks and hollows in the rock face was a city, a mighty city almost as old as the Darken Realm itself.

Rust Spire, the capital of the Steel Crag Mining Guild, was located upon the Giant's Spine mountain range. The central portion of the city was situated at the end of the massive suspension bridge spanning the deep gorge between the Steel Crag mountains and the Giant's Spine. The local inhabitants of Rust Spire had dubbed the suspension bridge leading to the city the Giant's Arm.

The doors of the city opened directly onto the ancient bridge.

Tall, thick steel walls surrounded its main square. In the dim light, growing increasingly duskier, the walls of the city were a faint red, an oxidized rust color, a result of having stood for centuries, slowly corroded by nature. These walls were a monument to geometry. They met at perfect right angles, giving the entire city a rectangular feel. It looked as if a child had built the entire town by stacking wooden blocks together. The box-like appearance of the city sitting atop the chaotic, natural mountain range of sharp protrusions was an unsettling sight, one which made the city look out of place.

Just beyond the main gate was the central courtyard, the commerce district of the city, nestled against the sheer rock face of the Giant's Spine. The district housed several inns, dining halls, taverns, and shops selling a variety of wares. Branching off from the main square were a series of twisting stairwells and buildings constructed upon the jagged rock face of the Giant's Spine. Workshops and houses clung precariously to the steep rocky slope. The twisting stairwells followed fissures in the rock face, leading to the different buildings and hidden pockets of civilization. To the imaginative, the city of Rust Spire was a giant, three-dimensional maze built atop a mountain range.

The very top of the Giant's Spine was still covered in snow. An enormous palace, constructed of oxidized, rust-covered towers and steel plating, was built in the snow- capped reaches of the tallest peak in the Giant's Spine. This palace was the home of the Protectorate, the leader of the ruling house of the Steel Crag Mining Guild. The Protectorate was a title handed down from one generation to the next, and always kept within the ruling family. The Protectorate of the Steel Crag Mining Guild reported to an elected council of nobles and wealthy families. Together, the council of nobles and the Protectorate ran the city, a regimen which had been maintained for countless generations.

The Protectorate was one of the most powerful individuals in the entire Darken Realm. The Steel Crag Mining Guild operated a gigantic series of mines, oil wells, and petroleum refineries. The guild effectively produced the majority of the resources in the southern reaches. Their wealth and power were legendary. Their meddling in other kingdoms and nations was also well known. It was not uncommon for a wealthy family from the ruling council to bankroll a city official or nobleman in another province. The Steel Crag Guild's influence extended into almost every town, province, and kingdom in the land. It was even rumored that several military officials from other powerful armies were in the secret clutches of the Protectorate, controlled by him completely and influencing policy on his behalf. With their tendrils in every affair that could turn a profit, the Steel Crag Mining Guild controlled the western reaches of the Darken Realm, the very edge of the world, bordering the great wastelands.

Nightshade and Marion looked out at the city of Rust Spire across the ancient suspension bridge. The sun had almost set, and the two were still hurrying toward the gates of the city. Rushing across the mighty bridge held high above the gorge below, the two reached the gates just before sundown.

"You're just in time, ladies. You know better than to come back this late. You are lucky – we're just about to close the gates down for the night," a city guard brandishing an assault rifle spoke gruffly to the disguised Reaper Kai priestesses.

"Yes, we are *very* lucky." Nightshade smiled through her psychic disguise. The guard smiled back and they passed through the gates of Rust Spire. As they passed, the enormous doors swung shut, sealing the city off from the frost filled night drawing near.

Marion and Nightshade found themselves in the grand courtyard at the base of the Giant's Spine mountains. The courtyard was surrounded on all sides by the rust tinted, corroding city walls. Wooden buildings housing shops and inns clung to the interior walls.

"We should get a room for the night," Nightshade ordered, and Marion followed closely in her tracks. The two made their way into a nearby inn, guided by the sounds of drunken laughter and smoke pouring from the interior. Grubby men, covered in dirt and grime, were packed into the inn's dining hall, drinking strong beers and cursing loudly. The peasants of the Steel Crag Guild were typically miners, working east of the city in one of the great quarries or tunnels of the Gold Road.

Marion and Nightshade moved over to the front desk and a thin, lanky man eyed them oddly, his eyes passing over their bodies with a frightening, hungry look. Licking his lips, the innkeeper spoke to the women. "What can I get you two ladies this night?" His eyes sparkled as he looked them up and down once more.

"We need a room." Marion spoke in a direct tone, not liking the way in which he was looking at them one bit.

"We are all full for the night... but I got a special, just for you two fine ladies. For no fee, you can share my room this evening," the creepy innkeeper leered, lust flaring in his glassy eyes.

Nightshade had a twisted look upon her face. With a smile, she spoke to the innkeeper. "That sounds lovely. Let's have a look at your room right now. I want to get cozy for the evening."

The innkeeper smiled as nasty, wild fantasies took shape in his lurid imagination. "Right... this... way." He urged them to follow him into the back of the inn.

The grubby innkeeper pressed into his private quarters and the two ladies followed. As he shut the door behind them, Nightshade spoke in an eerie tone. "This will do nicely." The sound of steel clearing a scabbard echoed in the room. Sister Nightshade had drawn a dagger. The unsuspecting innkeeper never knew what hit him. The sinister Reaper Kai moved in behind him and covered his mouth with one hand, as she took the dagger in her other hand and plunged it into the innkeeper's neck. He struggled at first, trying to scream, but to no avail; Nightshade was strangely strong. Within a few seconds, the innkeeper ceased to stir and fell limp in Nightshade's grip. Throwing the dead innkeeper to the floor, Nightshade smiled with a sinister look upon her face. The twisted Reaper Kai had once again proved a theory:

Those who are evil always take care of their own.

Marion jumped back in alarm. The death of the innkeeper was so quick and brutal that it unnerved the young Queen. Nightshade was undaunted by her sinister act. She had slain a person on a whim and was none too sorry about the act. Without a second thought, she stepped over the dead innkeeper and approached

Marion. Startled, the young Queen stepped back in fright.

"Let's head into the city. Now that we have a room for the night, we can carry out our mission. Before the sun rises, the water supply of Rust Spire will be tainted with this!" Nightshade pulled a steel tube from her belongings. Stroking it lovingly, her disguise faded. The boils erupted once more upon her face. Blood seeped from cracks in her lips. Pus dripped from her eyes. Wrinkles sprung forth on her face likes cracks upon a shattered mirror. Her visage grew ill as she looked lovingly upon the steel tube in her hands. "This plague should do nicely. With the water supply contaminated, the citizens of this city will be on the verge of death as our glorious army reaches the front gates. They will not be able to withstand our might!" Hissing, she smiled, and Marion shrunk back further from her.

With a calm breath, Nightshade continued to smile as the disguise of a young woman washed over her form once again. Within seconds, the vision of death disappeared, and the lovely visage of youth returned. Concealing the steel tube containing the deadly disease, Nightshade prepared to head out into the city of Rust Spire.

"The seeds of victory will be planted this night. Take notice, young Marion: this is how you win a war." With a sneer, Sister Nightshade pushed out of the inn room, passing into the night with the traitorous Marion Toil in her wake. Their goal was the city water supply. With a glimmer of pure evil racing through their hearts, the two Reaper Kai priestesses intended to contaminate the drinking water of Rust Spire with a virulent pestilence. With any luck, half the citizens of Rust Spire would be dead by the time the Biogtech army arrived.

Chapter 33
The Great Plague

The air was chilled and moist. A deep fog had settled about the Steel Crag range. Swirling forward, the wall of fog rolled amongst the snow covered peaks. Globulus and Carla had not spoken a word in over an hour. They had pushed out from the Gold Road and were drawing near Rust Spire. The entire journey was filled with a deep anxiety. The voyage through the Gold Road had been strange. They had not seen a single person in the entire expanse of tunnels or mines. With gold and iron being the lifeblood of the Guild, it was strange that no one was working in the mines. It was quiet, too quiet, which had unsettled the mighty mutant hippo and the usually bubbly Carla. Both knew something was not right.

The fog was rolling across the great gorge in between the Steel Crags and the Giant's Spine. As it reached the gorge, the fog fell downward into the deep pit. It almost looked as if the mist was pouring off the mountains into the gorge. The only place that held the fog was the mighty suspension bridge made by the ancients.

The duo had taken up a defensive position at the base of the giant suspension bridge. Neither felt comfortable charging across the open, unprotected bridge without first gaining some information about the strangely quiet city ahead. Globulus eyed Carla and motioned her toward him, whispering, "Take your scope and have a look across the bridge. Let me know what you see."

Carla crouched down, as did Globulus, both scanning the territory ahead of them in the fog. They were concealed upon a rock outcropping just above the concrete roadway. Pulling the mighty sniper rifle to her shoulder, Carla peered through its scope. As her eyes scanned back and forth, the wisps of fog constantly clouded her vision. Swirling about, the fog obscured most of the city ahead, and she only managed to gain fleeting glimpses of its front gates. Shaking her head in concern, she dropped the rifle from her shoulder and spoke to Globulus in a whisper. "The front gate is open, but there are no guards. I have been here hundreds of times and the front gates are always manned by troops. I don't like this."

"I don't like it either. I have a lump in my stomach and it's getting bigger. This is the same way I felt on the night Rasheed fell. Evil is at work." The mutant hippo spoke in concern. "Be on your guard, young Carla."

Globulus drew his brace of shotguns, palming them like a pair of pistols. With hesitation, the mighty hippo took a step forward into the fog, placing one foot on the edge of the ancient suspension bridge. Carla followed close behind with her own weapon ready, eyes scanning the fog. The only sound in evidence was their own footsteps on the cold concrete bridge, echoing in the dense fog. Globulus's heart began to quicken, his pulse racing; his fear was mounting as he took each step forward. Nothing greeted them except for more indecision. It was as if Rust Spire had been abandoned. Carla brought the weapon closer to her shoulder as her hazel eyes scanned the barren city ahead.

It took several minutes to cross the bridge, an interval that seemed like hours. Pushing out of the thick fog clinging to the bridge, Globulus and Carla found themselves at the front gates. One of the two mighty steel doors was standing ajar, allowing passage into the city. "Here we go," Globulus whispered, and Carla nodded back with a staunch look of concern.

The duo moved into the city. The courtyard, the main business district of Rust Spire, was devoid of life. Nothing stirred, no sounds could be heard. Globulus motioned to an adjacent building hiding in the dense fog, apparently housing an inn. Carla ran softly across the giant courtyard and took up a position behind some wooden barrels lining an alleyway. The young sniper trained her weapon on the front door of the inn. Globulus held his weapons at the ready and moved toward the door. With a mighty kick, the mutant smashed through the door and rushed inside.

Bursting inside quickly, Globulus stumbled over something in the dim light of the inn. Crashing to the ground, he rolled over quickly, feeling terror overtake him. The stench of death wafted through his nostrils. Rotting flesh filled his nose. The smell was so overpowering, he had to fight to control himself, struggling to avoid retching. Surveying the dark inn, a horror filled his view. Dozens and dozens of corpses were piled inside the building. Horrible sores and bloody boils covered their flesh. None of them stirred. Retreating like a frightened child, Globulus crawled back across the floor with wild-eyed fright. As he crawled, he found what he had tripped over. A man, with pus-filled eyes still open, was looking at the ceiling. Rigor mortis had taken the corpse, its face covered by bloody boils. A scream filled him, and he could not restrain it. Scrambling out of the inn, Globulus let out a frightful yell. Carla almost shot the fleeing hippo as he burst from the inn.

Retreating even further away, Globulus fought the bile rising in his throat, forcing the horrid smell from his lungs.

Carla rushed to his side in alarm. "What is it?" she quizzed, secretly yearning *not* to know the answer.

"They are all dead..." he gasped. "The inn is piled with dead bodies all covered in sores and boils. It looks like some sort of plague has erupted in Rust Spire. I fear pestilence has taken this city."

She looked on, horrified. It was now evident why the city was so eerie. Not wanting any part of the corpses piled in the inn, Carla backed away while spinning around in the fog, feeling as if something was watching her. With spine tingling and goose flesh rising on her arms, she fought the fright that was building in her mind. A plague, a horrid disease, had ravaged her own home years ago. The fragile minded sniper was not prepared to face a similar horror, especially one of such magnitude.

"Let me collect my thoughts," Globulus whispered, forcing the gruesome sight from his mind. The fresh, crisp air was filling his lungs, replacing the stench of rotting flesh. "Let's push onward. *Someone* had to have survived..."

"Let's just go, right now." The young sniper spoke in a frightened tone.

"We need to get to the palace. We must find the Protectorate immediately, and locate any survivors. With this plague in the city and the enemy marching on us as we speak, hope is fading fast."

Carla agreed with haunted reservation. "Follow me. I think the palace is this way."

The duo pushed into the heart of the city quickly, passing an endless series of silent homes and abandoned shops. Minute after minute went by and there were no signs of life. Globulus had a grim look on his face. He was beginning to believe that no one had survived the plague.

His mind began to play tricks on him. Out of the corner of his eye, the mighty mutant thought he caught a glimpse of movement. When he turned to confront the vision, it would vanish in the swirling fog. The mist and shadows were becoming a new enemy, which hindered their progress and filled them with a deeper dread.

Pressing into the maze of passages and curving streets, the duo ascended twisting stairwells, snaking upwards through the city. Many moments passed as they struggled in the mist, until, finally, Carla and Globulus found themselves in front of the palace. The gates had been sealed from within, barring passage into the courtyard. Carla and Globulus stood before the gates and looked at each other in despair.

"Hello?" the mutant hippo yelled.

Silence was the only response.

"Is there anyone here?" Carla yelled at the gates.

Another eerie quiet followed. Globulus looked at Carla with concern. He was convinced the entire city was dead.

Finally, a weak, distraught voice responded. "This place is doomed. Flee while you can!"

"Where are you?" Globulus yelled back.

A form emerged at the top of the gates. The man was moving slowly, evidently struggling. The face peering out from the fog was covered in bloody boils. He coughed softly and looked down from high atop the gate. "The only ones left are holed up here, inside the palace."

"I am Globulus of Rasheed, and this is Carla of the outlands. We bring news for the Protectorate. We seek his council immediately," the hippo yelled up at the guard.

"Leave while you can, spare yourselves this horrid fate," the guard replied. At the end of his speech, he fell into a fit of coughing, blood and mucous dripping from his open mouth.

"We have traveled far, and must be allowed to speak with him."

"So be it, fool, but I fear you will fall ill as well, and suffer a similar fate." As the guard spoke, the gates to the palace opened with a creak.

Globulus and Carla moved inside. In the thick mist, forms shambled about, coughing softly in the darkness. The courtyard was littered with hundreds of sick and dying victims of the virulent plague ravaging the city. The horde was huddled around makeshift campfires, trying to stay warm. Radiating an air of despair, the afflicted citizens turned their eyes to the newcomers with hatred. The duo was untouched by sickness, and each infected soul envied their condition with frightening anger. Globulus pushed on without giving the sick a second look; he knew better than to look upon them. Carla, on the other hand, was oddly fascinated by the scene. With hurried, quick glances, she took in the masses with heartfelt compassion. The infected looked back with a mixture of silent pleas and venomous hatred. Finally, Carla looked away, only allowing herself to keep her eyes upon the mighty hippo heading into the palace.

The palace of the Protectorate was enormous, and revealed itself to be another scene of agony. Thousands of additional ill people were littering the bottom floor of the palace. Cries of agony abounded. Globulus refused to look at the afflicted, and moved forward with a resolute look on his face. He had been in the palace before, years ago, when King Toil conducted a diplomatic visit to the Protectorate. Making haste, the duo reached the gold inlaid doors of the throne room.

Globulus pushed open the doors to the throne room of the Protectorate, but was ill prepared for what he found. Upon the mighty throne was the Protectorate of the city, lord and ruler of the Steel Crag Mining Guild. His lifeless body had already begun to spoil upon the throne. A wail of anguish echoed in the grand room. A ten year old boy was crouched before the throne, crying in despair. Sadness and madness both had taken the youth. With the Protectorate dead, the ruler of the city was this small boy, lost in grief, crying in the lap of his dead father.

Globulus shook his head in disgust. "Reaper Kai treachery…" It was just like Rasheed. An army of enemy troops was about to lay siege on the city, and the leadership was dead. The scenario was too similar to the fate of Rasheed to be a mere coincidence. Half of the population was dead, and the other half was on the verge of death.

"Globulus, what do we do? This city is lost. The army of the enemy will be here within days. No one here is in any condition to fight." Carla spoke in dismay, fighting back the tears as she watched the frightened boy before his dead father.

A moment of silence passed between the two. Wailing in anguish, the young boy tugged at his father, dead upon the throne. Shaking his head, his anger rising, Globulus knew that he had to do something.

"I cannot let another tragedy rip this land. I will not abandon this city to the enemy. No matter what happens, we must find a way to fight the Reaper Kai marching on this city." A flash of anger illuminated the mutant's eyes as he spoke.

"Fight them?" Carla said in shock. "How? You and me? Fight an entire army?"

"What's more powerful than an army of human soldiers defending this city?"

"I don't know. What are you getting at?"

"An army of *my* kind," Globulus said in a resolute tone.

"Your kind? They're so far from here. I am not sure we can reach the village in time. Will your people even fight?"

"We have got to try. It's our only option. I cannot let another empire fall. I cannot allow this," Globulus said in a rage of frustration, smacking his fist into the palm of his hand. "Come on, Carla, we don't have a moment to waste."

Globulus and Carla moved out of the throne room of the

Protectorate. As the doors shut behind them, the small boy let out a horrid wail, lying at the feet of his dead father, a once strong and powerful man who could have defended the populace against the army of Biogtech soldiers now marching in on the plague-ridden city of Rust Spire.

Chapter 34
The Crushing-Fist Tribe

Running forward, making haste, knowing every minute was precious, Globulus and Carla bounded along the old worn trail that had taken them out of the heart of the Steel Crag range into lush and fertile lands just south of the great mountains.

The companions took a brief moment to stop at the base of a thundering waterfall to refill their canteens. The mighty waterfall descended thousands of feet, crashing against the rocks with a spray of white mist. In the heat of the day, the mist from the falls was refreshing. A pool of water collected at the base of the mighty falls, filled with an icy chill liberated from the snowfields of the Steel Crags.

Carla, who had removed her sniper suit due to the heat, and was now dressed in standard military issue combat fatigues, crouched near the cold water, filling her canteen. The paint on her face had been removed early in the day when it became blistering hot in the foothills of the mountains. Now that the war paint had been removed, her face displayed delicate features, with a nose hooked slightly upwards. Her short brown hair fell so that it nearly covered her ears and the base of her neck. She had childlike features and a gently whimsical look upon her face; it almost seemed as if she was smiling all the time, her warm eyes bright and cheery.

Globulus was exhausted. He filled his canteen, then jumped into the cold water rolling off the mountains. With a jolt, the icy water hit his travel-worn body. Swimming around like a natural, the hippo dove deep into the pool and then surfaced once more. With a gasp, his nostrils flared as his head emerged from the water.

Carla was smiling as she watched the beastly hippo swim about the pool. "You are keeping your end of the bargain. You were beginning to stink!" she giggled.

The dip in the pool was refreshing. The hippo now had the

fortitude to continue onward. "Let's get moving. We have but a little further to go, if memory serves me well."

The companions recovered their gear and made haste once more toward the village of Marsh Falls, leaving the shadow of the mountains far behind. Pushing away from the soothing waterfall, the trail descended rapidly into a flooded valley. Dozens of streams and waterfalls rolled out of the mountains and hills, fed by snow and spring rains. The streams converged in a low spot just below the foothills. The result was a flooding effect that turned the entire area into an enormous marshland, lush and green for miles and miles. It was in these lands that the tribe of the Crushing-Fist, the tribe that gave birth to Globulus, made its home.

The rocky hillside was gone. The land was plunging rapidly into the flooded, lush valley. Green plants emerged from the waters of the marsh and rose skyward, catching the rays of the sun. Miles of waterways snaked amongst small islands of soggy mud, covered with wild grasses. Large, spiky trees, a mutant variety, clung to the edge of the marshlands, acting as a natural fence, holding back the world beyond. Just past the perimeter of the marsh was open desert. On the western edge of the marsh, a dense line of dead trees, choked by the sand, held back the dunes from smothering the fertile wetlands. The ecosystem in the region was extremely fragile; slight changes in the environment could lead to an ecological disaster, plunging the wetlands into utter ruin.

Globulus and Carla kept up their frantic pace, quickly reaching the end of the trail. Standing dumfounded, young Carla looked at the deep waterways with despair. The water was too deep for her to wade through, and the vegetation was too dense to swim through effectively.

"Now what?" she whined.

Globulus sighed and shook his head at the dumbfounded Carla. Pulling his weapons aside and placing any gear he didn't want soaked into his backpack, the mighty hippo started to wade into the deep water. Crouching down, Globulus got on all fours like a beast and eyed Carla with a strange look.

"Climb on my back," the hippo instructed Carla.

"Seriously?"

The mutant did not respond; he only looked at her with a dubious look on his face. With a broad smile, Carla mounted the mighty hippo, climbing onto his back while giggling.

"Get moving!" Carla laughed while kicking the hippo lightly in the ribs as a one would spur a horse forward.

"Knock it off or I will drown you," the hippo grumbled. With a graceful push, they were off. He swam magnificently through the waterway, and soon, they were making excellent time.

"Tell me about your people, Globulus, about this valley, about their way of life. I have heard of this valley all my life, but never imagined coming here," Carla said in a dreamy tone as she rode upon his back.

Taking several deep breaths and extending his head out of the water as they traveled, the hippo collected his thoughts and began to spin a tale about the valley of his birth.

"Our tribe was born out of mystery. Our oldest legends, dozens of generations old, speak of the Progenitors, a wise and powerful race of people who were said to be as powerful as the Gods. It is whispered in our legends that the Progenitors knew the secrets of life itself. It is said that from their wisdom and knowledge of ancient science, they could create life from vats of chemicals. Our people are all descendants of forty mighty hippos. These mighty hippos had no knowledge of their parents. Not a single one of them could remember being raised by other hippos. Instead, it is whispered in our legends, this race of super humans who survived the apocalypse raised all forty of our ancestors in pens and cages. When all forty reached their teenage years, they were set loose in the wilds of the earth. Under the direction of one of the Progenitors, they traveled here, to this valley, and began the mighty Crushing-Fist Clan. Our tribe has no Gods. Instead, once a year, when this great valley floods, we hold a ceremony to pay homage to the Progenitors, our creators." Globulus recounted the tale and Carla was enthralled.

"So none of these original forty hippos had any knowledge of their parents? Don't you think that is strange? It's almost like none of your ancestors were ever born." Carla was mystified.

Globulus laughed. "Indeed. According to our legends, the Progenitors gave us life. Another part of our legends, passed down through the generations, tells of other mutant animal species spawned from the holy ruins of Godhome. These legends also tell of other animal species that had hands like a human, walked on two legs, and had enough intellect to speak. Many in our tribe believe that we were created by the Progenitors, just like all other animal mutant species that inhabit the Darken Realm."

Carla was amazed by the mythical tale as she rode upon the hippo's back. "I have never heard such a story. What about this Godhome, these ruins, do you know where they are?"

"Their location has been lost in the passage of time. Most of the mutant animal species of the Darken Realm live in a pattern, almost like a circle. It is rumored the ruins of Godhome are somewhere in the center of all the mutant tribes."

Globulus fell silent as something caught his eye. Just ahead, along the waterway, were three figures, all very similar to Globulus but much smaller in size. The mutant hippo trio had not yet taken notice of young Carla and Globulus; instead, they were concentrating on collecting plants. Standing in the waterway, the hippos worked diligently, cutting reeds from one of the small muddy islands. The trio was harvesting a crop of dew weeds, a sugary plant that grew abundantly in the wetlands. A giant net was already filled with a clutch of dew weed.

A tremor of fear rolled through Globulus. These were *his* people, his race. It had been a lifetime since he had seen another of his kind. Shaking with hesitation, Globulus stopped his advance, eyeing the trio of hippos before him with reservation. A knot formed in his stomach. Carla sensed his distress and patted him on the back. "It will be fine. Don't worry."

One of the trio turned around suddenly, staring in amazement at Globulus. The village of Marsh Falls was small: only about ten thousand inhabitants lived in the region. The hippo farmer looked oddly at Globulus; he had never seen the warmaster of Rasheed before. Concerned, the harvesting hippo alerted his two companions, and all three eyed Globulus with suspicion, as if they were looking at a ghost.

"Greetings, my countrymen," Globulus said with his heart pounding. The homecoming was truly uncomfortable.

They simply stared back. The village of Marsh Falls was small enough to ensure that everyone knew everybody. This hippo before them was an outsider, and his presence put them on edge. Not knowing whether to trust him or not, one of the workers quizzed him. "Where did you swim in from? I have never seen you before."

"I am Globulus of Rasheed," he responded hesitantly. His mind was screaming to simply flee, swim away as fast as he could.

"Globulus? The beastling given to blessed King Toil all those years ago?" The suspicious hippo spoke in surprise. Hearing the name of King Toil put Globulus at ease. King Toil had rescued the tribe years ago from starvation, and his kindness was not easily forgotten.

"The very same," he responded.

The hippos were equally set at ease. They swam over and greeted Globulus and young Carla.

"Your father will be pleased with your return," one of the hippos said earnestly. "It has been a great many years since you left."

Globulus was silent. It had been a long time indeed. More than twenty years had passed since he was given to King Toil's house. It would surely be an uneasy homecoming.

"Follow us," one of the hippos said in an excited tone. The homecoming of the child sent to Rasheed as payment for their act of compassion was a legendary day for the tribe, and all three of the hippo farmers were excited. It would, without a doubt, be a day long remembered.

With that, all four of the hippos moved off toward the village, with Carla still riding upon Globulus. It took but a few minutes for the company of hippos to reach an island in the middle of the marsh. Smiling, Globulus rose from the water and surveyed his home from so long ago. Many of the residents were stunned. None had ever seen the mighty hippo before, and his size was unnerving. Globulus was so enormous that the warriors guarding the edge of the island backed away with hesitant looks. For where tender feasts of fine grasses from the marsh had bulged their bodies with fat, Globulus rippled with muscle; he was an impressive sight.

The guards gasped and looked on in awkward suspicion. Seeing the alarm in their eyes, one of the farmer hippos spoke immediately to alleviate the tension. "This is Globulus of Rasheed!"

"Globulus?" They looked on in awe. All in the village knew that long ago, Globulus had been given to the kingdom of Rasheed as a gift of gratitude for King Toil's compassion.

The word spread quickly throughout Marsh Falls. It wasn't every day they had visitors, and even more miraculous was a visitor of legend, the beastling sent to live in Rasheed. The entire village converged upon Globulus and a curious mob formed. The town was enthralled by his return. He didn't know what to think. Globulus had been dreading this return, and he had put it off for years, feeling that he would be viewed as an outsider. Contrary to his expectations, the village received him with open arms.

Smiling in contentment, Globulus looked around at his people receiving him so lovingly. If he could blush, he would have been doing so.

Urgency suddenly took over; he remembered their frantic quest, and was resolved to locate the chief of Marsh Falls. One of the guards moved through the crowd and stood before Globulus. "Your father, the chief, has asked for your company."

"The chief is your father?" Carla asked in a confused tone. A chill shot down her spine. The homecoming would be tense indeed. Long ago, it was the chief of Marsh Falls who had made the decision which male child would be sent to Rasheed as payment for King Toil's generosity. The chief had chosen his own son as payment. Carla shook her head in amazement. Globulus simply looked at her with tension upon his face.

A silence spread through the crowd. Globulus was uneasy, and his face displayed this feeling with a grim expression. It had been years since he had seen his father. A mixture of emotions was rising to the surface. Globulus had lived a fortunate existence in Rasheed, but he had always felt some resentment about being sent to live away from his people. The members of the crowd could see his pain and they looked at him with compassion. The crowd moved away, allowing Globulus to pass. Carla smiled up at him and he looked back with hesitation and fear in his eyes. Sighing, his breath became erratic. He was nervous and took a shaky step forward. Moving slowly, his mind swimming with wild thoughts, he progressed toward the giant lodge in the center of the village. He stopped at the entryway and turned back. The crowd was still silent as they looked at him; many of them nodded at him, urging him to enter the lodge of the chief.

Globulus moved into the lodge. It was handsomely decorated with animal pelts and finely crafted wooden statues. The interior was dark, but at the center was a fire pit with glowing embers from a dying fire. Memories of his childhood filled him. The lodge was his home as a child, before being sent to live in Rasheed. Trembling, stunned with emotion, his heart pounding, Globulus moved inside, searching for his father.

"Is that you?" A voice sounded in the darkness. It turned into a boom. "Is that my boy?"

Globulus sensed movement in the darkness. A hippo dressed in animal hides moved forward. His skin was coppery brown and had seen the marks of war. Great scars covered his body. His eyes were small, narrow, and worn with responsibility. Though not as tall as Globulus, Chief Stoneskin was an impressive presence, with a sturdy frame and thick muscles.

Squinting in the dark, he moved forward and stood before his son. A smile covered his great, toothy maw. Tears welled in his eyes, breaking the confines of his eyelids, rolling down his cheeks. Clutching Globulus, his father gripped him tightly and hugged him. Globulus stood silently, not reciprocating the affection. A mixture of emotions flowed through him. Not knowing what to do, he shook with anxiety. But as several moments passed, suddenly, years of sadness and grief boiled to the surface and evaporated. The harsh feelings disintegrated and happiness emerged. Tears rolled down his cheeks also and he hugged his father tightly. In that moment, it didn't matter. The years of uncertainty had vanished. They had been reunited, and the reunion was joyous.

"My boy!" Chief Stoneskin grumbled. "You are so big!" He began to laugh, slapping his boy on the shoulder.

Globulus laughed and smiled at his father. "Yeah..." he said while wiping the tears from his eyes.

"It has been so long, my boy. I have waited a lifetime for you to return home to us." He gripped his son's shoulders as he spoke. "Please tell me you are here to stay."

Globulus had a distant look in his eyes. Many thoughts were flowing through his mind.

His father could see the concern and spoke again. "What is it, my boy? What has happened?"

"King Toil..." He shook his head in renewed pain. "King Toil is dead. The city of Rasheed has been destroyed."

Chief Stoneskin took the news with shock. Frustration and sadness coursed through him. It had been King Toil's kindness that had saved the entire Crushing-Fist Clan from starvation years ago. With a heavy heart, the chief collapsed into a sturdy wooden chair. His eyes were grave and sullen. "That is ill news indeed. His entire empire is gone?"

"His daughter betrayed him, she betrayed us all. The city is now in the hands of the Reaper Kai. The entire empire of Rasheed has been destroyed."

"Rasheed cannot be gone..." The chief shook his head in disbelief.

"It's true."

"Damn that Asagara. Damn that Reaper Kai witch. Like mother, like daughter, eh?" Globulus's father shook his head in frustration. The tale of Asagara Toil and the revolt of Dune Station was well known in the southern reaches of the Darken Realm.

"The legacy of old tales never die, they simply evolve," Globulus boomed in a distraught voice. "The evil and treachery of Asagara Toil has been reborn in her hate-filled daughter."

"Is that why you are here, my boy? You want the story of our people and the people of Rasheed to survive? We have a strong history, our two nations. I cannot in good conscience let the memory of King Toil's kindness die. Is that why you are here?"

Globulus was silent at first, then nodded in agreement. "Yes, father, I am here to request your aid."

"Aid you will have, my boy. Years ago, we should have pledged our support to rid Dune Station of the foul presence of the Reaper Kai, but we didn't. This time it will be different. In memory of King Toil, we will pledge our aid to your cause. We will retake Rasheed and slaughter the foul Reaper Kai that infest the city!" Chief Stoneskin growled in anger, pledging his support to his boy.

"Rasheed is lost, father. What I want is your help in this region. Your neighbors now need your support."

"Our neighbors?" Globulus's father was confused.

"The Reaper Kai unleashed a plague, a plague that has decimated the Steel Crag city of Rust Spire. Half of the population has died already, and an army of Biogtech troops, the same army that pillaged Rasheed, is only a few days away from a full siege on the city. I want your aid defending the Steel Crag Mining Guild."

"Hmm… those greedy bastards have finally caught the eye of the Reaper Kai?"

"Not just them. All nations are being destroyed by the Reaper Kai. Dozens of kingdoms and villages were already destroyed prior to the siege of Rasheed. The enemy's goal is absolute. The complete subjugation of all races in the Darken Realm is at hand. The Steel Crag Guild is simply the next target."

"I never cared for those damn miners much, but we have lived in peace. So the enemy that sacked Rasheed is marching onward to Rust Spire? The enemies of King Toil are enemies of mine. I will rally an army to protect the Steel Crag Guild on one condition." Chief Stonekin looked at his son with a serious expression in his eye.

"What is it?" Globulus quizzed, still barely able to comprehend that his father was now standing before him.

"The condition is that my son, my long lost son, marches into battle by my side." Smiling, Chief Stoneskin slapped Globulus on the shoulder as he spoke.

Globulus smiled back and hugged his father. "I wouldn't

have it any other way. I am home for good. I want to be with *my* people." The years of indecision and anxiety had come to an end. Instead of fear and worry, Globulus felt a kindred fire ignite in his heart. He had been reunited with his father and his people, with a heartfelt homecoming. Globulus was not the outsider that he feared he would be. Instead, he was welcomed back into his father's house and tribe with open arms.

Chapter 35
The Siege of Rust Spire

A deep fog had once again covered the Giant's Spine mountain range in a clogging mass of swirling white wind. The Iron Kai veteran troops from the battle of Detro Tech City had made their way to Rust Spire, and just in time. Half of the populace had been killed by a gruesome plague and the other half was weak, barely able to walk, let alone fight.

It hadn't taken long for the educated Iron Kai field medics to isolate the source of the plague to the underground holding tanks that fed the city's water supply. The field medics forbade the drinking of water from the city supply and instructed the local population and the Iron Kai troops to only drink water from the melted glaciers outside the city. Following their advice, the populace that had survived the pestilence was well on its way to recovery. With three thousand Iron Kai veteran troops and only about a thousand healthy residents acting as a crude, untrained militia, the defenders of Rust Spire were sparse.

It was afternoon, nearing sunset, when the attack came.

Amongst the swirling mist came the eerie sound of marching. An enormous army was approaching. The fog was so thick that the other side of the gorge could not be seen. The mighty suspension bridge, the Giant's Arm, was shrouded in mist. About halfway across the bridge was as far as the defenders could see.

"Soldiers to the wall!" Field Marshal Graves, a seasoned Iron Kai field commander, issued an order into his radio headset. He could see next to nothing from his vantage point behind the walls, but knew the time had come. The enemy was *somewhere* in the swirling clouds of fog. "Artillery crews at the ready. Load your weapons and fire only on my order. No one fires on a target without direction." Field Marshal Graves thundered purposefully down a mighty stairwell into the great courtyard behind the corroded walls that defended Rust Spire from outside attack.   He moved confidently, with a serious look on his face. All the troops manning the defenses watched him with a sense of unease. Gathering his thoughts, the Iron Kai field marshal moved to rally and inspire his troops.

"I have fought for over thirteen years in the service of the Iron Kai. In that time, I have spilled blood on many battlefields. Today will be no different. We all stand stalwart, here and now. We all stand here bravely to defend this city and this country from heartless slaughter and tyranny. The enemy outside those walls is just that, an enemy. Show no mercy. Do not surrender. Our goal this day is absolute victory."

The troops could feel their blood begin to boil.

"In the thirteen years I have led troops on the battlefield, there has never been a defeat. In all those years, our enemies have always been overrun and destroyed. This day will be no different. We will win this fight, but we must be disciplined to do so. In the chaos of battle, you must trust my orders. Without sound leadership and strong decisions, we cannot hope to survive this day. Put your trust in me and my experience. We will defeat the enemy this day."

Field Marshal Graves fell silent and eyed the troops. He held his hand high and shouted: "Death to the enemy!"

With fire in their blood, the defenders of Rust Spire cheered and sounded heated battle cries in response. Field Marshal Graves head been successful; the troops were rallied and were prepared to defend the city.

As the battle cries died down, the enemy responded with an equal fury. Demonic trumpets sounded in the fog. Sinister laughter drifted ominously close.   The Biogtech soldiers were cackling, sending a haunting melody throughout the mist.

"All troops, to your positions! Give them hell!" Field Marshal Graves yelled and the troops obeyed.

Graves went up to the wall and brought his binoculars out, scanning the fog. Rays of sunlight punched suddenly through the darkness. The fog was beginning to lift. As the bright rays of the sun burned the fog away, the enemy was on the move. It had taken them mere minutes to assemble their artillery. As the mighty gorge cleared of fog, Graves looked out and felt a lump in his throat. Over five thousand enemy soldiers were assembling on the far side of the canyon. Full artillery batteries, armored personnel carriers (APCs) and a war host of Reaper Kai battle priests faced him defiantly.

Graves surveyed the enemy command group with intensity. The banner waving in the breeze depicted a skeletal horseman, bearing a curved scythe and riding upon a rotting steed. Graves knew the insignia and shook his head in dismay. The banner was that of Sister Nightshade, Matron of Pestilence. The plague that had gripped the city was no longer a mystery. It was now evident that Sister Nightshade was responsible for the horrible disease that had been unleashed upon Rust Spire. Sister Nightshade was not just the mother of plague, but also a sinister military tactician. Graves knew that this fight was going to be tough, one that could end in ruin for the unified forces if even a single mistake was made.

"Artillery batteries!" Graves spoke loudly into his radio headset. "Lay down a volley on those enemy cannons before they get assembled." With a single order, war erupted, with the first shots being fired by the unified defending forces, the Iron Kai troops and Rust Spire militia.

"Yes, sir!" a sergeant responded into the headset.

Several loud booms tore the air. Artillery shells screamed across the gorge and slammed into the condensed enemy troops with frightening damage. A dozen Biogtechs were slain in the explosions. The artillery blasts were devastating to the enemy infantry but did not damage the Reaper Kai artillery batteries making ready to attack.

"Adjust your guns and hit them again," Graves ordered another barrage.

The Iron Kai artillery screamed again. and the deadly explosives rushed across the canyon. One Reaper Kai battery was hit with two shells, destroying the position utterly. The cannon had been reduced to a smoking crater.

A whistling noise erupted as the first of the Biogtech

artilleries returned fire. The shells were not aimed at the soldiers manning the walls, but rather at the front gate. Several hasty shots rammed into the walls around the gate leading into Rust Spire. Shreds of metal shrapnel rained down with a clatter.

The Reaper Kai seized the advantage provided by the ensuing chaos, and several armored personnel carriers started rushing across the bridge. Graves was astonished by the rush, and frantically formulated a plan of action. The Iron Kai field marshal had no idea what the armored cars contained, but he was resolute in his decision not to let them get anywhere near the city. The Reaper Kai artillery slammed into the front gate. Buckling under the enormous explosions, the gates began to strain under the impact; the soldiers protecting the courtyard beyond the gate ran for cover.

"Artillery, light up those armored cars on the bridge!" Graves yelled into the radio as the enemy vehicles rushed forward.

The Iron Kai gunners obeyed their orders and fired a hasty volley at the APCs rushing across the bridge. Explosions tore the bridge, sending fragments of concrete flying. Two artillery batteries struck true, their deadly projectiles slamming into the APCs. With mighty explosions, the two armored vehicles exploded into smoking ruin. The other vehicles in the convoy, screaming across the bridge, swerved around the wreckage and went straight for the gate.

Another volley of cannon fire struck the gate. The assault pounded the enormous steel doors once again, this time ripping large holes in the gate.

"Damn it! Wipe out those vehicles!" Graves screamed, and the gunners fired in vain. Not a single shell hit.

A final volley of shells rocked forward from Reaper Kai artillery batteries. Two more shells hit the gate, while a third round went clean through, exploding in the courtyard beyond. Several Iron Kai soldiers were killed in the blast, their torn bodies thrown high into the air.

Boom! Another shell exploded on the gate. As the fiery concussion of energy and shrapnel leapt on the gate, a sharp sound of metal tearing seared through the air. The battered gate was collapsing in a pile of twisted steels. Both enormous sections crashed down, leaving the gates wide open for attack. Graves was stunned. The ensuing assault was quick and brutal. As the Iron Kai leader looked on in horror, the enemy armored carriers rushed inside the city, and their deadly cargo was unleashed. A host of the damned, a full war party of Goat Minions, rushed from within the vehicles and bolted toward the defenders.

Dozens of crazed and brutal Goat Minions hurled themselves at the stunned defenders. Clutching an assortment of metal hand weapons, they attacked with a terrifying ferocity. Driving ruthlessly into the soldiers, they bayed and bleated as their weapons tore flesh. Within mere minutes, the unified defense was under heavy attack.

Graves was feeling fear creep into his mind. The sounds of dying soldiers were intense. Within a matter of seconds, the Goat Minions had slain over thirty soldiers, with no end in sight. Even when mortally wounded, the Goat Minions continued to fight as the blood poured from their shredded bodies. Their blood-crazed battle frenzy was unstoppable. Swinging away like mindless killing machines, the Goat Minions drove deep into the defenders of Rust Spire. Many of the soldiers were caught off guard and began to flee from the horrid scene, while the Goat Minions, drenched in blood, murdered their kin without mercy.

The situation was grim, but it was about to get much worse.

A living carpet of metal was rushing forward. Over one thousand Splicers had been unleashed and were charging across the bridge. Like a pack of skittering cockroaches they came, moving rapidly and purposefully toward the front gate.

"Artillery, constant fire on the bridge!" Graves yelled in urgency. The artillery batteries opened fire and dropped a continuous bombardment of artillery shells upon the bridge. A massive barrage of explosions blanketed the bridge with fire and fragments of concrete. The horde of Splicers were scattered and mangled by the blasts, but remained undaunted, rushing forward with tentacles probing the air for viable hosts, victims to splice and take control of. The living carpet of moving metal spiders rushed over their slain brothers, charging through the rubble and craters amidst the rain of fire pelting the bridge. Despite the destruction of many of the Splicers, the sound of screams continued to rise from the courtyard. Whirling around, Field Marshal Graves caught sight of a chilling scene.

A soldier was screaming in terror, his legs sheared off at the knees, trying to crawl away from the host of Goat Minions. As his life blood rushed from his severed legs, a gore stained Goat Minion, red eyes bulging in rage, rushed forward, closing fast on the downed soldier. With a scream of fury, the black furred Goat Minion swung his axe repeatedly into the wounded soldier's back. Screams of agony rose out as the soldier was mutilated by the sinister minion of evil. Shaking his head in dismay, Graves knew he had to do something fast. The chaos caused by the Goat Minions was turning his army into a frightened huddle of soldiers led by indecision, not discipline.

Already, over fifty dead soldiers littered the courtyard. A host of sinister Goat Minions were still fighting, killing like crazed machines bent only on bloodshed. With a grim look, Graves grabbed a pair of hand grenades. Pulling both pins with his teeth, he lobbed the projectiles into the middle of the Goat Minions and his own troops. The weapons detonated, shredding friend and foe alike. The sacrifice was a minor one; Graves knew all of his soldiers at close range to a Goat Minion was most likely dead anyway. The remnants of the Goat Minions were surrounded and gunned down by the defenders of Rust Spire within a matter of seconds. With the courtyard now under control, Graves tried to collect his thoughts. Returning his attention to the shattered gates, he was just in time to see the first of the Splicers rush inside the city, hungering for a host.

"Form a perimeter around the gate! Drive them back!" the field marshal yelled, and the troops responded by forming a crude horseshoe shape around the fallen gate. Several hundred Splicers were destroyed in the artillery barrage, but hundreds more had survived the attack and were rushing through the gate at a frightening speed.

Opening fire, the soldiers shot bursts of lead at the charging Splicer horde. At first, the troops managed to hold them off, but as the full bulk of them reached the gate, there were just too many of them. The Splicers crashed into the soldiers holding the courtyard. Screams of terror pierced the air. The Splicers began to overcome their new hosts. As the silver legs plunged into the spines of the soldiers, the copper tentacles ground into their brains. Hundreds of soldiers crashed to the ground, thrashing around as the Splicers took control of their bodies. The mechanical devices sent impulses into their new hosts, taking control of their will and nervous systems.

Boom! Reaper Kai artillery fire slammed into the defenders manning the walls of the city. A series of well placed shots tore into the walls of Rust Spire. The explosions were dire, and many defenders manning the walls died in the blasts.

The battle was turning into a nightmare. Splicers were taking control of unified troops while artillery shredded those defending the walls.

The soldiers overcome by Splicers rose from the ground, turning their weapons on their kin and countrymen. Acting under the will of the robotic disks integrated into their bodies, the new slaves of the Reaper Kai brought their weapons to bear on the defenders of Rust Spire. A heated firefight erupted in the courtyard between the defenders and the spliced slaves. Brother killed brother, ally killed ally. The Reaper Kai had turned the unified troops on themselves.

Just when the battle seemed most dire, Sister Nightshade ordered a full advance. Five thousand Biogtech soldiers began to march across the battered bridge toward the besieged city of Rust Spire.

The artillery was slamming into the walls, spliced slaves were killing rampantly, and Biogtech soldiers were on a full advance. Field Marshal Graves needed a miracle: he needed more men and needed them fast. The city of Rust Spire was quickly being overrun by the Reaper Kai. Victory for the enemy was imminent.

Chapter 36
Charge of the Crushing-Fist

In the dim light of the battlefield, the crosshairs of the weapon fell upon Sister Nightshade. The sun was beginning to set and the darkness of the night would soon be at hand. With steady movements, the crosshairs came to rest on the target, centered on the neck of the evil Reaper Kai Matron. Holding her breath, Carla held the sniper rifle still and squeezed the trigger. The high caliber bullet sped forth with reckless fury. A twinge of alarm rose amongst the Reaper Kai priests. They knew something was wrong. A Reaper Kai priest, one of Nightshade's military advisors, extended his hands, and a blue barrier of energy surrounded the command group. The rifle round slammed into the energy barrier and was stopped cold, batted away by the psychic obstruction.

"For the glory of Rasheed!" Chief Stoneskin, the leader of the hippo clan, sounded an echoing war cry. Just over one thousand mutant hybrid hippo warriors grunted in response to the war cry. The mighty army was in full advance. The ground shook as the horde of hippo warriors charged the Reaper Kai command group.

"Damn them!" Sister Nightshade hissed. "Retreat, you fools!" The Matron of pestilence ordered her command crew to run for cover. The mighty army was close, and the Reaper Kai command group, numbering only five, knew they could not hold back the flood of mutant hippos charging the field of battle.

Fleeing, Nightshade, Queen Toil, and three other Reaper Kai headed eastward along the main road, aiming for the mountains near the besieged city.

The hippo army did not follow the command group, but rather, prepared to charge the main threat, the five thousand Biogtech soldiers engaged at the front gates of Rust Spire.

"This is how to win a war!" Stoneskin yelled with a glimmer of madness in his eyes. Cackling, the chief slapped his son,

Globulus, on the shoulder. "Prepare arms!" the chief yelled, and the front rank of the hippo army produced a dangerous assortment of heavy machine guns. The beastly hippo warriors were so large that many carried heavy fifty caliber machine guns or fully automatic mini-guns. With over fifty mutant hippos in the front ranks, each with the full firepower of a machine gun bunker, the odds were definitely improving for the entrenched defenders of Rust Spire.

The Biogtech army, having lost its leadership, blindly charged forward toward the battered gate of Rust Spire, firing upon anything that moved within their field of vision. Holding the gate with a faltering morale and heavy casualties, the Iron Kai army, along with the Steel Crag Guild soldiers, fought a desperate battle. Field Marshal Graves had been wounded by an artillery barrage but was standing fast, giving crucial orders and rallying the frightened soldiers.

"Take out those artillery positions! Gunners, form up on my flanks!" Several squads of mutant hippos charged each of the Reaper Kai artillery positions with an assortment of huge hand weapons. The Biogtech soldiers feebly defended their positions. Their gunfire hit several charging hippos, with minimal damage. The tough, thick hide of the hippos protected them from the bullets. Enraged and caught in a bloodlust, the hippo warriors slaughtered the Biogtech soldiers, dismembering them in a crazed fury, effectively nullifying the enemy artillery positions.

Meanwhile, the gunners formed up on Stoneskin's flanks. Globulus and his father each carried a fifty caliber machine gun in their mighty hands. With a front of nearly twenty warriors across, each with some sort of heavy machine gun, the Crushing-Fist clan advanced quickly upon the rear flank of the unsuspecting Biogtech army.

The mighty bridge shook as the hippos pounded forward with machine guns at the ready. Several ranks of Biogtech soldiers turned around just in time to be caught in a hurricane of gunfire.

"Gunners! Open fire!" Stoneskin yelled. The twenty-some odd hippos wielding their heavy machine guns starting shooting. The carnage was immense. The high caliber rounds slammed through the Biogtech soldiers with frightening damage. The bullets were so powerful that many of them would pierce multiple ranks of troops. Like dominos, the back ranks of the Reaper Kai army sustained heavy casualties. As these ranks fell away, the hippos marched forward, spraying the robotic soldiers with hot lead.

Responding to the attack, the Biogtech army split in two. Half the army continued to assault the front gate of Rust Spire, while the other half turned around to meet the gruesome assault of the hippo army.

Caught between the Iron Kai on one end of the bridge and the advancing hippo army on the other, the Biogtech army was fully surrounded and was getting battered without mercy. Heated gunfire was exchanged as the hippo army slowly advanced, dumping a heavy shower of bullets into the ranks of enemy troops. Mowing them down in a fury, the Crushing-Fist clan was shredding a wide swath through the Biogtech soldiers. Grinning all the way to victory, Globulus and Chief Stoneskin led the charge, slaughtering all enemies in sight.

The battle upon the bridge raged for what seemed like an eternity. Finally, amidst the barrage of artillery, assault rifle fire, and heavy machine gun fire, the Biogtech army was utterly destroyed. The hippo army and defenders of Rust Spire alike also sustained losses. Six hundred defenders in Rust Spire had fallen, and nearly one hundred hippo warriors were slain in the battle.

As the last Biogtech soldier fell, the darkness of night had washed over the Steel Crag Range. A triumphant series of chants began from humans and mutants alike. The Biogtech army had been crushed, all due to Globulus and his plan to unify the region against the enemy.

Both Field Marshal Graves and Chief Stoneskin had survived the battle, and their armies were feeling a rush of excitement as they stood upon the remains of the fallen Reaper Kai army. A wild exhilaration flooded the ranks of the victorious. Globulus slapped his father on the shoulder and smiled at him with a grim look. "It's good to be home," the mighty mutant said to his father.

"It's good to have you home, son!" Stoneskin boomed

gruffly, gripping his boy with a mighty hold.

The adrenaline of victory was short lived.

With a frantic burst of movement, a lone figure was running quickly along the end of the bridge which opened to the Steel Crag mountains. There was panic in the person's steps as they moved in haste toward the hippo army stationed on the bridge. The cheers of victory fell silent as the lone person charged forward. In the dim light of the dusk-filled sky, Globulus and Stoneskin made out the charging form as that of young Carla Reins.

"Don't just stand there!" Carla screamed in panic. "Run for it!" The young mercenary, dressed in her sniper suit, ran through the middle of the hippo army, heading for the safety of Rust Spire.

Boom. A thud rocked the earth. "So much warm flesh!" a voice roared in the darkness, somewhere near the edge of the bridge. A sickly feeling of fear washed over the hippo army.

As uneasiness washed over the army, a cackling rose around the sinister voice. Biogtechs, thousands more of them, were lurking in the darkness, with something worse than the darkness itself.

Nightshade was cackling. She was looking at Queen Marion with a smile upon her face. "This is how you win a war, young Toil." Sneering, the matron of disease motioned to her advisor. The advisor nodded and issued an attack order. The Reaper Kai had left its most powerful troops in reserve. The Abomination of Beldarmordain, demon from the netherworld, led a fresh army of five thousand Biogtech soldiers against the startled defenders of Rust Spire.

"I hunger!" The Abomination roared. It moved against the hippo army with frightening speed. As the mighty demon drew near, a panic rolled through the hippo army. Chaos and fear erupted immediately. None could look upon the fearsome demon. The creature's powerful demonic magic made it impossible for its opponents to gaze upon it, a trait which made fighting the fearsome demon nearly impossible. As it moved into view, none could behold the mighty creature. Averting their eyes from the charging demon, over half of the hippo army retreated toward the safety of the ruined city of Rust Spire, demoralized and frightened beyond belief.

"Hold your ground!" Chief Stoneskin roared. He felt the strange twinge of panic in his own heart, but he stood resolute, not wavering, wanting to stand as a strong example to his people. Trying with all his might, he fought to view the strange creature charging down on his clan upon the bridge. No matter how hard he fought, he could not force himself to look at the demon.

"Rally yourselves! We must stand against our foes!" Globulus yelled. A fresh boom of artillery rocked the bridge. Several artillery shells struck the heart of the hippo army, impacting with horrible results. Many proud hippo warriors were slain and torn to pieces in the explosions. The enemy troops had retaken their artillery positions and were slaughtering the hippo tribe without recourse. Strike after strike tore into the Crushing-Fist Clan. The sounds of death and the charge of the demon were too much to stand. Not being able to look upon such a foe was a terror in itself, but seeing one's countrymen torn apart by artillery fire was an unmatchable horror.

Within a matter of seconds, the once proud army of mutant hippos was scattered. Only four hundred warriors stood upon the bridge, facing the advance of the Abomination and five thousand Biogtech soldiers.

There was a grave look upon the visage of Chief Stoneskin. Globulus' father had made a decision, a tough but wise plan of action. He sighed in despair and looked upon his son. "Promise me something, my boy." His eyes were soft and the tears were welling up in his eyes as he spoke.

Globulus felt a pain hit his heart. He knew what was about to happen, and he didn't like it one bit. His father was going to try to save his people.

"We are outnumbered, and the creature leading that army is beyond comprehension. Promise me to lead our people." Stoneskin spoke softly, gripping his son's shoulders.

"Don't do this," Globulus responded, with tears welling up in his beastly brown globes; he knew that his father was planning to face the Abomination in combat.

"I must. The armies of the enemy are too strong. Fall back

and evacuate the city. Travel north along the Giant's Spine and escape into the desert."

"I can't do this. I am not leaving your side. It took me a lifetime to gather up enough courage to find you. I am not going to give you up now!" Globulus responded like a frightened teenager.

"We don't have much time, son. I can slow it down, I know it. I can slow it down long enough for you to evacuate this city." Stoneskin smiled grimly.

"Please, no..." Globulus pleaded.

"I must do this. Take our people and those of this city and flee. Do not sacrifice all of the defenders so needlessly. Live to fight another day. This city is lost. Save all that you can."

A boom of artillery struck the remaining hippos still cowering in fear, killing dozens more. The Abomination had breached the perimeter of the hippo army and was slaughtering at will, pummeling and squashing any hippo warriors it could find.

With that, Chief Stoneskin of the mighty hippo tribe rose to his feet. His scarred body rippled with rage as his muscles flexed. Gritting his teeth, Stoneskin drew his hand weapons. Taking a step forward, still trying to look upon the foul form of the demon, he gripped a sledge hammer in each hand. Despite his courage and force of will, the black magic of the demon was too strong. Closing his eyes, he let the sounds of battle fill his mind.

Globulus looked on at his father in terror. He knew that the wise thing to do was to survive and lead the shattered armies. Shame began to fill him. As he swallowed his pride and resisted the urge to stand with his father, common sense and duty were his companions. He had to pull the remaining troops back, or they would all be lost. It was the hardest thing Globulus would ever have to do: flee with the survivors as his father faced the Abomination alone.

"Rally to me!" Tears were streaming down his face and his voice crackled. "Retreat with me! Flee to the city!"

The mighty Crushing-Fist Clan, under duress, gripped with indecision, listened to his orders. Swallowing hard, Globulus looked back one last time at his father bracing to fight the Abomination on his own. Turning, with tears rolling down his face, the mighty hippo led his people away from the carnage and the scene of death.

Listening to the battle, Stoneskin heard all the sounds around him. He kept his eyes closed and clutched his hammers, ready for the battle at hand. A keening wail rose from the battlefield around him. Hundreds of voices were gibbering and wailing in terror. All of the trapped souls bound into the body of the Abomination were making a host of frightful noises. A heavy thud echoed from the concrete. The Abomination moved forward, eyeing the defiant hippo in disgust.

"So, once there was a fallen hero, long ago, in the land of my birth. I was a tyrant, holding an unholy vigil over my lands. A lordling did once move to challenge me. I smote him and cleaved his body with the force of my wrath. You will be no different," the demon directed a hateful taunt at the hippo chieftain.

The voice pierced the darkness. Stoneskin knew that the demon was now before him. The sickly smell of rotting flesh filled his nostrils, the panicked wail of the lost souls rang in his ears. All these signs gave the hippo warrior a chance. Taking advantage of the opportunity, he charged the demon with a sledge hammer flailing in each hand.

The charge was so stunning to the demon that it was unable to react in time. Moving forward and uttering a mighty battle cry, Chief Stoneskin assaulted the creature. Swinging like a crazed juggernaut, Stoneskin charged, listening to the sounds of the creature. While charging and swinging wildly, the hippo closed in on the monstrosity. Finally, he reached his target and his hammers struck flesh. The attacks were brutal. The mighty sledge hammers slammed into the beast. Roaring in pain, the Abomination staggered back, reeling from the damage wrought by the reckless hippo chieftain.

"Fool!" it screamed. The tormented souls trapped in its body yelled pleas of salvation. *"Kill us…"* they whispered. *"Save us…"* they pleaded. *"Deliver us from suffering…"* None of the trapped souls could stand another moment sealed inside the beast, many of them having being trapped for a hundred years or more.

As the pleas of suffering rose out from the demon's body, Stoneskin continued the assault, using the sounds of their voices to direct his attacks. The mighty hippo thundered forward and struck the beast several more times. With hammers flailing, he struck and splintered the mighty leg bone of the beast. The bone bent and broke under the attacks. Crippled, the Abomination fell to one knee, roaring in agony, its one leg shattered and broken. *"Finish off the beast..."* a tortured soul yelled. *"Yes, slay him, end our suffering..."*

Stoneskin attacked once more, battering the demon, striking it relentlessly.

The Abomination had had enough. Regaining its composure, it swung its mighty cudgel at the hippo. As he was unable to look upon the demon, the hippo was caught unaware. The cudgel struck him in the chest, breaking his ribs, tearing his flesh. Gasping, Stoneskin swung again in desperation. He missed completely, and the Abomination struck him again, this time dropping the mighty chieftain to his knees.

Gritting his teeth, the chieftain, turned away from the demon, looking toward the ruined city of Rust Spire. No troops manned the walls, no defenders could be seen; all the survivors of the attack were now fleeing, escaping certain death at the hands of the Abomination and the imminent attack from the horde of Biogtech soldiers. "Good boy..." the chieftain whispered, thinking of his son. Globulus had evacuated the city. As his body failed and his life began to ebb, Stoneskin knew that the defenders of the city had been given enough time to escape and live to fight another day. Stoneskin's plan had been a success; he had stopped the Abomination's charge long enough to save many of his own people.

Another blow hit the hippo. Darkness took him. Collapsing to the ground, Stoneskin felt his shattered body grow cold. The last thought that filled his mind was the sight of the lush marshes, far to the south, his young son standing at the edge of the water, smiling up at him, far from the sounds of battle, far from the horror of war.

"My boy..." Stoneskin whispered as the life went out of him. With a final gasp, the mighty monarch passed into death.

Chapter 37
Slide Toward Ruin

"How did the enemy get several thousand troops out of their capital under a full siege? It just doesn't make any sense." Gunther shook his head in disgust. The mighty monarch moved over to the windows in the Truce Hall and looked out upon the lake below. The wind was blowing and the waves on the lake were breaking with white caps. A storm was pushing across the lake. Black clouds and thunder were entering the region.

"I am not sure, my lord. The number of troops that attacked Rust Spire was in excess of the number that laid waste to Rasheed. *Something* is not right," the war advisor affirmed Gunther's unease.

"Our spies have said that a garrison of two thousand troops holds the city of Rasheed. I still cannot fathom how all those robotic soldiers escaped the Reaper Kai capital without us knowing." The monarch watched as the storm moved in, closer and closer. "What of Nova 7?"

"We have not heard any news of Nova 7 for quite some time. They have disappeared. Monitoring the enemy radio transmissions has also yielded nothing. The Reaper Kai have no idea where they are either, my lord."

"I am worried about them, but I feel elated that our enemies know nothing more about the matter than we do. What news of the front around Detro Tech City?"

"Our troops are holding out. We are fighting a stalemate. The enemy produces troops every day and we destroy roughly an equal amount. The free peoples are rallying to our flag. The refugees from Rust Spire and the hippo clan have pledged their support as well. We also have additional recruits still pouring in from smaller villages and cities. Our ranks are beginning to swell and we have more than enough troops to hold our ground for a long time to come." A new note of distress crept into the advisor's voice. "On a grimmer note, the Reaper Kai now have control of the richest steel and petroleum deposit in all of the Darken Realm. If we cannot break their supply lines, we have little hope of stopping their troop production. With all of the fresh resources, the enemy will be able to produce thousands of additional soldiers. It is critical that we stop these resources from reaching their city."

"Agreed. We must send commando teams into the Steel Crags. Wipe out the train route out of the mountains. If they can't move the resources by train, we can minimize the transport of materials to the enemy factories. Without a viable supply route, it will take months and months for the enemy to get the resources to their factories. By then, hopefully, we can break their supply lines, and the production of enemy troops will end and ensure our victory."

"Without the support of the Steel Crag Mining Guild and Rasheed, the southern reaches will be fully open to enemy attack. All of the smaller provinces and kingdoms are doomed," the advisor responded in a concerned tone.

"Unfortunately, that is true. We cannot withdraw our focus from the production facilities. If we do, the enemy will produce more troops than we can handle. We have about a year's time to break the enemy. After that, I doubt we will have the resources or manpower to win this war. I only hope Nova 7 is still out there somewhere." Gunther spoke with a grim look.

"Nova 7, my lord, is a long shot. For hundreds of years, our troops have scoured the battered earth and never found an intact nuclear weapon. The ancient weapons no longer exist. We must put our faith in tactics and brute strength to win this encounter."

"You are wrong. This Nova 7 has defied all odds thus far. They escaped Rasheed, where all the other Nova teams were eradicated by the traitorous Marion Toil. They have escaped countless attacks by the enemy and eluded dangerous mercenary teams hunting them. They have a strange momentum propelling them. If there is still a viable nuclear weapon out there, Nova 7 will find it and deliver us from the enemy," Gunther said in a confident tone.

"I hope you are right, my lord. With only a year to win this war, every day counts."

Gunther fell silent and turned away from his advisor. The conversation was over, and the advisor knew that he was no longer welcome. Taking his leave, he left the Truce Hall.

The monarch of the Iron Kai moved over to the windows overlooking the lake. Crossing his arms across his chest, Gunther looked out into the violent waves of the enormous lake. Stroking his fiery orange beard, he felt a sense of foreboding wash over him. The enemy troops who sacked Rust Spire did not hail from the Reaper Kai capital. *Something* was wrong. The monarch knew that his army could withstand the enemy troops in Detro Tech City for one year's time. But if extra Biogtech soldiers were thrown into the mix, the odds of surviving the enemy would be slim. If the Reaper Kai had something else up their sleeve, it would take a miracle to win this war. It would take the insane possibility that Nova 7 would actually locate a nuclear weapon, somewhere out there, in the battered ruins of the ancients.

Chapter 38
A Dream of Ill Intent

Gasping in fear, Mineera stepped back from the horrid scene. Her mind could not comprehend the grisly image before her. Shaking her head back and forth, the psychic maiden fought to control herself. Grief and frustration coursed through her, mingling together. A rage, a hate-filled pressure, was building up inside of her.

Jared, his sword stained in blood, turned around. At his feet were the remains of Banion. His eyes were filled with hate and he gazed at Mineera with disgust. The strange totem around his neck was glowing intensely, its red eyes hungering for more blood, more suffering.

When Mineera tried to run, her legs would not move. The tribal youth moved toward her, hate burning in his eyes. When she tried to yell, her voice would not sound. The youth moved ever closer, gore stained blade in hand...

"No!" Mineera screamed as her eyes shot open. The stars twinkled in the heavens, but otherwise, all was dark. The smell of burning wood filled her nostrils, and chill air pressed against her skin. Recovering her fragile sanity, the psychic maiden looked around in alarm. Banion was seated on the other side of the fire. He was awake, and eyeing Mineera with suspicion. She had been having bad dreams lately, dreams that she was convinced were a portent of the future. Banion had other thoughts. It had been many months since Nova 7 had rescued her from the Reaper Kai slave convoy. Ever since her liberation, she had been strange, almost psychotic, often rambling on about her horrid visions.

With an uneasy tension in his mind, Banion sighed at Mineera's distress. Her 'visions' were becoming all too frequent, and more and more twisted.

"Don't look at me like that." Mineera spoke in an authoritative tone. "I *know* what you're thinking, and it's wrong."

"Is it?" he quizzed.

"I spent a lifetime trying to find you. All my life, I dreamed of you. Now, you are before me, and I am not going to let *anything* happen to you." As her body shook and her blue eyes gazed at him frantically, Banion felt she was beginning to lose her grip on reality once more.

"What was it this time? Your vision? Same as before?" he asked softly, not wanting to wake either Tani or Jared.

"Same as before." Mineera shot a look at Jared, sleeping near the fire. "I don't trust him..."

"Because of your visions?"

There was a silence. Her eyes swept back and forth, darting about like crazed hornets. The blue orbs never settled; they were always on the move. An inner turmoil had taken her.

"I won't let him kill you," she said in a resolute tone.

"Jared–" Banion looked over to make sure the tribal wasn't awake. "Jared is not going to kill me. Your dream is just a bad dream, nothing more. I don't doubt that you can see the future – that much is clear. In the four months we have been traveling across the wasteland, your visions often came true. But you have been through quite a lot. I'm still not sure Tani extracted that damn Splicer from your brain and spine correctly."

"I am not *crazy,*" she said in a fierce tone, lashing out.

"Sure you're not. What makes more sense? Jared is not *really* Jared? He's some sort of spy?"

"Why can't I sense him?" Mineera said triumphantly. In her fragile mind, the logic of her argument was flawless.

"I am not going over this with you again. I know you are concerned for my safety, but this is too much," Banion said harshly. His eyes fell upon her with a gradually simmering rage.

"I'll tell you why I can't sense him. He is one of the enemy. He's not really Jared, he's some sort of Reaper Kai, masquerading as Jared. Only another one of our kind can withstand our powers." The psychic seemed to be tottering on the edge of reality as she spoke.

"Shut up!" Banion had had enough. Anger flashed upon his face. "I trust him more than I do you!"

There was a moment of silence. Mineera retreated for a second, before the twisted gears in her head began to grind again.

"Why won't he tell us of his journeys after he disappeared? Huh, tell me why? What is he hiding?"

Banion was fuming. He was so angry he could barely speak. With an intent, silent desire, Banion wished she would just knock it off.

"I really don't care." He shook his head in disgust as he spoke. "It's none of my business where Jared was. For all I care, he could have been shacking up with whores the entire time. It's none of my damn business and it's none of your damn business. Let the matter drop."

"I can't. If I had dreamt it once, it would be different. But almost every night, I see the same thing. Jared will kill you!"

There was a heated moment of silence. Banion was grinding his teeth in a fury. He shot Mineera a hate filled look, then began to speak. "I will give you a choice." Pausing, he waited till Mineera's eyes met his own. "You stop this nonsense, or you will continue on alone. I will not compromise this mission or the lives of Jared and Tani for you. You are on the edge of insanity, and if you don't stop this nonsense, we will go on without you. Those are your options, your only choices. Stop all this bullshit or continue alone, by yourself. You got that?"

"Yeah..." Mineera was feeling ashamed.

"Just bad dreams. Plain and simple. You are just having bad dreams. They don't mean a damn thing," Banion asserted sternly while maintaining eye contact with the psychic.

"I am sorry." Something changed in her demeanor. She no longer hunched over, and the frantic twitch was gone. It almost seemed as if someone else was now talking with Banion. The same old Mineera they had all known before her capture was returning. Sighing, she gripped her hair with her dark skinned hands and shook her head. "I don't know what's happening to me..." She sighed again, looking at Banion. "I feel strange... almost like something is here with me, inside of me. I can't put my finger on it, but I feel out of sorts."

"Whatever it is, you need to get it under control. I cannot risk the fate of the Darken Realm for someone who is losing their mind. There is way too much at stake. I need you here, with all of us, on *our* side. We will not make it through all this if we doubt each other, even for a second. We must trust each other absolutely, with no questions." His gaze never wavered as he spoke to her.

"I am sorry," she said again.

"No more of this." Banion pointed his finger at her.

"No more, I promise, I just feel a little out of sorts. I will get it together," Mineera promised with a beseeching smile. "Thanks." She smiled again.

Shaking his head in frustration, he sighed. His decision to take an enemy, a former Reaper Kai, into the ruins of old was beginning to seem like madness. Banion secretly wished he had never taken her with them.

Sensing his indecision, Mineera said, "I won't let you down."

Banion grunted under his breath, feeling that the psychic was assuming a dangerous semblance of reason.

"I'm gonna get some rest, and since you are already awake, you can take the next watch," Banion ordered Mineera and she nodded in agreement. "There are only a few hours left until dawn. Use them to reflect on your actions and your state of mind. When the sun rises, I don't want to hear another word about your dreams, you got that?"

"Yeah..." Mineera replied, feeling ashamed. She would make a concentrated effort to regain her composure.

Banion tipped his hat over his face and settled in for a quite sleep. The fire crackled in the night. The team, Nova 7, had settled for the night on a small bluff overlooking an ocean of white sand. Mineera wrapped her arms around her knees, pulling her blue robes about her body. For the moment, she was under control; the strange presence that prodded her toward madness had been driven back, for the time being.

With guilty feelings, she turned to look at the tribals, lying upon their handmade sleeping mats. The two had acquired supplies about a month back and crafted two new sleeping mats. Smiling, she basked in their innocence. It was almost comical to watch them sleep. Tani was lying in a fetal position, clutching his laptop. Jared was sprawled out, arms flayed about him, the strange totem resting on his chest...

She gazed at the totem intently. It seemed sinister to her. Even though she could no longer feel Jared's thoughts, from time to time, another presence was revealed to her, a powerful one centered on Jared. It was almost as if a potent spirit had taken up residence in the strange bird totem made of charred wood. It was a deceptive presence, only making itself known on rare occasions. Nevertheless, despite Banion's warning to get her actions under control, Mineera still felt suspicious of Jared. The recurring dream of Jared standing over the corpse of Banion could not simply be pushed from her thoughts. In her own mind, all of her dreams were significant. Mineera could not discount the vision altogether.

An owl, perched upon a cactus, hooted in the night. Its low screeching sound was haunting. Mineera gazed out, surveying the owl upon the cactus with a bemused stare. Brown feathers with white spots covered the animal's body. Its barren, scrawny legs rested peacefully upon the top of the cactus, whose sharp quills protruded between the creature's toes. The owl looked back and stared at Mineera. When she stared back, the owl did not avert its gaze. It somehow appeared as if the owl was initiating some sort of competition with the psychic maiden. Without breaking their gaze, the two combatants fought not to blink. Finally, Mineera blinked, and the owl screeched once more, proclaiming its victory in a hoot of defiance.

Sighing, Mineera let the environment of the night fill her. Ambling through the valley below, a coyote slunk through the darkness with its tail between its legs. The canine hunter probed the white sand with its nose, searching for the scent of prey. It moved erratically, head bobbing from side to side, sniffing the sand. Finally, it grew tired, yipping in a dull growl and moving off to find its burrow.

The owl upon the cactus hooted once more at Mineera, but she avoided its gaze. Instead, she sighed and shifted her vision upwards, into the heavens. Bright pinpricks of light broke the veil of darkness, twinkling in the blackness. Wisps of light, tendrils of forming stars, stretched across the night sky. For a brief moment, Mineera suddenly felt very small. The heavens glittered, filling her with a sense of humility.

"Where are you?" she quizzed the darkness. Nothing responded. It had been many months since the holy, glowing entity had come before her. Since then, her dreams had been tormented, wracked with suffering and indecision. Wanting to feel the comfort of the noble spirit, Mineera called out once again in a whisper. "Comfort me. Please..."

The night responded; instead of the heavenly being rushing forth to comfort the psychic maiden, the owl hooted defiantly again, this time bobbing its head up and down in a taunt. Her frustration mounting, Mineera forced the loneliness from her mind, imagining the warm glow of the holy being that had come to her on many occasions since her betrayal of the Reaper Kai. Secretly yearning for heaven to save her from herself, the psychic maiden wandered aimlessly in her thoughts until the sun rose once more over the wasteland, bathing the earth in a sweltering heat.

Chapter 39
Green Isles

Nova 7 trudged onward through the burning wasteland. It had been just under four months of travel since the companions left the fishing village of Shape Home. Since then, it had been an arduous journey across the battered ruins of the old world. Moving from haunt to haunt, ruin to ruin, the ragged mercenary team had pushed deeper into the wasteland, further than even the most seasoned expeditions and treasure hunters had ever pushed.

It was midday. Banion led the tribals and the traitor of the Reaper Kai across the white sand. A rain storm had blown in from the western wasteland, leaving the desert cool and moist for a short time. As the dark storm clouds pushed ever eastward, Nova 7 rejoiced in the relief from the burning desert sun.

Small plants and cacti found favor in the earth and grew plentifully. Many of the cacti were in bloom after the rainstorm, leaving the desert crossing pleasantly filled with the fragrances of blossoming plants. Birds and insects were also abundant after the rain, taking full advantage of the life-giving moisture.

"This is it, kids," Banion said triumphantly. Just ahead were several mounds of rock and earth erupting from the surface of white sand dunes. Each pillar was mushroom-like in shape, and was connected to the other spires with wooden plank bridges. The hills were colored bright green as vegetation covered the broad top of each pillar. Small earthen and wooden huts lined the strange pillars as well, about thirty feet above the sand floor. At the base of each pillar, the sand was flooded and covered in water. It was as if the village was set atop toadstools growing out of a pond.

"Weird," Jared said, dumfounded by the sight ahead of him. The appearance of the village was surreal and almost comical.

"Leave it to Banion." Tani smiled, shaking his head in disbelief. "Are you sure this is the right place, Banion?"

"What are you talking about, bookworm? Of course this is the right place," the deranged rancher added with a thick tone of sarcasm.

"Well, it looks too normal for the kind of places where you usually like to go. It doesn't look dangerous enough for a Banion O'Neil vacation destination. Where are all the explosions? Where is all the gunfire?" Tani was grinning as he spoke, poking fun at Banion.

"Real funny, bookworm. You finished?" He glared at the tribal youth. Jared himself was smiling as he listened to Tani, trying to avoid laughing outright at Banion.

"What a beautiful place," Mineera whispered. Sending out her psychic powers, probing the land ahead, she felt at peace. The village was a place of solitude.

"The village is called Green Isles. Water from the mountains to the north travels and congregates in this spot. It floods the base of the rock formations, creating a natural lake. The inhabitants built their homes up upon the spires to avoid the flood zone," Banion told his companions as they all continued onward.

"It's so serene and peaceful here," Mineera said, feeling happy.

"Yeah, it's the last place of refuge for about three days travel. West of here, up that mountain pass, is the end of the road for most people. After pressing out of the mountains, the earth falls away into the Rift Valley, an unstable patch of land rocked by earthquakes and volcanic eruptions." Banion was relating the tales he had heard about the region.

"That's more like it," Tani mused. "Volcanoes and earthquakes are definitely appropriate for a Banion O'Neil vacation hideaway."

Jared burst out laughing, giggling at his friend's taunting of Banion.

"Yeah, yeah…" he said, blushing.

"Beyond the Rift Valley is the city, the ruins of the ancients?" Jared pressed.

"The Iron Gate ruins lie beyond the Rift Valley. The ruins of the city are flooded with boiling tar and fierce steam vents. The city is inhospitable for miles and miles, almost as far as the ocean. The Iron Gate ruins are an underground network of passages that press into the heart of the city. From there we reach the Concrete Barrens, the home of the Runner."

Mineera sighed and looked distantly onward to the mountain pass. "This Runner, he is the one who knows the location of the nuclear weapon?" she asked.

"Supposedly. This Runner is the best weapon merchant in all the reaches of the Darken Realm. No one has actually seen him, but legends abound about his guild, stationed in the Concrete Barrens."

"If he's such a powerful arms dealer, why doesn't he have a nuclear weapon already?" Jared asked in a confident tone. He had become more accustomed to voicing his opinion with the group over the last few months.

"Yeah, why doesn't this Runner get it himself if he knows where it is?" Tani added, finding favor with Jared's question.

"That topic also makes me uneasy. That's why we have to be careful when we deal with him. A nuclear weapon is the greatest prize in this sick world," the deranged rancher concluded.

Nova 7 finally reached the edge of the pristine pool of water surrounding the village of Green Isles. High above them, the villagers had congregated at the edge of the mighty spires and were now looking down at Nova 7. Many were waving at them. It wasn't often they got visitors, way out in the western edge of the world. Mineera waved back, feeling a genuine sense of happiness from the villagers.

A wooden platform extended from the edge of the pool to the base of one of the rock spires. Banion moved onto the platform, as did his companions. One of the inhabitants lowered a rope ladder from the top of the spire, allowing access into the village.

Banion steadied the ladder and let Mineera ascend first. The tribals quickly followed, leaving Banion to climb up on his own power.

Nova 7 reached the top and looked around at the village of

Green Isles. The earth that they stood upon was spongy. Just below the surface, the inhabitants of the village had labored for centuries, collecting fertile soil and depositing it upon the tops of the spires. Over countless centuries, the roots of the plants had packed the earth densely, preventing the top soil from eroding. The result was the strange mushroom shaped towers, consisting of rich topsoil and a thick mass of roots.

"Amazing," Tani said with a wild look of fascination in his eye. He had dropped to one knee immediately and was probing the spongy earth with his stumpy fingers. Banion kicked the tribal youth, causing him to stand up in alarm. The villagers were waiting to make their introductions.

"It has been ages since we last had visitors." The village elder, tall and lean, with heavy set wrinkles, moved forward to stand before Banion. With a look of humility, the famous mercenary stood at attention, stepping forward to greet the chief of the village.

"Thank you for accepting us into your village," the deranged rancher declared while bowing in respect to the elder. The elder furrowed his brow and looked him over as he spoke.

"You are welcome here on one condition. We are a peaceful race and abhor violence and bloodshed. As a result, you must surrender your weapons here, or return back into the wasteland," the elder explained, eyeing the tribals and Mineera with reservation.

Banion almost snorted in defiance at the request. Instead, he simply gazed at the aged chief with a look of suspicion. The deranged rancher was none too keen to surrender his weapons.

Mineera moved forward, probing the chief with her mind. There was no ill will or intent within the chief. He honestly did not want any armed mercenaries walking about in his village. Mineera felt comfortable with the request, and so made the first move.

"Of course." The psychic maiden was the first to make a gesture by handing the elder her knife. The remaining members of Nova 7 relinquished control of their weapons. It took several minutes for the three men to give up their weapons. All three were heavily armed with automatic weapons, explosives, and an assortment of hand weapons. Jared was the last, hesitating before handing over the mighty Scar Blade.

"Feel free to enjoy the sanctuary of our home." The elder bowed to Mineera as he and his advisors moved away with the enormous bounty of weapons liberated from Nova 7.

Jared and Tani had a look of wanderlust. They turned to Banion and he nodded his assent, acknowledging their need to explore the village. The tribals responded by waving and heading off to view the strange village, leaving Mineera with Banion.

The tribals made haste, escaping deeper into the village. It had been weeks of travel through the wasteland, passing through small trade outposts and villages. Green Isles was the first real place of notice on their path, a large town with the amenities of the Frontier. Excited, Jared and Tani quickly moved away, wanting to get lost and enjoy some much needed down time.

"You know what tonight is, don't you?" Tani quizzed Jared.

"Yeah, the ninth full moon," he responded triumphantly. "I wonder if this place has a bar?" the warrior said with a smile.

"I hope so," Tani responded with a mischievous look on his face. In recent months, both the tribals had acquired a taste for liquor, a nasty habit taught to them by their deranged mentor, Banion.

"Almost halfway there," Jared said, feeling hope return as he thought about the rising of the ninth full moon. The exile was long, but was nearing the halfway mark. Only eleven more moons would have to rise before the tribals could return home.

"Yeah, and we are still alive, even after all of Banion's insanity," Tani said, and both almost burst out laughing. Even though his words were meant as a joke, there was a sinister reality behind the statement. Being with Banion was a dangerous way to travel.

They both chuckled and felt the strain of the journey start to wither. The strife since the ruin of Rasheed was gradually becoming a contained memory. It had been many months since the horrid night, and both had put most of it behind them. On occasion, a bad dream would take them, but the events were seeming more and more like another life, a secret life that they could disengage from, resorting to their original, pre-trauma personalities.

"Hey, check this out," Tani said with a look of astonishment. While wandering the streets of Green Isles, the two tribals had come across a map shop. The young scholar was already poring over the maps with a look of astonishment.

"This one shows Rasheed," Jared said, pointing at a finely crafted map.

"Look at this one, it shows Turner's Corner and Shape Home."

"It's missing some information a little to the north..." Jared said cryptically. The missing portion of the map contained the village of Song River, the location of the strange monastery dedicated to a mysterious hero known as Navezgane. Thinking about the church atop the mesa, Jared's hand fell to the totem around his neck. He rubbed it lightly with his hand, almost daydreaming.

A moment of silence passed between the two. Tani felt his friend's hesitation and eyed him curiously. Finally, Jared snapped out of his trance and spoke. "We should buy some of these maps, Tani. It would be great information for Scarskin when we finally return home."

Tani agreed and selected several of the larger maps. "You take dollars?" Tani asked, holding several of the maps before the vendor. She smiled and nodded her head in agreement. The scholar bought the maps and looked at Jared with a dubious look.

"I think it's about time to figure out what the hell happened to you out there, don't you?" Tani asked, looking through his wire-rim glasses with a serious expression. "Let's find a bar, get drunk, look at these maps, and you can tell me what happened to you out there after the boat sank."

Jared had a sheepish look on his face, almost on the verge of denying the request. Then, with a sigh, he nodded in agreement. "Yeah, I think it's time to tell someone what happened."

Crossing over one of the wood and rope bridges, the tribals found themselves above the pool of water, which glistened as it lapped over the white sand. They took a brief moment to look downward, a sense of dizziness filling them as they did. The pristine pool of water reflected back their images, and they felt a sense of peace looking at their own reflections.

"You all right?" Tani quizzed Jared, who nodded back meekly.

After crossing the bridge, the tribals found what they were looking for. A cantina made of mud and wood spread out before them, taking up almost the entire spire of rock on which it rested .

Tani grabbed a table and spread out the map of Turner's Corner and Shape Home. His stumpy hand came to rest on the map, pointing at the region just to the north, listed on the map as open desert. A look of nostalgia washed over Jared. He sat motionless for a few moments, then called the waitress over. Ordering a round of drinks, Jared drank down several strong swigs of beer, then began to retell the tale of his fateful journey through the wasteland. He described the mighty Rattle Hydra, the strange church upon the mesa with its crude prophetic diagrams on the walls, the tale of the mad priest, the crazed shaman, and finally, the magic totem. Tani sat enthralled, almost unable to believe what he was hearing. It took several rounds of beer to finish the story. By the time the tale was over, young Tani sat silent, tense, stunned, and somewhat drunk. Several moments of silence passed between them, the sated laziness of the day beginning to give way as the uncomfortable topic was finally brought out in the open.

"I don't know what to say..." Tani mouthed.

"Me neither. Now you know why I didn't tell any of you. It was just too strange."

"I agree..." The scholar sighed while shaking his head in disbelief.

"Not a word to the others," Jared said in a matter-of-fact tone.

"Not a word, Jared," Tani agreed.

And so they sat, the tribals from Scarskin, outside the cantina, on the patio, soaking in the calm of the village. The day grew long and the sun pressed toward the western horizon, a timeless event which had occurred for ages before a record of such things ever existed. Washed with brew, the tribals sat and waited in reverence. The sun set, plunging the wasteland into darkness. The chill night air settled over the desert and the tribals remained in their drunken stupor, ordering an extra round of drinks. A major aspect of their religion was about to unfold, and both tribals wanted a front row seat.

The glimmer rose first amongst the dunes. A thin white splinter of brilliant light erupted along the edge of the sand. The splinter grew, and the silhouette of the moon pushed upwards from the horizon. As it moved, the tribals watched silently, feeling a fear rise in their stomachs. So perfect it was, rising out of the darkness, glimmering like a beacon in the night. With each passing second, the tribals grew more anxious. In their secret thoughts there was doubt, a doubt about what they were seeing. With anticipation, they both watched, yearning to see the full body of the moon emerge from the darkness. The fear of a partial moon was gradually lost, a fading tremor of dark doubt. With a triumphant exuberance of glee, the tribals viewed the natural event in awe. The blazing white light of the moon was now fully exposed in the dark sky, and the moon itself was perfectly round. Smiling, neither of them said a word. They just looked up into the heavens as the full moon shone brightly, bathing the wasteland in a holy glow.

Chapter 40
A Peaceful Truce

White light flooded in through the open window. The full moon had risen, bathing the wasteland in a peaceful, warm light. Banion rested quietly within the confines of the small inn room, lying on the bed with his shoulders pressed against the wall. A cool breeze rolled in through the open window, and the deranged gunfighter drew in the night air with a deep breath. Satisfied, he exhaled with a sigh.

Banion's thoughts were peaceful, for the moment. With soft emotions filling him, he let the calm of the evening flood over him.

The door to the inn room opened. Mineera stood in the doorway, eyeing Banion with an expression of distress upon her face. With a quizzing look, the deranged rancher considered the psychic maiden. Over the past months, Mineera had been wracked by horrid visions of darkness. The psychic maiden seemed to be losing her mind, caught in a tortuous downward spiral of decay. Banion had a front row seat for the entire show, watching her slowly come apart.

The distress in her eyes was clearly apparent. Mineera gave the impression of being wracked by some inner turmoil. Her lip trembling and her eyes welling with tears, she stood in the open doorway like a frightened child. Staring straight ahead, she wished with all her might that someone would take pity on her.

Sighing, Banion smiled at her and extended his hand in her direction, coaxing her to enter. The first step she took was labored; she moved forward slowly, like a frightened animal. The distress upon her face was beginning to mount. With each step forward, more tears rolled down her cheeks.

A look of concern covered Banion's face as he watched her move. The scar on his face wrinkled as his eyes grew soft and he gazed upon her with compassion. The door to the room closed, swinging silently shut.

Mineera halted in the center of the room, too wary to advance any further. With eyes soft and full of warmth, Banion smiled. The anxiety collapsed. The young woman resumed her progress, still shaking. She halted at the foot of the bed, staring at Banion. The deranged rancher moved forward, reaching out to her. Clutching her hand softly, Banion caressed her soft skin with his rough, sandpaper-like skin. Initially, she recoiled at his touch, wanting nothing more than to flee from him. Mineera was not herself, and the torment she was experiencing made her feel weak.

Urging her forward, Banion pulled her onto the bed. Their eyes locked, the blue mirrors set in her dark skin gazing into Banion's harsh stare. As they looked at each other, the fear began to wither inside of her. She was home; they both were. Still holding Banion's hand, Mineera fought back the stream of tears rolling down her cheeks.

In the soft, warm moonlight, Banion reached out and caressed her cheek, drawing the tears from her face. With a smile, she responded, gripping his hand tightly. Moving forward, she crawled near Banion.

He did not flee her advance; instead, he welcomed her close. Like a frightened child, Mineera pressed her head against his chest, resting lightly upon him. Banion pulled her closer. She responded by collapsing on him, clutching him tightly. He kissed the top of her head, upon her jet black hair, touching her softly, gently pulling her hair through his rough hands.

As she trembled, the inner conflict Mineera was fighting came once again to the surface. Feeling a fresh flow of tears soak into his shirt, he clutched her lovingly, once again kissing her, trying to wish away her pain by the sheer force of his will. Banion knew she was tormented, and instead of scoffing at her suffering, he embraced her weakness.

In the arms of Banion, Mineera found peace. It was the very thing that she had been yearning for, hoping to avert the influence of the voices within her mind. Clutching him, there were no voices, no anxiety, no visions of darkness. It was as if a sickly haze had been pulled from her soul.

And so they rested in each other's arms, bathed in the light of the full moon, feeling the wash of cold air rolling in from the wasteland. The quiet truce between them had grown into something much greater. It had evolved into a restless peace between two battered souls clutching each other tightly, feeling warmth and compassion within the other. In that moment, Banion and Mineera were the only two people in the world who understood one another, a truly amazing bond to exist between two who were once the fiercest of enemies...

Nova 7 was nowhere near an inn. In fact, they were camped along a ridgeline, close to the mysterious Concrete Barrens. The tribals were sleeping peacefully. Banion on the other hand, was wide awake, keeping watch over the camp as night clung to the world. His eyes narrowed as he stared in anger at Mineera. She was evidently dreaming about him again, and was calling out his name in the darkness. Every time she thrashed about and whispered his name, the sinister gun fighter became angrier and more wary. The psychic maiden's obsession with him over the last few months had made him extremely edgy.

In the beginning, Banion had been suspicious. Now that suspicion had evolved into a sinking feeling in the pit of his stomach. Her insane visions were about to take her across the threshold into madness, a place that Banion was fearful of. A normal person on the verge of madness was bad enough, but a psychic losing her grip on reality was dangerous.

Banion knew that he himself was gripped by a deadly obsession, a ruinous emotion that could bring his companions to disaster. He understood her all too well, and this was the reason Banion was on edge. One member of Nova 7 gripped by obsession was dangerous enough, but *two* could end their crusade.

Banion resolved to watch Mineera closely. Either she would get better, or else she would shatter completely. The deranged rancher felt in his heart that it would be the latter. In either case,

Banion was attempting to prepare himself for the outcome.

"Banion…" Mineera mumbled, still dreaming.

Banion sighed in response, his hand dropping to his gun belt instinctively as he watched the fragile Mineera tormented by her dreams. His hand brushed across the weapon as he stared at her. Whatever the outcome of her madness, Banion would be ready.

Flailing about in her bedroll, she called out again. With each call and whisper, anger flashed inside of him. Attuned to his own dark thoughts, Banion knew that her madness was overcoming her. Shaking his head in disgust, he fought an internal struggle. If he came to believe that her condition was about to compromise the mission, the deranged gunfighter was ready to take any means necessary to stop her.

Banion shook his head with a quiet sigh of dismay. The responsibility for their quest was a daunting task. Not knowing what to do with Mineera, he pressed his palms over his ears, blocking her whispers from his mind. Staring out into the night, he shook his head again, still agitated, watching the flickering of the campfire as Mineera thrashed about in the shadows. Madness was a sickness, a plague Banion was willing to eradicate if it came down to it, regardless of the price to himself – or to others.

Chapter 41
The Rift Valley

The group had finally ascended the jagged trail that clung to the ridgeline. Banion led the way, pushing over the mountain pass leading into the deadly Rift Valley. The companions stood silently as they breached the mountain range and surveyed the battered earth ahead.

Giant cracks were torn in the landscape. Canyons and deep rifts split the ground like cracks on a shattered mirror. The city built by the ancients, once proud and strong, lay in absolute ruin. Hundreds of years of earthquakes and volcanic activity had worn away most of the buildings to mere stubs of failed grandeur. Steam vents erupted from the cracks at uneven intervals, washing the landscape in a haunting fog. Volcanic vents had also erupted, sending plumes of liquid, molten rock hundreds of feet into the air, and bathing the wasted concrete buildings in orange flame. Pools of sickly, bubbling tar flooded many of the ancient roads and byways. The black sludge clung to the ruins for miles and miles.

In the center of the ancient city was a circular, barren patch of ground several miles in diameter; ages ago, a nuclear weapon had reduced the center of the city to a burning cinder, leaving a circular blast mark. Black earth, devoid of all life, was the focal point at the middle of the city.

A chill of anxiety rolled through the tribals as they surveyed the alien landscape ahead. It was the first time they had ever beheld the ruins of a once great city, laid to waste by a rising plume of pure energy and charred ash. It was clear that Nova 7 was in an unholy land, a world irreversibly scarred by violence long past.

"May God help us," Mineera whispered. The tribals looked on silently.

The companions stared in awe at the ruins before them. The uneasy feelings turned to panic as Banion caught sight of a threat moving toward them at great speed.

"We have got to seek shelter before that hits us," Banion said, pointing up at the sky.

A set of low-lying storm clouds had cast the world into shadow. The cloudy mass was dense and sinister, swirling about like a maelstrom on the sea. Even though the clouds were turbulent, the air was strangely calm. With a sky tinted dark grey, shading into a near purple hue in certain sections, the coming storm was clearly an event to be respected and not underestimated. A rumble of thunder sounded dully from the violent clouds.

"I suggest we run," Tani said hastily.

"Yeah, the last thing we need is to be drenched in radioactive rain water," Jared agreed with a look of fear in his eyes. The storm, after all, was swirling about the city, and there was a good chance that the clouds would produce radioactive rain.

Nova 7 picked up the pace and was pounding down the trail in the darkness of the pulsating clouds. They moved swiftly, all eyes uneasily tracking the approach of the sinister storm. While still on the ridgeline above the Rift Valley, the companions felt panic rise in their hearts.

The clouds began to swirl about more intensely. The clinging stillness of the air began to quiver. Rotating more and more rapidly, the purplish-grey clouds heaved and pushed. Something violent was about to happen.

A dark cone erupted from the bottom of the clouds. Spinning tightly, the cone snaked downward, toward the ground. The wind increased dramatically as the storm front released a massive amount of energy. Debris was thrown free as a tornado touched down, creating a swath of chaos down the ruined streets of the once mighty city.

Dust clouds formed at the contact point on the ground. Plumes of dirt were thrown into the air, causing Tani to shake his head in despair. "If we breathe that contaminated dust, we are done for!" The scholar's estimation was essentially correct; the tornado had kicked up a radioactive swarm of contaminated earth charged by the nuclear blast ages ago. However, thankfully for the team, the tornado was miles away, and they faced almost no danger from the dust. In his panicked state, the young scholar's rational thought was beginning to waver.

Seeking shelter, Nova 7 came across a shallow cave set in the rock face along the ridgeline above the ruined city. Moving quickly to the back of the cave, Banion and the rest of his mercenary crew huddled together, hoping to avoid the coming storm.

The tornado tore at the earth, and heavy rains began to fall, crashing down and wetting the ruins with a fresh splash of radiation. The rock around the steam and lava vents sizzled under the deluge of water falling from the sky, as the high temperatures from the core of the earth itself burned away the newly falling rain. The tornado increased its intensity, tearing across the ruins. The force of the wind generated by the tornado was immense. Tani shielded his face with both hands, looking like a frightened child seeing his first thunderstorm.

"Look, another one!" Jared said in disbelief. The tortured clouds heaved again. Another cone emerged and twisted toward the ground. Two tornados were now ravaging the ruins. Spinning around, the two twisters courted each other in a sinister dance, intertwining while ravaging the skeletal remains of the concrete buildings.

"Yeah, this is more like it. You scare the hell out of me, Banion. You actually think we can find anything living in those ruins, let alone a legendary arms dealer?" Tani's tone was quite hostile.

"This is the place. We have to wait out the storm. The Runner supposedly lives on the western side of the city, near the ocean," Banion responded.

"How do we get to the western edge of the city? The ruins are covered in lava and tar pits. The center of the city is a radioactive crater, and must be too contaminated to travel across. How do we get to the western edge of the city?" Mineera was also stunned. This was by far the most hostile environment she had seen in her travels, and she had seen quite a bit over the years.

"The tunnels," the crazed gun fighter responded. "Beneath

the city there's a network of passages: old subway routes, sewer pipes, and access tunnels. Below that blast mark..." Banion pointed to the site where the nuclear weapon had scoured the city ages ago, "...is a labyrinth of tunnels. The passages are known as the Iron Gate ruins."

"Do you know the way through the tunnels?" Tani whined, not liking the idea of continuing further even one bit. The ruins were a hostile place, and he was none too keen to meet anything that actually lived in those ruins.

"No, but we will find our way. The contacts I made in Shape Home provided a map of the city." A bolt of lightning streaked across the sky, accompanied by a loud boom of thunder. Both tribals jumped at the sound. Seeing their discomfort, Banion became irritated. "We don't have an option this time, bookworm. We have to find our way through. Otherwise, no Runner, no nuke."

Bolts of lightning streaked across the sky. The purple storm clouds heaved and churned. Thunder clapped, stirring the already restless Nova 7. Moments passed as the frightened tribals looked out at nature unleashed. With a mixture of anxiety and wonder, Banion, Tani, Mineera, and Jared stared out of the cave. The concert of natural disasters that had battered the city over the centuries was impressive. Each of them thought silently about the ruins, and each wondered in awe how *anything* could still be left of the once great city. Many moments passed in silence. Finally, the young warrior from Scarskin, with knees pulled tightly to his chest, spoke to break the silence.

"I miss Scarskin," Jared said in a somber tone. The others looked at him with quick glances.

"Yeah... me too," Tani admitted. "I miss my family." Sighing, the tribal scholar watched the tornados ravage the ruins. "I hope my parents are doing okay."

"I bet they are," Jared said with a twinkle of hope. "They are probably having a picnic near the northern edge of the village, past the corn fields." The tribal warrior was misty eyed as he spoke.

Tani smiled and let his mind wander. Thoughts of Scarskin and his family filled his consciousness. Breathing more softly, the young scholar felt at peace.

Mineera sat quietly, seeming to lose herself in hidden thoughts. "I never knew my parents."

A silence passed between the companions. The statement Mineera had introduced into the conversation put Banion on edge. A wary look covered his face, and he stared at the psychic maiden in discomfort.

"Why not?" the tribal warrior asked. "What happened?"

Banion shot Jared a look instructing him to let the subject drop. Jared shrugged, not knowing why he should stop.

"My kind does not have families. They are bred into existence using slaves. The high priests impregnate the female slaves in the breeding pits. The offspring are our people."

Tani was wide eyed, as was Jared. Banion shot them both a look of disgust.

"The youth are sent to live in dormitories, each one led by a high priest or priestess. Young Reaper Kai are sent to train in the defiled temples. At age eight, any child not able to harness spiritual energy is slain, after being declared as weak. Not a single Reaper Kai lives past the age of eight unless they have psychic ability. The ones who live are sent to training communes, war houses where they learn to master their dark powers." Mineera was lost in thought as visions of her youth filled her mind.

The rest of the group looked on with uncomfortable gazes. "I should send you out into the storm," Banion said to Jared. "You and that damn bird necklace of yours."

Jared fell silent, avoiding the eyes of both Mineera and Banion.

"The practice of slaying those without psychic abilities seems like a potent selective breeding practice. It's no wonder the Reaper Kai have advanced their abilities so strongly," Tani said, still engrossed in speculations about the Reaper Kai.

"A sickening practice, using slaves to further their race," Banion said, his tone brimming with contempt as he eyed Mineera, who had fallen silent.

An uneasy silence washed over the group. The tornados had

receded back into the swirling clouds. Suddenly, a violent boom rocked the landscape. A quake shook the very earth. A spout of fire flared upward in the valley amongst the ruined buildings. A fountain of molten lava erupted from the ground. Spraying high in the air, the molten rock flared like a firework, as clumps of molten rock rained down in chunks. A low grumble was emitted from the lava spout as it flared.

Lost in silence, Nova 7 viewed the power of the earth in awe. It took several moments of stunned silence for the team members to collect their thoughts.

"The rain is over." Jared pointed outside the cave. The storm was dissipating, moving off toward the east as it pressed over the jagged mountain range. The companions rose and looked around them as sunshine pierced through the holes in the clouds. Rays of light touched the ruins, and it was an eerie sight to observe warm light touching the wounded earth.

Banion moved out first, and the others followed. The trail was narrow, only allowing them to pass single file. Following the fading ridgeline, the trail descended into the violent valley. The edge of the city was coming into view. Ancient structures clung to the hillside along the ridgeline, survived only by their frames. The wooden walls and planks had long since been burned away by flaming eruptions, or worn away by the slow decay induced by the ceaseless rains. In any event, the battered houses of long ago reminded one of a battlefield beset by crows or other carrion feeders, rending all flesh from the bones of fallen warriors. The hillside was a graveyard where the skeletons of civilization, remnants of the ancient people who had thrived in past ages, remained on display.

An uneasy feeling came over the companions as they descended deeper into the Rift Valley. Passing through the aged city made each of them seem small, insignificant. The wonders of the ancients were truly awe inspiring. Leaving the trail, Nova 7 pushed into the heart of the city itself.

The wafting stench of sulfur filled their nostrils. Steam seeped from wounds in the asphalt, wafting up from the volcanic tunnels below. A thin fog rolled through the ruins. Steam mingled with a thick mist rolling in off the nearby ocean. An eerie silence, thickened by the fog, clung heavily to the ruins.

As they walked down a broad street, the echo of their footsteps resounded through the fog, echoing off the concrete buildings. Shops of old lined the street. Corroded signs and shattered glass littered the sidewalk. Old world cars, rusted down to the frames, clogged the streets, a haunting vision of the fatal, long-ago day when the citizens had tried to hastily evacuate the city; their cars still remained in the very place in which they were left, hundreds and hundreds of years ago.

"It's not far." Banion spoke in a whisper, holding his revolver in one hand, scanning the collapsed buildings around him. Jared and Tani were also on edge, each fondling the weapons at their belts.

Pressing onward just a few more blocks, they came across a gaping hole gouged in the street. As if a giant scoop had pulled away the ground, the wound in the street fell away, leading down into the depths, the underground labyrinth of the Iron Gate ruins.

"This is it," Banion said.

A foul stench rose from the pit. A mass of twisting pipes and cables surrounded the entrance to the tunnel. An ancient subway car, smashed in several places, lay below the slope leading into the ruins.

Mineera gasped as something strange filled her senses. A vivid impression of the ancients clouded her mind, filling her with old memories. Her head pounded intently as a buzzing sound filled her ears. A wail, mixed cries, and the voices of millions began to dully thud in her mind. The ghosts of the dead, millions of lost souls, were still trapped in the ruins, entombed by the violent nuclear blast ages ago.

Staggering backwards, Mineera eyed Jared with suspicion. Her face twisted and she seemed to look different. Scowling, she gripped her hands tightly. The voices, whispers of the dead, filled her consciousness. Shaking her head back and forth, Mineera's eyes narrowed. *"I won't let you do it!"* her mind screamed as she stared at Jared.

"Hey!" Tani shouted. Mineera blinked several times, coming out of her trance. The look on her face changed dramatically. "What are doing? Did you hear me?"

"Huh?" she stammered.

"What are you doing? Banion and Jared already went in. You coming with us or what?" the young scholar asked in annoyance.

Jared was nowhere to be seen. She blinked several more times. Just before she had lost control, Mineera could have sworn Jared was standing in front of her. "Yeah... let's go."

Mineera followed Tani down into the darkness of the abandoned subway tunnel. As they moved away from the entrance, she looked back and felt a fear creep into her soul. The entryway leading back into the open air was getting smaller, further away. With every step she took, panic built within her. Whispers rose from the darkness, clawing at her mind from the shadows. From every direction they pounded at her: voices of the dead, voices of the lost souls who had died in a blinding flash ages ago. Shaking, trying to remain in control, Mineera fought to keep up with the tribal scholar, pushing ever deeper into the passages, with more and more whispers and voices accumulating in her mind.

Chapter 42
The Iron Gate Ruins

"No way!" Tani said with a look of disgust. "No way in hell am I going in there!"

Jared was shaking his head, worry and anxiety apparent in his face, as well. Mineera was standing at the back of the party, talking to herself. From time to time, the psychic maiden would flail her hands about, as if to drive away an unseen swarm of flies. Banion eyed her suspiciously, wishing he had never taken her on the journey.

"Come on, bookworm, it's not all *that* bad," the deranged gun fighter cajoled, with a hint of hesitation. Though tough and travel worn, even Banion was a little rattled about what lay ahead.

Tani was holding his flashlight, passing its beam across the room in wide sweeps. The room was just beyond an abandoned subway tunnel. A long-ago earthquake had torn a rift through the center of the subway tunnel, collapsing it, but leaving a fissure leading away from the main passage. The fissure grew significantly in size as it progressed, over thirty feet across at its center. A foul stench wafted from the tunnel, smelling of sulfur and other volatile chemicals. Bubbling out of the floor of the fissure was black, viscous tar, superheated by the volcanic activity in the region. Pieces of flat rock and concrete were placed in regular intervals in the tunnel. Someone had long ago placed footstones as a crude path across the tar-filled room.

Jared held his nose and laughed. "It smells like your room back home."

Tani shot Jared an annoyed look, but then shrugged in agreement; the space did smell like the scholar's room back in Scarskin.

"Mineera!" Banion shouted. The psychic maiden turned around, startled by his voice. A frantic look covered her face.

Mumbling, she moved forward, gripping her hands tightly.

Jared shook his head as he stared at her. Tani narrowed his eyes, looking on with suspicion of his own. Banion was on the verge of shaking some sense into her. Suddenly, a shift occurred in her demeanor. Pushing the hundreds of voices from her mind, Mineera regained her composure and took control of her consciousness.

"Sorry..." she whispered in an apologetic tone. The other three members of Nova 7 were not amused.

"You ready?" Banion asked her, his eyes widening in impatience.

"Sure," Mineera responded, still feeling ashamed. The last few days had been spotty at best. The voices in her mind had become increasingly stronger, and more potent. She knew reality was slipping away, and was unable to fight against the downward slide into madness. She knew that if she could not force the voices from her mind, something dire would occur, and it would be her fault.

Banion sighed, looking at the stepping stones which were partially submerged in the boiling tar, small islands set amidst a black sea. With a resolute look, the deranged gun fighter leapt to the first stone. It held fast, and the rancher jumped to another, then another, making his way slowly across the tar pit. The fumes erupting from the sludge were toxic, almost overpowering. Banion tried not to breathe in too much, feeling dizzy as a headache formed in his temples almost immediately. With a final bound, Banion reached the other side. Turning around, he urged the others onward.

The three remaining companions stood at the other edge, hesitating.

"Just don't fall in!" Banion shouted.

"Great advice!" Jared yelled back, shaking his head.

The tribal warrior looked first at Tani, then at Mineera before he spoke. "Here we go." Jared bounded across the stones like an agile cat. His sense of balance and strength quickly brought him to the other side of tar pit.

Mineera and Tani stood at the other side. With a deep

breath, Mineera gathered her robes about her, taking care to avoid slipping on them. Hopping across, the psychic maiden made it with little trouble.

Tani stared at the bubbling pit of tar while shaking his head. His green eyes were wide as he surveyed the room. Sweat was pouring down his face, and his hands were trembling.

"Come on, Tani," Banion ordered.

Tani held back, stuck on the edge of the tar pit with a look of horror on his face. Shaking his head back and forth, he spoke in a frantic tone. "No way, Banion. I am not going across that!"

"Tani, you can do it. Just relax," Jared coaxed his friend. He knew that the young scholar had issues with feats of physical courage.

"Maybe you should come back for me..." Backing away, the tribal scholar shook with fear.

"Damn it, bookworm! Get your ass over here!" the crazed rancher shouted.

With a staunch look, the scholar wrinkled his nose and prepared to jump. Clutching the straps on his backpack tightly, Tani launched across to the first rock. He landed and stumbled, almost tripping over his own feet. He fell to one knee, stomach lurching in terror as he eyed the bubbling tar just a few feet away. Bracing his hands on the stone, he could feel the blood pounding in his temples. Steadying himself, he rose to his feet and eyed the next flagstone in the tar.

He scrunched up his nose once more, sweat poured down his face. The tribal bit his lip as he concentrated on leaping to the next stone. Banion, Jared and Mineera, were silent, not wanting to distract him.

Tani jumped to the next stone. He landed awkwardly on his right ankle. Taking a step backwards, he lost his footing. Jared gasped as his friend lurched backwards toward the edge of the stone. Flailing his hands wildly, the tribal shrieked and squawked like a frightened bird. He felt his legs go out from under him. Tani was falling backwards, not knowing how close he was to the edge of the stone. Panic filled him. Each inch he fell backwards seemed to last a lifetime. The tribal landed hard on his butt, a mere inch away from falling into the boiling tar. He felt the ground hit his rump, not the hot ooze of viscous tar. An elated sigh of relief erupted from Tani's mouth as he realized that he had avoided falling in the sickly black muck.

Banion saw the tribal fall down, and a smile graced his lips. Slowly, the smile grew, and the rancher began to cackle. At first it was slow, but then, it turned into an all-out explosion of laughter. Within a matter of seconds, Banion was buckled over, laughing uncontrollably, gasping in short breaths between bursts of laughter.

Jared smiled and chuckled, more due to Banion's response than to seeing his best friend scared out of his mind.

"You got an extra pair of pants, Tani?" Banion smiled, still gasping, trying to keep from laughing further. "I think you just messed yours."

Tani, embarrassed, could feel the sting in his cheeks. His pride wounded, the tribal youth fought to keep from exposing his emotions. He jumped to his feet and bounded from one stone to the next, each leap accomplished with shaky moves, but with growing confidence. The tribal had little pride left after the ordeal, and he had to appear courageous to save what little dignity he had left.

Banion slapped Tani on the back; the tribal's cheeks were still flushed in the dim light. "Let's get going. I don't want to spend any more time down here than we have to."

The group moved on. Jared walked beside his friend with a grin on his face.

"Just shut up," Tani reacted with a mixture of anger and levity.

Jared just looked back in the dim light, shaking his head, trying not to laugh.

Nova 7 pressed onward into the bowels of the underworld. Passing through a catacomb of passages and tunnels, they moved deeper and deeper into the earth. Each step took them further from safety, closer to the hidden dangers of the Iron Gate ruins. It took nearly an hour of trudging through tunnels to reach a sight that would forever fill each of their memories.

A rush of water resounded in their ears. Mingling with the sound of rushing water was a hiss, a serpentine sound of steam rushing upwards. Abruptly, in mid-tunnel, the floor fell away. Nova 7 had just discovered a natural wonder, a place that few in the Darken Realm would ever see or ever imagine.

The room was enormous, several hundred yards across. Carved out of the naked rock, the walls of the cave were jagged, the result of colossal seismic activity. A waterfall, rushing from an underground river pouring out of an old world sewage pipe, was cascading downward, several hundred feet into the cavern below. The rush of water met the blood of the earth. Pouring into the void below, the water crashed into a quickly flowing river of lava, a bright orange rush. Pumping through the veins of the world, lava tubes had bored through the rock. The water hissed in anger as it smashed into the molten rock. The result was a rising column of steam rushing upwards through the chamber.

Bathed in an eerie yellow light, shimmering through the plume of rising steam, a crude bridge stretched across the sinister void which gaped like a wound in the earth below. Spanning the entire distance, the crude steel bridge stretched to an opening in the wall, on the far side of the chamber.

"It's almost time..." A whisper tugged at Mineera's senses. She spun around, wide eyed with fear. Nothing and no one was standing behind her. A buzzing sound filled her ears. The psychic maiden began to sweat profusely, as bright yellow spots filled her vision.

Banion gazed at the bridge in fascination. The tribal scholar had come to his side, staring at the bridge as well.

"I don't know, Banion. It looks awful rickety," Tani said, shaking his head.

"Yeah, I know." Banion stretched one foot before him, his combat boot testing the edge of the bridge. It held fast under his weight. Looking ahead, Banion eyed the rising vortex of steam rushing past the bridge in the tremendous updraft of rising air. "If my skin burns off, don't follow." With a twisted grin, Banion's dark eyes flashed with madness.

The rancher moved onto the steel bridge spanning the cavern below. Stepping cautiously, he moved toward the middle of the bridge, washed in rising steam. Grimacing, and preparing for a possible burn, Banion crossed the center of the bridge, passing into the plume of rising steam. He moved through quickly, protecting his face with his long coat.

The steam plume was heated, but not beyond human endurance. Banion passed through unharmed and urged the remainder of Nova 7 to follow. Tani took a bold step ahead, not wanting to be the last one to cross this menace as he had been with the boiling tar further back in the ruins. Bounding forward, the scholar crossed quickly.

Jared stood in front of Mineera. A strange look covered her face. Ignoring the psychic maiden, Jared bounded across the bridge toward Banion and Tani.

Mineera stood in a daze, watching Jared move across the bridge. Twitching, she stared at the tribal warrior in suspicion. *"You must save Banion..."* A voice erupted in her mind as she gazed at the unsuspecting tribal. A vision of Jared standing before Banion's bloodied corpse filled her mind. She shook her head in defiance, trying desperately to drive the horrid vision from her mind. *"You must do it... kill him..."* the voice echoed once again in her mind. Another vision flowed through her, and she was powerless to resist it...

"Damn it, Mineera!" Jared screamed, his cheeks flushed red. There was a crazed look in his eyes.

Mineera stared at Jared dreamily. Her subconscious was screaming that something was wrong. "Jared?" Mineera asked in a confused tone. The hotheaded youth had Banion's revolver in one hand and the mighty Scar Blade in the other.

"Wake up!" Jared shouted angrily. "Snap out of it. We have a job to do."

Mineera looked around and found her surroundings unusual. Old, corroded rusty metal walls and steel girders rose around them.

She spun around and caught sight of Tani sitting on the floor, leaning against the wall. There was a look of shock on Tani's face.

"He's gone!" Jared said in a matter-of-fact tone. "There isn't a damn thing we can do about it now. We need to get moving…"

The dream flashed into another image, the image of Jared standing over Banion's corpse with the mighty Scar Blade drenched in blood…

The vision fell away and she felt herself losing control. As she awoke from the waking dream, Jared had crossed the bridge. With a wild look of panic and anger on her face, Mineera, driven by both voice and vision, felt her fingers tingle and her mind splinter. Something unclean had emerged within her spirit. A foreign presence, a powerful entity, was making itself known, driving her to do its bidding.

"Kill him, Mineera, slaughter the boy…" The Voice hissed in her mind. *"Banion must be saved, or all is lost… do it… kill the tribal before he brings harm to your love…"*

Mineera had succumbed to the Voice. With a flash of madness, her body twitching, the psychic maiden charged forward across the bridge. As she charged, the glow of the lava below lit her face. No longer was she a child of the light. Instead, bathed in the yellow glow of the tortured earth, she had become a tainted thing, washed by evil, hungering for the kill. With a battle cry, Mineera charged young Jared with the intent of killing him.

Chapter 43
Scent of Darkness

A blast of frost erupted from the bird totem around Jared's neck. The emerging chill was more than enough to startle Jared and the others who were standing nearby. Both Banion and Tani jumped as the totem sprang to life, its hungry eyes glowing red with anger, sensing impending danger. The burnt wooden animal totem vibrated violently. Jared knew something was wrong and cleared the mighty Scar Blade from its scabbard.

Turning around, Jared was just in time to catch sight of Mineera violently swinging a dagger toward him. The tribal sidestepped the attack with a stunned look on his face. A frosty wind was encircling him, protecting Jared from the whiff of darkness flowing from the disturbed psychic maiden.

With a flash of madness in her eyes, Mineera screamed at the youth. "You will not kill him! You hear me?!" Her dark hand rose in the air. As she shook with rage, the dark presence inside her lent its aid, feeding her anger, fueling the psychic maiden with a fresh rush of spiritual energy. Flexing her hand forward, she elicited a spark from her fingertips, the electrical cinder growing as it sped forth. The blast of energy arced across the air with a crackle. The lightning blast struck the tribal.

The totem responded. A rising vortex of wind absorbed the blast, throwing both Mineera and Jared to the ground. Banion was stunned, and it took him a moment to fumble for a weapon. Tani stood mortified, unable to comprehend why the fragile minded Mineera had attacked his friend.

Rising from the ground, her eyes narrowed and her lips twisted in a sneer. Holding her hand forward, she conjured telekinetic energy. The focus of her action was Banion's revolver. With a tug from her mind, unseen energy pulled the gun from its holster. Flying through the air, the revolver spiraled toward her outstretched hand.   Mineera was fully prepared to use the firearm on the fallen Jared.

The weapon was gripped tightly in her trembling hands. As the gun sights focused upon Jared, an internal spiritual battle was raging in Mineera's mind and soul. The trigger on the weapon twitched as the hammer began to slide back. Banion trained his submachine on her chest, fighting a battle of his own. Not knowing whether to kill her or not, he wavered. The event was so unexpected that it drove him into a panicked state.

"Kill him, slay the boy! Save Banion!" The Voice screamed in her mind. Tears rolled down her face. As she whimpered like a scared child, the weapon remained raised, with Jared as its target. Her spirit was fighting the foreign presence that had invaded her mind and soul. Shaking her head, trying to force the entity from her, Mineera was losing her grip on reality. It would be so easy to listen to the Voice, so easy to pull the trigger to appease the will of the spirit.

"Don't do it!"   Banion ordered, getting a solid aim on Mineera.   His own trigger finger was twitching.   The deranged rancher was only a few seconds away from opening fire.

"No....!"   she whimpered, crying in both rage and fear. "Stop it..." Her words were broken by the darkness taking her soul.

"If Banion dies... all is lost... you must do it." The Voice spoke once more, throbbing in her mind like a wedge of glass piercing her brain.

Screaming, Mineera dropped the revolver. With indecision and an evil spirit filling her soul, she pushed through the trio and into the dark tunnels of the Iron Gate ruins.   The stunned companions looked on in fright as her screams echoed in the twisting tunnels. Within seconds, all was quiet, and Mineera had disappeared, gripped by madness, driven deeper into the ruins.

Tani made a move to go after her, but was stopped by Banion.

"No, Tani, leave her," he said in a guarded tone.

"We have to go after her," Tani protested. "She needs our help."

"If you didn't notice, bookworm, she just tried to kill your friend."

Jared rose from the ground with a confused look on his face. "I am not sure we should go after her."

"She's not right in the head. We have got to do something," the scholar responded.

"Do we? Why?" Jared said, anger rising in his voice. The reality of what had just happened was sinking in. The tribal warrior was none too keen to go running off into the ruins after someone who had just tried to kill him.

"Let her go. I refuse to sacrifice our mission over her. Let her be. She has a battle of her own ahead of her. None of us can fight it for her." Though his voice was quiet, Banion still spoke with authority.

"How can you be so calm about this?" Tani was irritated by both Jared and Banion's indifference.

"It will all work out," the rancher said in a matter-of-fact tone.

"What?" Jared said sarcastically. "Since when did you become a foolish optimist?"

Banion held the tribal warrior's gaze, staring him down until Jared had to avert his eyes. After beating the youth into submission with a glance, Banion fell silent for a moment, collecting his thoughts.

"I have been out here a long time. Ever since I was a teenager, I have been out here, in the wastes, selling my skills to the highest bidder. In that time, I have seen some amazing things. I have seen fierce combat and desperate acts of survival. And in all that time, I have never witnessed anything more amazing than what the four of us, this Nova 7 team, has achieved. You two little brats just don't get it, do you? You don't get what this is, what we are." Banion stopped speaking, eyeing each of the tribals in turn. Too scared to look away, Tani and Jared obediently listened.

"When I close my eyes, I can still feel the fire coursing through my veins." He shook his head and let the images fill his mind. "I can still feel the adrenaline and the wild burst of freedom

when I fight my way through my enemies. In those fleeting
moments, I am alive, truly alive. You know what amazes me?" he
quizzed the youths. They did not respond, only looking at him in
silence, feeling their skin crawl and their hair stand on end.

"What amazes me is that the feeling of fire is nothing
compared to what I feel when *we* fight together, when *we* stand side
by side, against the world. I cannot fathom the series of events that
enabled *all of us* to survive to reach this very spot, under the world,
secluded in these tunnels, fearing the next step, the next curve in the
road. Don't you find that amazing?" The tribals still did not
respond, but felt a strange twinge at the edge of their souls.

"When *we* stand as one, nothing can stop us. I marvel at how
strong each of us is, all of us, Mineera included. Don't you find it
amazing *we* are all legends, each with unparalleled ability?
Whenever Tani's banging away at his computer or incinerating
something with explosives, I feel a fire in my blood. When I see
Jared spinning through our enemies, remaining unscathed where
lesser men would fall, I feel my spirit leap. When I watch Mineera
fight against all the darkness of the world, battling the devil himself
in her dreams, I feel the hair on my neck stand on end. And when I
face the world with all three of you at my side, I don't just feel the
fire in my blood, I feel something much greater. I feel as if the
whole world could press against us and we would hold it in place.
Our goal is insane, our quest is beyond comprehension. We cannot
complete this journey without each other's strength. I have no doubt
that we will find a nuclear weapon and force retribution upon our
enemy. So in that respect, I am an optimist, but I am no fool. We
will succeed and we will do so with Mineera's help. We are all
legends and will face our worst fears through this journey. Mineera
is fighting her battle, she will win, and she will be with us at the end
of this crazy road. Stay here, hold your ground; she will return when
her battle is won."

Tani and Jared stood in awe. For the first time since they had
met Banion, they felt hope. No longer did they fear the future; it was
now a thing to be embraced and ushered in with a reverent fury.

Consoled by Banion's heroic speech, the tribals stared at him in awe and felt at peace. Jared and Tani both believed Mineera would return. An eerie quiet passed between the companions. The only sounds in the enclosed space of the chamber were the rumble of magma coursing through the earth and the hissing plume of rising steam beyond the doorway.

Still lingering in the seclusion of their thoughts, the trio made camp just beyond the doorway leading to the chasm of fire. And there they waited, each saying a silent prayer, lending their spiritual aid to their companion who was lost somewhere in the ruins, battling the very will of the darkness.

Chapter 44
The Battle Within

The ruins were dark, an imposing prison of shadow. Mineera had retreated into the twisting tunnels beneath the ruined city of old, having fled for what seemed like an eternity, deeper and deeper into the ruins. She ran down many ancient halls and abandoned passages in a fit of madness, driven into an insane fury, a journey into the darkness of both her physical reality and her twisted thoughts. With visions driving her, the maiden had passed through utter darkness, voices guiding her where her eyes could not see. In this blinding crusade through the dark ruins, she had passed into the inner reaches of the ruined city.

Her body was wracked with a constant flurry of spasms and convulsions. Vomit clung to her lips and nose. While running, she had retched all over herself, the result of a mingling of panic and exhaustion. Feeling her heart racing, the psychic maiden collapsed against a concrete wall, letting her back slide along the wall. As she came to rest on the ground, her head was wracked with pain, a fierce blinding agony centered at the base of her neck.

Feeling the darkness around her, she let the icy cold invade her senses. The numbing silence of the black tunnel was truly inviting, a welcome escape from the madness driving her soul toward a shadowed rage. Breathing softly, chilled by the cold of the ruins, Mineera tried to regain her composure. In her fading memory, the last thing she could recall was trying to kill young Jared. It seemed like madness now, but at the time, it was the only option, the only way to stop the death of a man who had haunted her dreams all her life.

She felt truly miserable. Even in the dark, yellow splotches of light filled her vision. Whimpering, she rolled over, holding her shaky hands ahead of her. The bile rose in her throat. Leaning over, Mineera vomited again. Tears welled up in her eyes and she wept quietly in the dark tunnel. Her panic was returning; the presence had found her once again.

"The boy still lives..." The Voice stung her mind once more. The presence filled her as the pounding in her brain increased. It felt as if her head was going to explode.

"I can't do it!" Mineera responded, convulsing on the floor amongst the rubble.

"You must. The boy is dangerous, he is the enemy. You think it's just a coincidence that your powers do not affect him? You know all too well he is the enemy, one of your kind..." The Voice spoke once more, enthralling the crazed Mineera.

"LEAVE HER BE, SPIRIT." With a haunting rasp, another voice sounded in her mind. The psychic maiden shook in terror, trying to force all of the voices from her fragile consciousness. Try as she may, Mineera was too weak to win this battle. "THE BOY IS INNOCENT."

"Is he? Trust your own dreams, Mineera. You know your visions to be true. If you do not act, Banion will die and all will be lost. Remember what happened before? Remember the palace? It was my will that saved Banion from death... without my help, he would have died."

"YOUR WILL?" A faint hum erupted in her mind as the other voice spoke.

"Stop it!" Mineera yelled, trying to hold back the tears.

"Trust in me once more, I will not lead you astray. Go back... find the boy, kill him and save the one you love. It is your fate to save Banion, not lose him to that boy..."

"THE BOY IS NOT THE ENEMY. YOUR LACK OF CONTROL, YOUR FADING SANITY, ARE THE REAL ENEMY. YOU MUST FIND THE STRENGTH IN YOURSELF TO RESIST WHAT YOU HAVE SEEN. YOUR VISIONS OF THE FUTURE HAVE BEEN TAINTED. DO NOT TRUST IN THE VOICES, NOT EVEN MY OWN."

"Silence! How dare you oppose my will? Be gone, demon, I will not let you corrupt my child!"

"I don't want to be a pawn. I only seek to do what is right," Mineera whimpered.

"The right thing is to save Banion... do not let the boy kill him. He is an agent of the enemy. His powers are strong, but you are stronger. End his life and the shadow of darkness will lift."

"I WOULD NEVER SEEK TO CONTROL ONE OF MY CHILDREN. THOSE WHO WISH TO FIND TRUE FAITH MUST DO SO WILLINGLY. TRUST IN YOUR OWN JUDGMENT, NOT IN A VOICE WITHIN YOUR SOUL."

"Fool! Your lies will not deceive my child. Do not listen. I am your only salvation, trust in me, do what is right, save Banion."

"TRUST IN YOURSELF. THE KINDNESS IN YOUR HEART IS THE ONLY THING YOU MUST TRUST IN."

Shaking violently, Mineera strained to force both voices from her mind. Feeling a calm come over her, she began to meditate. She sensed an unclean spirit taking residence in her heart. She focused on her faith, silent prayers rolling through her mind. A warmth of light flooded over her. The violent, sick feeling was beginning to dissipate. The longer she meditated, the better she felt. Suddenly, a twinge of anger erupted inside of her.

"I don't think so..." it hissed at the edge of her mind. Another wave of nausea flooded through her. Fighting to avoid the sickness, the psychic maiden responded by channeling serene energy through her being.

"Be gone!" Mineera shouted.

"It will take more than a simple prayer to drive me away... how foolish you are... I have spent an eternity collecting an army of servants, and you will be no different. I will never yield. In the end, you will be back in the fold, back in my family, where you began your wretched existence."

"I cannot go back to such an existence. I will not slay young Jared. You have sent me false visions. What I have seen is not a portent of the future. It was nothing more than a corrupt dream, sent by a tainted being."

"Not a vision of the future... your folly shall echo through

the ages and will be known to all of this world. Your dreams are a reality, one that has yet to be played out. In the end, Jared will kill Banion."

"Enough!" she shouted once more. Forcing the thoughts out of her mind, she focused on serenity. Dropping into a deep meditation, she imagined the sickness leaving her body. The sickness responded with an air of retribution. A prick of pain rocked her spine, a foul tingle intended to force her into submission. The will of the foreign spirit was strong, but the psychic maiden was stronger. The feeling of peace washed over her in waves, slamming back and forth against the waves of sickness. And so they fought, soul against soul, until a victor emerged. With a shiver, and an intense will, Mineera finally drove the perverse spirit from her body, a thing that had been slowly plaguing her ever since being spliced by the treacherous Guillotine, many moons ago.

The sickness was gone. The Voice was gone. At last, it was driven back; the unclean spirit departed, defeated but not forgotten. Mineera felt the pain of her torment slip away. The nausea had subsided, the pain in her neck was gone, the piercing agony and blinding yellow spots scouring her vision had been driven away. Mineera rose to her feet, alone in the icy blackness of the tunnel. Powering on her flashlight, the psychic maiden surveyed her surroundings. A series of eerie, abandoned passages stretched ahead in all directions. Staring at each passage, unable to discern from whence she had come, Mineera looked around in confusion, free of the evil spirit but lost in the ruins, uncertain where to go in order to find her lost friends, friends she had just betrayed in a fit of madness.

And so she traveled into the haunted passages, trying to find her way back home, back to her companions. Her senses had returned. A clean feeling coursed through her. No longer was she under the tainted rule of darkness. Instead, Mineera had driven back the will of evil itself and emerged victorious.

As the psychic maiden passed through the ruins, a twinge rose at her senses. Something wicked, something of the living world, was at the edge of her perception. She could feel its hatred, which was directed toward her companions. Letting her psychic powers stretch outward, she could feel a presence in the ruins, watching her friends. Somewhere in the tunnels, evil plotted, scheming to destroy her companions. Dropping into meditation, she tried desperately to discern the ill intent approaching. Pushing forward, a familiar presence entered her mind. A snarled snout filled her mind. Yellow rotten teeth were exposed in the creature's toothy grin. A long tail coiled and flicked the ground. Two piercing black eyes filled her mind. In the vision, the creature snarled as it watched Nova 7 from the darkness. Whispering, the creature said over and over again: "Oh yes, oh yes, indeed!"

Her eyes opening in panic, Mineera gasped in fear. "Guillotine…"

Knowing that the sinister mercenary was close to her companions, Mineera, with flashlight in hand, lost and alone, rushed through the tunnels and abandoned passages, searching for the companions she had just betrayed, seeking to save them from the sinister Guillotine, who was stalking them from the secluded darkness of the abandoned tunnels in the Iron Gate ruins.

With Nova 7 falling to pieces and the sinister mutant lying in wait, the fate of all free peoples was growing more dismal by the moment. Knowing that every second was crucial, a jolt of adrenaline coursed through Mineera. If she could not save the rest of Nova 7 from an ambush, the crusade to locate a nuclear weapon would fail without a doubt.

And so she ran through the maze of passages, urgency biting at her heels, and hope her only companion.